KISSING
PATRICK MOWBRAY
WAS TREASON!

Slowly his hands slid up her sides, over her ribs, his thumbs spread below the swelling curves until they met in the center of her body. If he touched her breasts, Christin knew she was lost to . . . everything.

"I didn't like it!" she gasped.

Patrick stilled his hands and locked his eyes with the gray ones which blinked mistily at him. A grin teased his lips, and he steadied his breath. "You're a magnificent liar," he said huskily and pulled himself upright.

She nearly fell on top of him. Steadying her with a hand about her forearm until she could regain her balance, Patrick's smile broadened. He touched the tip of her nose with a finger.

"Good night, my lady. I daresay you will think about that after I leave."

Dear Reader:

We trust you will enjoy this Richard Gallen romance. We plan to bring you more of the best in both contemporary and historical romantic fiction with four exciting new titles each month.

We'd like your help.

We value your suggestions and opinions. They will help us to publish the kind of romances you want to read. Please send us your comments, or just let us know which Richard Gallen romances you have especially enjoyed. Write to the address below. We're looking forward to hearing from you!

Happy reading!

Judy Sullivan
Richard Gallen Books
8-10 West 36th St.
New York, N.Y. 10018

The Satin Vixen

LINDA SHAW

PUBLISHED BY RICHARD GALLEN BOOKS
Distributed by POCKET BOOKS

Also published by RICHARD GALLEN BOOKS

Rhapsody
  by Jessica Dare

Passion's Heirs
  by Elizabeth Bright

The Rainbow Chase
  by Kris Karron

 A RICHARD GALLEN BOOKS *Original* publication

Distributed by
POCKET BOOKS, a Simon & Schuster division of
GULF & WESTERN CORPORATION
1230 Avenue of the Americas, New York, N.Y. 10020

ISBN: 0-671-43163-3

First Pocket Books printing June, 1981

10 9 8 7 6 5 4 3 2 1

RICHARD GALLEN and colophon are trademarks
of Simon & Schuster and Richard Gallen & Co., Inc.

Printed in the U.S.A.

To Virginia
who always loved me.

Chapter One

England, 1318

Christin Winchelsea's hands would not stop shaking. She sat her lathered horse expertly and straight. Yet, when she sought a firm rein, her fingers trembled. Grasping the pommel hard, she forced them still.

She formed a stunning silhouette on the crest of the Yorkshire hill—her chestnut hair lustrous and wind-tossed, her green skirts luxuriant and billowing. The terrors of her flight, however, had her gasping for breath. She swept her gray eyes across the valley like an alarmed monarch surveying the worsening plight of his armies.

"Murdering Scot thieves!" she cried, her outrage snatched away by the wind.

Only this morning a friendly May sun had dried the dew from the glen surrounding Northallerton. It had warmed the earth, freshly brown from the plows. Now, the sky was roiling with the smoke of carnage, the land flooded with hundreds of men. Strewn weapons cluttered the fields, and Saxons were mangled until one could hardly be distinguished from the other.

Christin's home, the tiny village of Miron, lay only five miles down the Ure River. If she could reach there before the Scots, Miron could bargain for its survival. Many towns, if they offered enough, bought reprieve from Scots torches.

Christin bent low, blending her body with the churning muscles of the horse beneath her. Her hair streamed down her back as if its freedom would somehow quicken her ride. As Persis plunged downward to the green floor of the Ure valley, Christin's eyes flicked to the side.

"Of a mercy!" Her shock jerked the reins and forced Persis to a shuddering standstill.

At first the soldiers were nearly indistinguishable dots. Then they swiftly took shape, nearing with an echoing thunder which swelled to a tempest.

As if she smelled the danger, Persis lunged forward and lengthened her stride. But Scot hobins were bred for speed. Few mounts alive could match them. As the arm of the Black Douglas lifted, Christin's darting glance caught the menace of his signal.

A death sentence! Even if she hadn't recognized the fluttering standard, Christin would have known her peril. James Douglas, the terror of children's nursery rhymes, pillager of churches, burner of towns and the nightmare of kings. The general of Scotland's armies.

A cluster of nearly twenty men detached itself to streak across the glen. In mere minutes, with desperation's own means of clarity, Christin saw the hopelessness of her race. Gone were thoughts of alerting Miron. The Scots swiftly encircled her, and Christin hastened to prepare her soul for death.

"Holy Mother, hear me now in the hour of my need."

Above the labored snorting of sweaty horses rang trappings—metal scraping metal, the threat of long-shafted axes slapping the saddles. A deliberate hand grasped the reins of her horse.

Christin whirled, striking blindly and jerking Persis upward to cleave the air with thrashing forelegs. Let it come from the back, she prayed. Please let it come from behind.

"Stop!"

2

The driving command jarred her, but it didn't seem remotely relevant in her mad frenzy to escape.

"Arrêt!" the same virility demanded in French, only this time just behind her head.

Christin, dissolving now with panic, expected the deathblow to immediately cleave her skull in two. Loath to watch it hack its bloody path, she shut her eyes and slumped over the mane of her horse.

With a force that bruised her ribs, Christin felt herself dragged from her mount and across a scarred leather saddle. Her head was pounding. For several seconds she lay limp beneath the mastery of a strange hand, her efforts to breathe painful.

"Foolish Southron wench!"

Even in her defeated position, the rebuke spurred Christin's defiance. Escape was impossible, but Christin's drive for survival blessed her with amazing strength. She tried to claw at him, and in the effort displayed flashes of petticoats, knees and thighs as she kicked at him any way she could.

Christin's face was shoved downward by a hand little interested in amateurish heroics. The small hook which attached the Scot's iron girdle to his saddle—that plate of iron which he used to bake his oat cakes around the bivouac fire—gouged into the tender flesh of her shoulder.

"Ho-ooh!" a Scot swore as Persis's cries rent the mist.

Christin glimpsed a man swing from his small Border mount to the back of the terrified creature.

"Have a care with that beast!" ordered a deep voice above her and Christin swung a futile arm at his chest.

In the moments that followed, her exquisite embarrassment wasn't inflicted by her enemy, but by the hook attached to his saddle. As Christin abruptly tumbled over the shoulder of the Scottish gray, none but she heard the defeat of ripping linen before she landed upon moist English soil.

She was bared almost to her waist, with the shreds of her sleeves fluttering mournfully to her elbows. Stunned, as if she had never seen them before, she gasped at the desolation of pale, thrusting breasts. Their curves gleamed in the waning sunlight, horribly eager to betray her. Her fingers grew clumsily inept as she struggled with the linen.

"Ohh!" she moaned and crossed her arms, bowing low to shield herself.

Oaths she had never heard grated hoarsely above her head. Then—nothing. So gripped were the men-at-arms at the glimpse of this inadvertent delicacy that Christin could distinguish their ragged breathing over the noise of the distant soldiery.

Was she now to be tortured with indignities by these barbarians? Only wide-eyed girls behind locked doors giggled about the atrocities of Scots; everyone knew Scots were heathens.

"Get up!"

Christin wanted to beg him not to look at her half-nakedness. But an honorable Saxon would never crawl to a Scot. A Saxon would die first. William Winchelsea had drilled valor into his children like a catechism. She refused to move.

Momentarily, a rough hodden tunic dropped to the grass beside her. Hugging protective arms across her bosom, hiding behind her curtain of hair, Christin still refused to rise.

"Well, is your fine English back too good for raw Scottish wool?"

"Nay," she whispered.

"No man will look upon you," he lied.

Nearly a thousand men in number, the rest of the raiding company halted in the valley to wait for her. Her—Christin Anne Winchelsea, who in eighteen years had done little except adorn her beauty and behave as she pleased.

Parted legs positioned themselves beside her, almost over her head—strong legs in rawhide boots, criss-crossed with leather thongs reaching nearly to the knee. A massive sword hugged one thigh and, insanely, Christin was struck with the elegance of its inlay. The man impatiently shifted his weight from one leg to the other, unconcerned with her misery.

Modesty finally became more important than a show of bravery. Christin swiftly straightened her back. Her smooth satiny flesh, about which she had cherished such secret girlish vanity, seemed to be her curse now. Her quick efforts to snatch the tunic into place did not suffice.

The roughened breath above her head was confirmation that the warrior had insolently taken his pleasure of her with his eyes.

"Now get up."

Fury, renewing and righteous, made Christin plunge her fingers deep into the sod she had been taught from birth to respect. With a small toss of her riot of hair, she arose to face her captor, her fists tight.

Christin Winchelsea, bred of fine, willowy stock, was taller than many women. She was proud of her mother's Norman blood which had given her a slender neck and high cheekbones, a narrow waist and long, slim legs. But her father's steady Saxon wits were what she needed now—a fourth-generation pride in her Yorkshire nobility.

As she stood, she studied the sun-browned fingers curved about the hilt of the the sword. They were lean and ruthless. Then Christin stared up into the most arrogant brown eyes she had ever seen. He had to be thirty, and in a flicker of seconds, he missed nothing about her: not her stance, nor the pulse in her throat, nor the quick rise and fall of her breaths.

"The Douglas would know your purposes, mistress."

"The Douglas will roast in hell for his evils, Scot! You'll all roast in hell!"

His brows lifted with disapproving interest. "You are quick with judgments, English. I think I may need protection."

He moved suddenly, and Christin flinched. But he only removed a leather-covered helmet and ran his fingers through curly blond hair. The gesture was uncalculated, and her thought was satisfying: the sunstreaked locks were a trial to him.

Disdain curled one corner of his mouth into a stubble of beard, and his eyes narrowed, revealing fine creases at their corners. Unruffled, his face would have been handsome in its way, were it not for a certain derisive expression about his eyes which said: I trust nobody but myself.

Catching the edge of one brow, sweeping upward across his forehead, a scar disappeared into his hair. Christin inanely hoped some English blade had drawn that line.

"Do you know you're trespassing ninety miles across our border?" she defied.

He seemed to weigh his words, and Christin had the distinct notion that this man had never done anything on impulse.

"In our judgment it was worth the risk. We hoped to steal the queen."

"Your judgment? By what judgment did you find Northallerton worthy of your torches?"

"By the same judgment as your king when he proclaimed me to be a traitor to the English crown." Pausing, he inclined his curly head in a tired, mocking bow. "Patrick Mowbray, mistress."

Christin doubted there was anyone in England who did not know the name. Patrick Mowbray was hated almost as much as the Scots king, Robert Bruce.

London and Bristol gossips whispered broadly that Patrick Mowbray turned rebel because of his Scottish mother. Some said it was because Cecil Mowbray left his fortune to Patrick's older half-brother, Malcolm. Few sympathized, for whatever reason, when Patrick Mowbray turned to his mother's people and allied himself with the rebel king.

Edward II took Patrick Mowbray's defection as a personal affront as well as treason. Not only did the pope excommunicate Patrick, but Edward placed a price of twenty-five hundred pounds upon his head.

"You . . . bloody traitor!" cried Christin.

With the unwise reckoning of a fledgling champion, her fists hurled their clods of dirt squarely in his face. Before she could regret it, the open palm of a large hand struck her hard across one cheek, and only burly Scots arms kept her from sprawling to the ground again.

"Where were you going?" he raged at her.

Christin, scrambling to right herself, was stunned senseless; not only from the blow, but that he had struck it.

"Mi—," she moistened her lips. "Miron, but—"

"Get her ahorse," he flung over his shoulder, fitting his boot into the stirrup of his saddle.

Christin thought if she had been a man, she would have rushed after him, probably to her death. Now she was like a punished child, put forcibly—and embarrassingly—in her place.

"Ah, you begged for that one, lassie!"

Whirling toward the remaining man, a massive figure with a patch over one eye, Christin trembled with bone-deep humiliation and the fury of a spitting cat. He offered to help her mount.

"Don't touch me! I can do it myself!"

"B'heaven, lass, you'd best hold your tongue to his lordship."

"Keep your advice, blackguard invader! How *dare* you savages come to York? Edward will hang you all!"

His laugh rumbled. "Don't count on't, lassie. Come along now." He jabbed a thick thumb toward the company which waited.

As she clambered into her saddle the renewed chance of escape beckoned a tempting finger. The half-blind Borderer shook his head.

"Nay, don't be daft, mistress. It would do no good to run. Sir Patrick would take my head if you bolted, and a blade could still find its way between those bonny ribs."

He grinned through his beard, and Christin's eyes fluttered shut. He had no idea just how much she *had* asked for this. None of this should have happened. She was to blame. She was a Scottish prisoner, and it would be Miron that paid.

"Curse the wretched lot of you!" she muttered, dejected.

"Aye, mistress," he returned just as dourly.

Invaders had hammered at England for four years. Deeper and deeper they had ventured, past the Cheviot Hills, until today they were ninety miles past the border. The war of Robert Bruce since Bannockburn had been a war of recognition. Peace was not enough. The Scots were independent, and they had a king. To the world they boldly declared he was Robert Bruce, not Edward II of England.

Until England and the Roman church recognized the Scottish king, Bruce's officers plundered and were plundered. Northern England was paying for the war by mail—heavy ransoms estimated by some at forty thousand pounds a year.

Southern England was existing well enough, thought Christin bitterly, as Persis jostled her within a tight escort. They didn't have to live here. They didn't move their families and herds out of Northumberland every raiding season. They didn't see blameless Saxon peasants fleeing to the moors while landed gentry and clergy remained to bargain for their homes.

William Winchelsea was a landowner, a raiser of sheep. His respectable brows twitched as he swaggered lovably about his duties as sheriff of Miron. He had always said Miron didn't really need a sheriff. Today it did.

But William wouldn't be at Miron to help her; he was in London, protesting the taxes upon Miron's fleeces. The rule of her father's household was simple and indisputable. No woman rode from the mains of Greystone Manor unescorted, not after the wheat was up. Scots raided when there was good forage for their horses.

She had wheedled Laurence to let her ride to Northallerton. It had been weeks since she had seen their sister Margaret. With grave misgiving her brother had finally agreed, though their father would be furious if he ever discovered it, Laurence had warned.

Magnificent heroics flashed through Christin's mind now. She must do something completely splendid and memorable, something grandmothers would recount for generations and monks would speak of in somber tones. She would be a martyr, here in the glen. But the hysteria edging her own voice horrified her. An unkempt Borderer riding beside her stared as her words rambled to no one and to everyone.

"Do you think you will trade me for rights of passage? We know your kind." She was as effective as a mewling kitten taken from its mother. "You'll set no torches to Miron. Do you think we're trinkets to be bartered? You Scots trade us for mail and hold our people hostage. We're not cattle for sale to the highest bidder!"

Christin's eyes flickered to faces that were as sealed as crypts.

"Well, that's why you didn't kill me, wasn't it? To trade me for the sheep?" she shrieked. She was embarrassed and wished she could stop. "You thieves don't even honor each other. You burn a town for whoever pays the most. Saxon or Scot. We're not animals to be traded, do you hear? We're not—"

"Shut that woman's mouth!" shouted a voice beyond her.

Christin dropped her head. She would not break, she vowed. "We're not animals," she whispered.

Patrick Mowbray was hungry and weary. The Borderers had eaten nothing since early morning, and had eaten precious little then. Sparseness of diet was a necessity. Mobility and speed had won them Bannockburn and the attention—if not the respect—of the English crown. The men about him were hardened to discomfort. Years ago they had learned to eat little and to sleep in the saddle.

He cast disciplined eyes far to his right. From time to time he could just see the reddish-yellow mane of Christin's hair. Realizing the object of Patrick's glance, the young man beside him spoke. A broad grin etched white crinkles across his dirty face.

"A bonny wench, m'lord."

The comment was affectionate, for Gideon was intensely loyal. Patrick frowned that his thoughts were so obvious. When it came to women, he prided himself on a singleness of purpose. A few careless seconds of daydreaming could cost a man his life and the lives of the men who rode with him. Patrick rarely indulged himself.

"Aye, bonny." He frowned.

Patrick swerved aside to overtake several ranks of galloping horsemen. He needed to talk to Douglas. James Douglas thrived on taking the offensive when he rode the Borders. He wore his efficiency like a sturdy garment which made him invincible. And his men devoutly believed that he was.

"She lives there!" Patrick shouted.

With military cunning they gazed at squares of tilled Miron farmland framed by gray Yorkshire crags. Small patches of higher grazing land speckled the panorama with the puffy bundles that were sheep. The pace of the raiding party didn't slacken.

James nodded his head in the direction of Miron.

Smiling grimly, Patrick wiped grime from his face. "I can get a ransom with two hundred men."

"And the girl?"

"Yes."

Ransoms were always preferable to cattle on foot. With Christin as hostage, the outcome of any bargain was inevitable. Preoccupied, Douglas was considering the more lucrative abbey further south, Patrick knew.

"Take Finney and Gordon. We're too far from home.

This will be the last of it. We'll make camp. You go back when you can," he called, waving orders with gloved hands and watching the company divide into ranks. They had done this many times, and with far fewer men.

Patrick swiveled in his saddle to search for Christin, only to find her eyes wide and fixed upon him. Reading fear and much bitterness in them, he absently found himself admiring the way she sat her horse. She was handling herself well, considering her circumstances.

He swallowed a faint sense of shame. He shouldn't have struck her face; she was only a girl. But her rash discourtesy scraped against his temper. These Englishmen didn't teach their children the value of prudence.

With an efficiency born only of hard-won repetition, his two hundred men formed themselves into three units. Patrick drew the centermost men slightly ahead. Without any action on her part, Christin found Persis led from man to man until she was maneuvered to the side of the outlaw. Patrick didn't smile when he called over the sound of hooves.

"What's your name?"

She shouted back. "Christin Winchelsea."

He grimaced. "I'm about to use you, Lady Winchelsea. For that I apologize."

He drew his gray hobin until it nearly touched her own mare. "Also I apologize for slapping you."

"I do not accept it."

"As you wish," he replied wryly.

Yanking his reins hard, he pulled away from her hatred. Just beyond them the tiny burgh of Miron snuggled in the arms of the River Ure.

Already mist was settling, and the spire of the small church speared in and out through the haze like a tapestry needle. Not more than half a dozen buildings were in the town, and only a portion of an ancient wall. Miron had no military strength at all.

Patrick scorned Edward's neglect of his northern counties. Wasn't he aware they were crying to be looted?

Bargaining wouldn't take long, and Patrick was anxious to ride northward to the Low Highlands. He clucked to his horse. No sooner had the first hooves touched the worn stones of the bridge fording the Ure, than Patrick spotted the half-expected truce emissaries.

Only the snorting of horses and the jangle of Scots trappings broke the silence. Children hid behind the skirts of their mothers, not daring to scream. Sparsely scattered plowmen stared at Northallerton's smoke and cursed the lack of time to flee. Only their dogs were missing—up in the hills with the sheep.

One lone man and a garbed priest, the only Englishmen on horseback, separated from the villeins.

"Gideon, see if Finney and Gordon have forded the river yet." Patrick stayed his men. "I want the net to be a tight one."

"Aye, sir. I can see Finney's flank. No sign of Gordon."

"This playlet will be short. We'd best make it a good one," Patrick said, squaring his shoulders. "The sacrificial lamb approaches. David, protect our rear. No surprises now."

The Scot seemed to relish the disease of the town's fear. An English purse was about to yield the price of Edward's refusal to recognize the Scots as a free people.

"Hold your position, Scotsman. We come to parley." Laurence Winchelsea's hands shook on the reins, but the sweep of his eyes gave the impression of haughtiness. "You expect to take Miron with . . . these?"

He nodded his head to Patrick's men behind him who were waiting near the bridge, their swords drawn.

Patrick's mount sidled and he blinked, rubbing at the edge of a tooth with his tongue, unbelieving. He might as well be staring across at the English girl he had made his prisoner. They were identical—the same chestnut waves, the set of gray eyes above high cheekbones. The twin was finely boned and slender, perhaps more than she, and considerably taller, though the girl was not small.

"They're more than enough, Saxon. Northallerton will burn for days. A few minutes will sack this one. Very few."

The priest smiled, though his eyes didn't give the impression of tranquillity. "Miron has elected to meet the terms of a truce."

"Do you speak for this town?" asked Patrick.

"These people have no part in your war. Settle your dispute with the king and his army. Leave them in peace."

Patrick frowned. Then he raised his voice so all could hear.

"You have one quarter hour to agree to ransom and twenty-four hours to deliver it. If the terms of truce are not met, this burgh will be razed to the ground."

"This is an outrage!" Laurence shouted. "State your terms. Miron's sheriff is at court. We are honorable people. Your terms will be considered and negotiated with your . . . king." Then he added, "In a civilized military fashion."

Patrick's laugh was rich and insulting. Laurence had refused to call him "sir."

He smiled. " 'Tis unexpected, the sending of an infant to convenant for a town. Let *them* speak. They will tell you. Ask your townspeople."

"If you don't wish to speak with me, gladly return from whence you came. If you have a price, then by God's blood ask it!"

Patrick was determined that his anger would not master him, but Laurence's arrogance was infuriating, as was Christin's. Mowbray's white teeth showed in a grimace, and he slurred into a thick Border burr.

"Eight hundred mar–rks, then, your lor–rdship."

"Eight hundred marks," the echo whispered through the crowd like dying leaves rustling on the ground. Lord Penmark, next in rank below Lord Winchelsea, took a timid step forward and faced the panicking town.

"Be still," he cautioned, his voice quivering with age. "Be still and stay alive."

13

"Man, are you daft?" Laurence demanded. "We could never raise such a sum."

"Eight hundred, Southron," Patrick repeated coolly, watching the nervous priest. Thinking he meant to speak, the Scot paused, then warned, "Gently, father. 'Tis not my wont to unhorse a man of the cloth."

Smoothing his robes with a reproachful gesture, the priest set a vexed mouth, but he made no move at all. Patrick nodded, acknowledged the visible forces of Finney and felt the town's defeat. Strategically, hoping for haste, Mowbray reached for the leather gauntlets behind his saddle. Laurence wiped sweaty hands upon his breeches. The outlaw finished pulling on one of his gloves with his teeth and, turning, alerted his men for attack.

"Hold!" shouted Laurence. At his cry a dog streaked from the group of stunned people. It plunged straight for the legs of Patrick's horse, yelping furiously and causing the gray to skitter. Despite his mother's cry a boy, hardly nine years of age, dashed for the animal, the child's mother rushing after him. Alarm vibrated through the cluster of villeins, and more than a few crossed themselves.

Already Patrick's men had begun their charge, weapons ready. Snatching up the dog, the boy turned and ran headlong into his mother's arms, directly under Patrick's stirrup. Both of them trembled with their white faces glued to the tall Borderer.

His sword out of its scabbard, Patrick let his breath out slowly, the dry feel of cotton in his mouth.

"Go, madam," he spoke with the precision of an executioner.

"God bless you, m'lord," she sobbed.

Laurence had not moved. If Patrick had had fewer years of bitterness in his past, perhaps he would have pitied the boy's unenviable dilemma. How did this English have the nerve to hesitate?

As Gordon's rank drew closer from the south, the

silence was once again shattered by a woman's cry. But this cry twisted Laurence in his saddle.

"Christin?"

Patrick watched his lips form the name with no sound. He drew rein to charge.

The younger man's composure crumpled, acknowledging his peril of two equal dangers. His eyes continued to strain for the source of Christin's voice as Gordon's ranks parted. Laurence's eyes widened, then they flashed back to Patrick.

The strange tunic Christin wore was as shocking as some despised banner fluttering in their midst. A sword could only kill the twin, Patrick thought. His own tunic could bring Laurence to his knees.

"Are you ready to bargain now, mayhap?" taunted the Scot. For dangerous seconds he sat, the object of Laurence's astonishment. With slow deliberation, he moistened his lips; then he grinned broadly.

"In God's name," choked Laurence, "I'll smear your blood from here to—"

Patrick shook his head and Laurence faltered.

"Don't be a fool," counseled a voice at Laurence's side. "No one could have foreseen this. What sane person would have imagined Scots would come this far?"

"We don't have eight hundred marks!" the young man blurted. "We'll give you the sheep. In good faith. Only return the girl. I beg you." He paused. "Sir."

Patrick smiled, and his order did not hesitate. He didn't want the sheep, and a year wasn't what he wanted, either, though he might be persuaded to take one or the other. He would soon see.

"Gather the sheep!"

Immediately his men began to divide, mingling among the townspeople, some of whom cried for compassion, some of whom cursed, and some of whom retreated in haste, not daring to turn and run. Hoarse commands rang through the gathering darkness, and men were dispatched to go into the hills for Miron's woolly

15

wealth. Small children screamed and crouched behind anything large enough. The older ones stood by their parents, white-lipped with fright.

"No!"

Christin's voice echoed through ranks of men and strange warriors. The two years of pestilence which had taken Miron's sheep were fresh in her memory. If the villeins hadn't eaten the flesh of horses and the dogs, they would have starved. The loss of sheep three years in a row would see them all dead.

"Let me go!" Christin flailed at the hands which reached to restrain her. "Take me for the ransom! I'll be your hostage. Don't take the sheep. Have that much mercy."

Laurence, caught in a tragedy his years were ill prepared for, leapt off his horse.

"Laurence!" shouted the priest. "Play the man. He is baiting you. You'll take a sword through your chest for your trouble."

"By the Virgin, not my sister. Take me. Eight hundred marks, I vow it. My father is an honorable man. Don't destroy this people." He bowed his head.

Their confrontation was too swift, over before it had hardly been fought. Christin saw that she and Laurence combined could not match the skill of this veteran extortioner. The town would not blame Laurence; yet the appeasement shouldn't have happened so quickly. Her fate would be swift, she was certain. Time was a commodity the Scots never squandered.

Patrick Mowbray guided his horse forward until he was only inches from her twin. She hated him for Laurence's shattered innocence.

"You cannot inspire a town's honor as well as your sister, English weedling." Patrick's voice was icy. "It's either everybody or one woman."

At the mercy of an insensitive hand upon the reins of her horse, Christin's secure world crumbled about her; a castle whose mortar has suddenly ceased to hold it together. Persis's hooves clattered on the bridge. Laurence stepped through the horses to grasp Christin's foot in its stirrup, and a white-aproned woman detached herself from the villeins. She ran, clasping and unclasping her hands, her linen skirts flapping about her legs.

"Mistress!" she cried, her voice shrill with resolve. "I shall come, too."

Patrick's brow rose, and Christin opened her mouth to object. The woman was near enough to touch the rawhide of his boot. Her bow was decided, brief and honest.

"I'm known as Tildy Grey, m'lord, and I've been with me mistress since the day she was birthed. An' it please your lordship, I would come with m'lady. I will do any labor asked me, only don't take m'lady with none to tend 'er. I beg of you, sir." The brown eyes Tildy peered into seemed strangely sympathetic. "She's a gentle-bred girl, m'lord," she added softly.

"Aye, so be it," Mowbray hardly waited for her to finish speaking. "Quickly, see to the personal needs of your lady. One pack mule only. And come with one man to the copse yonder before midnight."

He raised his voice. "In the name of Robert Bruce, we spare your town. We do no sacrilege to your church. One year from this date, a ransom of eight hundred marks will be paid for Lady Christin Winchelsea. We claim the rights of safe passage through Miron of York for the same period. I will prepare a signed decree for your man who comes with the maidservant."

To Laurence, Patrick said, "I will arrange safe conduct for one servant through Scotland. You may send a season's garments for your sister. And letters. No more."

"Laurence?" Christin's whimper was drowned by the clamor of departing Borderers.

Thinking she would at least be allowed to embrace her brother, Christin fumbled to dismount. She needed to hold him, to let the strength of his man's body flow into her own. The fear that pressed tightly in her chest

17

was foreign and defeating. Miron must not see her weeping as she left.

But the thick hand of a passing Scot recaptured the reins of her mare, and Christin could only twist back, reaching outstretched hands until she was drawn far away. Laurence's shoulders said he wished he were being taken instead. He loved her and was sorry he had let her disobey their father's law.

Christin's eyes filled with tears, and she blinked vigorously. She had been born into this war. She was not part of it. Yet she was paying for it because an English monarch and a Roman pope refused to attach the word "king" to a man who had already won freedom for his country.

"God go with you, Christin!"

The anguish in her twin's words would go with her to the grave.

As darkness brought a heavy mist, Christin's guilt plagued her. How could God go with her when her very own disobedience placed her in hands which handled horses with more sympathy than people? She had disobeyed by going to see Margaret. Christin and her sister had snatched up the children and crouched in the firs with aching legs at the first sign of trouble. Maggie had wept for her husband Richard when all they could hear was the shouting and cursing of battle. Richard could be dead. Or a prisoner like she was.

Now, in the thicket, the horses were finding little else but spindly grasses and heavy moss, so most of the Borderers eased hungry hobins into the richer grasses of the glen. Friends of the darkness, the Scots divided themselves into closely strung clusters between the copse and the distant hills. Christin obediently took what rest she could as they awaited Tildy and her personal necessities. Apparently this company intended to ride all night, and it could, for no booty weighed it down except her. She wouldn't be permitted to stand in their way.

Borderers carried few supplies—little more than a

small bag of oats which they mixed with water and baked on their iron girdles. Otherwise, they ate what they found. Their mail, if they wore it, was very light, and their horses small and remarkably fleet. The hobins could maneuver through bogs which would suck under a large English destrier in minutes.

When Christin was a child, she had thought Scots were magic. But Sir Mowbray was certainly no figment of a fairy tale, with those legs which never seemed to compromise and those eyes which left one no pride. Patrick Mowbray was a thief who used people's need for food and shelter for his own ends.

There was a word for the kind of mail these Scot robbers extorted. It was black mail—as black as The Bruce who conceived it and as black as The Black Douglas who enforced it. Christin understood now why Robert Bruce and his barbarians were cursed in England's churches three times every day.

At the noise of approaching horses, Christin's head snapped upward. The tunic she was wearing had scratched her raw below her neck and under her arms. She prayed they would allow her to change her clothes.

"Who goes?" a strange Scot demanded gruffly into the mist.

"Tildy Grey and Creagen Smith."

Creagen! A great hulk of a man whose image had never changed in Christin's memory from the time she had crawled about his big leather boots. From Creagen's shoulders she had looked out on the whole world.

He forged the wrought-iron fences about Caroline Winchelsea's grave. From Creagen the twins learned to saddle their horses. And, when William Winchelsea threatened to switch her legs for bloodying Laurence's nose, Creagen coaxed her into apologizing. His concern was that of a lifetime, broad and uncomplicated.

Patrick Mowbray bent his head to Creagen; yet he studied Christin until she withdrew behind the safety of Tildy's back.

"I'm Creagen-the-smith, your lordship. If it be the

same to you, I want to go with her ladyship. My needs are simple, and I do the work of two. I don't lie and never pick a fight. Her father's a good man. If you'll allow me, m'lord, if you were in 'is place, you'd wish someone to see that the lady . . . wasn't spoiled in her bloom. If you—uh, m'lord."

"A long speech," observed Patrick. "Contrary to opinion, Scots are human, born of women and capable of loving their children. We even know somewhat of human nature. Your treachery would never occur to me."

He settled his swordbelt to the line of lean hips.

Creagen offered a stiff bow from his waist. "See that her woman stays on her horse. You'll find our pace a fast one. If there's trouble, do what you're told."

"Aye, m'lord."

Patrick turned his back without hesitation, though Creagen could take on most any two men at once with no difficulty. In the moments of preparation to leave, Christin changed her clothes. With an economy of flurry, the signed terms of truce were given to a messenger from Miron, the pack animals arranged for travel, and Christin assisted into her saddle.

"Lady Winchelsea," the sober officer ordered when they were once again within sight of the glowing horizon of Northallerton. "Ride here. Beside me."

"I warrant you'll strike my other cheek if I refuse." With some difficulty, she reined Persis nearer.

"Aye. I might." He settled his helmet.

Christin obeyed, uncertain at this point whether he really would or not.

Only once did the party pause to rest that first night. Even then, the most Christin could do was pull up her knees and lean her cheek upon them, distraught and afraid. The men slept, and two guards passed her as they trudged, knitted scarves wound over their beards, dirty hands fondling spears.

Once remounted, Christin could no longer worry

about Tildy. Sometime before dawn, Creagen lifted the collapsing woman to sit behind him. At least she could rest against his back and gain a few moments of sleep. These men could sleep as they rode, and they paced the hobins expertly, steadily eating up the miles toward the Cheviots.

Christin clung to consciousness. Every few minutes, she thrust the sleep from her head with a shake. Aching all over, she refused to let Patrick see her cling to the support of a man's back. Behind those blond lashes, she knew he was aware of every move she made.

Wrapped in the flowing mantle Tildy had brought— a small touch of velvet obscured in a Northumbrian night—her consciousness waned. As Persis swerved hard into the galloping horse beside her, Christin sensed herself falling.

Before she could even cry out, her hand brushed the rawhide of Patrick's boot. She grasped for anything as she felt her cloak sweep the speeding earth. More than one horse shied, and somewhere in the confused prancing and yelling, Christin came wide awake. Then she screamed, seeing herself trapped in the dark beneath sharp, thrashing hooves.

Patrick was merciless with his horse as he grabbed for her. And Christin, nearly dragging him off his own mount, clawed at the straining Borderer. Urgent fingers buried into the muscles between his legs, making Patrick wince with surprised pain.

"Don't kick the horse!" he shouted above the pandemonium. He closed his legs tightly about the small hands trapped in the most intimate of places. It took all his strength to grab her below the curve of her buttocks, and the mark of his hands would take days to fade. Strenuously, Patrick hauled her across his lap. For a second time, Christin lay draped on her stomach before him, knowing every man was cursing her as they came to a halt.

In a moment so brief that she later wondered if she

had imagined it, Patrick bent his mouth to touch her ear.

"I've long favored honey-haired lasses," he whispered and released her hands from between his legs. "Now, Mistress Winchelsea," he snapped, all frivolity discarded, "get yourself up behind me. You've delayed us enough for one evening. Half of Yorkshire is probably looking for us by now."

Stung with embarrassment, Christin bridled. She could have been killed!

"Don't talk to me like that! I didn't choose to come!"

"So you didn't, and I weary of your rebellion. Now do as I say, or I'll put you behind Weryn."

Weryn was undoubtedly the man with the patch over one eye. She couldn't bear for another Scots hand to touch her. Already a Borderer stood beside them, his hand cupped, waiting to assist her up behind her captor.

In miserable disarray and much discomfort, Christin climbed up behind Patrick Mowbray. Before she could even settle her skirts, they were moving. Aching from the wet cold, she wished terribly to cry.

"Put your arms about my waist," he ordered.

"No!"

"Do it, woman! And lean against my back and go to sleep. Faith, I'm beginning to wish I'd left you back in Miron!"

"Well, so do I, you . . . thief!" She gritted her teeth.

His sleeveless mail hurt her face when she leaned against it, and after much shifting about which she knew annoyed him, Christin at last found a half-comfortable position for dozing. His body protected her from some of the chill, and presently she began to warm. Patrick sighed as he felt her weight slump against his back.

Minutes slipped past, and he envisioned the repercussions he was sure to hear when he rode into Scotland with her. This girl would be a sensitive hostage: not important enough to be considered a trophy, not unknown enough to be negligible. Her father, through the English king, would give him trouble. Patrick could depend on it. The Bruce was growing very diplomatic about hostages: returning critical ones when it would make him look generous and make Edward look like an assassin.

Edward II an assassin? Compared to his father, he was a choirboy. Patrick remembered the moment when he began to hate Edward I with startling clarity. Patrick had been sixteen. He had sat on his horse in the snow and stared up at Isabel Buchan hanging half-frozen in an iron and timber cage.

Edward I had hung Isabel from the prison tower of Berwick Castle like a wild beast. For nearly four years she suffered exposure to summer's heat and winter's savagery. At least the king granted that a privy be placed in the cage, but he forbade that Isabel speak to another Scot. Her crime? She had placed a small crown of gold upon the head of Robert Bruce.

And for this she paid eventually with her sanity. As the years passed, even calloused Englishmen could hardly bear to look at her.

But Patrick had often looked at Isabel. It was in his eighteenth winter that he stood before her with tears freezing on his face. Many who knew him thought that Malcolm's inheritance of the family wealth sent him to Scotland. No. It was the sight of Isabel in her cage that reached down into his soul and brewed an anger bitter as gall inside him. He felt it now, with this English girl sleeping against him.

What would he do with Christin when he arrived at Warrick? Would he put her in one of the dungeons? If she were a man he would. Or have her labor like Creagen. The two woman were in no way alike, Patrick reassured himself to the rhythm of thrumming hoofbeats. To compare them was illogical. Isabel had been the brunt of Edward's outrage; his own motives were much different. Christin would not be mistreated, only traded for mail. This was war!

Christin's face tilted slightly, and her breath blew warmly on the back of Patrick's neck, whispering into the curls beneath the rim of his helmet. Trembling, he muttered a long, appeasing oath that he reserved for special occasions.

Sure hooves drew them nearer the Cheviots and the Border. Loosening in her slumber, Christin's hands draped innocently between Patrick's legs. *Must the wench persist in doing that?*

A wisp of chestnut hair whipped across his cheek. Patrick shook it aside, only to have it return across his eyes. Reaching to toss it away, he impulsively lifted the end of it to his lips. The fragrance of it teased his thoughts, causing him to remember her with her back bent, the slender shape of her ribs, her crossed arms covering her bosom in an age-old gesture of womanly protection.

His recollection was a weakness—momentary and unwelcome. In the past, women had served an uncomplicated need, and he liked it that way. One didn't expect to find a beautiful girl half-naked in an English glen—that was all. The sleeping girl sighed, her cheek instinctively searching for a more comfortable pillow along the curve of his shoulder.

"Damnation!" Patrick muttered, grinding his jaw and choosing to ignore the odd trembling of his hands. A danger was here, he thought pensively. If he were not careful, taking this hostage could turn out to be a great mistake. It was quite possible that in the end he really would wish he had left Christin Winchelsea in Miron.

Chapter Two

A mossy branch above Christin's head dripped ill-boding dew, forcing her awake. Gray mist bathed the landscape. The valley below was thick with lethargic clouds straggling as if they were lost. Stiffly huddled against Tildy for warmth, as she had the past two nights, she pretended to be asleep.

Slumbering men stretched full-length about her—twenty-five, thirty, perhaps—some wrapped in blankets, some without. Carved hilts of longswords or spear shafts lay within a fingertip's reach of all. As if she inspected the workings of a trap, Christin glanced from form to form, seeking one in particular. Yes. There.

His helmet carelessly removed, Patrick lay on his side with one knee pulled upward toward his chest. He looked taller when he was stretched full length. Even in slumber his fingers rested upon the shaft of a spear.

The wariness about Patrick's eyes was gentled for once, and Christin grinned halfheartedly, noting that the dew had made his hair even more curly. His hair was streaked nearly white from the sun. His body was hard. She could scarcely forget how hard his back was, for she had never been so physically close to a man before. The palm of his hand on her cheek was hard, too, she remembered, her anger rekindling.

During the past two days and hundred miles, Christin had imagined herself escaping a dozen times, and in as many ways. She was always brilliantly heroic, and the Scots always shook their heads at her cleverness in outsmarting them. Then her eyes would meet the reality of Patrick's, and she would feel like a small girl who had to look up at grownups as if they were giants. She was convinced he knew her every thought and was secretly laughing at her.

Christin slowly closed her fingers about Tildy's shoulder and shook her. The woman jerked awake with a sudden start.

"Shhh!" warned Christin.

They sat perfectly rigid as the Scot nearest shifted in his sleep. With a noisy smacking of his lips, he settled back to a soft snore.

Tildy's mutch had slipped off her head, all limp and soggy, and her braids were comically awry. The fright in her eyes was earnest enough. Distinctly forming the words, Christin shaped a soundless message.

"Let's get out of here."

"Nooo." Tildy shook her head in such emphatic dissent that her braids tumbled down altogether.

"Well, I must have some privacy away from these men."

Christin ruffled her locks vigorously with both hands and gave her head a shake to free the tangles. Tildy stared at the set of her shoulders, the slim ivory neck that was so like her mother's.

"Very well," Tildy sighed. "Come along, m'lady."

They crawled on all fours from the motionless camp, literally drenching their skirts with dew. Once they were some yards past, both women stood. Christin yawned hugely. The day before yesterday her clothes had been blue; now they were a dingy gray.

"You wait here," she commanded stoutly, "and let me know if anyone so much as makes a sound from that camp. Then I'll watch for you. I'm starving!"

After some swift minutes of straightening garments,

rebraiding hair, and brushing away dust and debris, the two managed to restore themselves. Still, no sounds of arousal drifted from the camp beyond.

"I'm not going back."

Tildy drew herself up and frowned at the young jaw, set with such injured dignity.

"Aye, but you will. What about Creagen?" she demanded with the strictness of a mother. "You can't just run away and leave him to be punished for your escape."

"They won't hurt Creagen. It's me they want, and they won't find me. We'll hide in the trees. They're in a hurry and can't afford very much time to look. As soon as they get across the Border, we can go home."

"Walk? Back to Yorkshire? Oho, m'lady. You've lost your senses."

When Christin twisted her mouth out of shape, it only drew attention to its perfection. She was desperate. She wouldn't deny that her scheme was irrational, but she simply couldn't go back and suffer at the hands of Patrick Mowbray for an entire year.

"They starve political prisoners, Tildy. And sometimes they kill them."

"Mistress, be sensible. You've never had a mother, and I done the best by you that I knew how. But if Lady Caroline was here, she'd tell you, the same as me. His lordship seems a fair man, for all his reputation, considerin' we're at war. It could've been a lot worse than it's been. At least he spared Miron. It's certain you're better off with the Border rogues than wanderin' about in Northumberland to get caught by Irish Jack and that band of English outlaws."

Bright tears of vexation stung Christin's eyes.

"How d'you dare defend that gutter knave to me? I'm the victim, if you'll remember! Well, go back to them, then. But I refuse to be mauled and disgraced at their hands anymore. His lordship, his lordship! God in heaven, Tildy, the man is a criminal! Fair indeed. He'd as soon kill a woman as look at her, if it suited his mind."

27

The uncertainty of inexperience made her face bleak. Christin battled for a maturity that came only by living the kind of life she had been protected from.

"They'll hurt me, Tildy," she said, beginning to lose the last of her control. "You weren't there. My kirtle— it was torn to pieces, and they all gawked at me. They'll wait until the time is right, and then they'll hurt me. I'd as soon die in Northumberland as like *that*."

Christin's mind was whirling. She had even overlooked bringing her mantle. But she was far past caring, or thinking logically. She could survive somehow, if she could only put some distance between herself and the Scots.

Yanking her skirts high, she impetuously began to run like some bright-haired wraith skimming through the trees. Before losing sight of her, Tildy grudgingly gathered up her own wet skirts and began to trudge after her mistress.

A half dozen paces was as far as Tildy went. An armed and mailed figure stepped from seemingly nowhere to plant himself across Christin's path. Clutching both hands to her mouth, Christin paled and almost crashed headlong into the guard. He was a full head shorter than she. For some compelling reason, however, the shaggy beard and blue eyes pierced her almost as sharply as his spearhead threatened her.

Christin cursed herself. She immediately realized the folly of her ways. The entire affair now appeared to be the mad caprice that it was. What had she been thinking?

" 'Twould seem you've lost your way. If you'll allow me, I'll escort you back to camp . . . m'lady."

She squinted, trying to decipher the burr. But his manner was so insulting and his politeness so ridiculous, that she didn't need to understand his words. Grappling for some means of persuasion, she pulled her stomach very flat and stared down her nose.

"I don't suppose you'd consider—"

He blinked and stared pointedly.

"Look, Scot"—she grew earnest—"my father is not

28

a poor man. Not a rich one exactly, but if you'd help me escape these men . . . you'd never want for another thing the rest of your life. Anything. He would protect you from them." She paused, urging him to reply with an arch of her brows.

Only his lips moved when he replied. "Nay."

"I thought not," she said and slumped with a sigh.

As they returned to the breaking camp the smell of heated fat and scorching oatcakes hung heavily in the mist. Patrick chewed pieces of unleavened cakes and washed them down with some brackish-looking liquid. Christin tried not to fidget, but she had almost reached the screaming point when he finally motioned for her to sit. She refused.

"It would appear, Lady Winchelsea," he began with the monotone of a monk, "that you find our company undesirable. Perhaps your appetite won't be too proud to partake of our humble fare."

"Tildy may eat if she wishes. I will not."

Rubbing the blond stubble of a moustache with the tips of three fingers, Patrick narrowed his eyes. Effortlessly, then, and without seeming to move rapidly, he was beside her.

"Eat it, mistress!" he gritted, setting her head thrumming. "Now!" Then he explained more politely, like a tight-lipped parent. "I don't wish a fainting woman upon my hands, and time is dear. This area that neither country controls crawls with lawless Saxons who delight in butchering their own kind."

Their eyes met, and with astonishing authority he repeated calmly, softly. "Eat it."

Christin's youth and her lack of skill dreaded the battle of wills she knew was catching fire like tinder. But Saxon honor, misguided or not, spurred her resistance further. She would not bend to him again. The quiet which gripped the camp was treacherously, murderously alert.

"You're not my lord and master, Patrick Mowbray.

I may be your hostage, but I'm not your serf. I'll not take orders from any underling knight of Robert Bruce."

The angry muscle in Patrick's jaw admonished her as it flexed. "Don't press me, Lady Winchelsea."

As an open indication that he had no intention of enduring a tirade, he spun about and bent on one knee to continue his eating.

"M'lady," whispered Tildy as Creagen watched in agitated silence. Tildy stepped beside her mistress to press the small oaten bannock into her hand. "Don't anger him," her soft plea fell on deaf ears. Aloud she soothed Christin, trying to repair the damage. "Eat something, mistress. You'll feel better."

Christin took a few tasteless bites. If Patrick Mowbray had said he respected her difficult position and would be as fair about it as possible, she would have relented. Perhaps he relished this confrontation. Perhaps she did, too. With symbolic abandon, Christin threw the precious food into the flames.

"Feel better? Feel better?" she cried. "This wretch expects us to go marching tamely into Scotland with him, making obeisance to that pretender to the throne. Well, let me tell you something, *Sir* Mowbray. The day will come when you'll wish you'd never heard of Robert Bruce!"

Creagen dug holes in the dirt with his boot.

"Why, the man's a fool! Look at the stupid mistakes he's made. The very idea, making Edward Bruce king of Ireland. Even the idiot himself realizes the folly of that. And you, an Englishman, trailing along behind the man, and even The Douglas—a blacker villain there never was—waging some little boy's war. I use the word 'Englishman' lightly of—"

Patrick's wrath was so brilliant that even his own men froze, their food poised in shocked fixation between hand and mouth. The man Weryn stepped forward to Christin, his astonishment drawing craggy concern across his features.

"Lady Winchelsea," he gasped.

"Stay where you are!" Patrick thundered and jabbed a hard finger of caution at Weryn. "And, Mistress Winchelsea, I hardly need any advice of military conduct from a silly female brat hardly out of swaddling clothes!"

Tildy started mumbling her prayers and drew back nearer the trees, covering her head with both hands as she moved.

The distance between Patrick and Christin closed in three steps, and she, realizing she had gone too far, tasted bitter remorse in her mouth. This man had brought Miron to its knees. This was what he did best.

"Edward the First was a tyrant, mistress," he said. "He interfered in a country's own business when he should have kept still. Edward the second is different only because he isn't half the man his father was."

"Edward may be weak, sir." Christin felt embarrassment heaving below her breasts. She feared she looked ridiculous. "But we English know where we stand. Our king doesn't pledge allegiance to one and serve another like Robert Bruce."

She watched Mowbray's mouth draw downward, his weight shift to one hip, his intake of breath which mocked her.

"Edward the Second isn't the crown, Mistress Winchelsea. Hugh le Despenser controls the crown of England. Do you realize where your father's taxes go? To furbish the wardrobe of the king's lover! You take food from the mouths of hungry children and put jewels on Despenser's fingers, gold in his vaults."

Christin had no argument. Not even Edward I had been successful in keeping his son from flaunting his lover. After Edward II's earls murdered Piers Gaveston, the young king's first favorite, Hugh Despenser the Elder craftily used his own son to seduce the English crown. When Despenser pandered to the king's weakness for men, he incurred more hatred in the realm than his predecessor, Gaveston. Edward II was the puppet of Hugh Despenser the Younger, and Hugh Despenser the Younger was the puppet of Hugh Despenser the Elder. England's earls, through Parliament, wanted to rid themselves of all three.

"People have no choice about the taxes they pay!" Christin spat her words. She was beautiful, which made the wound of her words more cruel. "Shall I become a traitor like you?"

The flash of the Scot's brown eyes should have warned her. Even Tildy read the danger simmering in their depths. She resumed her prayers, drawing farther away.

Patrick's mouth was tight as he spoke. "Perhaps Edward's earls will still do us the favor of murdering Despenser as they did Gaveston."

Christin refused to be forced into apologizing for Edward.

"You're awfully free when it comes to someone else's life, Sir Mowbray. Scots are different, I suppose. They kill only women and children. They burn only the homes of people whose worst crime is to live in northern England."

Like two magnificent wild creatures determining to not be broken, they locked eyes. They drew themselves tall and proud, refusing to bend.

"Perhaps you are more like Edward than we realize," Christin said. Even as she spoke the words, she knew they were false. But the accusation fell with deliberate weight, like drops of water upon a white-hot stove. The tension increased beyond bearing at the insult to his manhood.

The scar across Patrick's forehead whitened. Deep lines drew from the edges of his nose to the sides of his mouth—a mouth compressed in bitter fury. He wouldn't take this from her. A large hand lifted, and Christin could not prevent the damning words with which she sealed her fate.

"Half-Scot," she whispered. "Half-man, do you think?" Then she closed her eyes, knowing she had stepped beyond any hopes for mercy. She braced her

slender shoulders to receive his blow, thinking wooden-
ly that the horror on his face had been worth it.

Hypnotized, all observed the grave drama; a war
not just between man and woman, but between English
and Scot. Christin had not drawn a breath, and she
yelped as Patrick's fingers bit into her arms. He pinned
them and lifted her off the ground until her face was
just below his. And his breath fell upon her open,
startled mouth as her neck snapped backward.

"Don't you dare faint!" he snarled through a terrify-
ing smile. "You're not equipped to play this game, my
lady. Didn't your mother teach you the ways of wisdom? Even a wanton would think twice before she
questioned a gentleman's manhood before his own men."

Christin whimpered a protest.

His voice tightened. "Just so you won't make the
same mistake twice . . ."

Grasping her head in the fingers of one hand so
fiercely that Christin feared he would crush it, Patrick
forced her mouth upward until it almost touched his
own. For a few seconds she thrashed, but his mouth
ground down upon hers in a kiss so cruel that she
tasted the saltiness of blood.

Christin's mouth was virgin territory; the most daring
kiss had been a nervous peck on her lips. Gripping her
to his body and holding her fighting hand outstretched,
Patrick's tongue thrust unforgivably against her clenched
teeth. Inarticulate protests strangled in her throat, but
the angry man ruthlessly ravaged his way into her
mouth. As Christin strained, freeing her hand entirely
by accident, she grabbed a generous handful of blond
curls and pulled with all her might. Slivers of pain splintered through Patrick's head, and he released her for the
seconds it took to strike loose her hand.

"You don't know when to give up, do you, lamb?"

"Please, I—"

"You beg my forgiveness now?"

"No!"

Winding her hair through his fingers, Patrick jerked

her head back until he could observe the fright turn to
hatred in her eyes. The Scot didn't like what he was doing, yet he was strangely eager to have her despise him.
He allowed Christin no chance to speak before he took
her mouth again. This time he forced her head still and
tasted what no man ever had—plundering, taking, strip-
ping. Nor did he gentle his assault when he felt her spirit breaking. Her eyes brimmed with tears; she couldn't
possibly understand.

When it happened, Christin felt his surprise, but she
didn't really comprehend when her mouth was yielding instead of fighting. Her inexperience didn't know to
warn her when desire began to harden him against her
belly. She couldn't think at all. Unexpectedly, even to
him, Patrick freed her hands. Once they almost reached
upward toward his face, but then they dropped, as her
bones seemed to melt somewhere within her.

For a man seasoned as he was to war, to hardship,
and yes—even to women, Patrick was irritated to realize that he had seemingly lost track of time. He hadn't
meant to do that. In truth, he hadn't meant to kiss her
when it started—only to make her regret her slanderous
remark.

The first thing Patrick saw when he came to himself,
realizing uneasily that the taste of her mouth was pleasant, and that kissing Christin Winchelsea was a thing
he would like to toy with a good deal longer, was Gideon's obvious delight. And Weryn's reluctant embarrassment.

With a frown, Patrick put the subdued girl from him.
He knew he had hurt her and no remorse wavered his
glance at Creagen. Nor did he offer explanations, but
turned on his heel, presenting his back to Christin as if
he chose to ignore what had just happened. He bent to
reach for his mail without comment while she covered
her mouth with a trembling hand.

Through the Lowlands of Scotland, Patrick seldom
spoke to Christin, but she often caught him staring

darkly at her, forcing her, in the end, to lower her eyes. The terrain grew craggy, yet more lusciously green, once they left the barren wilds of Northumberland. The sun was enshrouded in clouds as if, she mused, it was offering some celestial disapproval of the return of the Borderers with ill-gotten gains. Then it seemed to blur confusingly with each new day. With the skies in a constant state of drizzle or downpour, her mind ceased to count the hours. Staying alive seemed a burden.

Dispiritedly she observed fragments of what wealth Scotland possessed. Even in war, some of its buildings were magnificent. Bruce and Douglas had a way of destroying Scotland's vast fortresses, however, for once an enemy became entrenched in a castle he was almost invincible. Many incredible ruins told the war's story. Peel towers, cylindrical refuges stuck out in nowhere, were half destroyed or toppled entirely.

Nearer the Highlands, poverty manifested itself on every side. Bruce's efforts to reclaim productive lands didn't seem to be working very well. Even though England's cattle and sheep had suffered a plague, Christin didn't think Patrick's land was faring any better.

"It was last year's wheat crop that broke their backs," Gideon offered during one of his efforts to be friendly. Her brows questioned. "It looked good, filled out and fine. But at the threshing—nothing. A third of what it should have been."

Peasants existed in miserable black houses. She saw many huts from her horse—timber, wattle and turf barely hanging together. Stones had been placed upon the thatched roofs to keep them from rejoining the environment during Scotland's sudden and savage storms.

Christin observed Patrick's hands upon the pommel of his saddle as they threaded the worn reins. These Borderers had no splendor. They were tough and grim, like the land they lived in. Scot battles had been won by men who treated war as a grisly business.

Their numbers steadily reduced as men dispersed homeward. Until the next time. When hooves were no longer pounding until one could scarcely shout above them, the remaining company dipped eagerly into a broad valley swathed in flowers.

Clattering across a crude, aging bridge, two abreast, Christin viewed the somewhat battered edifice of Warrick Manor. Clustered fir and spruce, a small loch beyond which emptied into the River Ardle, also caught her eye. Timbered docks stretched from the rear of the manor to meet the river.

Gideon reined up beside her, and Christin shivered at the infectious exhilaration of returning home. While they might be conquering heroes, she was in exile, cut off from those who loved her. Had she not been so proud, Christin would have pulled the edge of her mantle over her face as Tildy did. Great choking sobs could be heard in the woman's throat.

"Warrick Manor once belonged to a Norman knight," the young man said, smiling. She didn't reply. "Edward the First sent a great many Normans and Saxons after Alexander the Third was killed. He was determined to make Angles of us, you ken?"

Christin nodded, thinking it was a pity Edward hadn't succeeded.

"English owned Scots land and lived here, in Scotland. Scots owned English land and lived there. Like The Bruce did. Sometimes a man didn't know a friend from an enemy."

Laughing children, barefooted and wiry, skipped beside the prancing hobins to receive a bauble or two and a chuckling response from weary thieves. Greetings were shouted, and men quickly dismounted to scoop up white-capped women with a hug.

Suspicious villein eyes raked Christin as she struggled to endure her position beside Patrick with coolness and dignity.

"An English lass!" marveled an older woman whose step was as springy as a child's. " 'Twould ha' been better t'bring the mail."

Christin wanted to scream, "But we didn't have the mail! Do you think the English are made of money?"

"Aye. Three English mouths t'feed for a winter. And us barely keepin' body an' limb together."

"Immoral it is, to boast an uncovered head so."

The stern reprimands tightened Christin's mouth. She wished to heaven that Tildy would stop sniffling.

Creagen's face was unreadable. Her own mother would have been like him and stiffened her back and stared them all down like a queen. Christin was too tired to be majestic, and she wished it didn't matter. But it did matter; it all mattered terribly.

"Ho, Dan! Paddy MacMinn!" Patrick bent nearly out of the saddle. Young boys ran to touch his horse or his boots with awed fingertips. Astounded, Christin realized that the peasants loved this man. How could they? Didn't they realize the kind of man he was?

Patrick's laugh was a clear, hearty sound as he tossed his helmet to the youngsters who scuffled for it. Her own misery was acute, bending her forward as if she hurt inside. Surely he would turn now and tell her what to do. She waited; she wanted it; she even opened her mouth to speak. But Patrick had dismounted and was speaking with Weryn. Long strides took them toward Warrick, and he never once turned to look at her.

Gideon, whom Christin was beginning to trust, stripped off his mail and scratched at a head of rusty hair and beard. Issuing a few terse instructions to the remaining guards, he bowed stiffly to Christin.

"You may dismount now, Lady Winchelsea, and I will escort you to your quarters. You"—he indicated Creagen—"follow them to the stables."

With a friendly hand, Gideon swung Christin from her saddle, and as Tildy continued to rub her eyes, they walked toward the manor. Then it dawned upon Christin where she was being led.

"No!" she whispered.

Her offended eyes swept across the broken tower, sandstone scattered upon the ground and vines reaching upward to sympathetically hide the scars. They surely wouldn't put her in some cell below the ground. She would die.

"Please, I cannot stay there." She tried not to plead.

"But, your ladyship," argued Gideon, "a chamber is being provided for you. It's the wish of Sir Mowbray that you don't suffer undue discomfort."

This surprised her, and Christin's mind took quick advantage.

"I will not stay in that manor!" she bluffed.

For the first time, Christin became aware of the girl behind him, her arms filled with Gideon's mail. He grinned sheepishly, realizing that Christin had caught a glimpse of his pat to the girl's backside as he drew her forward.

"Lady Winchelsea, may I present Glynnis? We're soon to be married." Glynnis flushed hotly, curtsying.

Christin smiled. The girl couldn't be much younger than she was. Yet, for some reason, Christin felt much, much older.

"I'll stay in one of the wattle houses," Christin offered heavily, returning to the problem. "Or there, perhaps. The cottage behind your kirk." She pointed to the tiny neglected church. "One of those. Anything. But I'll not live in the manor house."

Gideon sighed, shrugging at his unexpected problem.

"Very well. Wait here, and I'll see." He set off at a brisk pace toward Warrick, laughing boyishly with his sweetheart.

How surprised Gideon would have been to know Christin's thoughts. She envied him. Her homesickness plagued her greatly. Once she had been where people loved her and laughed with her. Now what was she to do?

It was almost dark when Patrick discovered Tildy resting against a tree with her eyes closed. Christin wandered idly about the kirkyard. She seemed very small, very alone as she paused to brace herself against a worn stone marking a grave older than both their ages together.

Patrick's first impulse was to draw back and study her unobserved. As disheveled as she was, she was quite lovely just now, the shadows of dusk catching her in relief against the sky. She appeared strikingly fragile—transparent, ephemeral.

Then she saw him, and he strode to her with steps which pretended impatience.

"As usual, mistress, there seems to be a problem."

"I'm sure there's a well-put insult somewhere in that."

"Your tongue, m'lady, lets blood far too easily."

"And your behavior persists in whetting it. Aside from discussing my political position here, I refuse to live in that . . . place." Christin gestured toward the hall with flippant fingers.

"I have chosen the cottage nearest this church." She doubted that he was impressed with her independence. "And I wish water for Tildy and me to bathe. Food for our stomachs, too, if you don't mind. Other than that, if I don't see you again for the coming year, I shall be able to endure."

Turning a step toward the tiny hut, she whirled back. "Your lordship," she murmured sarcastically, as if she had forgotten.

"Cease, mistress," growled Patrick.

"Of course, *sir*."

She smiled brilliantly. Patrick wanted to slap her.

Hands rammed in his belt, the Borderer strode stormily toward the old stone dwelling. Before the mass excommunication of Scotland, the thatch-roofed affair had been for the priest. But no priests came now; even vicars were in short supply in Scotland. Defying the pope made them understandably nervous.

Stooping to enter the dingy room, viewing the central hearth and what had once been a rush-covered floor, Patrick snorted. Perhaps the little witch would drown when it rained—an unsatisfactory opening in the roof served as a chimney.

"It's hardly fit to live in," he diagnosed. Christin began to roam about, and he unexpectedly found himself trailing behind her.

"You would be more comfortable in the manor hall."

"Isn't it a bit late to begin worrying about my comforts, Sir Mowbray?"

A brief uncomplimentary obscenity escaped Patrick's lips, and he stepped to motion to the guard outside.

"Take her dame and instruct her how to see to her ladyship's needs. Send some women to see to the cleaning of this place."

"Nay!" cried Christin, gesturing wildly. "I don't want people here who hate me." She grew agitated. How could she explain pride to a thief? "I will do everything for myself," she began again. "Don't give orders to Tildy, and don't tend to my horse, and don't clean . . . Just leave me alone, and—"

Patrick motioned the guard on with a nod of his head.

Christin was *so* tired, and the plight she found herself trapped in was making her capable of most anything. Her fists clenched, and as she thought back upon it later, she realized that she had had no intentions of striking at him.

But Patrick just stood there, lounging in the doorway of that miserable hovel—so smugly, so complacently. Before she thought, she stepped to the chest before her and began pounding against it like an angry toddler battering its head against a wall. Positive that he was mocking her, she then began to weep soundlessly. Once she started crying nothing could stop the tears. She must have looked ridiculous, standing there pummeling his chest and calling him all sorts of garbled names between her sobs.

Either because Patrick Mowbray was a fairly wise man after all, or else he wished to see just how big a fool she would actually make of herself, he calmly let Christin spend her wrath. He didn't say a word; he didn't try to stop her. Finally she raised a limp hand for the last time and dropped it listlessly to her side. It was very dark outside.

"Are you quite finished now, Christin?"

"Don't use my name. And I'm not sorry."

"I didn't expect you were, and I shall call you anything I please." Both were dirty and exhausted, and Christin's face was tear-streaked and drawn. But his tone lifted her eyes to find him studying her so intensely that she became alarmed.

"I warrant so," she breathed, her lips parted.

"I will caution you this one time, Christin. And if you disobey me, you have only to reap the fruits of it."

Her eyes snapped then. "What?"

"No plans to escape, lassie," he cautioned, his head shaking gravely. His authority was so complete that it infuriated her.

"Imbecile! You should have thought of that when you brought me here. I'll never cease trying to escape this horrible place. Laurence will send men for me. He—"

"Don't be a fool, Christin. Laurance Winchelsea will do nothing of the sort, and the sooner you stop fighting the reality of this war, the better off we'll be."

Gazing down at the top of her head, Patrick shifted his weight uneasily and reached for her slender hand.

"Come here."

Christin strained against him. Barely holding his temper in check, Patrick gave her a small jerk. He took her face between his thumb and forefinger and forced her face upward toward the narrow slits of light glowing from the stone manor.

"Do you see that window there?" he demanded. "The first one off-center, to the left. Do you see it, Christin?"

Silence.

"Answer me!"

"Yes, yes! I see it!"

"That is my chamber, Christin Winchelsea. Now do you see the one beside it?"

She nodded against his fingers.

"That will be *your* chamber if you make one attempt

to leave the valley. A guard will be posted outside the door and will watch your every move. I might warn you, lamb, by then it might be too late. Scots are not immune to laying pretty wenches in the grass, and my authority holds only within my own lands." He paused. "I don't want any man touching you."

"You're contemptible!"

"I'm warning you now, for after a decent night's rest you'll doubtless have fancies of backsliding into your old habits. And I'll always bring you back." He smiled. "I need the eight hundred marks."

Voices were nearing, and he released her jaw, his fingers brushing down her neck to bury themselves into the thick tangled locks. Christin's eyes widened as Patrick's hand cradled her head. She couldn't force her eyes away as he studied her mouth.

"You have yet to recant the charge you so unfortunately made against me," he said.

"I recant nothing. You'll not hear me say those words. Not ever." Her voice dwindled to silence.

He chuckled, and Christin flushed hotly as his brown eyes ambled over the curves of her breasts, down to the taper of her waist. She knew he deliberately made his grin lewd, to see if she would defy him as she had in the presence of his men. With one hand, she attempted to remove his fingers from her hair, but he caught her wrist. She dared not struggle against him.

Presently he relaxed, smiled and dropped his hands.

"You shall say the words, lassie," he promised. "You shall, you shall."

Chapter Three

"I hate this wretched fire!" Christin shrieked, rubbing her smarting eyes and beating her apron at smoke which persisted in fondling her face.

Staggering to the doorway to gulp huge drafts of air, she stamped her foot at the offending cottage. The opening in the ceiling let more rain in than it drew smoke out, and its Scottish inadequacy only damned it more. Why had Edward's armies not subdued these savages years ago? Then she wouldn't be here, glaring at Tildy as she stirred vegetables and herring in a blackened old pot.

Tildy smothered a smile into her collar. Even now, in Christin's bleary rage, hands fanning about a tiny waist and her mouth puckering in a pout, Tildy adored her. The woman was not so daft, either, that she had failed to notice the number of Scots eyes reflecting the same sentiment. A number had habitually stopped to savor the sway of Christin's skirts the past two months. Warrick Manor and its crofts had seemingly sired a number of comely lasses, but Christin was fairer than any. Much to Tildy's disquiet, her lady knew it all too well.

The laird of Warrick had promised twenty stripes upon the back of any Scot who made even a lewd remark to Christin. Tildy knew it was true, for Creagen had confided it. She had never told her mistress, however. Lately the mere mention of the Mowbray name was apt to induce such a state of fury that all her cajoling becalmed little or none.

"There's only one thing I hate more than this house," Christin grumbled, blotting red eyes.

"Och!" sniffed Tildy, who had heard this tale for the hundredth time. "Well, m'lady, if you'd be halfway civil to the laird, your plight mightn't be so hard. You must admit, you've more than a bit of your brother's blood in you. How such a sweet man as your father managed to raise such spoiled children . . ." Sorrily, she shook her head.

At the mention of Laurence, Christin's stare became fixed. Her bonds with England and her family were fraying, crumbling irreparably. She absently flicked mortar from between the stones of the wall.

"Oh dear. I'm beggin' your pardon, mistress. Truly, I didn't mean to grieve you. There, there, now. Be a good girl and skim the milk that Glynnis brung you. Faith, but I've taken quite a likin' to that youngster." She laughed. "Why, the way those two carry on, there's a fine chance a weddin' will be earlier than they—"

Christin scolded with her wooden ladle. "Hush, Tildy. You know it's a sin to gossip. And besides," she giggled, "I think it's sweet. Gideon's a fine young man and will make Glynnis a good husband. Sometimes I can even forgot he's a Scot."

That was about the most generous praise she could bestow these days. After poking a bent finger into the thick cream, Christin popped it into her mouth. Her sooty lashes lowered as she sighed.

"Heavenly. Just heavenly." Her mood changed without warning like a sudden squall. "I wonder what Laurence is doing today. And Papa. And Margaret. The last time I saw Richard, he was running, buckling on his sword. He yelled, 'Take the children, Maggie, and go to the woods. Run and don't look back.' Margaret started crying, vowing she wouldn't leave him, and he started out the door. He yelled at me, 'Make 'em go, Chrissy. I depend on you!' "

Christin's shoulders grew heavy with the burden of memories. "I don't even know if he's alive. I suppose it's possible that Magaret doesn't, either. I wonder how many really died in Northallerton that day."

When she turned to Tildy, the grief twisted Christin's face so badly the older woman moved to hold her like a child.

"It was all so stupid, Tildy. If I hadn't been so willy-nilly and gotten myself caught by those savages, none of this would have happened."

"All of it would have happened. They would have taken the sheep instead of you, and Miron would be starving. Why don't you ask Sir Patrick about Richard? I think he'd be honest with you."

"I'll not ask that knave anything, and that's final! I wish to heaven you'd stop hinting at that. Even if he knew, he wouldn't tell me. Nothing delights that man more than looking at me in that condescending way he has. *Eight hundred marks,* by the saints!"

With a clandestine peep out the door, Christin lowered her voice. The only person in sight was the everlasting Scots guard, whittling now under the branches of a comfortable spruce.

"I'm planning an escape, Tildy," she whispered. "It's foolproof."

"Ahhh! You can't leave trouble alone, can you, m'lady?"

"Stop scolding. I told you only so you'd have a choice. If you stay here, the Mowbray wretch will figure you knew all the time and didn't tell. Then he'll have you scrubbing sheets in the river."

"Begone, Christin Winchelsea! It's a foolish, foolish child you are, and I'll not listen." The clank of her spoon on the pot assured Christin that wheedling was useless.

With one final sigh of crossness, she caught up her

skirts and swooped out across the kirkyard. She had absolutely no patience with Tildy's cowardly ways. For two months, Christin had hardly seen Patrick Mowbray of Warrick Manor.

Her belligerence whirled her about to suddenly catch her watchdog ambling some distance in her wake. The lanky Scot, for some silly reason, always tried to pretend he just innocently *happened* to be in the vicinity. As if they didn't both know better. Sticking out her tongue, Christin lifted her head like a duchess. The imbecile could just follow her all over the valley.

Far into the distance, Christin could distinguish tiny figures working the fields. Much of a Borderer's farming was done now by the women and older children. The men's absences were lengthy during growing seasons, when they were needed most.

Three small fishing craft were drawing into the tiny inlets off the River Ardle, and gulls were squawking with curiosity. The catch would be salted down, for Scotland's rivers abounded with salmon and its streams with trout. Though Christin had never been fond of fish, she was fast acquiring the taste. It was either learn to eat cullenskink, a dish of boiled fish and stewed vegetables—or go hungry. Soon enough she had tired of porridge and shortbread, finally managing to choke down the fish.

Bored, restless, her deep blue skirts marking a wide swath in the dew, Christin strolled toward the docks where the laundry maids were already at work. It wasn't at all logical, she thought, glancing at the manor's broken tower and south wall in a chronic state of disrepair. Such a pile of stones shouldn't boast clean linens, but it did. Far better that they attend to the clothing of the fishermen and the sawyers. Her fastidious nose could smell several, even yet.

"Mornin', Lady Christin." A laundry maid's head bobbed. After two months, the animosity had lessened until the servants tolerated her.

"Good day." Christin was smugly pleased, as if she

had finally maneuvered a handsome man into flirting with her.

Ambling to the weaving room at the back of the manor, Christin received a grunt of acknowledgment from the she-goat Dame Renney. But a toothless smile from Dame Haggitt drew Christin like a bee to the comb. The frail woman gave the spinning wheel a turn and worked the fine wool through gnarled fingers. Bending impulsively, Christin bestowed a hug about the stooped shoulders, fluffing at the crushed mutch perched upon her head.

"There, now," she laughed, " 'tis a first-rate beauty you are, Dame Haggitt."

A dry cackle deepened the grooves about Dame Haggitt's mouth until she looked like a wise old bird.

"Eh, lassie. Come to take a spell at th' wheel, now?"

"I wish I had one," Christin sighed.

"Eh, lass?"

"I *said* I wish I had a wheel. It would give me something to do."

Dame Renney's snort was pessimistic; she didn't believe Christin had ever done a day's work in her life.

"Ask th' laird, lassie. He be th' one to see," croaked Dame Haggitt.

"We'll see, we'll see," Christin shrugged. "Good day, Dame Renney," she called, certain that good breeding was English armor against such a nasty-tempered old crone.

And, she thought, once she was away from them, she would ask the laird for nothing. These people lived and breathed that man. She would ask for nothing, even if it slew her.

Smoke curled from the chimney of the smithy, and Christin peered back at her guard. She marched deliberately into the noisy building. It was really more of a shed than a building. Creagen raised a shaggy head at the sight of her. His shock was as great as he was.

The three-sided building was extremely warm, and both smiths were soaked with sweat. Their heavily muscled arms reminded her this was a place of work owned by Patrick Mowbray.

"M'lady, you shouldn't be here," sputtered Creagen. Christin waved him back to his work.

"Nonsense," she disputed. "Of course I should. No one has told me I can't. Even the Mowbray heathen knows I'm here. Besides, I'm a prisoner too, you know. I should be laboring like the rest of you."

She giggled, the uncertain grins of the men still not overly amused at her remarks nor her presence. Casting Creagen a queer glance, the Scots smith returned to his work.

"Go on, go on." She shooed Creagen's frown with her fingers. "I'm just going to watch you for a bit. Now, will you *please* continue?"

Grudgingly the man obediently picked up his hammer and began to shape a strange-looking piece of iron he withdrew from the coals. Tappity-tap-tap. Tappity-tap-tap.

Smithing didn't appear so difficult to Christin—just a hot dirty job, if one could stand to bounce a hammer off a piece of iron for hours at a time. She should learn the skill. She would probably be the first woman smith in history.

The scandalous reports of it—whether it was a girlish antic or not—would lift some eyebrows when they got back home to Robert Bruce. One of his favorite knights making a highborn English lady slave over an anvil? The benevolent Bruce's reputation tarnished?

Scotland was a very small country, and news traveled fast, even through the rebellious Highlands. This could well earn Patrick Mowbray a public censure from the king. Edward Plantagenet was watching her situation with interest, Laurence's first letter had said.

Spying a single glove lying in the hay, carelessly tossed aside without its mate, Christin picked it up. It was many sizes too large, of course, but she slipped her fingers into it and fussed about until she found a small piece of iron to stir in the coals. The iron hissed impressively when she poked it into the water. She soon grew tired of that.

"Would you like me to pump the bellows, Creagen?" she inquired sweetly.

Busy, concentrating on the stirriups that Sir Patrick had designed for him to make, Creagen barely heard her.

"If it suits your fancy, lass," he replied absently.

Christin gave the big bellows a pump or two. More strength was necessary than she had at first thought, and besides that, black smudges of soot streaked her arms. And one upon her cheek that she was unaware of.

My, but it was hot in here! Her hair was growing damp, curling wisps clinging to her forehead and sticking to her cheeks. Roaming about, peeking into this and that, Christin's original idea grew more and more intriguing by the minute. Why not? If she caused only one prick of political embarrassment to the good laird, it would be nothing like what he had done to her. He deserved it.

Grasping the hem of her skirts, she immodestly caught them up from behind, between her legs, fastening them in her waistband like a fishwife. Her knees were showing, and her bare calves gleamed.

"May I try that?" Christin peered over Creagen's shoulder as best she could.

His side vision, catching a glimpse of his mistress and the undignified manner in which she had pushed up her sleeves and hiked up her skirts, to say nothing of the soot on her, caused the big smith to slam down his hammer with a crash.

"An' the good Lord be my witness, mistress! I be ready to give you a paddlin' if you don't remove yourself. Sir Patrick will stripe my back proper, he will. Now get yourself home, lass."

"I shan't, and you can't make me!" Then she softened. Creagen could never outlast her girlish pleas. "I ought to be here, Creagen. He brought me here like a slave, and I will act like a slave. Now, are you going to show me how to do that, or shall I make do on my own?"

Realizing she was decided to the point of stubbornness, Creagen didn't miss the smothered grin of the man at his side. Aye, what a hot-blooded lot the Winchelseas were!

"Oh, lassie," he moaned, "d'you wanna be the death of me?"

"He won't do anything, silly, except perhaps shout a little. But that never killed anyone. He yells at me all the time, and I'm still in one piece, aren't I?"

Creagen glanced at her legs and sighed ruefully. There was no doubt of that.

Very much against his better judgment, Creagen relented. Truthfully, a good deal of crooked grinning and feminine giggling floated about the smithy that day. What a sight she was! Twice she had burned herself, gritting her teeth tightly, swearing to heaven she wouldn't complain of the angry red streaks if she keeled over dead. Sooty black, her blue kirtle was hopelessly ruined.

Still, her little piece of iron had been shaped rather well, they all had to agree. Christin was immensely proud of it. This was the most enjoyment she had had since she had been taken prisoner. In fact, she paused to recall, this was the most enjoyment she had had in a very long time.

Several pairs of amused eyes peeped in the door that day, considerably awed by what they saw. By suppertime, the little burgh was buzzing about the highborn Saxon maid laboring away in the smithy's shop.

They had lunched upon hard cheese and shortbread, washing it down with cool ale brought by one of the kitchen knaves. Now, between pauses of his hammer, Purcell told them of the laird's prize mare, for which Creagen was now fashioning stirrups for a new saddle.

"The line runs clear back to Norway, it does," he explained. "Lady deMohr gave this mare's sire to the laird's mother before she died, God rest 'er. Quite a store he sets by that animal. Bred 'er to a stallion brought special. From Skye. She's the fastest mare abouts, and five foals she give. Champions, all of 'em. Aye, five champions."

Wiping her hands, Christin listened with interest. Lady Calla deMohr, was from England and had married a Highland chief. Reputed to be the most beautiful woman in Scotland, even at forty, this woman must be a legend, Christin fancied. Purcell continued explaining how fond Lady deMohr had always been of Patrick's mother and was still a fairly frequent guest since The Bruce had ceded the Warrick lands to Patrick for service rendered at Bannockburn.

Apparently, mused Christin, Lady deMohr was interested in more at Warrick than a favorite horse.

"Six foals, come this fall," grunted the smith.

"What's the mare's name?" Christin smiled.

"Triste."

"That's a beautiful na—"

A shadow fell across the entrance. Christin turned slightly, the half-smile hardening upon her face. She had wanted him to know; now he did. Still, her strategy was oddly laced with pangs of misgiving.

Patrick's disbelieving eyes didn't require more than a few seconds to determine what had transpired during his day's journey to Braedeen steading and back. Christin didn't suppose she could have torn her eyes from him if he had knocked her flat off her feet with his fist.

His trews were deep forest green, waist to toe, over which the rawhide boots laced firmly. She knew the slender line of his body was deceptive. He was very strong. Belted over the trews was a soft chamois tunic reaching to mid-thigh. He wore no cap. And as he filled the doorway with the waning light at his back, Patrick looked like some magnificent golden god. Christin swore he seemed seven feet tall. The most inane words slipped past her lips.

"You need a haircut, m'lord."

She shuddered. Realizing how perfectly guilty she

looked and how ridiculous her words sounded, Christin wished that she could simply faint.

The clean-shaven jaw bunched tightly. "Christin Winchelsea, I should thrash you here and now!"

"Why, m'lord?" she squeaked.

"Why, m'lord?" mimicked Patrick in an absurdly high voice. Then he barked at her. "Because I heard about this little comedy a mile away. That's why!" Patrick whirled to shout toward the churchyard. "Tildy Grey!"

Evidently, though Christin couldn't see at all past the towering man, her maid was coming, for Patrick snapped a curt order. "Fetch your ladyship a bath."

Mumbling something about how he should wring the guard's worthless neck, and if word of this got to The Douglas, he was going to wring hers, too, Patrick stepped into the dusk and yelled for Gideon.

"Take care of that bloody animal," he indicated his horse with a jerk of his thumb. Gideon stared at Christin, agape.

"And you, mistress, come with me," commanded Patrick. The mobility of his brow promised Creagen that the last of this had not been seen by far.

Fearing she had done quite enough for one day, Christin didn't argue. She would be a splendid martyr, she decided. Assuming her most injured posture, she tilted her head the proper amount, ignorant of the several patches of soot upon her forehead and cheeks. Only at the last second did it dawn upon her that the ludicrous manner in which she had tied her skirts would ruin the entire effect. She paused to fumble at the waist of her skirt.

"You needn't bother, Lady Winchelsea. You're not nearly good enough to pull this off. Don't you know we Scots never take the English seriously?"

"You'll take me seriously enough when news of this reaches Edward!" She strained against the punishing circle of his fingers imprisoning her wrist. "I'll walk. Leave me be."

Patrick didn't say he had begun to wonder already if he shouldn't have left her back in Miron. Spies of The Bruce had whispered to Douglas that Christin had a friend in the English court—a man of the clergy and a noisy one. Some thought his eight hundred marks would be paid before the year was out. Others said she would turn out to be more trouble than the money was worth.

"You look like a scullery maid, and I've half a mind to treat you like one. Jock! Damnation, that beggar knows he'll pay for this. Jock!"

"Aye, sir."

Christin didn't want to look at her guard Jock, nor the curious villeins who occupied themselves at their tasks, pretending not to watch. Patrick half-dragged her, and she knew they missed nothing. Everything would be reported—many times.

"We shall talk, Jock," promised Patrick as he strode. Christin could hardly keep pace with his reproving strides. "Count on't."

"By heaven, s-sir," apologized poor Jock. "She didn't try to bolt or nothin'. I didn't see nothin' to get upset about."

"Don't move from outside this door," Patrick ordered.

Jock grinned. "Aye. You can depend on me, sir."

Patrick withered him with a look. After pushing Christin inside the cottage, he straightened his tunic. His thoughts troubled him.

"Repair the damage you've done to yourself. I must be about seeing if I can repair what you've done to me," he snapped. He ignored Christin's consternation at the giggling kitchen girls who marched from her tiny bedchamber with empty buckets.

"I want some privacy with your lady, Tildy Grey. I shall have food sent. You may sup in the hall."

"Yes, m'lord. Sir?" she ventured, uneasy with his temper. "About the smithy?"

Patrick dismissed Tildy with a gesture. "I'm becoming quite familiar with how your lady's mind works. I don't blame you." He sighed, stepping into the night.

He had vengeful thoughts of threatening Christin with the cells below the floor of the manor hall.

Christin paused in the act of brushing her hair dry. Patrick dismissed a reluctant Tildy and posted a man outside the door. She heard him prowling about the room, making an occasional comment about their supper.

Repaired objects of furniture Creagen had unearthed were arranged in the cottage along with bits of pottery and flowers, even some knitting from Dame Haggitt's scrap yarn. Feminine touches helped make the room comfortable, but in Scotland it rained nearly every day. A thin blue haze of smoke always drifted back from the hole in the ceiling.

Scotland was like another world compared to England. The personal isolation of a lord from his fief seemed not to exist. Patrick's baronage didn't prevent his villeins from approaching almost as one would a member of his own family—in complaint or in common worry about the economy.

Perhaps the country's wild geography demanded such familiarity. It was conceivable that King Robert Bruce could come tomorrow for breakfast. And it was almost certain that in two days everyone for miles would be whispering that Patrick Mowbray was in this house—alone, at night—with his Saxon hostage.

Careful not to make a sound, Christin drew herself erect. She had surprised his lordship; she had been clever enough to place him in check. Even through his anger, she had glimpsed grudging respect. She wondered if Patrick was ever gentle. Did he touch beautiful things with care or watch puppies play? Did he laugh at silly, feminine teasing? Patrick was a puzzle, taking care with his fingernails yet threatening to destroy a town.

Waiting irritated the Scot. Christin grimaced at the impatience accenting his steps. Wth a small sense of doom, she stepped from the small bedchamber.

Christin's gown was a sultry black velvet—wide-sleeved, bodiced with a rust-hued jerkin which she had laced tightly. She was exquisite. As Patrick gazed at her girl-woman allure, he wondered if she had dressed that way on purpose. The room suddenly felt too warm.

Why did she have to be so damnably beautiful? Why couldn't Christin Winchelsea be plain and worth a lot of money?

Patrick hacked through his roast mutton, slammed down the knife and stared. Once he started to speak; then he dipped the tip of his finger in the mustard and sucked at it.

"I really should send you home," he muttered, resuming his slicing. "I should just forgo the eight hundred marks and send you home. The Bruce does it all the time. It makes us look less like barbarians, you see."

"When? *Tomorrow?*" Christin urgently stood before him, compelling him to look at her. "Sir Mowbray, if you would do this thing you would be rewarded in heaven. I swear it. Miron is such a small town. It will ruin my father to try and raise—"

"We're at war, your ladyship! I can't be concerned about your father's purse."

"But you said—"

"I said I *ought* to send you back. I didn't say I would. You have a distant kinsman, I believe, making a lot of threats. I may be forced to return you, in the end."

As if he didn't see her brimming eyes, Patrick turned from her distress, busying himself unnecessarily.

"That was really quite cruel, to dangle it before me like that. I don't know how you live with yourself. I would fear for my very soul if I were you, Sir Mowbray."

When he spun to face her, Patrick's eyes were glittering. Christin now saw his second spot of vulnerability. His soul.

"*A Borderer has no soul!* Don't you know that, my lamb? I'm damned for my politics. I'm forbidden the sacraments, marriage—even baptism for my children."

"The king takes holy communion. Glynnis told me so," Christin protested.

"The king believes in his rights, as a just monarch over this country. He has honorably fulfilled the conditions before God. He doesn't seek for himself."

Christin watched Patrick examine his hands.

"The English crown did terrible things to Robert's family. Did you know that Edward the First conceived of drawing and quartering? Hm? I'm not as certain of my rights, to defy a pope as The Bruce has done. Even so, he does it for Scotland. Robert and Jamie have been deprived of their privileges by right of Scottish birth. I suspect Edward didn't see me in quite the same position when he accused me of treason."

"Perhaps"—she didn't know why she was whispering—"perhaps the second Edward would reconsider what his father did to you then."

"Reconsider treason?" He laughed, motioning for her to take her chair. "High treason was what it was, lass. I'm where I belong. Don't see me as an Englishman anymore, for I'm not."

Christin had never perceived of Patrick being anything other than a man who took things. Everything spoke of taking: his hands, his eyes, the length of his step. That he would be troubled about his status with a church which had publicly denounced him, puzzled her. She would have pictured him as a druid, or something equally extraordinary.

For the first time, without any conscious deliberation, she used his name. "You're a very bitter man, Patrick."

He studied her with no hint of a smile, unmoving. Then he arose and jarred the table as he withdrew to the doorway. "Mistress, you surprise me."

"M'lord?"

"I mean, after that travesty in the smithy, I expected you to try and lop my head off with a sword. But to ask questions, as if you—"

Christin realized he had been about to say the word

"care," but it wouldn't have suited him. After he took his chair again he didn't eat; he only leaned back and watched her in that detached manner she hated. The silence was lengthy and laced with tension. Christin fancied he probably heard her heartbeats thudding.

"I never had a serving wench who did not pour me ale," he said without preamble. Her head tipped upward.

"If you're asking me to get up and serve you, Sir Patrick, my answer is simply . . . I'm not a serving wench. And if I were, I wouldn't serve a Scot."

"The circumstances tend to dictate otherwise, little Saxon."

Patrick smiled, but his brown eyes remained intent, refusing to let her look away. She had never locked wills with a man as strong as he. Had this been some-one else whose mouth formed the slow, sensual words, she would have emptied the contents of the table into his lap. Not daring to push Patrick that far, however, Christin gave the semblance of submission.

" 'Tis a point of no real issue," she shrugged. "You need to command. Without command you would die, for war is all you know."

He grinned. "It appears that you have spent consider-able thought upon me, Christin. First the state of my soul, now the motives of my heart. Do those grown-up thoughts tell you that I don't wish for you to serve me, but only to stand beside me?"

"Should that surprise me? Is not that the way of all men?"

"I'm not most men! I deny myself much, but in this one thing I wish you to stand here beside me."

It was a game. She saw it clearly, now—her girlish high-lady to his flesh-and-blood man. Christin wondered how he had caught her up in it so easily. Nevertheless, she arched her brows high and continued to play.

"Pour me the ale, Christin," he said softly.

"As you wish, my lord. But since we're being so honest, though I confess I don't know why, I will tell you that I submit only because I wish to do so. If I didn't wish it, I warrant you could drag me by the hair, and I still wouldn't do it."

His power was a large physical thing—like those wild Scots fortresses two hundred feet straight up the cliffs. She reached carefully across his shoulder to pour ale in the flagon he held. Standing beside his arm, yet not touching, she waited. He drank deeply. Caught up in her own boldness, the strange power she seemed to wield, she murmured, "Do I please you, m'lord?"

She played on—foolishly, dangerously. "Would it please you more if I rubbed away the tiredness, m'lord?"

The muscles in the back of his neck were sunburned and hard. Christin's fingers warned her she was ill-advised as she smoothed them across the leather of his tunic. She drew firm circles, feeling the tautness gradually relax as his back relaxed beneath her hands. Then she moved down both sides of his spine. It was symmetrical and competent, as she had known it would be.

"You know that you're beautiful, Christin," he said lazily: a simple statement of fact.

"Yes."

Patrick's laugh was partly at himself. "I think you're playing me for a fool, but for the life of me, I cannot detect the reason."

"Do you oft play the fool, sir?"

"No!"

At his words, Christin felt strength surge across his shoulders, and he lurched to his feet, causing her to step back. He towered over her with such virility that she stiffened with quick fear and stepped backward.

"You have no experience with men," he said. "I know that, and yet I would wager fifty pieces of gold that you know how much I desire you."

"I warrant so," she said softly. "Your lordship."

"Stop calling me 'my lord' and 'your lordship.' I know you're also aware of how that irritates me. Do you play chess?"

With a careless gesture, he rested the tips of his fingers lightly upon her collarbone, but his eyes fell to the laces of her bodice.

"I'm quite skilled at it." She smiled with honeyed sweetness.

Patrick removed his hand from her shoulder, and his chair scraped harshly against the rushes. Several feet separated them, but she read desire glowing in his eyes, and other things—pride, distrust. She had been unwise to play his game.

"I could take you, Christin," he said gruffly, taking one step for the one she had retreated. "Don't you know that? Here, on this floor. And you would be powerless to stop me. No one would come to your aid."

Meeting his brittle scrutiny with a forthrightness that didn't come easily, Christin demanded that she be as strong in this as he.

"I don't doubt it, but you won't."

"You're that sure?"

"You want me to like you, Patrick." Mockery teased the corners of his mouth, and she feared he was winning this game. "Aye, perhaps you even want me to love you. And I won't, for I'm coming to know you very well. You would turn upon a lover when it filled a need— and the lover would be in pain, not you. If you did that to me, I would always hate you, and you don't want to be hated—not by England, not even by me. That's why you will not force me, Patrick."

The only sound was the hiss of the rushlight and the distant barking of a dog. Minutes lengthened. Finally Patrick's teeth flashed in a smile.

"I've been wrong about you, sweetheart. You're old, not young. Ancient, in fact. I don't know if I like being read by a suckling babe with the mind of a sage. I'm going to kiss you now and leave. And I shan't think about it once I've left this room."

At that Christin laughed. Gravely.

"You place much trust in your charm, Scotsman. I said that I would not lie with you, but that doesn't mean

I will kiss you. If you force me, you *will* think about it when you leave here. There is some honor in you somewhere, I think."

"You should be burned as a witch," he observed drily. "What is the price of a kiss from those sweet lips? Can you be bought, fair Christin? Or is it that I don't have enough to buy you?"

Christin hesitated. Did she dare? Could she best him after all?

"Aye, I have a price." She trembled at her audacity. She was flirting with disaster. Swiftly the game grew lethal, and then it wasn't a game anymore. "You see, I've already grown Scottish in the time I've lived here. I do indeed have a price, Patrick Mowbray."

"And that makes you common, my sweet, like the rest of us."

"Perhaps."

"The price, lamb. My patience grows fragile."

Christin's words grew sluggish as she found it difficult to express her thoughts. Her lack of courage began to tell.

"I would have news of a man," she blurted, struggling to appear poised and credible, but betraying herself by lowering her eyes from his gaze. She could almost hear his thoughts racing.

"I see," he breathed. "A lover, perchance."

"Don't play the simpleton. In fact, don't play at all. Oh, I wish I'd never started this." Her words spilled out too hastily. "I wish to know if Richard Hartley is still alive. He is, or was . . . *is* my sister's husband. He was at Northallerton. I know what I'm doing is wrong, but I must know!"

"Ahh, you would sin for Richard but not for me."

"Yes!" she cried. "Take the wretched kiss. I only wish to know if the man is dead."

A determined arm reached for her, for Christin had twisted about, preparing to leave him in spite of her words.

"No, no. Not so easily, lassie. I fear you've mis-judged my honor. I'll make inquiries, yes—but I'm no saint, if you were gambling. I will have a taste. Without the battle this time."

The kiss would have nothing at all to do with Rich-ard Hartley, that much Christin realized by the sudden tension of Patrick's body. If she said no—that she had changed her mind—would he listen to her?

Slowly Patrick rotated her by the shoulders. The hour was late, and she stared blindly at the smoking light past his head. Her vulnerability was painfully obvious, and Patrick's large hand already spanned the width of her back.

"You're trembling."

Christin made herself rigid and stared hazily at his Adam's apple. When his other hand closed about her jaw, she let her eyelids flutter shut.

"I've wanted to do this for a long time," he said and forced her face upward toward his own.

Nothing happened. For some minutes, Christin didn't dare open her eyes, aware that his waist was higher than hers, that her fingers could easily touch his leg. When he didn't move her eyes finally flew open.

"There you are," he smiled. But his eyes, beneath their lazy blond lashes, were a dark glistening brown, al-most black. Christin thought he would release her, but his fingers began to undo the laces of her bodice with an ease that astounded her.

"No!"

She spun from him with a whimper and drew herself into a confused huddle against the wall. Patrick stood without moving, only chewing his upper lip and waiting.

"I can't!" Christin moaned.

Patrick moved then, and pressed her into the wall with his weight. He cupped her face in both his hands, and Christin grabbed them. *He had killed her people with those hands!* Pulling them down, she trapped them tightly between her own.

61

"It's not fair," she whispered. Patrick slowly removed his hands until he was holding hers.

"No," he murmured. "It's not fair at all."

As if he were explaining why, Patrick drew Christin's hands down to touch him, imprisoning her fingers around the hard masculine flesh. Trying to twist from his embrace was as hopeless as struggling to remove her hand. His curly head bent, and he groped for her mouth. Christin drew a quick breath of affront, but Patrick smothered her open lips with his, refusing to let her shut them, exploring with his tongue until her mouth belonged to him.

Christin managed to free her hand, thinking in some isolated part of her brain that she must not succumb to the warmth of his kiss which was driving strange blistering fire through her veins. Kissing Patrick Mowbray was treason!

When he finally did lift his head, Christin could not speak. She could do no more than drop her head against his chest, so oddly drained of strength she could hardly stand up. With his weight pinning her to the wall, that ever-present shaft speaking of the intense need he had for her, she succeeded in tipping up her face. He was flushed, and he grinned down at her. There was nothing she could say, even if she knew what it was. He knew exactly what he had done to her; he had opened her awareness to entirely new sensations she had not known of.

Slowly his hands slid up her sides, over her ribs, his thumbs spreading below the swelling curves until they met in the center of her body. If he touched her breasts, Christin knew she was lost to . . . everything.

"I didn't like it!" she gasped.

Patrick stilled his hands and locked his eyes with the gray ones which blinked mistily at him. A grin teased his lips, and he steadied his breath.

"You're a magnificent liar," he said huskily and pulled himself upright.

She nearly fell on top of him. Steadying her with a hand about her forearm until she could regain her balance, Patrick's smile broadened. He touched the tip of her nose with a finger.

"Good night, my lady. I daresay you will think about *that* after I leave."

Chapter Four

The two men who approached Warrick's iron-studded door were about the same height and were darkly garbed. One was a guard from the outpost of the village lands, a crossbow in the crook of his arm. The other, a stranger to Warrick, had an English longbow slung over his shoulder.

The sleepy sentinel stirred, and in precisely eight minutes from the time the stranger was first stopped, he peered up into Weryn's glowering one-eyed face.

Weryn adjusted his patch, intensely suspicious. The stranger had no cause to believe that Warrick's lord would welcome a night audience.

Only Weryn ever entered Patrick's chamber in the middle of the night with no warning sound. After many years on the Border, he knew Patrick's habit of rolling from his bed—naked, deadly with his sword in hand when unexpectedly awakened. Patrick's lightning agility was his finest quality in battle, second only to his ability to outbluff his enemy.

Realizing it was Weryn who spoke his name, Patrick automatically began to dress. No words were necessary; this was not the first time he had been summoned from sleep in this manner.

The dark trews, an old leather tunic, and a knitted

64

stocking cap pulled low over blond hair hinted at an invisible danger—a much different danger from that of night raids on horseback. Patrick cross-laced his boots. Carrying his spurs and a packed leather bag, he soundlessly followed Weryn down the narrow flight of stairs to the vast hall below.

Ten minutes later, the stranger retraced his steps with the same outpost guard, and Patrick hastily broke his fast with cold mutton, cheese and ale.

"I don't like seein' you go alone," Weryn frowned. He always said the same words, and his face always clouded the same way.

"Keep a close watch on the sheep, my friend. If these fleeces don't make it to Flanders, you know we'll go hungry. The nearer the shearing, the more tempted the thieves grow."

"How long will you be away?"

"Five days. Maybe a week."

Patrick left the hall through the kitchens, past the pantry, out toward the docks. It was two hours past midnight, and when he ran headlong into Glynnis, he almost struck her in his surprise.

"What are you doing?" he demanded.

Roughly he set her from him, barely recognizing who she was in the thick darkness.

"Beg your pardon, s-sir. I—well . . ."

"Are you just now finishing up, lass?" Patrick grinned. "Everyone else was done hours ago."

Warrick's rules were strict regarding the protection of its housemaids from prankish mauling. Gideon had already been fined once for dallying with this lass. His next fine would be heavy. In a hurry to get home, Glynnis gathered up her skirts.

Patrick tweaked her hair. "Off to bed, lassie. And no sleeping late."

"Aye, m'lord. Thank you, m'lord."

A mild dusk found Christin at the boat docks, listlessly watching the river slap murky waves against the pier.

Thick mist swirled greedy fingers inland, and the faint stench of decaying fish drifted from somewhere upriver.

Days ago, as if it were of little import, Christin had casually asked Dame Haggitt of the whereabouts of Warrick's laird. Sally Buchanan, a plain, big-boned woman with hands larger than a man's, had been assisting Dame Renney at her vertical loom. Neither had looked up at Christin's question, but rather at each other.

The laird was in Edinburgh, Dame Haggitt claimed with a lisp. Rumor had it that siege was planned for Carlisle. Christin watched their fingers fly and held her tongue. Carlisle was one of England's most important Border strongholds, and Edward II would waste his entire army before he would see the town fall.

"More to it," Dame Renney added then, the irritable thrust of her shuttle an indication that Christin's presence annoyed her, "she's probably more bonny than most. Five days he's been gone now."

As if she hadn't heard the words, Christin left, walking very fast, cold fingers pressed against flaming cheeks. Not understanding her anger made her even more angry. It was true, exactly as he had said. He could kiss her, then leave without thinking of her again. That Patrick Mowbray's lovers should even matter to her was humiliating. His list of unforgivable errors was constantly lengthening.

Situated inland, Warrick was fairly safe from attack and was not strongly fortified. Its assets were its limited farmland and its sheep. Any fortifications were designed primarily against intrusion by fellow countrymen who might be thieves or feuding neighbors. Inside Warrick's wall was the great hall with two stories and its mysterious compartments below the ground.

But it was what went on in the village that interested Christin. Greystone, her home in Yorkshire, was a manor house, too—not a great castle holding. She had always roamed the tiny hamlet of Miron with Laurence, and they poked interested noses into all facets of daily life.

These days, from her wattle cottage behind Warrick's kirk, Christin viewed the laboring villeins. She watched small vegetable gardens being tended, cows get milked, children chase ducks and hunters skin meat. That was when she became homesick enough to heave open the heavy door to the church and slip inside.

Greystone's days had always begun with mass. All their years revolved about feasts and holidays and bells from the church. Here, in this miserable country under interdict from the pope, Christin felt her soul in dire distress. But there was little solace to be gained from this church.

Warrick's spiritual decline was Patrick's fault, she decided. Just because he was excommunicated didn't mean that his people should be cut off from their right to pray. If he were conscientious, he would see to the education and spiritual interests of his people.

The interior of the kirk was a shambles. Crude benches dug into a smelly earthen floor, and the altar was almost destroyed. If she judged by the evidence, she would say that grain had been threshed in here. She decided to talk to Glynnis.

"Oh, no one's used the kirk for years," Glynnis explained when she brought Tildy their milk and cream. "We had a skinny little friar for a while, but when th' laird found out he was robbin' the farmers, Sir Mowbray threatened to cut off the man's thievin' right hand if he ever came back."

Christin gasped. "Don't you even celebrate Michaelmas or Easter?"

"In the hall we do. Every year. I don't mind helpin' you clean up the poor old kirk, but it won't do no good. The vicar's scared of Sir Patrick and won't come within miles of Warrick."

Christin rolled her eyes at Tildy, who had already told her she was meddling where she had no business.

"I need something to do, or I'll go mad. I thought I might clean up Warrick's church. Maybe the king will hear of this and send me home. Perhaps even the pope."

Laughing, Glynnis remembered Christin's last hornet's nest at the smithy. Everyone knew that The Douglas had spoken of it to The Bruce and had watched Warrick with a thoughtful eye ever since.

So, asking no one's leave, not actually meaning to become so involved, Christin attacked the kirk with a frenzy. The labor and the weariness was medicine to her heart. With a turban pinned about her hair she cleaned, clearing out aging clutter, scraping her hands and choking on dust.

This had once been a place where souls had come to pray and confess their sins. Ironically, it was now a symbol with which she would purge her aching heart of loneliness. Christin would make it a penance for her disobedience to her father . . . and for the treasonous pleasure she had spent in the arms of her enemy.

What linens remained and were not rotted, she washed. After cleaning the furniture, she shoved a makeshift scaffolding to reach the spider webs in the rafters. Grime rained into her eyes and mouth.

Christin bent double, pressing her face into her apron to cough from the filth. Lifting her head she gave a small cry of alarm to find a man less than ten feet away from her. He was rather grotesque looking with not a hair on his head. He was very, very old, and obviously blind.

"Oh!"

"I didn't mean to frighten you," he said in a burr so heavy that she had even more difficulty in understanding him than understanding the other villeins.

"I'm sorry," she managed to gasp. "You will have to speak slowly."

"You're th' English lass?" He spoke as if it were a question. She watched the skin move across his cheekbones like aged leather.

"Yes. I'm just cleaning up a bit. Do you mind?"

"Nay. I knew you were doin' it. Everyone knows you are. I came to see it."

How can you see it? was on her lips. But he began to

move about in his unnerving fashion, smelling the clean rushes on the floor, touching benches as if they could tell him things. When he reached the higher level of the tiny altar, he stopped.

"There was a man killed here," he recalled. "Ivan was his name. He had words with the Norman lord who once lived here. Th' lord killed him with a sword. I had my eyes then. The stains of 'is blood are still here, I warrant."

He wanted her to come and look, and Christin, still fearing him, drew near the old man. Hearing steps that hardly whispered, he held out his hand for her. She responded, moving beside him as he smoothed his hand along the rail.

"Here. It should be here. D'you see anything?"

Christin bent nearer. There was a slight stain precisely where he indicated.

"Yes. It's darker and about this big." She spread his hands apart.

"Thank you." He turned his body in her direction. "They call me Tag. I've fished this river for over sixty years. They won't let me near it now, o'course. I make nets instead. If one of th' young fishermen has time, he'll take me out. But life is too hard to waste time with a useless old goat."

"You're not useless."

"You say that, lassie, 'cause you're useless, too. We make a pair, don't we?"

His laugh was knowing and rather frightening, for she did consider herself as useless. When he touched her face, Christin gasped.

"I won't hurt you, lass. I don't have any other way."

Grasping the altar rail, for she felt nothing except horror that he would actually touch her, Christin submitted. The gnarled hands measured her height, the width of her shoulders, inching their way up her neck to the line of her jaw. The sensitive touch to her face seemed connected directly to his brain, and when he smiled, feeling the turban, then down her forehead to her nose, she shocked herself by smiling back. His teeth were incredibly perfect. When he felt her mouth spread in a smile, Tag laughed with raucous mirth.

"I'd say you're worth th' eight hundred marks the laird's askin'," he crowed. "I told 'em they'd best get you home before Edward the king comes lookin' for you."

Christin strained to comprehend his awful burr.

"I warned him he should send you home, I did. I told th' Mowbray laird that he's going t'stir up the fauns and Low Country fairies. He won't listen."

"What?"

"The unseen people, th' little ones. They won't like him bringin' you here aginst your will. His mother would ha' listened to me. She knew. She knew."

"Tag! I can't believe you're serious."

But Tag drifted back into his own dark world as abruptly as he wandered in upon her. For a moment she watched him feel his way out of the kirk. When she told Tildy and Glynnis about his superstitious little people, neither laughed.

"Stay away from that old man. He's crazy as a loon," shivered Glynnis. "Not about the little people. But don't worry. They won't come. It's the trolls I worry about. Ugly little things that came with the Norsemen long ago. They love to vex those about t'be married, you ken? Faith, I live in constant fear for Gideon and me. They steal babies and the like. Terrible things!"

"Glynnis! Stop talking like that! That's the most foolish thing I ever heard. You've been without a church too long up here."

"Havin' the kirk won't chase away th' trolls, m'lady. Nothin' can chase them away. They have t'be drowned."

"Stay and tell this nonsense to Tildy. I have to finish my yard work." Christin shook her head, amused at the thought of Warrick's English-educated laird arguing with his villeins over the threat of a fairy.

Christin pruned and trimmed, raked and weeded, wrestling with tenacious vines until her hands were sore.

When the work was almost done, as much as she could manage, she built a fire and cast in the rubble. She wondered if perhaps her sins were being consumed with the crackling brambles.

Some of the villeins watched her, too puzzled to offer a hand. But when Creagen replaced an iron hinge upon the thick door and repaired the broken clapper of the bell, it was highly fitting, she thought. At dusk the task was completed, and Gideon came to ring the vesper bell. For the first time in years the burgh of Warrick echoed the sound of a church bell over its plowgates and grassland, its moors and its bogs.

Now, just before dark, too weary to eat, Christin found herself at the docks. After three frenzied days it was done, and she rested against a post of the pier, worn smooth by the years. Depressed, she saw her life as the linens in the kirk which had fallen to pieces in her hands. Ashes to ashes, dust to dust.

Christin removed her shoes and sat down to dip her legs in the water. Wriggling her bare feet in the murky depths, she smiled at a setting sun as it finally lost its way behind a tangle of trees. The water grew cooler as it teased her knees. She laughed softly then and bunched up her skirts into her lap.

When boots trod lightly upon the timbers of the dock, traces of contentment still curved the corners of her lips.

The muscles of Patrick's legs flexed beneath close-fitting trews, and his face and arms were even browner than before. He looked tired and needed to shave. Scrambling, swinging her legs out of the wet, Christin wrenched down her skirts, then stood in a puddle.

"Oh dear!"

Her body was a taut English longbow.

"Perhaps not quite the greeting a man expects, but a bonny sight."

Patrick gave no indication that he had any intentions of touching her. As brown eyes searched gray, for what she didn't know, Christin's head suddenly filled with visions of some lovely faceless woman in his arms at Edinburgh. Images of his mouth reaching for lips more experienced than Christin's own stiffened her back. *That* woman wouldn't refuse those practiced fingers!

Bending, Christin tugged on her shoes, feeling oddly rebuked, as if everyone had known something but her.

"Did you?" His laugh came easily as she popped upright as a willow after it has been bent and released.

"Did I what, sir?" she snapped. Why were they here, in a place where this man had all the advantages?

"Miss me, and forget it. I can see you were devastated."

"I've been too busy to miss anything, Patrick Mowbray. Except home." At least she found equilibrium in his sarcasm. "I remedied some of the disgraceful shambles of your church, if you'd care to notice. Why should I miss someone who cares little enough to even say he's leaving?"

"I've already seen the kirk, and it seems that I must even purchase a civil tongue from you."

Christin deliberately paused in her offended march toward the manor, hoping she looked as if she was twenty-five. "You went to Edinburgh, they said."

"I didn't go to Edinburgh." She refused to ask why. "But I have news of Richard Hartley," he began.

If Patrick desired that Christin fall into his arms, she very nearly did. Her eyes sought to read things his mouth had not said.

"Yes, yes!" she shook his arm. "Go on. Is he alive? He's dead. Mother Mary, he's dead!"

Reaching to hold her face in both large hands, Patrick tilted it upward toward his own.

"Will you hush? The man is alive. Very much, I'd say. I haven't seen him, but Douglas told me that he broke one man's arm and cut up another before they even got him across the Border." He grinned. "I'd say he's doing pretty well. Douglas has him near Perth."

"Perth?" Christin repeated vaguely. She wasn't conscious of placing her palms upon the span of Patrick's chest. But he was—acutely so.

"Is that far?" she asked, worried.

"A good morning's journey, 'tis all."

"May I see him?"

"I think so. He's at an isolated castle where Wallace often used to hide from Edward the First."

Amazingly, as if fixed in slow-moving time, his grin faded. Christin watched with wonder as the familiar dull bitterness crept around his eyes and the edges of his mouth. Patrick's arms dropped, and his legs broke into a disturbed stride that taxed her to follow.

This man! One minute he was warm and humanly compassionate, the next hostile and cold. She would never understand him. She wasn't sure now that she wished to.

"Since Edward killed Wallace the way he did, perhaps the castle will recall memories of victory for you." His voice was snide and grossly unfair. "I daresay you'll remember his head carried on a spike all over England. I think that's a requirement in the education of young Saxons."

"I don't understand you!" she cried, catching up with his angry steps, digging her fingers into the back of his tunic until he stopped.

"Why do you turn on me like that? I didn't do it. Edward did, and it was monstrous. I won't defend the king for what he did. But Wallace tied people's hands and pushed them into a river, Patrick. I was a child so I don't even remember it. You blame *me* for political matters. I swear to heaven, sometimes I think you're a raving madman!"

Patrick's boots became rooted in his tracks, causing Christin's ire to waver. Emotions warred within him as he battled to swallow his pain. Images of vast human slaughter on both sides of the border slashed through his mind. Christin softened her voice, placating with him, endeavoring to quench their enmity.

"May we go?" Her composure was forced to the

point of absurdity, but Patrick knew she was trying very hard. "Does Sir Richard's family know he's alive?"

"That I cannot say," he shrugged and ran his fingers through his hair. "But I'll take you to see him whenever you wish. Tomorrow. The next day. It doesn't matter."

"How very nice. And extremely generous too, since Richard and I are here against our wills."

"Damnation, Christin! Sometimes I could just—"

"Just what, *you brigand?*" Her loose hair billowed wildly, and her tormented eyes ignited. "What would you do? You've stolen me. You've taken me from everything I love. Would you slay me now and have it done? Sudden death or slow torture? Tell me which."

The doorway to her cottage abruptly opened, spilling firelight, as Tildy stepped outside to empty a bucket of water with a vigorous toss.

"Oh, you startled me," she said, stretching her weary back muscles. "Good day, m'lord. We didn't know you'd returned. And I've been lookin' for you, m'lady. Your supper's cold."

"Sir Mowbray has brought news of Richard, Tildy. He's alive, not too far from here. If it pleases you, *sir*"—she curtsied—"I would like to go tomorrow."

Christin's theatrics always enflamed Patrick, and she knew it. He nodded curtly, his words were flat, coming with no effort and even less thought.

"If you wish. You need not suffer the journey, Dame Grey. She'll be quite properly escorted and well tended at the castle. We'll return the next day. Good night, ladies."

With a crisp bow from the waist, a small theatric of his own, he quickly disappeared into the mist.

"You could at least thank me for the kirk," Christin called toward the spot where he had stood.

"Why should I? It means nothing to me one way or another."

Her jaw clamped hard. "That's fine," she cursed him silently. "Just fine. Make me hate you. God knows I want to. That's easier by far than caring." Then Christin called him an extremely uncomplimentary name under her breath.

Storm clouds gathered above the entourage as it threaded its way toward Perth. Never had Christin found herself in such wildness. Violent gorges filled with frothing water and terraced slabs of rock defied everything. The gorges could flood in minutes with water from the hills but it was all breathtakingly beautiful.

Finally the southward slopes became gentler, to the land's Tayside. As if disapproving of the approach toward a castle once commanded by an outlaw, the heavens threatened to burst. Gusts of leaves and hurtling debris caused Persis to sidle, making it difficult for Christin to steady her nervous mare.

Patrick was moody. The few times he spoke, his words were brittle. Yet those dark eyes burned where they touched, and more than once Christin's flesh crawled beneath his stare. Her need for understanding from some source honed her temper. It would have cost him nothing to be considerate.

Lessening the tedium of the passing hours, were Gideon's good-natured quips in response to the barbed teasing about his courtship. Yet, his face fell somewhat when Patrick told him the last infringement was going to cost two weeks' wages. After a few minutes of considering, Gideon announced his verdict.

"It was well worth it, m'lord."

Weryn threw back his head and roared.

Lightning crackled loudly, startling Christin.

Patrick's cool scrutiny flicked her way. "Are you afraid?"

When Patrick frowned darkly, as he did now, the scar across his brow furrowed into a thin pale line. Christin had often wished to hear the story of that scar, for Douglas's prowess had miraculously avoided leaving any mark upon his face. "The bonny Douglas" the Scots called him, except when he was in the heat of

75

battle. Gideon said he was a terrible man when he fought.

Patrick wasn't what one would really call bonny. He was a rugged, handsome man—sensual and magnetic. But bonny? No.

"Are you afraid?" he repeated curtly.

Christin jumped. "Not of storms."

She had tried to keep her hair pinned up, but it was everywhere. Now she hid behind it. Presently, thinking him absorbed with other things, she covertly studied him some more. Patrick's mouth was mobile and reckless, always seeming to say things that she was not certain of. Well, she would have to admit that Patrick's mouth was bonny.

"Perth is just beyond, but we'll skirt it." He knew she had been watching him.

The secluded castle was not simple to approach. The riding was rough and tiresome. Christin used all her concentration to inch Persis down the rocky incline to the firth below. They stopped at a crude ferry, where Patrick dismounted and spoke with the wizened man who tended it. He was called Jeremiah. Aging joints, bent with years, belied his massive shoulders. He would pole them across the choppy firth.

Obediently, Christin submitted her hand to Gideon for dismounting. Weryn stepped on the barge with the horses, his powerful arms straining against the reins. As the ferry lurched, Patrick moved behind Christin, and she steeled herself, feeling him brace his legs against her own.

She was dressed in mossy green velvet and he in black trews and leather. Wood smoke still clung to his hair; she could smell it when his fingers tightened about her waist. She was ashamed of the tiny shocks which tingled down her body.

"It would please me if you found Scotland beautiful."

His voice, strangely congenial, whispered lightly in Christin's ear. The water slapped, and the horses fretted.

But all she could think about were his hands spanning her waist.

"I don't find it distasteful, Sir Mowbray, only—"

"Only what?"

"I—" She grew pained. "I don't know."

The jolt of the ferry ramming against the bank thrust Patrick tightly against her, and his arm moved upward, just below the swell of her bosom. A line of lightning streaked through the sky, but it might as well have darted through the top of Christin's head. The force of their touch startled Patrick too, she knew, for she felt him draw a quick breath. His heart was throbbing against her shoulder.

"Wait." He held her when she would have drawn away.

The men literally fought with the horses, half-dragging them off the ferry as peals of thunder panicked the thrashing animals. Christin, too, grew so afraid a cold sweat beaded upon her forehead. She took what comfort she could from Patrick's head balanced against her own.

"You're either blind or stubborn, my bonny. I don't know which. Stubborn, I warrant," he said, knowing that Christin understood exactly what he meant.

Fearful or not, Christin flung herself free of those hands and dared not let him see the burning of her cheeks.

The harshness of grating iron caused goosebumps to rise on her skin. Christin viewed the great portcullis slowly clank its way upward, giving entrance through a wide opening. Already fat drops of rain stung her cheeks, and the clammy dankness seemed like a warning.

Smells assailed her. The accumulated stench of many men, horses, the aroma of roasting meat. High overhead, falcons perched in the rafters, the heavy peals of thunder causing them to stir. A sleek hound sniffed at her skirts. Christin trailed her fingertips to pet the dog, but Patrick's hand firmly guided her by an elbow inside the walls. The approaching storm had already seen the rushlights lit, and they seemed cut off from the world.

Was Richard in this place? And was he above or below ground? For a desperate second Christin wondered if she had been deceived and if *she* was to be thrust into some dripping dungeon deep within the bowels of the earth.

Wide and high, the hearth framed a fireplace large enough for a tree to fit in it. She felt herself unceremoniously pushed down to sit.

"Wait here," she was commanded. Christin didn't reply. She only watched the chubby scullery boy slowly crank the spitted mutton—turning, turning.

Rain, beating in thick sheets against gray stones, could not be heard below the ground floor. Narrowly the stairs twisted, plunging into cold recesses. Carrying an acrid torch, a guard balanced himself against the oozing wall, glancing back to assure himself that the big one-eyed fellow would not lose his footing.

A scurrying in the darkness beyond, a muted curse, and a rustle from more than one cell told Weryn of other occupants in the God-forsaken hole. The guard's bare feet whispered upon the worn stones until he held the torch above the door of one particular cell.

"It seems a waste of good iron t'me," the large man mumbled.

The man behind the bars had been asleep. Instinctively, he lifted a hand to shield his eyes from the painful light.

"What is it?" the Englishman demanded in a clipped, educated accent. Weryn ignored the man rising from the straw pallet. Instead, Weryn held the torch high as the guard fumbled with his keys.

"How long has he been here?"

"Two months. Maybe longer," replied the guard.

"What is this?" snarled the surly English voice. Muttering a foul oath, he squinted to see past the light, then hauled himself upright.

"Never mind your questions, Southron. Come with me." Weryn reached out a meaty hand and closed it about an arm that wasn't quite as stout as when it had first come to this hellish place. "You're wanted above. Come along."

"Be still, y'bloody fools!" yelled the guard to a few not-so-gentle suggestions coming from adjacent cells.

Weryn snorted with scorn. "Go along, man." He gave the lanky Saxon a nudge up the stairs.

After an unsuccessful attempt at finding the steps, the prisoner slowly began his journey back into the real world.

Long minutes had passed for Christin, and voices had blurred. She could picture Laurence saddling his great horse, then mounting. Her father shrugging into his vest that never seemed quite large enough. Margaret's smile as she bent her head to the child in her arms. And, Richard's handsome face looming before her.

Richard's face! He was approaching hesitantly, measuring each step as if he weren't sure if his feet could navigate him. Yet, even now he moved with a certain aristocratic grace that was unmistakable.

"Richard."

Her cry rang across the hall, and voices lulled as her feet skimmed across the rushes, her arms reaching upward to twine about his neck. He was thin, and perhaps he was not quite as strong. But he was alive!

"Don't touch me overmuch, little one." His smile was rueful. "I fear more than one manner of creeping thing has found this frame. Lord, but you're beautiful! Is Maggie all right?"

Christin nodded vigorously, waiting as Richard got his bearings. His intelligent gaze searched the hall, obviously in quest of the one man to whom he would accredit his being brought from the interior of the earth. Richard's scrutiny paused upon the Scot who stood easily, one large hand resting upon the hilt of a sword. Man measured man, and Richard's eyes shifted, once more feasting upon the treasure of Margaret's sister.

"I confess I don't understand," he chuckled, "but I don't protest."

His brows lifted to Patrick, and the Scot stepped

79

closer. Guardedly, Patrick's leg positioned itself within the folds of Christin's skirts, and both men understood the implication of that one small movement.

"Richard Hartley?"

"The same."

"You're the prisoner of James Douglas, but I'm authorized to dispatch you, and the two taken with you, for England. You will be given horses and escorted to the Border. From there you're on your own. On foot."

Richard's unshaven face steadied, its eyes blinking and narrowing to juggle disjointed facts, frowning to make sense of something he could not fathom. "But—"

"Lady Winchelsea is my hostage," Patrick informed him, sensing the Saxon's unvoiced query. His own contempt of explanations sharpened his words. "Miron purchased truce."

"That much I know, sir, but Christin—"

"Is to remain here," Patrick finished brusquely.

Richard's mouth tightened. Tiny lines of wrath webbed finely above his cheeks. He shifted his weight in a deceptive slouch, and said with an easy smile, "Perhaps we might trade me for her. Or—"

"See to your person. You leave within the hour."

Following a movement of Patrick's hand, three men stepped about Richard. His dark head turned about, swiftly evaluating the situation and wisely acceding to Patrick's authority.

"As you wish."

"You make a harsh master, m'lord," Christian hardened her jaw at Patrick, "and now I suppose you want me to run along like a good little girl."

"Aye, that I do, Christin."

Patrick grinned and moistened his lips, not even trying to turn his eyes from the straining of her breasts as her breath grew labored. When she started to speak, he reached for her hand, which at this moment was tight-fisted with fury. Pulling it up from her side, none too gently, he forced open its fingers with his stronger ones.

Maddeningly, almost insultingly, he bent to place parted lips upon the soft palm.

He was releasing Richard because of her. Christin knew he wanted some small thanks from her, some flicker of gratitude. The yielding of her hand would be enough. But she couldn't.

Patrick dropped her hand and turned hard on his heel, leaving her standing alone. She was sorry. She wanted to call after him and say she understood what he had done. But she watched his back as it disappeared into a cluster of men some distance away.

When the storm passed, leaving the castle damp and shrouded in a slow drizzle, Richard's eyes scoured the busy hall for the man who presently controlled his fate. The outlaw stood beside great timbered doors which were swung open. His weight was shifted to one hip, a foot rested upon a section of log, his thumbs hooked carelessly at the back of his belt. As if he sensed Richard's eyes upon his back, Patrick looked over his shoulder.

Richard had bathed, shaved, changed his garments and eaten. His aristocracy was impressively apparent. The Englishman made no offer to speak, but stood politely, shifting lanky legs and gently clearing his throat.

Patrick hesitated. He didn't relish talking with this man. Explaining the reason for a certain behavior was like making an excuse, almost apologizing.

Patrick motioned Richard nearer. "It would satisfy me, sir, if Edward learned first hand that Scotland released you freely, without ransom."

"They told me who you were." Richard guarded his words. "This release is not James Douglas's affair, is it? It is yours. You surprise me, Sir Mowbray. Are you seeking peace with Edward?"

"No! It's not that."

"Christin's father, then?"

The Englishman realized he was on dangerous ground,

and Patrick sensed his courage. When their eyes met, the scales of indignation were balanced. One had as much right to hate as the other; one also had as much right to seek a common ground as the other.

"Perhaps," Patrick said.

"Sir Mowbray, realizing your generosity for my release, which I still do not entirely comprehend, I'm wondering about Christin. Has it occurred to you that it would be politically advantageous if she returned with me?"

"No." Patrick's decision came without consideration.

"I think I understand your position, sir, but a Winchelsea's word *has* been given for ransom. One of your own men told me that. You've nothing to lose, sir."

"It's not the ransom."

"For God's sake, man!" Richard forgot himself. "She's only eighteen. In all fair—"

"No!"

The two men, both strong-willed to excess, battled to save this encounter from ending in disaster. Patrick slumped against thick oak timbers. Then he swore. He couldn't force the concession from himself, though he'd thought about it constantly. He had walked out of England with a girl—not a queen, not a countess, but an innocent young girl. He knew Richard Hartley was right; he could and should allow Christin to go home.

"Ah, I begin to see, I think," Richard ventured.

"Do you now? Well, it doesn't concern you, Englishman."

"I'm her brother-in-law, Sir Mowbray. I say anything you do concerns me."

Surprisingly enough, Patrick's voice gentled. "I wish you to ease her father's anxiety."

"What of Laurence?"

"Laurence's opinions do not worry me. In the name of God! Can't you accept a simple fact? War is war, and politics is politics. I don't wish the girl to return, for reasons—"

"I warrant your reasons are neither."

The dangerously soft words were piercing. Patrick's fist ached to smash into the man's mouth for saying them out loud. Yet, Patrick, bore the silence and fervently studied the rain splattering in the courtyard. "You're right," he mumbled almost inaudibly. "You're right."

Richard's eyes widened, intuitively knowing that this was a rare admission for the passionate Scot. Patrick faced him then, and what Richard had not already guessed, he conjectured by the conflict drawing Patrick's features. Behind his incredible eyes, Richard observed more grief than a man twice Patrick's years should have ever known.

They were separated by too many years of war, too many wrongs to right, too many questions without any answers. Patrick doubted that his newly admitted emotions could span a line as impregnable as the Border.

"It hasn't been so long, Patrick, that I have forgotten what it feels like to want something as much as you do," Richard said. He used the outlaw's name with an easy familiarity that Patrick seemed not to notice. He continued, "It appears that you have charted a very stormy course. You realize, I'm sure, that almost anything you do at this point could destroy you. Your king's Highlands are always a threat to him. Now your own political indiscretion poses another threat. Take care, my Scottish friend."

Patrick's lips curled wryly. "That, Richard, I know how to do. It's all the rest that baffles me." Never in his wildest imaginings would Patrick have heard himself voicing his next words. "It seems that I am in need of an ally in England."

"I can see that," Richard agreed sympathetically, and his voice lowered. "At the expense of all my instincts, I accept."

Christin wracked her brain to fathom what was transpiring between Patrick and Richard. The hatred that should seethe between the two men didn't exist. Her life as it was now should be in two separate spaces: love and hate, black and white. This uncomfortable alliance between her captor and Margaret's husband blurred things.

Three Scots whom she had never seen before stowed gear, food, and wool blankets. Near the barracks, at the outer defenses of the hall, three horses were prepared for the departing English prisoners. Richard had bent to fuss with a contrary cinch. Christin, drowning in desperation as she viewed the minutes slip through her fingers, made a hasty decision to gamble one last time.

She strode briskly to the man whose head was bent in conversation with Gideon. The two were very nearly in the center of the hall, well out of earshot of the scores of men milling about. Gideon, taking one glance at her face, bowed.

"Uh, if you'll excuse me," he mumbled awkwardly, starting to say more, then turning with a shrug. Silently, Christin blessed him for his sensitivity.

"You've come to thank me." Patrick drew one corner of his mouth into a half-smirk.

"No, I didn't. I'm sorry. I mean yes, I am thankful to you."

His eyes enflamed her temper so swiftly that it exploded with bitter sarcasm.

"Saintsamercy! The whole miserable world thanks you. What would you have of us? *Patrick, please let me return with Richard!*"

Strategy was forgotten. It was far too late for gambling. Nothing short of begging would suffice, for men were already mounting. Her nails buried themselves into the muscles of Patrick's arm. Distress blanched her face.

"Do I have to get down on my knees and beg you, Patrick? If that's what you wish, I'll do it. I'm begging you. See me begging? Please let me go home!"

Her words caught in her throat. "I offer you a price, m'lord. I bought you once, with a kiss. Do you remember? Can't I buy you now? D'you see how low I stoop, that I would sell myself to go home? My virginity. I offer you the one thing you have not taken."

Christin nodded too eagerly, smiled too brightly. And

Patrick's countenance grew stormy as he watched her fingers lacing and unlacing.

"Don't," he growled. "Have you no pride?"

"Pride?"

The hall stilled as she moved to strike his face. But tenacious fingers closed upon her wrist, crushing it. Will battled will but his strength was stronger by far. Over and over his jaw knotted as he saw the misery cloud her eyes. The warrior in him compelled her into submission.

Gradually he gentled his grasp, but Christin's gaze was withdrawn. Her hysteria averted, Patrick witnessed the death of something deep within her. An oath breathed past his lips, and he let her go.

Richard held her, whispering words that didn't matter into her hair, kissing the pale cheeks good-bye. Presenting his back to a scene grown too poignant to watch, Patrick mechanically issued a few curt orders.

He felt as if he were somewhere else. He had felt this way before, but he had difficulty remembering. Then it came to him. He saw himself before a suspended cage. But it wasn't Isabel Buchan hanging in a snowstorm, it was Christin!

Ah, that was it! At last, the truth. He didn't want Laurence Winchelsea to have her, nor her father, nor England. Patrick Mowbray had imprisoned a girl because *he* wanted her. God in heaven, what was he becoming?

As Warrick's lord stood beyond the portcullis watching hooves bury in the soft mud and fling it back in clumps, he was aware of Christin. She was pale and so beautiful. Looking at the place where Richard had been, her lips barely moved to form the words.

"Tell Papa I'm sorry."

An uncommon numbness spread over Patrick's body, and he felt he would be sick. He saw himself, not as Patrick Mowbray, the valiant, wronged champion of Robert the Bruce. Rather, he saw himself a cruel, bitter monster-image of Edward I. Everything in the world that he hated was hidden in the unknown depths of his own heart.

He turned from watching Christin drag her body toward the narrow stairs. His throat constricted. Nothing mattered. He stumbled blindly to the kitchen, praying there were spirits there. He craved something strong enough to dull the pain until he couldn't feel it anymore.

Chapter Five

Patrick offered no explanation concerning the flask of murky liquid he took to his chamber. Dank and cheerless, the stone walls seemed no more devoid of compassion than his own heart. He filled a goblet to the brim with no self-deception. He hoped it had been made illegally and was potent.

"A curse on your bloody soul!" he punished himself.

The wall between his chamber and the one adjoining was as impenetrable as the inborn enmity between the woman and himself. What a mistake he had made! No amount of ransom was worth the conflict in his soul. But it was too late. Now she was here, and he couldn't make himself return her.

The scalding liquid ripped a gasp from between tightly clinched teeth.

Patrick knew he was very drunk. That fact was odd in itself as Patrick had only been drunk once before that he could remember, many years before this. His life was not his own . . . never had been . . . and now it was tangled in the slender fingers of a lass that didn't give a beggar's damn if he lived until tomorrow.

Drooping eyelids mirrored his heart. Darkness had long since taken the old Wallace hideaway when Patrick flung himself face down across the bed. He drifted into a dreamless stupor.

Christin had eaten a tiny supper only because Gideon brought it, insisting that Scotland was only holding her, not starving her. Then he had hovered over her like a warden until he was assured she would be all right.

Gideon's shock at Patrick's drunken state was no small thing. The lad had seen so much the last days that he couldn't understand, he was beginning to wonder if the end of all things was at hand. With a shrug, he departed for the hall below to pass the evening dicing and drinking with his friends. He wished dismally that he was back at Warrick, nestled in the hay with Glynnis.

At midnight a wistful moon finally peeped through the clouds, a sliver of ivory. Her eyes swollen and dry, Christin lay upon her bed, still fully dressed. She had awakened every few minutes, struggling to remember where she was and why she had come to be here. This stony fortress didn't want her, and Christin imagined herself to be Jonah in the belly of the ship before they threw him overboard.

She sat up with a lurch, her eyes flaring.

The door to her room was open, filled by a familiar form blocking out the faint light which ebbed through its portal. She gasped.

He looked unkempt and bleary-eyed, the fingers of one regretful hand reaching to soothe a temple. Christin felt compelled to scramble behind her bed, but she needn't have bothered. Patrick was in no condition to stand, much less do her harm.

"I'm as drunk as th' devil," he admitted freely.

Compressing her lips, Christin was reminded of a small blond waif proudly drawing himself up and announcing, "I'm five years old." His presence was astonishing after all that had passed between them this day.

"Well, then, get out of here," she demanded. "You've done enough to me sober, much less the disgusting torments you plan for me drunk. Get out of this room, or I'll scream my head off."

"Shh," he grinned blissfully. "D'you have anything t'eat in here? My mouth tastes like . . . weelll, it's bad."

With misgivings Christin frowned at the trencher Gideon had left and watched as Patrick carefully moved toward it.

"Oh," he paused forlornly, "I forgot t'shut th' door." Turning at that moment seemed such a burdensome chore, however, that his big shoulders drooped. Though halfway insulted, Christin was quick to realize that she had much less to fear from Patrick in this condition than ever in the past. Against her better judgment, she moved past him to shut the heavy door.

"I'm cold," he said simply. With grave care he seated himself on the side of her bed and happily ate cold fish and bread. Washing it down with some of the ale, he sighed.

"Y'look much better. I don't suppose you've f-f-for-given me."

"No, I haven't."

"I—oh, dear," he shivered and hugged himself. "D'you know I've always wanted straight hair? Like yours? I don't know where I got this hair. Malcolm doesn't have curly hair. Nobody in my family does, 'cept me. I wonder if my mother had a lov'r."

Christin smothered a smile. As best as he could, Patrick continued eating, deep in worry over his curls. Christin doubted that he had the vaguest notion of what he was doing. Who would have dreamed that the wretch she knew as Patrick Mowbray would be such an ador-able, fuzzy kitten when he was falling-down drunk? Too bad it wasn't the other way around, she thought grimly.

At last he finished.

"I know I'm terrible drunk, Chrissy. I'm sorry. I got drunk once. 'Fore this, y'understand. I don't think about it. I'm cold."

"Well, get up off the bed, and I'll take off the blanket."

Thinking she really should call Gideon or even try to propel Patrick to his own chamber, Christin removed the trencher from his hands. Patrick's attempt to stand was planned with the care of an attack. But in the end she nearly had to drag him off the bed. He had difficulty standing, and Christin, balancing him with one hand, snatched off a blanket with the other.

"Sit down."

Patrick meekly obeyed, looking up at her with the wounded trust of a small boy. After securely wrapping his shoulders Christin started when Patrick leaned half off the bed and nestled his curly head upon her bosom. He covered his mouth with his hand, and she staggered with the weight of his big body against hers. He mumbled something, and she reached around to pry two fingers off his mouth.

"What did you say?"

"I don't want you t'smell it. 'Twas h-horrible stuff. See?" He formed a small circle with his lips and blew at her.

Christin winced and agreed. "It is pretty bad. Here, drink some ale. It'll taste better than that poison."

He swallowed, then sighed softly. "Can you whistle?"

Christin nodded, struggling not to laugh at the completely guileless smile.

"I can't. I've tried an' tried, an' I jus' can't do it."

In spite of Christin's very real effort to nourish her offense, she giggled.

"Patrick, I can't hold you up any longer. I've got to sit down."

"Of course, lamb. Right here."

Adroitly for his state, she thought, the tall Scot pulled her to the bed, somehow managing to turn in her arms so that his head rested in her lap. He closed his eyes and, nuzzling his cheek against her belly, seemingly satisfied.

"Promise you won't tell how drunk I am," he whispered. "No one has ever seen me drunk. Not even Douglas. Sweet Christin," and he reached up to place a gentle kiss upon the velvet covering her breast.

Christin had already begun giving herself warnings

about the day following when he could possibly remember that she had not resisted his touch. Now, as Patrick lay cradled in her arms, half-nibbling, half-kissing her breast through her clothes, it seemed every nerve in her body centered in that one place. Her pride and her affections were at torn purposes. She seemed incapable of anything except sensation.

Though she didn't really know what she wanted from Patrick, it wasn't drunken caresses, no matter how tender and satisfying. She was a bit intoxicated herself, she thought, looking down at the curl of his lashes in the moonlight, daring to thread her fingers into his hair.

As if she couldn't possibly see through his cleverness, Patrick's fingers inched nearer and nearer the lacings of her jerkin. The universe shrank to the size of a hand, and only his slow tug on the laces was real.

Christin thought, her breath coming in small whimpers, that if he didn't touch her breast with his mouth, she would die. When he did, she thought she would die anyway. The wetness of his mouth, the warmth, the tiny teasing patterns he drew with the tip of his tongue— all began to drug her, to create a deep hurting need inside her. She felt shame for responding. An indefinite treason.

"You'd better go now, Patrick," she gasped. "Please, let me help you up."

"Ohh, don't make me stop. You feel so good. You're so bonny, Chrissy. So bonny."

Twisting himself about, Patrick raised himself on an elbow.

"What are you doing?"

"Takin' off my tunic, lambie," he explained sweetly, as if it were unnatural that she should ask. Except for a few wisps of silk from the center of his chest down to his waist, Patrick was smooth, his muscles lean and defined. Before Christin could object, he stretched full length upon her. He was hard and bold, flexing the muscles in his hips and moving upon her with a slow rhythm as old as time.

Christin's push against him was feeble and without conviction. He laughed softly.

"I'm too big, an' you can't push that hard. You're such an unskilled li'l lover. Put your arms around me. Yes. See how fast y'learn?"

Logic screamed in her head now, even as her fingers skimmed across the sinews of his back, pausing to memorize each hardness and curve and a few small scars.

"I don't s'pose you'd let me take off your dress."

"No."

"I've seen you," he argued. *"Part* of you."

Patrick cupped his palm about her breast. "See, it fits. I don't mind takin' off my clothes," he offered generously. "You can touch me all you want to."

Wriggling, pushing him aside like some deadly potion, Christin grabbed her bodice tightly closed.

"Patrick?" She needed badly to understand.

"Hm?"

"Why did you get so drunk, Patrick?"

"Oh, Christin." He rolled off her on to his back and rubbed his face with both hands. "I've put you in a cage, lassie, an' I never meant t'do that. I never did, I swear."

"Cage? What—I don't know what you're talking about."

"Someday, Chrissy. Tonight I'm drunk, an' I think in th' mornin' I'll kill myself. D'you mind if I jus' close my eyes for a minute? Just lie here with me for a wee bit an' don't hate me."

"No, tell me now. I need to know."

Patrick's brain was tired and dulled. He could hardly shape the words to explain what he meant. But between periods of silent, painful recollections she pieced together the story of Edward I's vengeance upon Robert Bruce. The executions were horrible, but mercifully brief. As Isabel hung in her cage upon Berwick's walls, the king's sister hung in another one upon the walls of Roxburgh. Fourteen-year-old Marjorie, his daughter, was hung in one and then removed to a more

92

humane imprisonment. For eight years Queen Elizabeth was held prisoner, separated from her husband and Marjorie.

Edward I's retributions bordered upon insanity, and he shocked the world. A magnificent king gone bad, they said.

When Christin grasped what Isabel and her suffering had done to Patrick, and that the Scots rebel could have a conscience and still commit his acts of cruelty, it seemed horrendous.

"Go to bed, Patrick," she said, gathering her clothes tightly and twisting herself free of him.

"Don't leave. Not like that."

He grasped only that she was taking away the comfort which in those few moments had been more dear than he could ever remember.

"Say y'understand why. That it's th' bloody war."

She shrank from the big hand that reached for her. "It's you and men like you, Patrick, that think it's only the big things that matter. Who cares about the little people in the process of your wars?"

He knew she didn't understand. When his hand grasped her skirt and Christin stumbled backward, and fell across him, some half-rational urgency possessed him. He didn't want her to hate him. He wanted to hold her and touch her and have her sympathize with his misery.

"No, Patrick!" Christin struggled to wrest his fingers from the resolute hold he had of her gown. "Let me go. Go to bed. We can talk some other time."

"Now."

He shook his head and pulled himself upon her. Christin never dreamed that Patrick would not comply. First his boyish sweetness, and now this more demanding Patrick.

If she thought his kiss had been compelling before, it was like a cousin's peck upon the cheek compared to his determination when he ground his mouth down upon hers. His tongue forced her teeth apart, and when she twisted her face this way and that, it only seemed to make him more intent.

Once Patrick pried her hands loose from her jerkin, there seemed no way Christin could prevent him from pinning her hands. His strength was amazing. With no help from either of them, her skirts twisted about her hips. He quickly had his hand between her legs, finding her, slipping inside her, discovering a virginal tightness that made her cry out.

Hot and urgent with arousal, he released her hands to fumble with his clothing. Shoving hard against his chest, Christin twisted her mouth free of his. In those few seconds, she knew she could scream for someone to help her. She could hardly believe it when she didn't. She only spat harsh, whispered words at him as he drove his knee between her tightly pressing ones.

"Force me, then! Be a king like Edward and force me!"

Patrick blinked as if she had struck him. Only then did it seem to dawn on him what he was doing. She might as well have kicked him in the groin. With a low moan he dragged himself off her, and he probably would have straightened her skirt, but Christin snatched it down and accused him with her eyes.

No words of remorse came from his lips. He lay flat on his back and adjusted his clothes with a melancholy sigh. For a moment, Christin thought he caught his breath to speak, but he only closed his eyes. She was about to ask him to leave, or let her call Gideon for help, but his breaths came deep and slow. His mouth slackened with an innocence she found both infuriating and defeating.

For many minutes, Christin lay still and listened to his breathing fill the room, remembering how terribly he had wanted her. In his sleep, he turned on his side and nuzzled his head near her face. She didn't move. And when he flung his arm across her waist, she lay so long, marveling at the weight of it, that her own eyes closed.

Her shoulders grew chilly, and she drew the blanket

beneath her chin. Unconsciously snuggling further beneath its warmth, Patrick moved his knee across her thighs. Christin's last waking thought was that she really should call Gideon for help.

Gideon paused, grimacing at the blinking of eyes that seemed much too large for his head. The hall was busy, its daily routine already underway. Early-morning hunters caused a stir near the portcullis as they returned with triumphant hounds and game for the spits.

Four men familiar to him busied themselves over their trenchers at the end of a long table: David, Rankin, Saul and Weryn. As Gideon had paused earlier outside the door of his lordship's bedchamber, he hadn't heard a sign of life. That was uncharacteristic of Sir Patrick. If he didn't arise soon, Gideon would be faced with the unrewarding task of awakening him.

Everyone was waiting for Patrick so they could leave for home. The reason for releasing three English prisoners of war the day before had not been explained. Nor the purpose of this entire journey. All had drunk too much the night before. Staring at his untouched food, Weryn drank deeply of his ale. Gideon took an unsteady place beside him.

"The sun's been up an hour," Saul complained. "The horses are ready to leave."

Gideon's shrug said it wasn't his fault.

An old woman, her white apron almost bigger than she was, shuffled to Gideon's side and placed ale, bread and ham with boiled eggs before him. The sight of it made him queasy.

Weryn's bloodshot eye didn't indicate any great comfort to be had from him either.

"Take it away," Gideon waved, having already dropped his egg twice. The old woman did as she was bid, grumbling under her breath about the doings of strange Scots who lived too near the Highlands.

"It's been a long time since I've seen his lordship that itchy," Rankin observed into his flagon. Weryn's warning scowl hushed the table immediately. Then, Gideon's quiet words cut sharply, especially since they were directed to a man older than he.

"Keep remarks like that to yourself, Rankin. It's a well-known fact that Sir Mowbray is not given to drunkenness. I warrant what a man does before retiring is his own business."

Pausing in the act of stroking his beard and overlong moustache, Rankin squinted at Patrick's defender. Again he bent over his trencher, sopped up the remaining food with his bread, swallowed and wiped his wet moustache on his sleeve.

"Makes no diff'rence to me. Or whose room he does it in."

Weryn's craggy head snapped up abruptly. "Hold your tongue, knave!" he growled. " 'Tis not the time."

"You mean, because he's half Saxon, that gives him th' right to sleep with a Saxon hostage? The Bruce will have his title for this."

Gideon found it impossible to reconcile Rankin's value as a Border mosstrooper with his foul humor. Gideon's short-bladed knife whirred as he stabbed it viciously into the table.

"You unsay that, Rankin! Where d'you think you'd be if it weren't for Patrick Mowbray? Still cleaning boots for Edward's soldiers at Berwick, with a starving wife. You bloody well know it, too!"

In his anger, Gideon was instantly on his feet. In the blink of an eye, he had the older Scot leaning back in his chair, the sharp point of the blade pricking redly upon his bared throat. Straightaway Rankin began muttering his apologies.

"Cease!" Weryn roared, his bellow ringing through the hall, his trencher clattering to the floor as he stood. "Put that thing away, Gideon. And you, Rankin, shut your witless mouth before it's emptied of its teeth. Now sit down, all of you! And no more about it!"

Shuffling to pick up the spilled food and glaring up at the huge man like an infuriated mouse, the old woman made Weryn fidget. Rankin submitted reluctantly, but David spoke politely, ignoring Weryn's authority.

"Rankin does have a point, Weryn. I'm as loyal to Mowbray as any of you. But you know how The Bruce feels about things like this. I'm not sayin' I'd do differently than his lordship. I respect him. I've seen him do the impossible more times than not. But the English won't pay if this girl goes back with less than she came with. Or with more in her belly. The mail belongs to us all, and I figure we have a say."

"Lady Winchelsea's maidenhood is in the same condition as it was when she was brought here, dolthead!" snapped Gideon, uneasily praying that he wasn't wrong.

David shrugged his slender shoulders, grinning a bit sheepishly. "Well, she is a right bonny little—"

"Marta would have your skin for that. You eyeing another, and her about to burst with that bairn of yours," observed Saul. He handled his food with the same precision he did a trowel when they weren't riding the English Marches.

"I meant only . . ." David endeavored to explain. "God's blood, if the storm takes the oats again or the wheat don't make, will we be able to keep from starvin' on fleeces and hides? We need this ransom."

Weryn frowned. David was struggling to keep a wife and a small lass alive while he raided most of the summer. Poverty was trailing in the wake of the forced war years. It was gaining upon the Scottish soil. With every passing year, the men lived more and more from hand to mouth. Provisions were so depleted that one capricious act of nature could starve them out in a season. They did need their share of Miron's eight hundred marks.

"The fleeces will see us through," Weryn predicted, reminding them the flocks of sheep now grazing on the upper slopes would be sheared in August. They all depended upon those strange taciturn men and their dogs for the wool crop shipped to Flanders every year.

"The man's not been born who can make money from

sheep," grumbled David. He lifted his head and stared, immobilized. Presently all four men followed his line of vision, absorbed in Christin's unexpected appearance.

She had paused at the head of the narrow stair, her garments in order, her thoughts somewhere else. Scots women, once married, covered their hair; the unsnooded tresses were a symbol of virginal purity. Just now the thick mass of chestnut waves, caught at the crown of her head to spill about her shoulders, glowed like flames caught in the shaft of light.

The fullness of Christin's green skirts, the tiny waist and flat stomach were breathtaking. The swell of her bosom tapering up into a long, proud neck made her a beauty they didn't often see.

Humorously, each man at the table appeared to read the thoughts of the other. Gideon's breathy oath provoked David's rebuke. "Turn your head, you devil. You're a betrothed man."

"You've no room to talk, a father within th' month. Mercy upon my soul, they do grow bonny lasses in Auld Saxony," groaned Gideon.

Weryn's gruff cough broke the spell. Scooping up her skirts, Christin made her way down the stairs with the precision of a graceful doe. Finally Gideon assisted her at the landing and slipped beside her at the table. Weryn nervously adjusted the patch over his eye.

"Ahem. Sir Patrick hasn't been down yet, m'lady, but you're welcome to begin without him. I've things to attend, if you'll excuse me."

"Oh, I wasn't looking for—"

Christin flushed, knowing already that every man was conjecturing all sorts of theories about the night before. Of course they knew Patrick had come to her room. In a week all Scotland would know, and no one would believe their innocence. Her cheeks flushed scarlet.

Gideon rescued her by placing a goblet of milk in her hands. This young man knew instinctively when she was about to fly into bits. She smiled gratefully.

After a moment or two of nerve-racking tedium, the

men attempted to make polite conversation. But, after dismissing several abortive endeavors, talk inevitably turned to politics. Things went quite well until Rankin muttered a disparaging remark about the pope. Christin's eyebrows flew upward.

"It was murder before the high altar, Scotsman," she murmured softly.

Every man turned to see if he had actually heard a woman voice an opinion in a man's conversation.

"Beg pardon, mistress?" David cocked his puzzled head.

Christin immediately realized her social blunder. It was done now. She swallowed down her timidity along with her mouthful of food. For too many years she had argued politics, religion, and social order with Laurence and her father. These men were thinking she didn't know her place.

"I *said* The Bruce murdered one of his own countrymen in the church. What greater sacrilege is there?"

"In the name of Saint Andrew, madam, it was no murder!" shouted Rankin, coming straight up from his chair. Gideon's motion to the hotheaded warrior was wasted. Vainly, he wished for Weryn.

"The Comyn betrayed the king to Edward after pledging his fealty, and tried to stab him in the church itself. The bishop heard the king's confession, mistress. That blood is not on the hands of the king."

"Aye," interjected Gideon, as intense as Christin had ever seen him. "King Robert received the blessing of Saint Fillan. Mark you, the Celtic saint of the Picts and Scots *blessed* him, mistress. And that blessing goes back to the eighth century. Before the Roman church ever was in this country."

"That's a fine play on words, if you ask me," Christin argued. She was annoyed and embarrassed to have ever allowed herself to be caught up in this senseless dispute.

"Words, mistress, may be life and death at times," interrupted David. "Scotland is a very small country.

The Bruce is always hard pressed to prevent civil war. Some of th' Highlands are still beyond control of the crown. The others, just barely. Words like yours are enough to burn a town."

Christin bridled. Censure from a young Scot was a galling thing to bear.

David's full mouth smiled coldly. He didn't approve of her having enough freedom to even sit at this table. If he had his way, he would keep her in the dungeons.

"I spoke the truth, sir, not a rumor," she declared in a tone which welcomed a change of topic.

"Evil rumors abound in Scotland, lassie," observed a deep voice behind her.

Twisting in her chair, Christin bumped into Patrick's knee with her arm.

"For example," he smiled, "a possible rumor of a shortage of blacksmiths in Warrick wouldn't surprise me. No greater distortion ever existed, did it now?"

She couldn't see his face, and she refused to lean her head back. "You may have my seat, Sir Mowbray. I think I've had about all I care for."

Arising suddenly, she sloshed ale from the flagons.

"Ah . . . I think I'll fast for this meal," Patrick returned wryly, nodding to his men. "I fear we'd best leave for Warrick before our hostage leaves more than one mess for the Douglas to mop up. Faith, lass! You do have a way of stimulating things wherever you go."

At that, Christin locked eyes with him. The slight pallor upon his face and her memories of the night before did not evoke the faintest shred of pity. The chagrin she suffered at the table vexed her, and now she brazenly jabbed Patrick in the chest with a finger. His eyes narrowed from the pain splintering his temples.

"Marry, sir," she said sweetly, "if you don't do the same yourself."

It was August. Dawn was broadening, burning away the mist hugging the manor and hovering over the river.

The heather was budding, preparing to bathe Scotland's heaths in purple.

Manors like Warrick depended on heather. The long stems were tied into brooms while the longer trailing stems were woven into baskets by Dame Haggitt and Peg MacKenzie. Heather and heath cemented with peat made their houses, and the peat was fuel to cook their food and warm their bodies.

Upon the second floor of the manor Glynnis and half a dozen other women were sweeping rooms and preparing beds. The king was holding a meeting of state at Perth. Beds would be filled tonight. Too many horses, too many mouths and too few servants, she thought.

She bent to give a pillow a lusty fluffing, yelping as someone grabbed her from behind.

"Och! You devil!" she swung a loving fist at his head, and Gideon ducked.

"Shh!" His fingers covered her mouth. "Old Renney'll hear you. If Mowbray fines me one more time, I'll be ruined. Can't you steal off for a minute for a little loving?"

Gideon folded the buxom girl into his arms and planted a string of hungry kisses down to her bosom. Then he lifted his shoulders impishly.

"Maybe if we shut the door. It seems such a pity, what with a perfectly good bed and all."

"Are you trying to get me ducked in the river? Get yourself out of here. I'll see you tonight when everyone's dancing and half drunk from toasting the Douglas's last conquest."

"Oh!" he pouted and slipped his hand into the bodice of her dress which was cut too high for his taste. "My word, what have I found?"

"Nothing that you didn't know was already there." She whirled from him and leaned out the window. Through the spruce trees they could see two small boys fishing in the loch. One side was reedy, its spires growing far out into the shallows. But on the farther side the

101

grass was deep and soft. Gideon knew what she was thinking.

"At nine o'clock tonight then, sweeting," he said pressing himself against her back.

"Gideon?"

"What, lamb?"

"What would you say if I . . . I mean, if I told you that I thought . . ."

"Thought what?"

Glynnis moved to look deeply into the frank eyes she had known since she was a tiny lass. Gideon knew her very well. He changed from the teasing boy to the real man eight years of war had made of him.

"You can tell me, Glynnis. You can tell me anything."

Glynnis smiled, then sighed and wrung competent hands which would never be those of a gentlewoman. Gideon grasped them and kissed them.

"My last time, Gideon. It never came. I'm almost positive I'm carrying a wee bairn in here."

"What do you want me to say?" He watched her chew at her lip, her hands pressed to her belly.

"What you feel, Gideon?"

"I love you. I'm glad you're with child. We've put this off too long. I just didn't want to leave a young widow to th—"

"Don't talk like that. What will we do?"

"We'll try to find someone brave enough to marry us. If no priest will, we'll live in common law. Half the realm is in common law, dove. We'll find a way. Kiss me."

Footsteps clicked down the hall. "Go now!" she whispered. "I'll meet you tonight, and we'll decide everything."

"You didn't tell me," he scolded, half in, half out of the room.

"Tell you what?"

"That you love me."

Quickly, certain they would be caught, she held his

face and kissed Gideon hard upon the mouth. "I love you, Gideon MacKenzie. Until I die. Now go!"

"I'm goin', I'm goin'."

When Gideon smiled from ear to ear at Dame Renney, she turned to give him a critical once-over. This younger generation was outrageously rude.

Gideon went to help see to the tuns of ale being brought up from the brewery. There were whole nets of fish cleaned and ready for baking. Several bucks from yesterday's hunt were already spitted, and numerous sheep had been dressed for roasting. Freshly baked loaves were carefully covered with cloths.

It was a good thing The Bruce wasn't a fussy man, for there were few candles and little aged wine. Bruce was a veteran fighter used to the hardship of caves and bogs. But the queen? Since her eight years as Edward's captive, Bruce denied Elizabeth little. Everything must be as gracious as Warrick could make it.

Gideon hoped there wouldn't be too many Highlanders traveling with the king. A few nearly always were, as the king persisted in trying to win their loyalty rather than kill them off. He always went the second mile with his enemies, accepting things his parliament would have tried for treason. Scotland's unity was more important than his feelings.

There was always a fight when Highlanders mingled with other Scots. The clans were nations in themselves, and Gideon hated the condescending looks and loose criticism that always seemed to come his way. He spoke with a Teviot drawl, and some half-sotted Highlander invariably referred to him as a low-born mosstrooper.

The Prince of Badenoch—Payne Comyn—for instance. The man was no more of a prince than Gideon was. Payne's uncle, John Comyn, representing the remnants of the conquered Comyn foe, was so unblessed as to have no male issue. The title of prince was an affront to The Bruce; a subtle proclamation that the Comyn clan still claimed descendency to the throne.

Payne Comyn owned a fleet of twenty galleys and

maintained an army of three thousand men, so Gideon supposed he could call himself a prince and get by with it. High-handed Northmen—heathens and druids, all of them.

Christin threw back the covers and shivered as she dressed. A noisy confusion had disturbed her sleepy memories of Patrick.

"What's going on out there?" she demanded of Tildy as the woman sat churning.

"The king comes today. Can you believe that, without any notice?"

"In this country I can believe anything. What is there to eat? My stomach is touching my spine."

"Porridge."

"Faugh!" Tildy made no move to help her, and Christin glared at the churn as if she would like to find it amiss and vent her temper. "Is *that* for the king? Good King Robert deBruce himself?"

"Aye, and six more like it. I'm helpin' Glynnis."

Christin sniffed. She wouldn't help with anything. Robert Bruce was at the root of every trouble she had.

Warrick seemed to be in the process of turning itself wrong-side-out. Every villein who was not in the woods with hounds or taking out the falcons, was busy at cleaning, baking, gathering rushes and an ample supply of peat. Everywhere she went, Christin found herself getting in the way.

In a pique, Christin swept up her skirts and ran to overtake Glynnis as she carried a bucket of milk in each hand. "Here, I'll carry one."

They walked so rapidly the milk sloshed in the buckets like moody white oceans. "It must be something to be a king and capable of causing such a stir," Christin said, her eyes automatically searching for Patrick and not finding him.

"Oh, it's not only the king, m'lady. It's the Douglas, too, they're sayin'. A regular party of 'em. One day's notice, and we all go stark-starin' to get everything ready. The kitchen maids have taken to screamin' already, and the laundry maids will be up all night, too. A body just can't expect to run a place this size without a woman. Not when the master is ridin' the Border near six months a year and slippin' out at all hours the other six."

"Slipping out? What slipping out? What're you talking about?"

Near the kitchen entrance now, beside the conduit that carried kitchen wastes and sewage to a nearby ravine, Glynnis rested her bucket on the ground beside her feet. Clearly, she had overstepped the bounds of discretion. She squirmed.

"Don't start something and not finish, Glynnis!"

"Oh gorry, m'lady. Gideon'll kill me for this. He says m'mouth has no beginnin' and no end. I had no right."

"Sir Patrick has a lady friend, does he?"

"Oh no, mistress. At least, not the kind you're thinkin'. That's not why he slips out. I'd stake my life on that."

Frowning, pained because she was straggling somewhere on the fringes of life, Christin turned aside. One never expected that feeling of exclusion. It was always a surprise.

"It's no business of mine," she mumbled, shrinking from the need to face the bustle of life going on.

"At least," Glynnis was oblivious to her need, "if it is a lady, she once put a knife in 'is back."

Christin gaped at the girl.

"It's true, m'lady. I saw the bandages myself. Much blood, much blood."

Realizing then that she was burying herself, the maid grimaced. Then, with a flutter of her fingers about her face, she lowered her voice.

"I've only seen him leave a couple of times when I . . . happened to be . . . up late. A fortnight ago he left, all dressed in black, ridin' by himself. I don't know what to make of it unless he does funny things for The

105

Douglas. Y'can never tell about The Douglas. Maybe it *is* a woman," she mused. Then she shook her head. "No, I don't think it's a woman."

No matter how dearly she would liked to have gossiped about Patrick, Christin knew it was inadvisable. "I think you'd better be getting about your duties, Glynnis. It would be wise if you didn't mention this conversation to anyone. Especially since you had it with me. I agree with you, though. I don't think Pat—Sir Mowbray—would slip out to see a lady. He wouldn't hide an affair with a woman. He'd be more likely to flaunt it, I think."

"Oh no, m'lady. He doesn't flaunt 'em." Glynnis reddened. "My mouth really doesn't have an end, does it? I'd best be about things now before I'm really in trouble."

Christin could envision any number of sordid situations involving Patrick's secret wanderings. But then, what if he were only exceedingly clever, deliberately allowing his villeins and household to believe that he strewed himself casually among the female race? Perhaps he actually was doing something insanely dangerous. What if the price on his head was all a ruse, and he was a spy for Edward? Or what if he were involved with an English duchess? What if he were a paid assassin to kill the English king? Faith, what if he were a Highlander paid to assassinate Robert Bruce?

This was absurd, and much too complicated. Grabbing up her cloak, Christin ambled along the hard street of the burgh. Wreaths of smoke curled from croft chimneys, smells of peat and porridge perfuming the air. She saw Tag hunched in front of a horrible black house, looping a fishing net with amazing accuracy.

"Lady Christin," he wheezed, "what are you doin' out? It's goin' to rain." Rain in this country meant a deluge. Anything less than a downpour was considered a fair day.

"Tag, I come from a town that raises the best fleeces in all Yorkshire. I'm off to Braedeen steading to see

Patrick Mowbray's sheep. Would you like to walk with me? I'll tell you where everything is so you won't fall or get lost."

Christin listened to Tag's tales as they ambled along, reminding him not to talk so fast. But either his burr had improved or her ear had, for she understood him. He spoke of wild Scots from the North, fierce little men. And women suckling wolf cubs and the sacrifices of small children to strange gods. Finally she shrieked for him to stop. With Tag it was difficult to tell where fact left off and fancy began.

They paused during their walk to chat with a close-mouthed shepherd and his two dogs. Then she described dry-stone dykes and stood beside Tag in the spray of violent, rushing water.

"There aren't any leaves on the ground," she marveled, holding Tag's hands, letting him pause to smell things.

"Ah, it rains too much, lassie. The leaves rot as soon as they kiss th' ground. God's country, this is. 'Ceptin' for the old North Sea, it's the most beautiful thing I've ever seen."

"I want to talk to you about Tag," Patrick's voice came abruptly from the doorway as Christin was bending over a pot of stew at dusk. She sprang upright so suddenly that she spilled the broth down the front of her bodice and flew to scrub at it with a rag.

"Don't ever walk up behind me like that again!" she cried. "You scare the life out of a person!"

"You're liable to get more than a scare if you wander off with that old man again."

Christin never knew Patrick's motives, and if she tried to outguess him, she was usually wrong and looked ludicrous. So she braced her fists on her hips and waited for him to explain himself. He wore leather, quite handsomely, and his brown eyes didn't hold any lurking comments of what had happened when he had

107

come to her room some nights ago. They had never spoken of it.

"The Highlands get itchy this time of year, Christin. I know Braedeen is a steading of Warrick, but I'd rather you didn't go there with any one but Tag, who is worse than useless. I'll give you back to Jock if you disobey."

"Why don't you like Tag?"

"I don't dislike Tag, woman. I just don't want you wandering about—"

"You wander about!" She clapped her hand over her mouth.

If Christin hadn't looked and acted so guilty Patrick would probably have let it pass. But culpability stained her face as crimson as the setting sun behind his back. His mouth was undisturbed, but his eyes glittered with suspicion.

At the same moment he stepped toward her, Tildy emerged from the small adjoining chamber, her arms full of clean folded garments. Patrick did no more than give her a passing glance as he stalked Christin backward against the rim of the table. She could go no further, and his legs pressed into her skirts.

"And who have you been gossiping with now, m'lady? Tag? Gideon? Jock? Ah, yes. Glynnis. And what did you two ladies decide? Would I be too bold to ask that?"

Christin, being reasonable enough to know that a few shared kisses with a man like Patrick Mowbray meant nothing, sounded more antagonistic than she felt. Her feelings, in fact, bordered more closely on worry.

"Glynnis believes in your honor far too much to see you victimizing women. I'm sure your midnight rides are of the highest order in her eyes."

"What about in yours?"

"Most men, if their intentions are pure, don't make early-morning assignations. Unless," she insinuated, "the lady already has a husband. Or perhaps she lives in a country where he is not welcome."

Hardly had Christin said the words than she regretted them. They were untrue and unfair; she knew it.

"You can't seem to make up your mind, lass," Patrick said evenly—deceptively, for she had no doubts about his vexation with her. "First you have me as a lover of men, then of married women. Marry, I'm losing count."

"Oh Lord Mowbray, she didn't mean it!" Tildy's interference was most inopportune.

"Dame Grey, would you be so kind as to find something to do outside this house?"

"Y-Yes, sir. I will do just that."

"Stay where you are, Tildy!" Christin's arms gleamed as she spread them wide to prevent Tildy's escaping. "You have no right, sir."

One look from Patrick and Tildy bowed low and disappeared quickly. The blunt of his brows disapproved of Christin's posture which was as haughty as she could make it. She looked once at his boots then forced her eyes to his.

"Well, we're alone," she gulped. "Say all the things you want to say, then go away."

Patrick managed a grim smile. "Oh, lassie." He smoothed the scar on his forehead with an absent gesture. "If I shouted at you, you'd know it. What am I to do with you?"

"Send me home."

"Why?"

"Because I'm not even a good hostage. If I were, I'd be starving myself or drinking poison or doing something brave like Antigone."

"That makes me Creon, I suppose." Patrick laughed lazily. Then he sobered. "Look, Christin, The Bruce will be here within the hour. All I want from you is reasonably good behavior. I'm not sure but what they want to see you more than me, anyway."

"I have to meet the king?"

"The Bruce is anxious about you. Edward's taking full advantage of this little incident and a few others by refusing the truce. The Douglas told me to catch you that day in the glen, and I did. Both of us are neck-deep in this quicksand."

All the time he had been speaking, Patrick's eyes brazenly roamed over her. When he finished talking and simply continued to stare at her, Christin was certain that he remembered everything of the night in Wallace's castle. She flushed.

"If that's all you had to say, please leave. Tildy will be back soon."

"If Tildy could read my mind, she wouldn't dare come back." He smiled and reached one lean finger to trace the line of her jaw.

"Patrick, please!" Christin despised her shaking voice when she wanted to hide from those eyes.

"Being drunk doesn't affect my memory."

"You make me so angry I could—" She glared at his back as he left.

The sun had dipped into the moorland glens when Tildy returned to find Christin dressed and fidgeting worse than a frustrated bride.

"Tell me what it's like." Christin pounced on her.

"Oh yes, dearie. Glynnis spent half an hour tellin' me of the guests. I was too tired to share her bustle, I'm afraid."

"Well, tell me! What does he look like? Is he wicked? How many men did he bring?"

Tildy rose to wash her hands and flick a bit of dust from Christin's gown. "You'll see for yourself soon enough. Th' laird'll send for you. The Bruce? He's a huge man, with large hands. An' he has freckles."

Christin smiled. "Go on. Is he vile?"

"Noo. I'd say . . . I'd say he's one of th' saddest men I've ever seen. A strong man, with a strong jaw, but th' sadness . . . It's his eyes, I think."

"Is he grand?"

"Faugh! These Scots don't go in for display, m'lady. Exceptin' that Highland man, who looks more like a king than the king does. Even Lord Douglas seems a simple man with a ready wit."

"He's a clever fox with the fangs of a wolf. Bruce brought the queen, I suppose."

"Aye, ladies enough. The queen, and one Glynnis said was the friend of the laird's mother."

"Lady deMohr. Yes, I'm not surprised she came. Is she really as beautiful as they say?"

"I didn't see her, m'lady. I didn't see the queen, either. The only reason I glimpsed the king and Lord Douglas was because they walked out to see that mare of Sir Mowbray's."

That didn't tell her too much, and Christin brushed her hair for the tenth time, continuing to pace and wait to be summoned.

Robert Bruce was indeed a large man with rebellious sandy hair, patient shoulders and aging eyes. His only jewels were in the chain that secured his cape and one garnet ring.

"How go the sheep, Patrick? Nearly time for shearing, eh?" The Bruce inquired as they prepared to be seated for the feast.

Not too far behind, men-at-arms kept their position. The king would have none of their security when he was among his knights. His entourage had been small, too—fifty in all. This far from the Border and almost as far from the Highlands, Warrick was as safe a place in Scotland as he could be.

"We shear soon," Patrick agreed. "God knows we need it. The grain has been better than last year. Still, we depend upon the fleeces until we have some gold in hand." Bruce quirked a brow at Patrick's deliberate mention of his forthcoming ransom.

Inside the wattle cottage, Christin's patience was at an end. She couldn't wait a minute longer. She stared down at Tildy's sleeping head drooped upon her crossed arms. How discourteous of Patrick to keep her waiting this long. It had to be nearly nine o'clock.

It was exactly nine o'clock, and music swirled down into the main floor from the balcony. Long tables

111

clothed in white were placed in a rectangle, cluttered with silver dishes and chalices, and some lesser ones not quite so fine. The movement of villeins was everywhere; familiar servants roamed about, seeing that the king and Elizabeth didn't want for anything Warrick could offer.

From the arched balcony, one could overlook the entirety of the hall and its guests. In one end of the balcony, musicians played for dancing, and several retainers lounged, enjoying the music, trying to best the other's adventures and throwing dice.

Christin moved slowly up the servants's stairway, keeping well to the shadows. Seated beside Patrick, her arm resting intimately against his, was the object of her interest—Calla deMohr. She wore a daring gown, cut low, with a high starched ruff. Instinctively Christin knew that the older woman's bosom would be firm and well-shaped, like her own.

Lady deMohr and Patrick shared things of the past, that sharing placing a familiarity upon the movements they made, their gestures, the careless touch of their fingers, their quick, easy smiles. Now Christin was positive of what she had only guessed at before. Patrick had been Calla deMohr's lover. Many times.

Jealousy had always been foreign to Christin. Now it was a monstrous pain inside her. All her girlish dreams of Patrick were ridiculous. His kisses seemed like a lash drawing the blood of her soul, bruising her confidence and making her curse herself for a stupid, loathesome idiot.

Patrick danced with the queen, then with Lady de-Mohr. The actual sight of him holding her in his arms was too much.

Once, his hands had forced Christin to touch the physical proof of his desire for her. No man besides him would have dared so much.

"You'll pay, Patrick Mowbray," she breathed. "You made a fool of me." Now Christin took everything about Patrick—things he had said, and things he hadn't said—to be a lie.

Without really thinking, she slipped past the musicians, entering the first empty chamber she found. She recognized Gideon's clothes. She was beginning to understand now what Patrick had meant when he said she was in a cage. The sense of shame was glowing inside her with a heat that increased until it burst with blinding vengeance. Christin backed against the nearest wall, craving, like some trapped animal, to attack that which hurt her.

If Patrick thought the smithy was damaging to his image . . . hah! The king wanted to see her. Well, by the rood, he would see her! For once, Scotland would listen to England!

She checked the hallway then closed the door with determined hands. In the darkness, Christin stripped off her clothes. Impulses of a lightning jealousy planned what she would do, and once she briefly thought she was being unreasonable. But she only brushed the guilty warning aside and yanked on Gideon's trews. They were awfully tight, but so much the better. Now, for some boots. She couldn't find any. No matter. Christin cross-laced the black-stockinged pants up to her knees. There was no mirror, but she knew every curve of her buttocks and legs left nothing to the imagination.

Now, something for her naked bosom. A tunic was no good. After a moment's thought, Christin grabbed the small jerkin she had laced over her long-sleeved kirtle. Of course, it reached only to her waist and had no sleeves. It was deeply cut, with a three-inch space between the bodice sides. Her bare abdomen would gleam through the laces. And her breasts would all but spill over the top.

Naturally, it was quite scandalous—hardly better than being stark naked. Worse, in fact. Not even a wanton would dare be seen like this.

Her hands shaking, Christin slipped out of the chamber to pause at the head of the main stairway. Two of the musicians caught sight of her, with her honey-colored mane billowing out like some fiery Amazon, her throat gleaming whitely down into the shocking exposure of her breasts. One by one they stopped playing. By the time Christin came to her senses and realized she was about to make a fool of herself, their silence jerked up the heads of the revelers below. In unison they searched for the source of the lull.

When her eyes, drawn by some guilty magnet to Patrick's, comprehended the danger of it, Christin would gladly have scrambled back up the three steps to Gideon's room. But it was too late. The queen appeared stunned, the king just stared at her, and Calla deMohr smiled with amusement at Patrick's reaction.

Christin had no choice but to continue down the stairs. In the silence, she half-heard the king's laughing remark to Patrick—something about Patrick having to fatten her up if he expected much smithing from her. The guests at the table chuckled and resumed their rapt observance.

Not one other word was uttered, but every eye followed her like a needle to the pole as she stepped to the table. As a swaggering man would do, Christin threw one foot upon the bench. The trews stretched tightly across her rear. Somewhere behind her a guard groaned loudly, and Patrick mumbled, "I'll have Pauly horsewhipped."

Christin picked up a chalice by its stem and twirled it. "English silver, by the saints!" she raised her voice. "Well, we English have always paid too dear. For everything, I warrant."

Robert Bruce met the eyes of his queen, and James Douglas doubled with laughter. Patrick bumped against the table, causing a startling clatter of dishes as he rose, and Lady deMohr gasped as wine sloshed into her lap.

Patrick muttered something resembling an apology to her and bowed his head to his king. "Lady Winchelsea, Your Grace."

"You should've asked more, Mowbray," vowed Douglas, leaning back in his chair to enjoy Patrick's blistering chagrin. "Eight hundred scarcely does justice."

"Hold your tongue, Jamie," muttered Patrick, his fingers already biting into Christin's shoulder.

"Leave her alone!"

The seriousness in Payne Comyn's voice creased The Bruce's forehead. "The lass is only doing what any good warrior would do: using the finest weapon she has for the hardest battle. I think she's magnificent."

Christin's eyes jerked toward the man walking around the open-mouthed servants like some triumphant Viking receiving his bride. Her jaw grew slack; he was exceedingly handsome. As he held his hand out for hers, Patrick was forced to withdraw his own. It was then that she looked at Patrick's face. There was no doubt he could have wrung her neck.

"M'lady," said Patrick in a strange voice, bowing slightly. "May I present Lord Payne Comyn of Badenoch?"

The tall blond man peered at the Highlander over her head. "Lady Christin Winchelsea of Yorkshire, a temporary guest who blesses us with a . . . uh, a display of her virtues."

"They would be obvious anyway," bowed Payne over her hand with a kiss she hardly noticed. When he straightened, he stood very still, as if they were the only two people in the room. She found herself quite unable to tear her eyes from his; they hinted of indulgence in pleasurable trespasses.

The king inclined his head, and the tension dispelled to a degree. "Pray be seated at our table, your ladyship."

When Payne Comyn drew Christin's hand through his arm, allowing his eyes to flit over the deep cleft of her straining bosom, Patrick involuntarily stepped forward. Only a movement from James Douglas prevented him from following.

"Music!" shouted James, winking at Patrick in a not-so-frivolous warning that this was neither the time nor the place for a confrontation with the temperamental Highlander.

Logs were added to the fire and fresh tuns of ale were opened for the lesser ranks of diners. At the king's table the wine goblets were refilled. Laughter rang at some observation by Robert that three of Edward II weren't worth one of his father.

Seated between the attentive Lord Comyn and Douglas's highest ranking officer, Captain Becket Swythen, Christin wished miserably this was all some dream from which she could wake herself.

"Your point was admirably made, madam," smiled the magnetic Highlander. Payne had a face unlined by the pain of caring or convictions, a face accustomed to follow the path of self-interest.

"I've often said that Highland lasses have more spirit than any women in the world. I've been wrong." She smiled sadly. "If you're uncomfortable, I'll take you to the stairs and you can change. No one will dare say anything to me."

"Oh, thank you. I would like that." She dropped her head.

Sullen, hardly containing his temper at all, Patrick found himself rudely neglecting Calla and fumbled to make amends. His distraction, however, was insulting.

"A man's reaction, such as you have displayed, my darling Patrick, can stem only from one of two sources."

Patrick frowned, watching Christin walk across the hall, escorted by a man not easily dismissed from one's mind. Her legs were long and perfectly formed beneath the tight trews. Patrick was aware, too, of the throbbing deep in his body at the sight of her—a feeling he probably shared with every man in the room except blind Tag.

"Your knowledge of men has never been amiss before, m'lady," he told Calla. "And what, say you, is the source of my anger?"

"Love or hate," she said. "They are closely related."

"You know me well. Which is it? I would like to know myself." He waited and gave her his attention.

Calla laughed. "I think I'll keep my opinion to myself. Are you coming to my room tonight, as always?"

"And what if my anger comes from love?" He propped himself on his elbows.

"It matters naught to me, whatever it is."

Patrick studied her—the long blond tresses twisted and piled high beneath a braided gold cap. Emeralds rested about her throat. Calla was as beautiful in bed as she was to the eye.

"We'll see," he answered softly, allowing his leg to rest against her thigh.

When Christin descended, dressed once again in her proper garments, her loveliness marred only by the sadness in her gray eyes, the room settled down to a noisy hum. Calla moved to speak with Queen Elizabeth, and Jamie placed an arm about Patrick's shoulders.

"We need to talk in a quiet place, Patrick. The three of us."

Patrick pondered for only a moment. "Come," he said, and led the king and his ranking general Douglas out the side gate of the manor toward the kirk. He leaned his weight against it, and the heavy door creaked open. Patrick hadn't been inside the building since Christin had cleaned it, and now it surprised him. Even in moonlight, one could see the order of it—its serenity. Had she come here to pray?

"Don't bother with a light," James suggested, and the king nodded.

"Keep your voices down," The Bruce warned. "Patrick, deHughes was executed three days ago. I just heard."

"Oh, sweet Jesu!" breathed Patrick and dropped to a bench nearby.

Jonathan deHughes was a knight of the earl of Lancaster who had secretly pledged his aid to Bruce's hopes for a truce. Through deHughes, it was hoped to reach the early of Lancaster who could be in a position to press the English king into a decision. Patrick was the liaison between deHughes and The Bruce.

"Why didn't he get word to me?" grieved Patrick, raking his curls. "I might have been able to prevent it."

"He was betrayed, Patrick," explained James. "By one of my very own men. I don't know yet who it was, but deHughes's wife got word to me in an attempt to save her husband's life. She didn't know who it was either, only that a man named Thomas Barber witnessed at deHughes's trial, declaring that he was informed by a Douglas retainer. Edward's troops simply surrounded the man's house and dragged him off on the charge of treason. His trial was held that very night. The next morning, he was beheaded."

The king sat then, burying his head into his hands.

"How much blood?" he mourned. "I've seen the deaths of all my brothers save Edward, of many men who have loved and served me. Isabel was driven mad. Now Edward Plantagenet begins to spill English blood on my attempts to end this war. Oh, the blood that is on my hands, Jamie!"

James and Patrick stood beside their monarch and comforted him with their silent presence.

"Patrick?" Douglas asked after a few moments. "I want you to find the man who told Thomas Barber about deHughes. If I try it myself, he'll learn of it and escape me. Or perhaps cause another death. It's dangerous even for you to try, as well kept a secret as that was. Who of your own men knew?"

"Only Weryn, and his word's as good as the king's. I'll do what I can—you know that. Jamie, about this hostage I hold—"

"Yes," The Bruce interrupted. "My spies inform me that the archbishop is harassing Edward to refuse negotiations of the truce if the girl is not returned, along with the priests we took at Myton. I know the ransom is needed, Patrick—I've taken enough with my own hands—but this has grown into more than blackmail. It threatens the best chance we've had for peace. I want you to return the girl to her family. I'll inform the crown that we are showing our good faith in the negotiations by making this gesture."

In the darkness neither man was too aware of the defeated heaviness of Patrick's shoulders. The silence grew even more weighty.

"Aye," he consented, a strange knot deep in his throat. "As you wish, sire."

"I'll take her with me to Stirling after my lords' counsel at Perth," the king continued. "When all has been arranged, she will be escorted back with enough flair to attract attention of the citizenry. His earls will press Edward hard, I think."

Christin, to be taken to Stirling? He would have her here only two days and nights, at the most. Suddenly Patrick wanted to be alone, so he could walk on the moors and think in quiet. But that was impossible.

"It will be done, Your Grace. Now, I suggest we return, or everyone will be suspect of us."

"Laddie," murmured James, as they walked behind Robert through the darkness, "had I known what all this would lead to, I would never have sent you after her that day in the glen."

Patrick didn't reply. He had lost Christin, after Richard's pressure, after his own conscience had smitten him. Nothing else seemed very important now.

Patrick had no chance to be alone with Christin that night; Payne Comyn never allowed her anywhere except by his side. The man was behaving like a suitor, completely aware of his host's displeasure. Christin didn't withdraw from his arm or rebuff his friendly touch. She laughed with him at times, and conducted herself with mature poise when Payne introduced her to the queen. She was anything but a girl, and everyone enjoyed her company but Patrick.

At midnight he flung himself face-down on his cot. Then he sat and repaired his clothing. With a loss of control he despised in himself, he slammed his clenched knuckles against the stone wall. When he stood outside Calla deMohr's chamber door, he knew it would open to his touch. She could ease the pain like no other woman he knew. Yet, even as he opened it, he swore under his breath. Christin had set the hook deep, hadn't she?

"I'm not without influence, m'lady." Payne's voice was hypnotizing granite. "I won't stand for you to remain here, a captive of a half-Scots savage. I wield a great deal of power in your homeland. You should be with your family."

They were outside the hall, walking toward the cottage, caught in a shaft of light from Warrick's window. Christin faced the man, observing his trimmed auburn hair and beard, the perfectly chiseled nose.

"You surely don't mean that you could send me back to York without ransom? How—"

"I've already begun doing it, sweet girl." His teeth flashed through his beard. He would be a fool not to use Bruce's plans to his advantage. "It pleases me to play chivalrous knight to such beauty. Your return is what I want. Why tarry?"

"But, Lord Comyn—" she began. For three months this is what she had wanted. Why did she hesitate?

"When I decide on a thing, Christin, I act swiftly. It's a characteristic of my family, unfortunately for some. You intrigue me very much. Your daring this evening was impressive. I thought to myself, such a woman deserves the best there is. Someone worthy of her beauty and who can compliment her strength. That is why I arranged your return home. My motives are entirely selfish."

The moonlight wasn't bright, and Christin paused outside the cottage. With a boldness she didn't expect from a man she had barely met, Payne pushed open the door and drew her inside. She was weakened from the ordeal she had put herself through. Much of it hadn't assumed a reality in her thoughts. When Payne began to fold her in his arms, Christin's confusion seemed to incapacitate her.

"You presume too much, sir," she objected feebly.

"I said I move too quickly. You wouldn't withhold those beautiful lips from a man who has just arranged your freedom, would you?"

"Of course. I mean, I'm much in your debt, sir, but a gentleman—"

"Never call me a gentleman," he laughed softly. "I'm a Scot, and you're an irresistible wench ripe for taking."

Christin didn't even know if Tildy was in the house, and she certainly couldn't call for help, for Payne swept her up in a hungry passion. He hadn't the coaxing gentleness in his mouth as Patrick. Perhaps he was even a little cruel. But his kiss staggered her.

"Sir!" she whispered when he finally lifted his head, and she lay back against his arm.

"It isn't often that I want a woman as much as you. I can offer you much, Lady Christin. Oh, I realize Mowbray has designs on you. I can read his eyes. Believe me, dove, I can satisfy you more than he could ever begin to. I know you better already than he does. He's insensitive to you. Trust me."

Again Payne drew her so close that she was struck by his virility. Darting fragments of thought flirted with her logic. But it wasn't until she was nearly fainting, that Christin begged him to cease. He was a compelling man. He would force her if he went much farther. Demanding hands seemed everywhere, never asking. Her lack of experience was undoing her. She had loved Patrick for so long that she should not be here. The unexpected clarity of her feelings—a sunburst of honesty—buckled Christin's knees. She collapsed in Payne's arms.

"M'lord, please."

"Only with regret." He finally placed her in a chair and knelt by her knee. "It's too soon, isn't it, lassie?

But I can scarce resist you. I go with the king tomorrow, with Mowbray. It will strain me from breaking his neck."

"Yes, yes. Certainly," she mumbled, unaware of what she was saying. Christin waited until Payne had gone before she wept. "Oh, Patrick," she buried her face in her skirt, "what have I allowed to happen to myself?"

Chapter Six

It wasn't as though Patrick had never been absent from Warrick before, Christin thought. However, she hadn't known then of love's complete lack of discretion. It was capricious and not to be trusted. Love had made a mistake. Now it must be smothered because it had touched a man on the wrong side of the Border, the wrong side of the law, the wrong side of custom and the church.

"I *asked,* mistress, if you intended t'eat anything today?"

"What? Oh, yes, I do, Tildy. The king dines here tonight. I will have to eat. My last night . . ." and Christin's words trailed off as she retreated into thought again.

"Praise God, yes! We'll be going home. It's been a bad dream, m'lady."

"A dream," Christin repeated, her monotone painting some private scene of pain. "A dream . . ."

But Warrick awakened from the dream, the return of its lord and Robert Bruce coming just as the sun faltered toward late afternoon. Chill clamped its fingers upon the river valley, and the sun did little to dispel it.

Christin's impulse was to search out Patrick, to see if his eyes held any comfort for her. Payne Comyn of Badenoch would have told her no.

He had watched Patrick all through the tedious discussion with twenty-two barons and ten earls. Now Comyn considered the moody knight—Patrick's obvious impatience to settle his guests before he broke into long strides out the doors. The Highlander frowned and smoothed his beard.

Patrick was explaining something to Gideon Mac-Kenzie as he proceeded, even before washing, toward the cottage behind the kirk.

"I said once that I would escape from him," Christin explained to the walls. "I should have. I may still do it."

"A girl needs a mother," Tildy sniffed, disapprovingly. "I done my best. You've disgraced your father's name with that foolish prank. Thank the Holy Virgin I wasn't there to see it."

Perilously near tears, Christin spun about as Patrick entered without knocking. The draft which entered with him seemed quite apt. Tildy carefully made herself busy.

"Why did you do it, Christin? Will you tell me that? You were going home anyway. Disgracing yourself wasn't necessary."

Tildy made some sound, and Patrick glared at her, his penetrating brown eyes sending her into the bedroom.

"Leave me alone," Christin said.

"I warrant I should. Or thrash you, as I once considered doing. You were obviously spoiled rotten as a wee child."

"Don't!" she cried, squeezing her eyes tightly to compose herself. Then she turned her back and he scarcely heard her words. "I was angry. Angry at you for bringing me here and making me watch you with . . . her."

The silence was heavy, and Christin never saw him reach to touch her and draw clenched fists back to his sides. "That's a very disturbing thing to tell me the day before you leave."

Christin turned, suspicious of the unpretended compassion in his voice. Their eyes saw now the enormity of the battlefields between them. Only a few grains of time were left, and they were too quickly seeping to the bottom of the hourglass.

"I've hurt you—"

"I wish I could say—"

A rapping on the door made Patrick's shoulders droop.

"What is it?" He didn't remove his eyes from hers.

"It's the mare, Patrick." Weryn's voice came hesitantly. "She's in trouble."

For the space of a second, Patrick seemed dazed. Then he snatched open the door.

"What about the mare?" He drew Weryn inside. "Is she about to foal?"

"Aye, Patrick. But something's wrong. It's not good. You'd best come."

Glancing toward Christin, who was struggling to focus her eyes, Patrick wordlessly invited her to come. She felt oddly needed. Taking up her shawl, she followed the two figures to the stables. Christin had never been inside any of these buildings except the smithshop and the weaving house. Everything was bustling because of the king.

Triste was lying on clean straw, her belly distended with its ready foal. At the sight of Patrick, the mare watched with dark, moist eyes, following his movements as if she knew they would help her.

"Ohh, she's so beautiful, Patrick."

As delicately as if she were touching a butterfly, Christin lowered herself beside the intelligent head and smoothed the silky nose. The purity of blood showed. Triste was a splendid bay—dark brown with black markings and black stockings. In response to the ruffling sounds of acceptance, Christin placed her cheek against the pointed ears. Triste twitched them and blinked.

"She's the last living thing between my mother and me. I don't mean to lose her," Patrick noted with determination.

Triste made a low, painful sound, thrashing about, behaving as if she wanted to stand upright.

"Hold her head still, Christin. Shh, girl. Easy now. What's the matter here?"

Patrick ran his fingers over the distension, trying to determine the position of the foal. "I can't tell for sure." Without hesitation he rolled up his sleeve and after some minutes, he unfolded himself and stood to clean his hands.

"Weryn, it's a breech. If she can birth it enough so I can get a rope about it, I think I can pull it from her."

"It's been a long time," Weryn frowned. "It should've come b'now."

Gideon, who was watching with several of the stable boys, knew how important this animal was to his laird. Christin's mouth slackened at the glances passing between the men; she had never seen Patrick afraid before.

"Gideon," Patrick said after consideration, "go fetch that warlock Tag. I must be mad, but tell him to get his weeds and whatever. Get back over here, and do anything he tells you to."

"Aye. You, Thomas, come with me," Gideon clipped his orders.

Telling them that she was in a distress for which there was no comfort, Triste continued to whimper softly. Then her head dropped back onto the hollowed straw, her breathing as labored as her need to bear a foal that wouldn't come. Very many hours of this would see mare and foal both dead.

Useless, frustrated, Patrick kicked at straw, swearing softly under his breath. When he moved behind the stall partition, Weryn's eyes caught Christin's, and she read the compassion of the older man. His lordship needed her, they said.

To Warrick's laird, losing this mare would be losing what fragile threads of the past he had. Christin saw Patrick Mowbray with striking clarity, not as a ruthless Borderer forcing his way through burning towns, giving orders to destroy and pillage. She saw a young lonely boy—hurt, shocked by a violence of war he never asked for, divided between two countries and belonging to neither.

She went to him, standing for some moments, measuring him as he sat brooding—elbows on his knees, his curly head in his hands. He didn't move or speak when her skirts brushed against his shoulder. But when her fingers lowered into his hair he leaned against the security of her thigh. Christin didn't think she had ever cared so much as when he wrapped both his arms about her knees and turned his face into her skirt.

"Patrick?"

"I'm all right." He smiled up at her sadly. "I just can't watch her suffer."

"Could she die?"

"Yes. I've known them to."

"If you can take this foal from her, will she live through it?"

"I don't know, Christin. I just don't know."

He drew her down beside him, and they huddled together like a pair of orphaned puppies. Patrick held one of her hands in his, absently inspecting its lines while his thoughts were far away. She didn't speak.

At the sound of Gideon's return with Tag, Patrick rose to find a silent, sullen man. Tag's dislike of Warrick's laird was no secret, even to Christin. Probably because Patrick refused to believe in his fairies, she thought wryly.

"Tag," Patrick led the man forward and drew him down to touch the mare, which by now had lost too much strength to even thrash. "I've heard talk about all these miracles you do with those weeds you have. Let me see one of them now, and you'll never want for a thing."

"Lass?"

How did Tag know she was here? Christin joined them, and knelt. "I'm here." Patrick's eyes grew wide as she took the old man's hand and placed it upon her hair.

"I do this for the lass," he muttered rudely. Patrick's mouth set, but Christin's restraining hand kept him from retorting.

Fishing about to untie a filthy square of cloth he must have carried for years, Tag spread out pouches and packets of dried herbs. Very carefully he smoothed a place for them, removed each one singly and laid them out: lobelia, hops, mandrake root and valerian. Herbs he had once gathered up and down the coast of the North Sea and the Continent. Then he moved his hands over the belly of the mare.

Patrick's eyes were nearly black—wet and glistening with distrust. "Can she foal? D'you know?" he prodded the blind man with the toe of his boot.

"Patience, m'lord. She might. She has a better chance than the foal, I'd guess."

Like some ancient Assyrian magician Tag took Christin's hands and formed them into a cup. He pinched an herb and smelled it or tasted, selecting one, rejecting another. Patrick mutely vowed if the old troll started muttering incantations over them he would kick him into the next stall.

"Mix that with water. We'll pour it down her," said Tag.

"No! Not until you tell me first. What devil's potion are you brewing?"

"I don't be your enemy, m'lord. I knew your mother. Your father didn't deserve her—"

"Get on with it!" Patrick growled, gesturing with powerless hands and glaring at the rafters.

"This will soothe the beast like a woman in travail," Tag pacified his lord.

With perceptive eyes questioning every move he made, Tag's herbs were prepared and, as Christin and Patrick forced Triste's mouth open, Weryn poured the liquid down her throat. The mare was so frightened that it took all of them to hold her. Then she presently began to settle.

Within the hour Weryn roused Patrick, who had

stolen a space on Christin's skirt and lay memorizing the rafters.

"D'ye want me t'do this?" Weryn had a short length of rope in his fist.

"I'll do it." Glancing at Triste's closed eyes, for a second Patrick thought the mare was dead. "What's this? What have you done to her, old man?"

Tag roughly pushed Patrick aside, as if he were a pesky youth. "She's only sleepin', m'lord," he said after leaning his ear to her belly. "Take the foal. She won't put up much of a fight."

Patrick hadn't thought it would be so difficult, but in the end he had to sit in the straw, his feet braced against the great bones of her rump and pull with all his might. Surely, he would kill the foal.

But he didn't, and Christin could hardly believe it when she finally saw the spindly legs move. Patrick and Weryn wiped off the membranes of birth, cleaning its eyes and perfect little muzzle as Triste would have done.

Drenched with sweat, his chest heaving from the strain, Patrick dropped down beside Christin. As Weryn finished, the comical colt managed to jut his hindquarters in the air with his back legs straight, but he couldn't quite deal with his forelegs yet.

Patrick laughed and slung his arm about Christin's shoulders without thinking, smiling and relieved. No one seemed to notice. It was dusk.

"Shouldn't Triste be stirring around a bit more, Tag?" asked Patrick.

"She will when she's ready. She's good stock, that mare. I remember when she come here."

"Yes," mused Patrick, bending his head for Christin to pick straw from his hair. "I suppose you do."

Accepting Tag's word this time without question, Patrick drew a weary Christin to her feet. "It's been a long day, lass. The king is waiting. Gideon, take Tag back to his house, and I'll make arrangements." Arrangements for what he did not say, but Christin thought that Tag would probably be wearing different clothes from now on. And perhaps even have someone to clean up the grubby hovel he lived in.

Triste made a muffled whinnying sound, and the colt stirred.

"I must have hurt Triste terribly."

They stood in the stables, dozens of men moving about, and Patrick appeared oblivious of their presence. They had shared something dear, and when their eyes met it was an embrace, a gentle caress.

"All mothering hurts," Christin smiled. "At least she lived, which is more than I can say for my own mother."

Patrick searched for the girl in her and found the woman. Without a reply he watched the forced straightness of her back as she disappeared into the orangey decline of another day. Her last day, he thought bleakly. He didn't want her to go.

Christin sat at a white-covered table, staring at the crusty efforts of the cooks: pastries, black bread, pies of wildfowl with strong gravy. Ale warmed on the hearth, and Payne Comyn's knee rested against hers beneath the table. He chewed venison and smiled dreamily.

"I had forgotten how beautiful you are, lass." He wiped his hands and touched her sleeve. "I like your dress."

Christin gazed into his blue eyes. Patrick never remarked on her dresses. She wondered if he even noticed them. He was awfully busy noticing Calla deMohr's dress which was as daring a gown as she had worn before, Christin thought ruefully.

"More wine, Lady Winchelsea?" Captain Swythen lifted bushy brows. He wasn't an out-of-the-ordinary man, rather squarish and quietly confident of his abilities.

"Oh no, captain," Christin covered the tankard with her hand.

"I would've guessed yes," he teased, reminding her of her scandalous entrance the evening before.

With a heavy frown at the man, Payne drew Christin up to stand near the fire.

The meal hadn't ended quickly. Christin was faced with the smiling task of accepting attentions from a man she must be courteous to. He was interceding for her; he was having her sent home.

"My lord, it's been a tiring day. I leave for Stirling tomorrow, and I still have things to make ready." She begged him excuse her.

He understood. "And I leave for Ireland, my bonny. For two months or more." He laughed at some private joke. "Edward Bruce needs me." Suddenly he frowned. "What is it you feel for me, Christin?"

Her breath catching, Christin watched his brows blunt. "Ah, Lord Comyn—"

"Payne."

"Yes. Payne." She stumbled in her thoughts. Did he now expect some payment for what he had done? Had that been his purpose all along? "I feel nothing but the very highest regard for you. Of course." She had difficulty in not lowering her eyes.

"But as a man," he urged, his discomposure making him slip a ring on and off his finger. "Do I please you? Am I in your affections, lassie?" He tipped up her chin which had gotten lower and lower.

Christin smiled prettily. "Certainly you're in my affections . . . Payne. You have—well, saved my life in a manner of speaking."

Knowing full well that Payne was sincere, Christin watched his head bow over her hand. His lips brushed the crest of her knuckles, then the tips of her fingers, one by one. When he lowered it, she curtsied and bowed her head.

"You honor me, sir."

"Wait, lass," he bade her hold when she turned. When he took a few steps forward he drew the attention of everyone at the king's table. Obviously, he wished to speak, and the room stilled somewhat.

"Your Grace," he bowed, "I would like to inform

Your Majesty of my intentions since this directly concerns the crown. Ordinarily I would not speak so quickly, but Your Grace remembers I have been commissioned to Ireland."

Robert Bruce listened carefully to his debonair Highlander. He could never afford not to listen to his Highlanders. "Pray continue."

"Christin Winchelsea pleases me much. I wish to take her to wife. I have no doubts that this can be arranged through Edward and her father, even with this unfortunate ransom pending. It will only give credence to your efforts for truce. I wish to be assured all your efforts will bend toward this end while I am in Ireland."

Coming through the controlled charm of his smile, his words were not unlike thunder, beginning with a murmur and ending with a crash capable of rocking a building. Christin stood, icy cold.

"Damnation, Comyn!" Patrick raged, not so afflicted. His disbelief swept the silver utensils to the floor in a gesture of passionate affront. "I promised this girl's return on my honor. By God, she will be returned! You have no right to interfere."

"Interfere? I hardly consider an arrangement of marriage to be interference."

Christin had no conception of the power behind Payne Comyn's name. True, his clan had been broken, but his holdings and influence were still quite strong. He seemed suddenly surrounded by Highland men.

"Surely you can find some enterprising wench to vent your lusts upon!" Patrick's insult twanged like a spent arrow.

"I hope you have enough blood to back that up," Payne snarled.

Bruce frowned wearily, and James Douglas kicked Patrick from where he sat.

"Sit down, you idiot!" he said between closed teeth.

Payne, having no way of knowing the depths of Patrick's feelings for Christin took his stand. But once it was taken, it was an object of whispers behind cupped hands. And conjectures exchanged between lifted eyebrows. He wasn't about to back down.

"I hate to resort to this, Your Grace, but my mind is set. If I don't see this marriage arranged with her family—legitimately, properly—I will raise a stir in the north the likes of which you have never seen."

The eyes of Bruce met those of Douglas, then flashed back to Patrick. His great shoulders squared, and his voice was exact. "You threaten the *crown,* m'lord Comyn?"

"Not at all, sire. There is no reason why it should ever come to that. I only tell you what is possible. My family remembers much, and still wields much influence among the clans. A mere spark could set off a civil war that would make your efforts to regain your western lands seem like a bairn's christening." He bowed graciously, as if placing an impressive gift at the Bruce's feet.

Christin was in shock, though she went through the motions of a curtsy to the king. Nothing seemed real, except the enormity of her folly which had placed her in such an incredibly dangerous predicament. And not only her, but an entire country. Marriage? To this strange man?

Elizabeth, seeing Christin's distress, touched her husband's arm. "Excuse Lady Winchelsea, Your Grace." Robert noded absently, and Christin blinked.

Feeling the same madness upon her as when the Borderers had taken her in the glen, she turned to flee the hall. She was only a few feet behind the king when Patrick prevented her. Payne stiffened, poised with his hand upon a jewel-hilted dirk. Comyn would try nothing here, Patrick knew. Yet Weryn, Gideon and David drew near, hands flexing about the hilts of their swords. Creagen hovered like some bereaved creature behind them, his heavy shoulders hunched with Saxon foreboding.

"She cannot wed you, m'lord."

Patrick's statement sliced smoothly, a well-stropped

blade cleaving open ready fruit. He could hear the gasps and feel the bright tension; he was at his best in situations like this.

"Oh?"

"She's not a virgin," he shrugged placidly. Before anyone could recover he made another announcement even more stunning. "Lady Winchelsea is my mistress."

The world moved beneath her feet, a nauseous shudder, and Christin fumbled to find Patrick's arm. Her legs seemed curiously detached from her body. None of this was happening.

"You little fool," he muttered under his breath. "I ought to let you boil in your witch's brew."

The Bruce turned to study this remarkable scene. Douglas was shaking his head, and Patrick didn't dare look at Weryn. Payne, settling into a visible determination to see this out, threw back his head and laughed richly. After staring at Christin for a few seconds he chuckled again, softly.

"I misjudged the coyness of her ladyship. In truth it only fascinates me more." He inclined his auburn head to Christin's slackened jaw. "It matters not a whit, madam. Nothing has changed."

The Douglas's small sound of displeasure and Patrick's quick intake of breath came at the same surprised moment. What did it take to stop this man, wondered Patrick, astonished.

"I'm afraid you misunderstand, sir." Spreading his fingers wide upon the bodice of Christin's gown, he drew her back against his body. She was trembling all over. "It's a little more complicated, I fear. You see," he paused as if he were remembering things, "she carries my bairn."

"You lie, you traitorous Englishman!" thundered Payne, his mouth twisting as facts battled in his mind.

The Douglas, as quick as he was, was pressed to keep the Highlander from rushing Patrick. His sword drawn, standing in a half-crouch, James readied himself. No one in the room doubted that Lord Douglas was dead serious. Comyn's fear was real.

"Patrick?" Christin whimpered, slumping against him.

"Keep your wits. Don't you dare go to pieces."

Even the servants forgot their duties. Food was burning on the spit, and Glynnis came to her senses enough to dash for the fire and drag the spit aside. She gave the kitchen knave a cuff aside his ear and wrenched her eyes back to Patrick.

"If the lass wishes to wed you, I can't prevent it, I suppose." Patrick spoke lazily. "But the child is mine. I will have it."

"Let her say it, you conniving Saxon! Better still, I will see for myself when I return. If no child is evident in two months, I will have proof of your infamy. Then I will kill you, sir."

"Ask her, then," grinned Patrick, wanting very much to draw his sword. "Tell the Highlander the truth, Christin."

His thumb was pressing into her back so hard that he was hurting her. As if to comfort her, he leaned his head into her hair. "Lives depend on this, lass. Do not fail me now."

Payne studied his foe before he challenged Christin, revealing his confidence that Patrick was lying. Straightening his shoulders, he gestured his men aside. He looked at the king as Robert twisted in his chair to face the shivering Saxon hostage.

In his younger days, Robert Bruce's courage caused him to burn his own lands and crops to starve out his enemy. He had defied kings and popes. But years had developed a control that didn't display excesses. If he was upset now, he concealed it, speaking with an unemotional candor.

"Lady Winchelsea, I regret this unfortunate matter," he said. "The entire war itself is to blame that you were ever placed in this circumstance to begin with. But now I have many lives dependent upon me. I would have a statement from you. If you do not carry Sir Mowbray's

135

child, I have no choice but to withdraw from the issue and to allow the Lord of Badenoch's family to approach Edward. I trust you can understand the delicacy of this dilemma."

The Bruce gazed straight into the glazed gray eyes, wondering if she was able to respond. Christin, humbled now and heartsick, allowed the remnants of a fleeing girlhood to crumble dismally at her feet. Feeling Patrick's shoulder just behind her own, she finally lifted her head to face Payne Comyn. For the first time in her life she would behave like a woman.

"I do pray that you will understand," she said distinctly. As a single man, the hall stood waiting for her answer. "It is the truth. I carry Patrick Mowbray's child."

By some unknown means, Patrick removed Christin from the confusion to the misty silence outside the hall.

"I can't believe this is happening," she managed to say before her feet stubbornly refused to take her one step further. As she slumped against him, Patrick swept her up in his arms. Tildy was following, and the faithful woman reminded him of a soldier who has seen too much battle.

"Lord have mercy upon us, Christ have mercy upon us," she kept repeating until Patrick finally demanded her silence.

"Take care of her," he ordered. "I'll come back, but first I must do what I can to mend this disaster. If it *can* be mended."

Placing Christin upon her cot with more gentleness than she expected, Patrick stood looking down at her misery. His pain for her was an old thing by now; he was at a new loss as to what he should do with it.

"Oh, sweet lassie," he sighed, sinking down to sit beside her, almost as stunned as she. "What have I done to you?"

"Enough," she whispered, lifting her hand to touch his large one. She really hadn't intended to hurt him this way. "I did the rest to myself, I think."

"What'll happen now, Sir Mowbray?" wept Tildy. "What'll your father do, m'lady? This'll kill him sure. Why in the name of the Virgin did you *ever* admit such a thing? *It's not true, is it?*"

"Of course it's not true, Tildy," Christin scolded. "Patrick, what if I . . . escaped? Creagen and Tildy and I could get horses tonight, and ride to the Border. It would solve everything."

"It wouldn't solve anything, Christin. Except to place you where I couldn't help you at all. Comyn would lose too much face to let you get away now. After all, he bared his intentions before the king and part of his court. No Highlander would allow himself to be made a laughingstock."

"But the truth will out, Patrick! One is or isn't with child, you know. What will Payne do then? What will *I* do then?" she wondered, whispering. Her fingertips couldn't seem to force the throbbing back into her head. Bracing a hand on the far side of her, Patrick smoothed the hair back from her forehead. It was a caress her father had often made, and Christin blinked hard to keep from weeping.

"Cursed Scots!" cried Tildy. Then she clapped her hand over her rash mouth and quietly withdrew, crossing herself, muttering that the world was coming to an end, that they would all be spewed out of the devil's mouth.

"Payne Comyn will approach the English king, sweetheart. Comyn the Red, the kinsman that Bruce slew at Blackfriars, really did betray Bruce to Edward the First. The Comyns are Bruce's most bitter enemies, and whatever the Comyns want from England, they usually get. It would be nothing for Edward to place your father in such a position that he would gladly marry you off."

"Father would never do that!"

"Don't be blind. He'd do anything, if it were a matter of your life. Don't try to play games with Edward. People who play with Edward lose their heads."

Christin rolled onto her stomach and buried her teary

137

face in the pillow. She felt her hair lifted and a kiss brushed against the back of her neck.

"I'll be back, lamb, when things have quieted."

The feast was virtually ended by the time Patrick returned to the hall. The Douglas had left with his men, Comyn and his Highlanders had disappeared to their quarters, and Weryn was having the hall cleared. The scurrying kitchen maids were putting food away, and the servers were waved away with impatient flourishes. Patrick thought he needed a strong drink of whiskey.

That James provided, dragging his blond friend up to the chamber provided for the king and queen. Robert immediately discarded any courtly formalities, and Patrick was vaguely aware of the queen's preparations for bed behind a thin partition with her ladies.

"Well, my lord Patrick Mowbray! This is a fine kettle." Robert Bruce threaded thick fingers through his hair. "All I need is an uprising in the Highlands. We can forget the truce, the lifting of the excommunication —everything."

"Is the girl really with child?" James's forthrightness was one of his most admirable traits. Now Patrick glared at it.

"Don't be daft," he growled.

"That's a pity."

A troubled silence ensued, during which the king sighed once, then sighed again. "I know this is trying to you, Patrick. But I, as king, must *not* interfere with this marriage, if that is what Payne Comyn truly wants. When he finds out the truth, he'll most certainly approach the English crown. We all know his pride. Prince Comyn, by the rood! Patrick," he gestured tiredly, "I demand that you don't meddle in this. As a knight of my realm, I forbid you to stop that marriage. What happens after she returns to England is none of our concern. You understand?"

"Aye," muttered Patrick, dazed with the magnitude of what he had just done to an innocent girl. How had a simple ransom, a practice common for two centuries, compounded itself into this tragedy? "It *is* my concern though, sire."

"Only in the fact that you acted during the course of war. There are always casualties in a war, and this girl is one of the innocent victims. Look at Thomas—twenty-six years when Edward hanged him because he was my brother. Sweet Jesu, the blood of the innocent!"

"She'll be doomed, sire. You know the kind of man Comyn is. I do believe he's had one wife already."

"Nothing more can be decided tonight, my lords. Go to bed. Second only to Berwick, the Highlands weary me greatly."

Patrick and James accepted their dismissal with a military bow and backed from his presence.

It was not yet midnight, and the night was a heavy, dark one, much like the texture of their circumstance, thought Patrick. Rain had begun to drizzle—Nature, washing herself. Well, this was one stain that would never come entirely clean. Patrick retraced his steps to the cottage, still undecided as to his course of action. Tildy was stiffly stirring the fire about, coughing from the smoke, and Patrick didn't receive even a reproachful welcome. The smoke burned his eyes, and he blinked.

"Dame Grey," he began slowly, "your lady and I have decisions to make. I'm sure you can find accommodations in the hall."

Tildy drew herself up timidly, her loyalty to Christin written between her eyebrows. "Sir Patrick, I've always tried to be fair with you, in spite of Miron. I've defended you to her ladyship, even when she was flamin' furious with you. But that girl never deserved t'be put through what she's had t'bear. I know you done what you felt should be, but I don't agree with it. Nay, I don't."

"You don't have to agree, madam. Now, please find accommodations and don't come back until you're sent for."

"But—"

"*Tildy.*"

He opened the door. Tildy clamped her jaw as she clumped past. Disheartened, Patrick lifted his head to see Christin, still dressed and pale, standing in the other doorway.

"Come." He motioned to the chair. "Sit down."

Men never suffered as much as women, she thought. He could force things to bend, while she was dependent upon caprice. She wished they would quarrel, but it took too much effort. When Patrick poured a bit of whiskey into a cup, she shook her head.

"Drink it, Christin. You're near to collapsing."

"And whose fault is that?"

"Yours, some of it, my sweet." Opening her fingers, Patrick forced the cup into them and stood above her until she choked it down.

Christin gagged, clutching her throat. "You've poisoned me!"

"Now you're a good hostage." Patrick tugged at his hair and dropped to his knee beside her chair. "Look, we don't have much time, lass. Damnation, Christin, *do you want to marry that man?*"

"Oh, Patrick." Christin's head dropped into hands that seemed unable to hold it up. Compared to this, leaving her homeland for a year was as nothing. A spurt of unreasonable jealousy, a few rash actions—this.

"There's a chance, then."

Christin's gray eyes were sharp and probing, vowing she wouldn't trust him. "You're mad," she said. "There's no chance for anything."

They didn't speak for a time.

"Unless you're barren, there is." Patrick was casually toying with the tips of her fingers.

Christin snatched her hand away, partly in anger, partly in offended modesty. No man had ever spoken so to her. All she knew about conceiving babies had come from Margaret, and though Christin had secretly wondered what it would be like to be in a bed with Patrick, what he was saying was unthinkable.

"Are you——" She cocked her head. Perhaps she had misunderstood.

"Yes, Christin." His brows were steady, hinting at hidden things about him she did not know. This new factor only made things more complicated, and she flung herself from the chair. He wasn't teasing her. How could he put her in a position of refusing him when she loved him? How could he dare suggest that she bear a criminal's bastard child? For a man to sire an illegitimate child was laughed about as virility. For a woman it was ruinous.

Her hair was in disarray, and Christin began flicking away stray tears. Patrick dismally wished they could go back to the time when they had stood in this house and she had pounded him with her fists. He couldn't stand to see her cry anymore.

"If I could undo all this, I would, lassie. I can't."

"But you've told me before that you can't marry. You can't baptize your children or give them your name. What do you suggest to me now? To disgrace myself before my family, before the whole world? What could possibly be worse than that?"

"Being wed to Payne Comyn."

"Well," she presently lifted her head to stare past him, "it really doesn't matter anyway. The king will take me with him tomorrow."

"Are you sick with your time?" He bent, trying to see her face.

Drawing from him, Christin gave him her back and flushed at his intimacy. She shook her head, and the years between them yawned. He was standing now, his hands on her shoulders, rotating her to face him. When he tipped up her face, he waited until she met his eyes. How could she have even thought Patrick was not bonny? He was untamed, and he was beautiful.

"If it's within my power at all, you will conceive this night," he said hoarsely.

The abruptness with which life could alter its direction dulled her wits. She was faced with catastrophe if she said yes, or if she said no. How did one choose between evils?

Minutes passed—fifteen, twenty. Patrick slouched in the open door and stared at the rain. Christin tried to be logical, but couldn't put two thoughts together. When she spoke, Patrick moved to bend over her.

"What did you say, lamb?"

"I said I'm afraid."

He smiled sadly. "So am I."

"I don't want to be married to him!" The words were whispered shrilly and rapidly. Her face twisted, her fingers pressing hard against her mouth as her eyes pled with his.

Her breath caught as he quickly held her. His search for her mouth was so desperate it overwhelmed her. As if he could never find her in the time he had left, his lips twisted upon hers, searching deeply. The salt of her tears was in their mouths, and from somewhere deep in his chest Patrick moaned a haunted urgency. She would be leaving, her mind kept weeping, over and over. It would be months before she would see him again.

"There are times, Christin," he released her mouth at last, his words husky and slow, "that I see things in your eyes, telling me that . . . well, that you care for me. I know this is true, because I—"

Patrick had never told a woman he loved her, and Christin stilled at the unnatural shyness in him.

"Aye, Patrick," she admitted. "I care. But I'm still afraid. Of Payne, of my father, of your king. Everything, I think."

Patrick scooped her up in his arms and stood with her above the bed. "If we did make a wee bairn between us, Christin, it wouldn't be so different than any other since time began. It seems the only thing to do. We might look back later and disagree, I don't know. But if our countries do declare truce, and the pope hears the appeal, perhaps it wouldn't be so long until I could marry you."

Tiny flecks of orange firelight reflected in his eyes.

"I don't think I can live with the thought of him touching you."

She reached to smooth the rebellious curls about his ears and touched the smooth blades of his cheekbones. They would make a beautiful baby. She wanted to cry again.

"I want you very much," he whispered, slowly lowering her to the bed, dipping his face to find her lips.

Patrick's kiss was strangely tender and wistful—nothing like the impetuous demands he had made of her before. Thoughts of future heartache drifted somewhere on a plane above her—out of the way, vague and unreasonable.

"If we did this, do I . . . I mean would I have to . . . undress?"

Patrick hid his smile. "Not if you don't want to, lamb."

Yet she didn't protest when Patrick removed his tunic and stretched himself the full length of the narrow bed. The wild desire to run her hands over him made her tremble, but she remained perfectly still. Conscious of her virginal timidity, Patrick moved slowly with her, drugging her with unhurried kisses and the slow hypnosis of wandering hands.

After a time, her lips red from the insistence of his mouth, Christin only faintly protested when he lifted her upward and slipped her kirtle over her head. When he began to gently remove her skirt she grabbed at his hands, whispering "no" in a constant, uncertain protest. Only when he kissed her eyes shut, whispering for her to hush, was he able to discard the hindering garment. As she clutched at the cover to shield her foreign nakedness, Patrick gave Christin her way, not staring and appearing unconcerned as he peeled off his trews.

Christin couldn't bring herself to look at him naked and snuggled deeper under the cover, making room for him to sit beside her. When he braced an arm across her, she still didn't look at him.

"Don't you trust me?" He bent to explore her ear with the tip of his tongue.

"I want to. I'm trying," Christin murmured after a time. Already her mind was sliding into some gauzy whirlpool, where nothing was familiar or real. His words grew distorted against her ear.

"You must want me too, love, or I'll hurt you."

She didn't really understand, and when Patrick inched the blanket from between them she touched her elbows and arms together and hid behind her hands. Gently, persistently, he forced them away and lowered his chest upon her. His flesh touched her flesh, and it was smooth and moving. It stilled, then changed again in search of a caress that was closer, more intimate in its learning of the other.

Christin's eyes—when they weren't closed—dared not look anywhere except at Patrick's face. When he gazed over the entire length of her, she stopped breathing. He smiled quickly, his own breath unsteady, and kissed her.

Once, in her mind, Christin had accused Patrick of taking, never giving. She had been wrong, for the care he took in bringing her body to the point of accepting him was unbelievable. He taught her first with his hands, rarely speaking, but always watching her eyes, swift to sense if he were moving too quickly. When he discovered her moist response to his play, he grinned at her rosy flush of surprise.

"You're so very much a virgin," he sighed, and she breathed a small moan of pleasure as his head lowered to find her breast.

Christin wanted to please him, but she didn't really know how, and her sensations were so centered upon the things he was doing to her that she could only receive what he gave. As inexperienced as she was, she sensed his eventual ebbing of control. She could hardly lie still when he drew his body upon hers. Only by instinct did she know what was happening, keeping her eyes locked with his. The slow tightness of his filling her made her gasp. It hurt.

"No," she tried to breathe, "please, no."

"I can't stop now." His voice was half-audible—not his voice at all. "Hold me."

When he took her virginity, he did it quickly, then stilled. She nearly crushed his ribs from the sharp pain of it. His rough whispers, when he paused and kissed her, didn't make sense. He said her name once, and though he moved slowly it seemed to cost him great effort. A smile flitted across her mouth, for his eyes never left hers.

The room grew terribly warm, and, as if she already knew how, Christin gradually moved to meet Patrick's gentle rhythm. Her very acceptance sent her upon a burning quest for something she wasn't sure of. Her only rational thought was, Patrick Mowbray is making love to me. He will place a baby inside me, and everything will be different. Even that awareness vanished. As if he knew something she didn't, he lifted her hips to him with a quickened intensity. Then he poured himself into her.

"Don't move," he said when he could breathe again. Patrick removed himself with care, pressing Christin's legs tightly together. Then he covered them and kissed her again.

"Patrick," she said, turning so her back was against his chest. Ever so slightly, she left a small space between them so they did not touch.

"What?"

"Did we do wrong?"

He lay silent for a moment. "I hope not, Christin."

"I'm . . . scared."

"It's not wrong to be scared."

She thought she had grieved him. How could she tell him that it wasn't conceiving a child that had made her do it? She could not say that which was perfectly clear to her—Patrick, I love you.

"Do you think we made a baby?"

Smiling in the darkness, Patrick fit his body to her back. "If you don't conceive this night, Christin Winchelsea, it won't be from lack of trying. You'll hate me before this night is over."

Twice he roused her with his kisses. When he took her again, Christin knew more how to help him. How could the hands of a Border warrior be so infinitely tender? There was no way she could explain the unreasonable pride she felt—that he was the first man.

Chapter Seven

The journey to Stirling Castle was tiring—taxing horse-flesh, soiling clothes and straining tempers. Christin struggled not to scowl at the Douglas's sandy head from where she sat, for she knew it made her unattractive. But she was certain that The Bruce or Elizabeth had ordered him to prevent Patrick from speaking to her. Patrick's dark mood tested the endurance of everyone, and even Gideon kept a safe distance.

Unfortunately, Payne Comyn's attentions were un-avoidable. He remarked upon her unusual paleness, in-quiring if she felt ill. He noticed her discomfort in her saddle as if he read her thoughts, as if he knew every intimate detail of what she and Patrick had done. And when he commented upon the tears dribbling into her lap, Christin said she only wanted to go home.

She and Patrick had taken a serious step, one that had seemed inescapable. But, in the honesty of daylight, were they only deceiving themselves? Were they using Payne Comyn as an excuse to appease a hunger that had gnawed at them since the very beginning?

Words crystallized in her mind: immoral, sinful, dis-obedient, foolish. What would her family do if they knew Patrick Mowbray had taken her virginity? No, he had not taken it; she had *given* her virginity to Patrick

Mowbray. She was not her father's innocent little Christin anymore.

What if Patrick had said, "Christin, I can do nothing to prevent Payne Comyn from taking you?" What if he had said instead, "Christin, I want to be the first man to have you?"

Christin studied the strength of Patrick's back as he sat his horse. She must not—would not—lie to herself. His words would not have mattered. Regardless of the uncertainties in her future, she would have taken him to her bed. Love for Patrick Mowbray consumed her, and it was her only excuse.

The lion rampant standard fluttered redly as the king's party approached Stirling Castle from the northeast. An outlying post of guards escorted them as they wound about Stirlingtown by the flat links of the Carse. Bogs and runnels, ditches and the Bannock Burn carved their pathway to the wooden Stirling Bridge. Beneath it wrinkled the Firth of Forth, widening toward the sea, for this was the last crossing.

The room where Christin was taken lay on the vast second floor of the two-hundred-fifty foot bulwark where the queen's ladies-in-waiting were housed. She was baffled.

"My rank has risen," she confided to Tildy behind her hand. "Somewhere near the priests of Myton, I warrant. I don't understand this. I expected to be shoved in with the laundry maids or the cooks."

"Shh, this pile of stones has ears, m'lady," Tildy frowned, glancing over her shoulders as if a Scots sword pricked into her back. "Take what fortune gives you. At least you're going home."

A stocky, close-mouthed squire guided them to a timbered door. "Lady Winchelsea," he announced, knocking three times precisely.

Calla deMohr appeared at the doorway, her frank eyes capturing Christin's for the space of an uncomfortable minute.

"I don't believe this," Christin breathed, shaking her head.

"It surprises you that our country can be humane, Lady Winchelsea? That we can be diplomatic?"

"There's much more to it than that."

"The queen wishes it so. Please have your tiring maid tend to your needs. We needn't stand in the hall."

Christin entered the room with the suspicion of a wary animal sniffing out a scent on a baited trap. Able to do little else, she motioned a sullen Tildy to begin unpacking. The journey had wearied Calla, and her years were now perceptible about the edges of her eyes.

"You don't have much to say," began the older Englishwoman, "for someone who almost caused a war."

Small, the chamber contained only two beds and a plain but well-made table for washing. Tildy glanced at the assortment of Calla's dresses, pushed them aside and found Christin a pair of slippers from her coffer.

"Perhaps I should have tried harder to cause the war," Christin answered levelly.

Calla laughed. "I can remember when I was your age, Lady Winchelsea. The war was not so bad then. The man I married was a magnificent Highlander, very like Payne Comyn. I had dreams of being the most envied woman of the realm." She paused. "It takes a special kind of woman to encompass two countries and be loyal to both."

Christin poured a bowl of water and freed her twists of hair from their coils. As she soaped and rinsed her face, Calla changed her own dress. She was quite lovely, tired or not, and Christin grew vexed that Calla's hospitality blurred the need to hate her.

"I have no intentions of being loyal to Scotland," Christin mumbled from the folds of her towel.

"I was always honest with myself, Lady Winchelsea." Christin kept her face buried in the towel. "Anyway, Scotland can't afford trouble right now. The queen wishes that you accept the courtesies of the court and return to your home with as much goodwill as possible.

She has entrusted you to me to ensure, I think, that Stirling doesn't witness any scenes like that we saw at Warrick."

Christin jerked her head from the linen and spun about. A small jar of cream crashed to the floor. Neither of them looked at it. "Are you giving me warning, Lady deMohr?"

Calla drew her lips downward at the flashing gray eyes. Then she smiled.

"I understand why you did it, Christin. I've known Patrick for many years. Take this as . . . advice rather than a warning. Learn from me, Christin. You're in a dangerous position here. Also," she sighed, "you're terribly young. Young, and very beautiful."

In the face of her compliment Christin felt foolish. Her shoulders yielded a fraction. "I didn't ask to come to Scotland," she parried a last defense.

A knock at the door was ignored.

"Then we have no choice but to understand you, do we?"

A knock rapped again, sharply. Their eyes riveted to the door. Calla answered, and it opened to reveal Patrick lounging disagreeably against its jamb.

When he straightened to lift Calla's hand to his lips, Christin steeled herself to not look away. Every movement of his body reminded her of the sensual weight of his legs and the way he roused in the night, reaching for her, pulling her into his arms. Deep, sleepy kisses reddened her cheeks. Calla deMohr had tasted those kisses, too, and lest Tildy grow more curious than she already was, Christin distraughtly fumbled with her hair.

"I couldn't believe that Christin was staying here," he shaped his words like an accusation.

Calla stiffened. "I don't think the queen trusted anyone else. Believe what you like, I didn't ask for the job. England is represented at dinner tonight, Patrick. By the clergy, I think. Since the king has already angered two of the pope's cardinals, Elizabeth is being careful."

"I fail to see how Christin's living quarters could affect Robert's reputation in Rome."

"They can't, my lord Mowbray," said Calla, "unless they're with you."

Patrick's brows blunted, puckering the scar across his forehead. He had discarded his leather riding clothes and wore black wool. Instead of the longsword which was usually belted about his waist, a small knife lay against his hip. Thrown back over his shoulers was a short, light blue cloak.

"Very well," he said slowly, "since you have been so appointed. I beg a few minutes of Lady Winchelsea's time, if you have no objections."

"If you force your way in here, we'll believe the gossip, Patrick."

"Think what you will. Christin, come with me."

Even if she could have, Christin wouldn't have denied his demand. Calla resigned with a shrug which said, *No woman will ever tame this impossible man.* Patrick held the door with an impatient gesture.

"Are you all right?" he murmured. His aloofness melted once he shut the door behind them.

Patrick, with a cautious glance up and down the hallway, drew Christin near a wall and closed his hands about the shape of her ribs. Presently her trembling stilled, but his smiling intimacy in the indiscreet passageway was so nerve-racking that he finally dropped his hands. He tucked his thumbs into his belt and they paced uneasily, their words stilted and senseless.

"I want to be alone with you for a few minutes," he said, finally facing her. "The Bruce is uncommonly determined about protecting your reputation, my sweet. And that druid—Payne—riding beside you nearly drove me to distraction. If I hadn't had such an aversion to being arrested, I would've unhorsed him."

"He's not mine, Patrick. And I scarcely believe he's a druid," she laughed. The hewed walls and floor sent her voice shimmering, then she grimaced, covering her mouth.

He grinned then, leisurely, as if time did not threaten. He brushed his fingertips from the base of her throat down across her bosom. No one within seeing distance would possibly have mistaken his intentions.

Christin gasped, fearing he would dare to take her in his arms. "Patrick, please."

"Please what?" he teased. "Please hold me, Patrick. Please love me, Patrick. Ple—"

"Please remember where you are!"

"Ah, lassie," his smile faded, "I hope you'll take your own advice. No tricks tonight. Be a good girl. No temper, no scenes." He waved an index finger beneath her nose. "You don't trust me very much."

"I've learned better. All of Scotland has learned better."

Patrick moistened his lips and took a breath. "You seem to have survived your first taste of womanhood, sweetheart. Never have I hated to see a day dawn so much."

Christin wrenched free of his hands, moved a few steps past, and twisted to face him. She had no control over her life.

"Why do you let them put me on display, Patrick? Why am I being used? 'See, Edward, see how nice Scotland is? See how polite we are?' What if Edward doesn't play your game and still refuses the truce? Is Scotland going to change its mind and come back to Yorkshire and snatch me away? I have feelings, you know."

Patrick was so plainly unhappy that she stopped her outburst and moved nearer to touch his tousled curls. As if they burned her, she snatched her hands away and looked behind her again.

"I probably know more about your feelings than anybody on this earth, Christin," he said, grabbing her fingers almost painfully. "I know everything is twisted around, but I didn't create this particular situation, and I don't command the crown. I want to marry you—don't you know that? You may be carrying my own flesh inside you this very minute. I want you, Christin. You belong to me. I—"

"Patrick!"

They drew back guiltily, their heads jerking upward to see James Douglas smiling, his strides long and unhurried.

"God's patience," muttered Patrick. "Meet me. Late, tonight. I'll come after—"

"Mistress?" Lord Douglas bowed. Christin scorned him with a lift of her chin. Douglas chuckled and faced Patrick. "His Grace wishes you to oversee the new armies when they dispatch for Ireland, Patrick. There're many details, I'm afraid. But never fear, Lady Winchelsea, you'll not be bored."

"I wasn't thinking of it."

"War games tomorrow. After a small hunt. The king extends his invitation, mistress."

Despite Patrick's cautious shift of weight, Christin ignored his warning. "Am I supposed to inform the English crown how capable your armies are, Sir Douglas? Is that why I'm being treated so civilly? I accept, then. I will count the claymores and mounted cavalry, and the bowmen and schiltroms. I'll brand them upon my forehead and repeat every detail with relish."

With a flurry of offended skirts, she brushed past them both, hearing Douglas's low whistle of amazement. The sharp slam of the door echoed down the empty portal, and Douglas's laughter rang after it.

"I should have slapped that man's face!" she cried, folding her arms and sighing resentfully at the ceiling.

"The Douglas?" Calla deMohr drew back in surprise and shook her head. "That's one man you don't want as an enemy, my dear. He's one of the best loved and the most dangerous men in Scotland."

"He's black and foul, and I hate him!" Christin vowed, unbuttoning her dress and snatching it over her head.

*　　*　　*

Only twice in her life had Christin been to court. Now, as she followed Calla deMohr down the twisting stairway to the great room full of people, Christin was afraid and surprised.

Candles sputtered upon tables. Numerous styles of dress caught her eye and foreign tongues her ear. A large number of clergymen's robes sprinkled throughout the guests, one of whom looked like her childish image of Moses: a huge robe tied with a rope and a wild white beard. He carried a crook something like a shepherd's and thunked about the hall, offending members of the more traditional priesthood.

Dressing had been a trial. Christin had deliberately selected the most modest gown she had. It was the black velvet, and she wished only to disappear into the crowd of people, eat what she could choke down and escape.

Robert Bruce was clever and prided himself on a balanced display of powers, she thought. He interspersed the rich with the poor, the strong with the weak. She found herself between an English Franciscan monk and Payne Comyn.

Across the court she caught glimpses of Patrick with a woman she had never seen before. When she lifted her hands to her necklace, which was nearly the only thing upon her bosom saving her from disgrace, Patrick didn't appear ruffled. Though he didn't seem abnormally talkative, he certainly wasn't uncomfortable with her flirtation.

Payne's careful politeness, together with the soreness of Christin's body, was almost unbearable. At one point, she simply closed her eyes and sat perfectly still, wishing it were over.

"I see the king is keeping his gallants well occupied this evening." Payne ate his raw oyster and drank off a glass of wine. He bent over Christin's shoulder and directed her gaze to Patrick now smiling at Calla.

"My family has ever accepted Edward the Second as Lord Paramount of Scotland," he offered. Seeing then, that Christin was not impressed, he nodded toward Patrick.

"Mowbray has been in her bed so many times since deMohr died, one wonders why he simply doesn't marry her himself."

"That, my lord, is unkind, if not untrue," she bridled. "I've heard the queen sorely dislikes her court filled with frivolous slander. And, could not the same be said of you and Lady deMohr?"

Payne laughed and touched her petulant lip with the tip of his finger. "Not in *her* bed, sweetheart. A Highlander has a taste for more tender fruit. I plan to spend my last two nights in Scotland indulging myself with you."

The Franciscan monk interrupted. "Her ladyship has enough fornication against her name, brother. Do not worsen a record already renounced by the apostles and even your venerated Saint Andrew."

As the priest fixed his eyes upon her, Christin shrank in horror. Guilt, and the added fact that Patrick's bold announcement was known even among the clergy, frayed her poise. She arose so quickly the goblets tipped. Those seated at the table grabbed for the wine that painted red portraits upon the cloths.

"Christin!" Payne strode after her as she swept up her skirts. "What did you expect after that grand display at Warrick?"

Christin paused, staring at Payne. Then with gritted teeth she composed herself. "Not censure from my own countrymen."

"Mowbray boasted of having you in his bed," he observed, trapping her against the wall. He smelled of expensive leather and wine, definitely not unpleasant.

"You haven't been in my bed yet. I would be gentle with you."

"My lord, I'm very weary and I have just been rebuked by a man of the cloth. I beg you to allow me this one night. We still have tomorrow."

Payne propped his elbow on the wall and cupped his

chin in his palm, secure in his beauty. "I would like for you to look at me when you speak," he said, moving his face until it was inches from hers. "And I wish you wouldn't go."

"You're very persuasive," she avoided his request and forced herself to smile. "But if you'll excuse me, Lord Comyn." She dared not turn on the stairway, for she knew Payne watched her with hunger in his eyes.

Christin lay in her shift, bathed, sweet-smelling and less sore from Patrick's invasion of her body. She was unable to sleep. At well past midnight, after she finally dozed, Calla's cry awakened her. The room was silent, pitch-dark and strange, except for Tildy's rustle of complaint.

"What?" Christin yelped.

"Who—is—in—this—room?" Calla demanded shrilly, as shaken as Christin.

"Jesu, don't wake the dead, Calla. It's Patrick."

"Patrick! Are you completely daft?"

"Yes, I think I am. Will you please lower your voice? How do you find anything in this place?" Patrick stumbled, sending a silver chalice clattering to the floor like a peal of thunder.

"Shh."

"By the mass!" Calla choked, scrambling about in the darkness to light a candle. Once it was lit, she pushed it beneath Patrick's face.

"Have you been drinking, my lord?"

"Get that thing out of my face."

"I'm sorry. Patrick, please leave."

Christin had never dreamed of a man bold enough to break into a woman's bedroom at Stirling. She became aware of her open mouth, and she closed it.

"I want to see you, sweetheart," he said, pointing a finger at Christin, starting toward her before Calla jerked his sleeve.

"You will have us all arrested!" Calla's eyes flared wide.

The shadow of Patrick's shoulders blocked out the candlelight as Christin grabbed a sheet about the flimsy shift she slept in and padded across the cold floor.

"What's wrong?"

"Nothing. Get dressed. Look, Calla," Patrick reached a hand in a comically boyish gesture. Calla stood very slender, very commanding, yet Christin knew she dared not seriously defy him.

"I'm looking."

"Have I ever asked anything of you?"

"Yes."

Patrick was a trifle surprised, and his jaw knotted. Surely they would not argue about something of this nature in front of her, thought Christin.

"One more scandal couldn't hurt me very much," he said tactlessly. "But I'm sure you don't want one."

"Oh, Patrick." Calla's lips compressed, and she placed the candle down with a thump. "You can be so rude when you wish to be."

"I just want to talk to her," he smiled, seemingly pleased with himself.

"You're lying, of course. I think you're both making a tragic mistake. I won't lie to the queen for you, Patrick. I will protect you from the servants, but not from Elizabeth."

"Bless you," Patrick bowed. "Christin, if I turn my head, will you *please* get dressed?" She did as he urged.

"Where are you taking me?" She pulled against Patrick's fingers about her wrist as he shut the door behind them.

"To the tower." He paused to place a peck on her nose. "And it cost me a fortune in bribes, lassie. Come."

"No," she wriggled, shaking her head. "Someone will see us, and The Bruce won't let me go home. I can't afford this."

"Hush," he said before he crushed her to him.

Patrick's lips forced hers to part with such honest hunger, such weary impatience, that Christin crumpled.

His hands reaching under her hips made her whimper, and he lifted her upward against the erect pressure of his passion.

"I'm dying," he murmured.

The shadows of the hall forced Christin to wrench her mouth free. "My lord."

Without another word he drew them through dark passageways, past silent rooms and an occasional menace of voices. As if he were comfortable with the intrigue of forbidden access, he preceded her up a winding stairway, far above where Tildy and Calla lay slumbering.

"I'm afraid," she managed to choke.

"You don't have as much to lose as I do."

Christin disagreed, but she didn't resist him any more.

After a full ten minutes, Patrick drew her into a tiny chamber that obviously belonged to someone of importance. Its walls were paneled, and two fur rugs were spread casually before a fireplace. No fire blazed in the hearth, and Patrick stooped to light one, for it was chilly so high up. A paned slit window was gouged into one wall. Christin peered outside but the night draped so thickly over the precipice that she couldn't see down to the Firth.

Hot wax sputtered, and Patrick paused to peel off a small bubble of tallow from his thumb. Then he faced her, without smiling, and waited for her to say something.

"You're so adept at this, Patrick." She studied her fingertips. "Have you had trysts with all the women in Scotland?"

"Would you care?" he ignored the question. His breath was ragged and uneven.

She listened to it as she roamed about the chamber, seeing nothing. This night would be the unfolding of what had begun the night before. If she weren't already with child, she would surely be after this night. There was no mistake.

"I wonder who has lived here," she rambled, wishing

158

to dispel the awful tension. "Perhaps a young girl from Germany whose father was secretly a famous poet taken captive by—"

"Christin!"

She swallowed, ceasing her prattle, glancing quickly at him and then away. "Things are moving too fast for me."

When he gathered her in his arms, she buried her face in the curve of his shoulder. "We need to talk," she protested. "We've never had time to talk."

"I love you," he sighed forlornly, as if he thought love might not be as crucial as other things.

"In the sight of heaven we're married, aren't we?" She leaned back against his arm and pleaded silently with him to say it. "I mean, even if people don't understand, *we* know how it is. We're not living in mortal sin, are we? *Are we?* Patrick, what will I tell Papa?"

Patrick tipped her chin upward so she was forced to blink back the tears.

"Things may not happen the way we want them to, Christin. Love is a risk however it comes. But know that I never meant to hurt you, even when I took you away. I want to keep you from a man that would drain the very life from you. I promise I will come to you. I'll tell your father myself what we did and why we did it."

His fingers were so skilled at the hooks of her dress that they startled her, yet his manner was thoughtful, solemn. He was a man with a price on his head. He was despised by every responsible person in her country, and he would be the father of her child. He had shed men's blood and taken things that didn't belong to him. But, she defended her need for him; people who hated him didn't know him as she did.

"Patrick? she whimpered, reconsidering, catching at the ribbons of her shift as he persevered in drawing them off her shoulders. "Patrick, would you want me if I hadn't stumbled into this terrible thing with Payne?"

He grinned down at her then, and his fingers began prying her hands open to release the ribbons. "Christin,

I've wanted you since you doubled up in that little knot with your clothes torn half off you."

"I'm so sorry about how messed up ev—"

"Shh, don't be sorry, Chrissy. Whatever you do, don't be sorry."

Patrick dropped to the furry pallet to remove his boots, sitting cross-legged with his shoulders and chest gleaming bronze in the firelight. Christin, standing with her shift clutched against her breasts, their spilling curves glowing pink from the flames, smiled down at the top of his head. She wanted to ask, as she threaded her fingers through his curls, how long it would be before he came to her in the openness of a husband claiming his bride. She wanted to know the future, but it was impossible. Patrick tugged at her underskirt until it slithered over her hips to the floor.

Standing naked before him was shattering. Christin choked down the frantic urge to cover herself. Patrick braced himself on one knee and slowly smoothed the lines of her legs from the curve of her waist to her ankles.

"Don't look at me," she begged, forbidding the demands of her own breasts with the palms of her hands. Their taut peaks throbbed for his touch, and Patrick reached to force her hands away.

His wet lips swept across her belly, and she stilled, gasping. Muttering some soft obscenity about time, he folded his arms around her waist and slowly lowered his head. Shamelessly he traced the line of her hip with his tongue, following the graceful shelf of her bones, ignoring the tiny protests when he closed his teeth into her thigh. Christin didn't have the will to stop him as he filled his hands with the curves of her buttocks. When he moved his head, when his mouth found the softness between her legs, the wetness of her own desire horrified her. There were too many things she didn't comprehend, and she struggled.

Patrick stilled, and lifted his lips to kiss the hands which pushed against him.

"Sweet Christin," he said. "The one thing I need I do not have. Time. Trust me." He placed her hands upon his hair and slowly drew her to him. Trusting him was easy; it was the invisible bonds fusing between them which frightened her. In the last moments of sanity, she wondered whether she could ever bear to part with him.

"Christin?" Patrick lay afterward with his cheek cushioned on her hair. Her eyes fluttered open. The embers glowed red in the fireplace.

"Hm?"

"I want you to stay here, sweetheart. In Scotland. Don't go home."

Christin tried to move so she could see his face, but Patrick pinned down her hair, and he didn't feel disposed to release it.

"Don't ask me that, Patrick. My mind is so torn now I feel as if I'm ripped in two. Neither of us have much to say on that score. Your king will send me home."

"I could find some bishop that would marry us, even if I couldn't, we could still be together."

Searching for her underskirt beside her, Christin covered herself as best she could. Patrick settled, moving his knee possessively over her belly and draping his arm over her bosom.

"It wouldn't be legal. It would be common law. You know I can't live like that, no matter how much I love you. There are certain rules of life a person must obey. You know that's true."

"You love me," he said, as if it were an argument.

"Yes, God help me, I love you, but—"

"Then, what will you do when you return to England and find my bairn in here?" He spread his large hand over her middle and nestled his nose against her cheek.

"I don't know yet, Patrick. I haven't thought that far. But I'll do something. Perhaps Papa can help us. I'm . . . not sure yet."

His mouth groped for hers, hot, demanding, though she hadn't finished talking. His questions were legitimate.

"Wait, Patrick," she protested even as his lips impatiently parted hers.

"No."

His flesh was blistering to her touch. He didn't take the time to cajole the garment from between them. Patrick flung it across the room and stretched his length above hers. Falteringly, Christin raised her head, realizing how boldly he wanted her. Of her own accord she closed her fingers about him, rhythmically moving her hand, not dreaming how swiftly she could enflame him.

"How can you leave me when you love me?" he groaned, filling her with himself, even as he kissed away any answer she would have given him.

Christin strained to him as closely as she could, and reality bore hard upon her mind. She knew then that life would not be gentle with them.

Christin awakened to an August morning which promised games and the charm of courtly laughter. Gallantries bandied about the courtyard, and men laid down their bets. Overeager hounds strained at their chains, baying for the chase.

Of all the outdoor sports, Christin liked falconry best —both as a sport in which her father had long indulged himself, and the more practical task of purging the fields of crop-destroying mice and hares.

Payne sent her a pleasant challenge as she lifted her face to the sun, her body still sated with unnamed sensations and dreams of the future. She must be more careful now. And cordial, she thought—not only for her own sake, but for Patrick's. The Comyns, so Calla curtly informed her, could field thirty knights and ten thousand men without even asking aid of a MacDougall or a Ross. The lithe Highlander was a dangerous man when he wished to be. He was capable of destroying Patrick.

"Ah, lass, you're beautiful when you smile. I would take you to Dundarg and hide you away for myself."

"I've been known to smile before."

"A face like that should never be in tears, by God!

Highland men treat their women like venerated saints, not extorted mail."

"I'm no saint, m'lord."

He laughed and caught her hand, threading its slender fingers through his. "Who wants his pleasure of a saint?"

They would both be spectators today, he explained, and drew her over the great flagstone expanse so Patrick could view them together. After one unspoken message to the tall outlaw who stood with one foot propped on a cask of ale, Christin lowered her eyes.

"I prefer the merlin myself," Payne nodded toward the fine hooded peregrine perched upon the king's arm. "Iceland has had the best fighting hawks for centuries."

"My father prefers the native hunters," she responded.

Elizabeth and the king mounted their horses as Douglas and Becket Swythen stood apace, pointing into the distance. Without a glance toward her, Patrick assisted Calla onto a huge black gelding. Christin refused to compare them; Payne in velvet and Patrick in riding leather.

"Thank you, Lord Comyn," she said as he possessively fastened the clasps of her cloak.

"My name is Payne."

"Oho!" Gideon reined in beside them as they mounted. "Just you wait and see! Sir Patrick's goshawk will misbehave for the king. I tried to talk him out of using her today, to use one which would show him to advantage. But his head was set."

"A common frailty among females, misbehaving," Payne admitted, his brow wrinkling at Gideon's presence.

Gideon didn't seemed disposed to leave her side, and Christin giggled at Patrick's guile. Gideon had been appointed her chaperon for the day.

"I caught the bird myself," the retainer chattered aimlessly, to the growing aggravation of the Highland laird. "After I located the nest and saw the fledglings, which took considerable time, I might add, trappin' 'er wasn't easy. I rigged a net and had a fresh kill every day. Aye, I spent many hours behind th' blind before I caught her."

"Didn't she peck your eyes, Gideon?" laughed Christin.

"Aye, just a wee bit. They're vicious little beasties, goshawks are. But after I got th' jesses on her and th' rufter over her head, she calmed down soon enough. This is only th' second time out. That's why I say, she'll misbehave."

"Why aren't you riding by your lord?" Payne smoothed his beard, his features continuing to darken.

"Lady Winchelsea's mare has never ridden these grounds. Sir Mowbray wished me to be nearby in case of trouble."

It was the worst possible excuse, ridiculously laughable. Christin tried—not too successfully—to hide her amusement.

With abnormal gregariousness, even for Gideon, he described his skill with the longbow. He would challenge his laird that afternoon, he bragged. Patrick was an expert with an English longbow. Few Scots could handle one, for the longbow demanded great strength. One nearly had to grow up with a such a bow, and Scots preferred the smaller, less mobile crossbow.

"That should be splendid fun," sighed Payne.

Gideon, Christin thought, had learned more from Patrick than the skill of the longbow.

Mounted on light horses, Patrick and Douglas led the hunting party through the woods southeast of Stirling to a long, but fairly low, open hill. At the east end, the hillock sank into the valley of the Westheath Burn. The hunting was to be done over the unplowed heath.

Hounds bayed and sniffed through nearby underbrush toward the burn. The predators were loosed to fly in hunting patterns overhead. Reeds drew a dark ribbon about the burn's edge, and when the hounds loped nearer, half a dozen fowls burst skyward. Christin caught her breath at the king's darting peregrine.

"Look!"

The dive was so quick that it could hardly be followed before the huntress struck her prey and swooped it to the ground. Under the massive talons, the kill was made instantly and cleanly.

"They always amaze me," Christin remarked absently, aware of Patrick's congratulating the king.

Most knights would have made an effort to leave a good impression upon their liege, but Patrick took the king's teasing of the poorer performance of his novice goshawk with unruffled composure.

After an outdoor lunch, a mock battle was staged between a company of Highlanders and the king's guard. In spite of the weather which threatened rain, targets were set up. Calla placed herself beside the queen on a grassy knoll near the main kennels and falconyard. Christin obeyed her wave to come and join them. Patrick ambled where Christin and Payne rested upon his spread cloak.

"Your lordship." Patrick bowed his head to Payne. The Highlander muttered some Gaelic remark Christin didn't understand, but Patrick seemed undisturbed.

"Gideon," he prodded, "do you have the strength to string that thing, now?"

"Watch me," laughed the younger man, attacking his bow with great energy. He chewed his tongue as his face grew redder. Muttering a few well-selected oaths, Gideon made several tries before he finally slipped the string into its notch.

"Ahh!" he groaned and slumped back beside Christin. Patrick chuckled, shaking his head. " I suppose you'll string yours now, sir, and make me ashamed."

"I have a crossbow that can outshoot that twig at forty paces," Weryn boasted, stepping near the group, ale in hand.

"Not with that eye you don't," Patrick disagreed.

"I think Sir Mowbray is about to perform for us," Christin said sweetly.

It was the first time they had spoken today, and Patrick's eyes contemplated her for such a long minute that conversation stopped. Crimson crept up her neck, and Payne chewed the edge of his lip.

"My performance will be a poor second to some," Patrick observed, buckling a leather strap about his wrist. His teeth flashed suddenly, causing Weryn to suffer an unexpected seizure of coughing.

The great bow Patrick carried would tax even him, Christin thought. It was all Laurence could do to string his, and it wasn't as long as this one. With a skill which made it look deceptively easy, Patrick braced the piece against his leg and neatly dropped his weight against it. The hemp went decidedly into place, as tight as a thrumming wire.

Gideon groaned, "Oh, m'lord. Why can't you, just once, have to do it the second time?"

When they knelt before the distant target, Gideon gave his best to defeating Patrick. This was one time Patrick's retainers could gleefully cheer against him, hooting their calls of encouragement to their younger companion. Though Gideon had flourished under Patrick's tutelage, he was far from the bowman Patrick was. He was easily defeated, and rowdily demanded he be allowed the best two out of three.

"Give us a show, m'lord," encouraged the queen. She was the daughter of the earl of Ulster, the greatest Norman name in Ireland, and she loved to see the bow used with skill.

"A man like Mowbray should never be encouraged, Your Majesty," Douglas said, shaking his head woefully.

Patrick gave them a comical bow and obediently went through his repertoire of skills. Both in distance and accuracy, he was phenomenal. His dry wit and lack of showmanship completely contradicted his blatant exhibition of cruelty at Miron.

Without comment, Payne observed Patrick hitting a target some could scarcely see, cleanly striking objects tossed in the air. Then, to please Douglas, Patrick executed a few gaudy tricks.

"Have you no shame?" shouted Douglas, refusing to let Patrick shoot the top off a wildflower placed in his hat.

The man beside Christin stirred. Rising, stretching long legs, Payne called to Patrick as he received the congratulations of the queen and Lady deMohr.

"M'lord Mowbray." He attracted the attention of the blond head.

"Sir?"

"Your performance with the longbow is admirable. Are you so good with a broadsword?"

"Douglas is better," shrugged Patrick.

"And you?"

"Sufficient, I warrant."

"To end a pleasant day, may I suggest a bout between the two of us?"

"And what shall go to the winner, your bonny companion?"

Laughter rippled through the crowd, which had by now swelled to comprise most of the townspeople. Lady deMohr and the queen drew to the sidelines, searching for a suitable place to view the knights.

"Only the honor of winning is reward, my lord," Payne dissembled his mounting distaste for the Bruce's favored knight.

"So be it," relented Patrick. "Gideon! Fetch us weapons!"

Dispersing into two sections, leaving room for the men to duel in the center, the party found places to sit and accept ale from the opened casks. Elizabeth motioned Christin to remain with them, though she didn't like this forthcoming combat and wished not to see it.

The Douglas didn't sit, but propped his foot on a rocky ledge. At the disarming of an opponent, he would call a halt.

Christin watched the two men belt on the heavy swords. Patrick was the lighter, for he was more slender

than Payne Comyn. Her hands were moist and trembling.
Would Payne be capable of besting Patrick with a
sword? Obviously, or he would never have challenged
him.

Both men buttoned their jackets—Payne elegant, Patrick less flashing, lanky and seemingly unconcerned.
Wagers were placed, swords were measured and arms
swung in practice slashes, judging the heft of heavy
steel. After shields were adjusted into place, and hel-
mets were settled on their heads, they positioned themselves, amid the relaxed calls of advice from the on-
lookers.

As the contest began, the valley grew earnest and concerned. Christin imagined the two men in different circumstances: a combat for blood, a search for victory
on treacherous bogs at night, their grim eyes watching
for the slightest feint which could preclude death. If it
weren't for her, they wouldn't be doing this. She shivered, feeling herself grow cold with anxiety.

After an afternoon which had threatened rain, the
sun came out, and at the commencement of ringing
blows it flashed off the heavy blades. Fighting with
broadswords without mail was a risky affair, for one
careless slip could easily sever a limb. Using the shields
required as much care as wielding the blades, and they
constantly thudded from the blows.

Soon, since broadswords were more a contest of
endurance than finesse, Payne's extra weight began to
tell. Patrick, his face moist with sweat, backed from
his opponent's sword and caught several of the thrusts
on his shield without parrying. Blades caught and held,
time and time again, then turned aside. Once he gained
a vantage, Payne pressed Patrick hard. For one faulty
instant, Patrick's attention diverted and, taking a surprised shattering against his head, he discovered his
helmet on the ground.

Nausea thrust upward in Christin's throat. She could
hardly swallow it down. There was no talking or banter
now; the valley was hushed.

Patrick, shaking the daze from his head, recovered—
but not easily. When he hurled himself toward the Highlander, it was with a technique far more of vengeance
than sport. Payne had no choice but to retreat from his
raining blows. Neither man smiled. The match grew
grueling. They dripped with sweat now, and neared exhaustion.

"Scotland has its own Border. Highland from Low.
You ken?" whispered Gideon, easing himself down
beside her.

She nodded, unable to speak. Still metal continued to
scream against metal.

The contest was overpassing the limits of sport, and
Patrick knew it. Purposely he began to relent, gradually
slackening his sword and expecting his opponent to do
the same. But Payne used no such discretion. For a deceptive moment he appeared to, but, in a movement any
judge would deem foul, he sent Patrick's withdrawing
weapon spinning to the ground behind him. The fair
Borderer stiffened with insulted outrage, planning to
sweep up the sword with a flex of his knees.

"Hold!" called Douglas. "A man is disarmed."

Lunging toward Patrick, Payne left little doubt that
he would draw blood if he could. Robert had always
forbidden this, having, he said, too few knights as it
was. Patrick's feet were the more agile, and he side-
stepped Payne's thrust, grinding his jaw to refrain from
sending his fist against the Highlander's head. Scots
might laze in the sun together or brandish swords together in battle, but in between time one didn't trust
another. Patrick maintained his crouch, uncertain
whether Payne would reject Douglas's authority or not.

"Hold!" shouted The Bruce. "My lord," he adom-
ished Payne, "I'm sure Sir Mowbray will cede you the
victory. There's no need for blood."

"I beg the crown's pardon, sire."

"Bare-shanked Highlander," grumbled Patrick within
earshot of Payne.

The auburn-bearded man was heaving for breath, as

169

was Patrick, yet at the insult he would have flown at his opponent. Patrick alluded to the Highland habit of fighting stark naked except for rawhide boots. Though Payne was not entirely divorced from tradition, he was sophisticated enough that the name rankled him.

Patrick, too, was of a mind to continue the battle to the death, but he caught his king's eye and stepped toward Payne with a displeased smile. "You wield your weapon like an artist, sir."

He bowed low—too low—and Christin drooped at the mockery in his manner.

To outward appearances, Robert Bruce was satisfied that his Highlander had taken the contest. Yet when he strode back to Stirling's ivy-crowned wall, Patrick found himself between the Douglas and the king. The king flung an arm about Patrick's shoulders, and Christin didn't fail to perceive Payne's stumble when he paused, nor his vexed intake of breath.

"Patrick," the Douglas laughed, "you might handle that thing better if you'd put on some weight." He clapped a large hand upon Patrick's thigh.

"I have too many worries to get fat," dismissed Patrick, half-turning to catch sight of Christin helping Payne off with his doublet.

"About that matter we spoke of, Patrick." The Bruce continued as if his low words were of little consequence. "In the kirk at Warrick."

"Yes, sire."

"I think that you should leave immediately," the king continued.

His jaw slack with wonder, Patrick stopped abruptly in his tracks. *"Now,* sire?"

"Aye. Comyn's temper is tightly drawn, Patrick. Keeping him at court has been a major victory. Edward's campaign in Ireland worries me. And, at the same time, I must rid myself of Thomas Barber's eyes and ears—whoever they are."

"Spying upon a spy is an honored tradition, Your

Grace," Patrick replied, his thoughts persisting in returning to Christin.

"I have only a handful of men I can trust with this, Patrick. And Jamie leaves tomorrow to raise ten thousand men from the Grampians. *If* he can."

"I will leave within the hour, sire," Patrick said.

Logically, Patrick understood why the king ordered as he did, but Patrick's heart stifled anger and a surge of rebellion. For too many years he had been a soldier, and obeying commands was a matter of personal pride. And national pride. He would do as he was told.

Before the hour was exhausted, Gideon tapped on the door to Christin's room. His carefree jauntiness was dulled as he stood before her, shuffling his feet.

"My lady, I have a message for you."

"What? What message?"

"Sir Mowbray was called to an important duty, and he said to explain it to you in person. His exact words were: 'He holds truce very dear.' "

Christin felt things dying—light, happiness, eagerness for another day. "Thank you."

" 'Truce and other things' he said." Gideon studied his thumb.

Chilling distractions swept her thoughts away. She didn't realize that she stood, staring through him. Patrick was gone from her life as unexpectedly as he had entered it. Her lack of control was humiliating. And intolerable.

"My lady, are you unwell?"

She blinked up at Gideon with the same wounded detachment she felt at Wallace's old castle hideaway. "Yes, Gideon," her voice dwindled, "I'm fine." Christin almost touched her face. "I mean, no, I am not unwell."

He sighed. "I'm to be part of your escort to England, Lady Winchelsea. You leave for Yorkshire tomorrow. His lordship said to wish you godspeed."

"Godspeed," Christin answered. Her laugh was pointless. "Of course, you'll be going. I shouldn't wish you godspeed." She turned in a daze, then remembered.

"Thank you." She faced the doorway again, but Gideon had gone.

Christin busied herself with packing. When she bent over her boots, scrubbing at the bits of Scotland's mud dried on their heels, she remembered Patrick's eyes searching for her. When Tildy turned her back, Christin fumbled for a clean corner of the cloth and blotted at tears which kept filling her eyes.

It was past ten o'clock when Calla informed Christin that Lord Douglas wished an audience with her in the castle's chapel. Christin's first impulse was to refuse. However, not being very confident of her leverage as a political pawn, she dressed herself and followed Calla down the ancient halls.

"Lady Winchelsea," the Douglas welcomed, bending to kiss her hand in a proper manner.

Standing very straight, her hair streaming, Christin wished she dared tell him not to touch her. Her caprice at Warrick with the trews put her at a tremendous disadvantage. Yet The Douglas now appeared to approve of her. When he didn't hint that she was a troublemaker, she grew suspicious. The Black Douglas was never sympathetic.

"My lord," she said crisply.

"On behalf of the crown, Lady Winchelsea," he moistened his lips, "I wish to say how much we regret your unhappy ordeal."

"You will now stop stealing English citizens?"

"Unfortunately"—his authority made her feel extremely inept—"that depends entirely upon your king. When Edward renounces the claims made by his father and surrenders his rights to suzerainty of this country, we will know he means his talk of peace."

"Whatever you decide won't change what I have suffered." Christin suddenly felt quite tired and searched for a place to sit.

James brushed off the end of a bench, declining to sit himself, but propping a foot and resting his arms across his knee.

"You're not th' only one to suffer, Christin." Two pairs of eyes locked at his familiar use of her name, but she only stiffened her back more rigidly.

"All of Robert's brothers were killed by the most hideous of deaths," James explained, his voice incredibly gentle. "I don't think I'll ever forget his grief when 'e learned Edward had executed Nigel. Nigel Bruce had the gift of laughter, Christin. When Robert was pressed beyond a man's ability to continue, Nigel knew't. His smile and his wit gave Robert the strength to forget his personal mistakes and t'place his people's needs first."

Lord Douglas's thoughts seemed to carry him somewhere back to a simpler age where men fought and died for an issue that was either black or white.

"I'm sorry, Lord Douglas. Truly I am. But I remind you again, I had nothing to do with that. Some of it happened before I was born."

"I know that." He cleared his throat gruffly and returned to his purpose. "I ask a favor of you, my lady. It's a terrible favor, and I grant we're not in much of a position to ask it. But you have a deep fondness for Patrick, I think."

She wished he weren't going to speak about Patrick. Dropping her head, Christin crossed her legs, then uncrossed them and brushed at nonexistent dust on her skirt.

"Patrick Mowbray's loyalty for this country doesn't stem from blood necessarily, but from a deep sense of . . . justice. If you really care for him, Christin, you'll return quietly and with dignity. You will not hurt him by making him look like some bloodthirsty heathen."

"I would *never* do that, Lord Douglas! *You have no right—*"

"I'm just making sure you understand me. Patrick is in love with you. A blind man can see that. His affections are hard won and run deep, and I don't want to see him destroyed. If you don't sever your affections with him, he could be torn to ribbons. Borderers don't always use good judgment when their hearts cloud the issues."

"I've heard all of this I intend to, sir!"

Christin arose awkwardly and hurried toward the door of the chapel. A rushlight fumed in its sconce, and she slowed her step, glancing back to see the Douglas still standing, watching. He only wanted to protect Patrick, and she knew it. They both loved him. The tragedy of it all made her lips quiver. She didn't want the Douglas, of all men, to see her cry.

"I'm sorry." She lifted her hands helplessly. "I don't want to see Patrick hurt either. I give you my word that I'll not embarrass Scotland. But I can't promise that I can forget Patrick. That's asking too much."

"He was a soldier before he knew you. He'll be a soldier after you leave."

He stepped nearer, and with a tenderness which stunned her, reached to wipe a stray tear from her cheek. For nearly two minutes, she stood staring blankly. The door seemed a distance away, and her feet felt heavy. One last time she turned to study his face.

"Just don't hurt him, lassie," he smiled at her. "I don't know if The Bruce can bear to lose Nigel all over again."

Chapter Eight

The escort from Stirling led Christin and the priests through the most populated roads of the southern counties: Falkirk, Linlithgow, southward through the Moorfoot Hills to Selkirk. Soot-blackened crofts didn't repulse her now as she retraced her steps toward the Border. The misery she suffered over being separated from Patrick held no promise of improving. She felt an unwelcome kinship to Scots women who waited during dark nights for the warriors to come home.

Even as far south as the Marches, gutted, abandoned manor houses grew up in weeds. What, or who, was to blame for the waste? Three months earlier, Christin would have sworn Scotland was to blame.

The priests, too, were pawns in the plotted exchange of prisoners. Yet their looks accused her of being different. The set of their shoulders offered no sympathy for Christin's bruised yearning. How dare they avert their eyes and censure her for yielding to a man who freely acknowledged his love for her?

As they neared the Jed River, the roads improved. Their destination was Jedburgh Castle, a scarred sandstone residence of David I. During the war it had become a menace, and English soldiers had garrisoned within its walls so many times that The Bruce often swore to raze it to the ground. Ten miles beyond lay the English border and the warmth of her father.

Becket Swythen dismounted and Christin tossed him the reins, remembering when Patrick had stood beside her horse. Before Gideon could dismount, she flung herself to the ground and dashed toward her twin with a cry.

"Laurence!"

"Oh, Chrissy, thank God! Thank God!"

The tall Winchelsea replica clasped his arms about her back and twirled her about triumphantly, billowing her skirts in a happy froth. Christin's relieved tears painted cold rivulets down her cheeks. Creagen was pumping Richard's hand. And, Tildy was behaving like a general, ordering two squires about the care of her belongings.

"Is Maggie all right?" Christin laughed, detaching herself from Laurence to throw her arms about Richard's neck. She returned his hard kiss upon her lips. "And Johnnie? And Sissy?"

"I had to threaten Margaret to prevent her from coming with us. She'll meet us later at Greystone," grinned Richard. He held Christin at arms length and inspected the accented hollows of her cheeks, the sooty depth of her eyes which hinted at lost sleep and vexation.

"Pembroke wants to see all of you across the Border as soon as possible." He lowered his voice. "I'm surprised the Scot didn't do something rash."

Troubled that she was so easily read, Christin stepped back. "How's Papa, Laurence?" she asked, looping her arm through her brother's.

Garrisoned troops, armed guards and servants watched closely, as if they expected trouble to strike since the ransom had still not been collected. The steward in command of the castle presented himself almost reverently. Christin bowed. Laurence, however, did not.

"Has Papa taken this well, Laurence? Your letter didn't tell me every much."

Laurence frowned. "Papa isn't as strong as he was, Chris. I didn't want to say anything before because there was nothing you could do. But you ought to be prepared that he isn't as . . . robust as he was."

"What're you saying? He isn't sick, is he? Papa was never sick a day in his life."

"His heart hasn't been right since you left, Chris. He has to be careful, that's all. Having you back'll be the best medicine he could get."

Laurence's smile was so grim and he was so obviously plagued by his guilt that Christin cupped his jaw in her palms.

"It wasn't your fault, Laurence. Don't keep torturing yourself that you should have done something. No one is to blame about Papa. Only the war."

Laurence stiffened quite suddenly, and Christin traced the path of his eyes. With an oath he loosed himself and strode to a Scot wrestling with ropes to secure Christin's coffer onto a pack beast.

"Out of the way, knave! Can't you see that's no way to do that? We'll lose the whole pack in ten miles, imbecile!"

He grasped the rope himself and began retying it. Except for a crossbow slung over his shoulder, the Scot was unarmed, and before Laurence was aware of the man's movement, he took the bow in both hands, like an ax. With all his force, he cracked it across the twin's hands. Laurence wrenched his numbed fingers to his mouth, his face livid with fury.

"Feeble-minded Saxon!" the Scot yelled. "Your blood will flow like bog water."

"Hugh!" shouted Gideon, and Richard sprinted toward his own brother-in-law with an irate curse. Becket deftly locked the Borderer's neck in the crook of his arm and twisted his arm behind his back. The exchange threatened disaster.

"I call a curse on your soul, Englishman!" roared the Scotsman.

"You sacrilegious infidel!"

If Richard hadn't stepped directly in front of Laurence, slamming his forearm in a backward blow to the other's chest, the impulsive twin would have attacked the man as well as Becket. He coughed from the untempered blow.

"Are you insane, that you would destroy in seconds what it has taken months to create?" Richard's mouth pinched at its corners. "Take one more step, and I'll run you through myself. Get these men mounted!" Richard tossed a thumb over his shoulder and advanced toward Gideon. The younger man's mouth was drained of color.

"I'm beholden, sir." He inclined his head. "The king would have had my neck if this exchange went sour."

"I don't recall your name," Richard said as they withdrew several paces aside. "You were at the castle that day, weren't you?"

"Aye," agreed Gideon. "I know your name, sir. Her ladyship has had a good journey. She's a wee bit tired, but we were careful not t'press. We had strict orders."

Their eyes narrowed and perceived things which would not be spoken aloud. And those voiced would be couched in riddles.

"Sir Mowbray remembers much," Gideon said. "And he is certain that you recall the intents of his mind."

"I remember quite well. Reassure him that the communications between England and Scotland aren't too strained to bear news of more domestic matters."

Gideon's eyes flitted toward Christin and back to Richard's face.

"I understand. These domestic matters, d'you see them spoken of by clergy and kings?"

"Such matters are best handled in small ways," smiled Richard. "The dark of the moon is the time of poets, I think. And small matters."

"Some might share your interest of moons and poets,

m'lord. His lordship has a friend, John, a Black Friar at Newcastle-upon-Tyne. Brother John has long been a student of th' moon, and small matters appeal t'him."

Richard's nod was wise. "I'm sure John of Blackfriars and I will see eye-to-eye."

"Aye." Gideon waved the tightly knit escort on to Jedburgh Castle. The contact between Richard and Patrick had been established.

"Our work is accomplished, then. James! Laurence!" shouted Richard. "We ride! The Border before night-fall."

Without another word, Richard mounted, leaving Gideon on foot with Becket standing a few feet beyond him. "We will stay the night, captain," said Gideon absently. "Tell the men."

Christin accepted Laurence's quick assistance into her saddle. Pulling her cloak against the evening chill, she glanced toward the Scotsmen etched against sand-stone walls. Becket Swythen studied her, his legs astride, and Gideon gestured with his arm at some command. As she turned Persis about, the young man grinned at her. Then, true to his character, he had the last word.

"Warrick will never be th' same, mistress!" he called.

Christin was sure her twin didn't understand the laughing wave she sent Gideon, nor the moistness that burned in her eyes when she looked away.

Three months and eighteen days had elapsed since Christin had last seen her father. The estate of Grey-stone Manor had been granted to William Winchelsea by Edward I, and its original structure had been severely small. William had built on corner towers and added a moat and drawbridge when Christin and Laurence were only babies.

Word of their return had preceded them, for the guards at the gate gathered expectantly, grinning at her and pulling Creagen into their ranks for a first-hand report on the raving heathens to the north. From where

Persis halted, creating small clouds of dust in the road, Christin saw familiar roses climbing on weathered gray stones. Fruit trees to the south reached skyward, losing their leaves now, and the beehives near the orchard had been robbed.

"Were the roses pretty this summer?" she asked.

Laurence's fierceness had subsided. "I think even the roses knew you were gone, Chrissy. Look, there's Father."

William Winchelsea approached on foot from a distance, leaning heavily upon the arm of his steward and carrying a small cane. Even from horseback, Christin could perceive how his illness had stooped him. His clothes hung on his body, and he walked with the halting gait of a man in pain.

"Papa!" she whispered. He didn't seem the same man. Without looking back, she slid off Persis and darted toward the gray-haired figure, grabbing up her impeding skirts. "Oh, Papa, I've missed you!"

They held each other closely, and Christin overflowed with the need to share Patrick. She wished to say, "Papa, there is a man I want you to love because I love him." But Patrick would divide them.

"I've prayed for you twice every day, daughter. You've returned to me, like Isaac spared for his father. I thought if I never saw you again, they could lay me to rest in the ground beside your mother. It would not have mattered."

The way he touched her hair drew tears, and the effort he made to appear stronger than he was made her determined.

"You've grown up, I think. You're not the willful little Christin I used to know. You're very much like Caroline. I wish she were here to see you."

Christin laced his fingers through hers and supported his arm. "I guess I have grown up a bit," she admitted. "A lot, in truth." She paused to let her eyes drift over the lines in his face that told her more than he would. "Everything will be all right now, Papa."

Maidservants blotted their eyes with apron corners, and menservants cleared their throats with gruff stamina.

"Patrick Mowbray was kind to me, Papa," she explained as they strolled, hoping to mellow his thoughts. "He's a good man. He didn't really mean to hurt us."

Suddenly William's smile faded. Moving away from her, he stared out at the hills where the sheep grazed.

"The fleeces were awfully good this year. Aye. There're coins in the coffers. Greystone burghers will have full bellies this winter."

It was as if he had struck her hands for mentioning Patrick's name, and Christin's soul shrank. Was this how it was to be, then?

Leading their horses, Laurence and Richard followed close behind them. For their sakes, Christin lifted her chin.

"See, Papa?" she forced a bleak laugh. "You can put a little weight back on those bones. I will make you my best roast mutton. Everything will be just the way it was."

"When Patrick Mowbray has paid for what he's done to this town, everything will be the way it was," muttered Laurence. "I want two extra men on every outpost on Greystone," he commanded the sentry beside the great double doors. "If the bastard thieves came once, they will come again."

"Laurence! There's no need," Christin protested. "Patrick Mowbray would no sooner attack this manor than he would attack the Tower of London. Don't be silly."

"Well, saints preserve us, sister. I don't know if I hear aright. Do I detect a tone of defense for the criminal? I vow they cast you under a spell in Scotland."

Laurence flung a hand toward the heavens, as if he were presenting his case. "I don't find excuses for the blackest outlaw this country has ever known to suit my tastes, by God! I'll double the guard and garrison the town if I think best."

Christin stood studying her twin like a column of

figures that refused to tally. "Double it, then! Patrick Mowbray is an honorable man. And that's the last time I'll say it."

"What d'you keep telling me, Christin? I would know what riddle this is."

"Stop it, Laurence!" demanded Richard. "She means nothing. The man released me when I was taken by Douglas, and Christin has been released without ransom. She's simply saying that Mowbray will not attack after doing that."

"Fools!" flushed the twin. "I think I have *fools* around me who have leagued themselves with the enemy! Of a mercy, the man would have burned this village to the ground and slain its women! And you dare defend him. To me? Why, I've watched my father nearly die the last three months."

How could she explain to Laurence that she loved Patrick? To hear Patrick's name slandered was painful. When William's shoulders slumped, Christin wondered what she had done to herself. She felt as if she had grasped a wild creature, and if she let go, it would tear her to pieces.

"Where's Margaret? I want to see the children," she said.

When Christin visited Margaret in Northallerton during November, she was surprised at her pain when she watched Richard with his children. Ever since they had been born, she had seen Margaret bathe them and nurse them. As Richard squatted down beside his twelve-year-old son, inspecting something the youth had found in the early snow, a craving gnawed at her soul.

"What's the matter, Chrissy?" Margaret made deep tracks, and Christin methodically placed her feet in them.

Shading her eyes against the blinding glare of the sun's reflection off the snow, Christin answered wistfully. "Richard's so good with Johnnie. I don't think I ever realized before what having a son means to a man."

"When Richard was in prison, Johnnie used to come and hold me." Margaret's eyes shone as she watched them frolic. "He was such an awkward thing, wanting me to comfort him, yet feeling he should comfort me. Christin, *what* is the matter?"

Margaret plunged after her sister, and they both struggled to balance themselves in the deep drifts. Christin stumbled toward the rear of the small manor estate nestled in a curve of stables, barns and sheepfolds. Margaret couldn't keep up, and Christin grasped the rough stones, bending double with retching. She scraped her hands to keep from falling.

"Christin!"

Like any good mother, Margaret held her sister's forehead until the spasms subsided. Christin knew she couldn't keep her secret any longer.

Withholding her own private judgment, Margaret waited until Christin could talk. Then she pulled her sister down on the snow-capped steps. They were in the shadows, and they both began to shiver.

"Are you ready to tell me now?"

"I'm carrying a child," Christin whispered. "Surely you guessed. I've known it for weeks."

The laughter of the children rippled across the grounds, and sheep made soft sounds from the folds. A rooster crowed. Christin had no relish for happy sounds.

"Yes, I think I already guessed. Oh, Chris, how has this happened to you? Does Father know?"

"He would be the last to know," Christin blotted her eyes with the frozen hem of her skirt. "Aren't you going to ask me whose it is?"

"It's Patrick Mowbray's, of course."

"I'm cold, Margaret."

Margaret studied the fullness of Christin's cheeks and the dusky smudges below her eyes. The straining of her bodice had already betrayed the new ripeness of her bosom—the one secret nature refused to keep. "Let's go inside. Why didn't you tell me before now?"

Moments later, Christin allowed herself to be pushed down into a comfortable chair. Margaret brought hot ale and smoothed the chestnut waves off her sister's forehead. Christin's gray eyes were shielded by frilly lashes, and her lips were dry and pale.

"I've thought a lot about why it happened. Besides the fact that we love each other. I think it was probably more my fault than his, Maggie. You mustn't blame him. If I had really said no, he would have listened. I wanted it as much as he did."

Margaret didn't interrupt as Christin explained about Payne Comyn and the attempts of the royal family to keep Patrick and her apart. Maggie frayed the edge of her cuff and watched Christin pick at her cuticles.

"Well, now that you know, Christin, what will you do?"

"Wait for Patrick to marry me. What else *can* I do?" Christin moistened her lips and tried to appear optimistic. "It may not be long now. Robert Bruce is working very hard on the truce. If the pope lifts the excommunication, it could be very soon."

Rising to her feet, Margaret took up her needlework, then put it down again. She sighed and arranged items on the mantel which didn't need arranging.

"Christin, you're my sister, and I love you. But that is absolutely the most insane thing I ever heard of!"

"What's insane?" Richard asked from the doorway.

"Where're the children?" Margaret snapped.

"Outside, why?"

"Richard, Chris—"

"Margaret, please. I didn't mean for you to tell. Not yet."

"Nonsense! Richard has to know. He can help you if anyone can. Then we must tell Father, whether you want to or not. Father *must* know immediately. I will help you tell him."

Christin wrenched herself from her chair, swayed with dizziness and slumped back down again.

"Will someone let me know what's going on? Tell William what?"

"Richard, Christin is carrying Patrick Mowbray's child."

"Good God!"

"Well, it's not a tragedy, Richard!" Christin cried. "You don't have to say it like that. Of a mercy, you'd think I was a common tavern wench or something. I swear no man ever touched me but him. I love Patrick more than anything in this world. I knew exactly what I was doing, and I want this baby very much."

Margaret knelt on one side of her chair, and Richard dropped to one knee, stroking Christin's cascading hair, wisp by wisp.

"No one's saying anything to you, Chris. I know Patrick Mowbray, much better than you think. I have no doubts that you are both as honest in this as can be. But you must surely see that you're in a very bad situation here. You have many problems that virtually have no answers, sweetheart."

Both their eyes held warnings. Christin also read pity for her plight. They didn't understand the kind of man Patrick was. She *had* to believe their breach of moral law was justified because they loved each other. But Margaret's and Richard's eyes were speaking of prices to be paid, and blame to be placed.

Seconds seemed to hang in time, refusing to pass. Christin battled to free her mind from her guilt like some butterfly trapped in a pool of honey. She fought, beating her emotions uselessly until her wings caught in her own deed, pinning her until she couldn't resist anymore.

"I can't even go to him," she confessed, weeping. "If I go back, the king will only send me home again. If I stay here, Edward will try to marry me off to that Highlander. And Patrick can't come into this country. He can't even marry me because the church says he's damned. Oh, Margaret, I think I'm going to die."

"Poor lamb," Margaret cooed and met her husband's

puzzled eyes. Over Christin's head, Margaret explained about Payne Comyn.

"Well, that does shut the door neatly enough, doesn't it?" Richard replied grimly. "Margaret's right, Christin. William must be told—immediately."

"But I can't bear that. Papa's sick, and this would kill him."

"What do you intend, then—to have this baby without a husband?"

"If I have to."

"And I, as your sister, have something to say about that. You can't disgrace this family, Christin. Papa's been through enough, to say nothing of the frenzy Laurence has been driven to because of this ransom. Richard, Patrick must be told, too. If he's half the man you say he is, he'll find *some way*."

"I'll send word immediately, love, but I must say I don't see very much that he can do. The truce is his only hope, and that may take years."

At that, Christin clapped her hand down over her mouth and dashed for the kitchen again.

"What is that girl to do, Richard? Does this Patrick Mowbray have any idea of the difficulty he's placed her in?"

"I figure he got her out of a worse difficulty only by the skin of her teeth. I doubt she'll try a harebrained stunt like that again. That display before the king and queen was uncalled for."

Margaret twisted her mouth out of shape. "That may be true, Richard Hartley. But if you'll remember back to the time you were eighteen, I think you'll recall a few harebrained things you did yourself."

"I wasn't a saint, but I never turned a whole country on its royal ear, sweetheart. You Winchelsea women have a stubborn streak that could wrest profanities from the archbishop himself."

Margaret insisted that William be told about Christin at exactly the right time. This wasn't something that could be told in the same breath with the weather, she said.

So, after the monies for Miron's fleeces were duly counted, the taxes paid and the profits divided, the Hartleys strategically invited themselves for a weekend to celebrate the end of shearing at Greystone.

Shearing was a good time of year for William; his masculine pride basked in seeing his money enhance Christin's loveliness. In an attempt to soften the blow of her unborn child, Christin sewed herself a new gown— expensive mauve wool with a high waist caught below her bosom. Reminding herself that Patrick would some- how manage to come the moment he received her mes- sage, she arranged her hair and made herself pretty.

At supper, though, Christin was drawn and haggard. She hardly ate anything and spoke even less. She sat breaking her bread in pieces, counting the dreadful, silly minutes of idle chatter until her nerves were raw.

Finally, they all retired to the intimacy of William's receiving room and opened a bottle of wine.

When Richard related Christin's ordeal in Scotland, he hesitated often. Everyone knew—even William— that he wanted to make Christin seem as honorable in her reasons as possible. Christin thought she would pre- fer a stoning to sitting with her hands folded in her lap and perspiration streaming down her waist and legs.

William listened quietly, then gazed into space as if he were somewhere else.

"I don't know what I did wrong," he muttered at last. "I promised Caroline I'd be a good father. I don't know where I went wrong."

"Oh, Papa," Christin wailed, jumping up from her chair. "Please don't do that. Please don't."

She crumpled at his feet, hugging the old knees and leaning her cheek upon them. As if he were taking the guilt upon himself, William placed his hands on her yellow-rust hair. Laurence paced the room, feeling like a wounded lion who has fought for a foundling cub, only to have it turn and bite him.

"I'll have you put in a convent!" he shouted, and Christin covered her head.

"Laurence!"

"If you don't remove that hand from my arm, Richard, I'll black those pious eyes."

"I've had enough of this!" Margaret shrieked at her younger brother. "Christin is our blood! She made an honest mistake with a man she loves. The problem is not was she right or wrong, but what will we do?"

"Kill the whoreson! That's the first thing! I don't care if it takes a lifetime," Laurence vowed, sloshing liquor into a glass from a sideboard and throwing it down his throat. He bared his teeth and sucked in his breath sharply.

As if she had no intentions of being outdone, Christin stared at the spirits. Struggling to her feet, she moved toward the sideboard. More like an offended patriarch than a brother, Laurence barred her way with his hand. Without hesitating, Christin smashed her fist smartly on his fingers and poured herself a healthy glass.

"Christin!" gasped Margaret.

The scalding liquid blistered her as it went down, and tears of pain gushed from her eyes. But she remained upright and gasped for tiny breaths until she could talk.

"Patrick Mowbray," she announced, "has more human . . . compassion than you'll ever have, Laurence. Even if you live . . . to be an old man. I'm proud that he loves me. If that makes me a harlot, so be it."

"Godamercy!" Laurence breathed. He began leaving the room, turning at the door and pointing a finger at Christin's head. "This is all your fault."

"I'll have no more of this." William heaved himself out of his chair, but he stumbled and groped wildly for something to hold to. Carefully, as if he were a fragile dying leaf that would crumble at a touch, Margaret led her father back to his chair.

"Get him some wine from the cellar." Richard waved Laurence on. "And be quick about it."

When Laurence returned, Christin's news had done its work. The room was silent. Their lives had all changed. William's gallant struggle with his heart subdued them, and it was difficult to know who was the more pathetic in their misery—father or daughter.

"How do I look? Divine?"

Patrick was afoot, preceding Weryn and leading his horse through closely set trees. Branches were stark silver fingers dipped in white frosting. Twigs snagged his rough leather jacket.

Weryn paused, his eye constantly searching for intruders. "Like a scurvy Viking swab."

A stocking cap covered Patrick's blond curls, and he bent to scoop up a handful of snow and dirt. Working it into his hands like soap lather, he dusted away the silt and squinted into the distance. His only weapon was a knife with an elkhorn handle tucked beneath his belt, out of sight.

"I haven't been to Scarborough in a long time," he mused, his breath creating white geysers and melting with Weryn's. "Give me one week. Then we'll see how quickly Thomas Barber talks when he finds himself in a Scots prison. My guess is he'll hold out awhile. The man is clever. Gillie dead, and now Logan."

"Fifty gold pieces says 'e knows you're lookin' for him."

"Aye, he knows it. I can feel it."

Patrick removed several items from his saddlebags and put them in his pockets. Wanting to be fed, his horse snuffled and nudged his shoulder.

"Everyone thinks they're doing me a favor, keeping me busy," he said. "As if I'd pine away when they took her back to England."

Patrick didn't look at Weryn when he spoke. They had never spoken of Christin, though both of them knew the brooding periods of quietness were because of her.

"They mean well," Weryn answered with uncustomary gruffness.

"Well, Barber or no Barber, there are a few matters I don't intend to put off any longer. Bruce has never sent me out in the dead of winter like this before. He knows I'll go to Miron the first chance I get."

"He's tryin' t'keep you from the hangman, laddie."

Patrick didn't reply. Christin had no way of knowing he hadn't seen Warrick Manor in two months. One of those months had been spent in Ireland helping Edward Bruce with his tottering Irish kingdom. And now this trip to Scarborough to ferret out the source of two more quiet assassinations.

"She probably thinks I'm dead," he said, half to himself.

Weryn grunted. "Take care, m'lord. A lassie makes a man afraid to die, and he gets too careful. Then . . . phfft! He's dead, sure enough."

A branch slapped Patrick across the face, and he flung it aside with a curse. They were nearly out of the trees. Far beyond jutted the outline of Scarborough's ancient Norman castle, its fishermen up and gone with the approaching dawn. With a nod to his trusted friend and a final pat on the rump of his horse, Patrick slouched. He gulped a deep breath of English air and ambled across the moor on foot.

Already plowmen stirred about the northern Yorkshire farmlands, and occasional hawks cried warnings in the sky. Peddlers didn't turn to notice Patrick as they filled the road with ox-drawn carts. If he were caught here, he would hang.

The North Sea port was crowded. In the harbor lay merchant ships docked from Flanders, Denmark and Belgium. Just inside the town gate were well-scrubbed taverns filled with customers. Patrick ate breakfast with genuine relish. The food wasn't served up in platters but on small spits, and men cut off what they wanted. Most elbowed and shoved their way to and from the fire and drank their ale from large drinking horns.

"Where do you hail from?" asked a heavy-jowled man

standing nearby, smoothing the well-tailored doublet of a merchant.

Patrick stared rudely and swallowed, wiping warm ale off his mouth with a sleeve.

"London." He had no doubts about the British twang of his Border accent.

The innkeeper watched all his patrons and their boots as if they were criminals. Patrick called to him loudly.

"I'm lookin' for a man called Barber. Where I come from, 'tis said that 'e hires enough swaggies t'outfit a fleet."

"Scarborough get 'em, don't it?" his host asked of the walls. "Gallows bait, all of you." His gesture swept the room, and his eyes narrowed at Patrick. "Not runnin' from the law, are ye?"

Patrick laughed. "I cover my tracks a bit better than that, matey. Where'd I find th' man? On the docks or in some wench's bed 'til noon? My pockets are empty, and in my youth I took a strange fancy to eatin'."

The man declined to answer but the merchant beside Patrick touched his arm, glancing about to see if they were being observed.

"You might ask Graham," he offered. "Graham is one of those cloddish Welshmen, and he operates these docks like a prioress defending a convent of virgins."

After blotting his lips, he tucked his kerchief carefully into his sleeve and continued, "I've never met this Barber fellow myself, but I've done plenty of business with him in my time. The man's a robber, pure and simple. Anywhere else in the world a man could ship for half the price. If you don't want t'be fleeced, my advice is to do business elsewhere—Hartlepool or Wearmouth."

Patrick frowned down his narrow nose. "Then why aren't you doin' it, mate? Besides, I never ask how a man makes 'is money. Graham, eh? I'm obliged."

"Move along when you're finished, lad. Men be waitin' to take your place," the innkeeper prodded.

Patrick, slamming down a coin, stuffed his hands into

191

his pockets and left. Looking like a slim-hipped ne'er-do-well, he clambered down the steep descent to the wooden docks. The teeming jostle of sailors and merchants made it easy to lose himself. At the northern end, almost hidden by stacked barrels of tar, Patrick located Graham in a low-ceilinged room that stank of sweat and rotting food.

"You Graham?"

Patrick searched the room as if he approved and waited for the man to close a smudged account book. As Graham inspected the size of him and the leanness of his build, Patrick chewed on a twig, shifting it, finally, to the other side of his mouth.

"What's your business?"

"Work," Patrick answered. "On the docks."

"The pay only comes once a week. A week's as long as most of you wharf rats stay anyway." The man eyed him closely and took a bite of his breakfast of cheese and raisins. "Where're you from, by the way?"

"London. But I've sailed the North Sea to the Mediterranean for fifteen years." Patrick was certain the man knew he was lying.

"Ah . . ." he began, trying to look guilty, "I'll level with you, mate. I ran into a bit of trouble in Bristol, and it took about every cent I had to escape the gaoler. There was this drunk hangin' onto the docks. Well, t'be honest I stole his money. Just say yea or nay about the work. I don't be about to get down on my knees and beg you."

For several minutes more Graham considered, then opened the book to note Patrick's name. Patrick told him it was Kestworth. After writing it down, Graham smirked disbelievingly and slammed the book shut.

"There's a frigate just in from Belgium, full of glass. Do what the captain tells you, and you pay for anything you break."

"Aye," grinned Patrick and tugged off his cap. "Thanks, mate. I'll give you m'best."

For four days Patrick followed Graham when he left

the docks. On the fifth day, after Patrick had parted company with Weryn in the thicket, he trailed through the noisy cobbled streets of Scarborough to a private two-story townhouse, tightly shuttered on all four sides. From a bakery several doors away, Patrick watched the front door open and close to admit his quarry. This was Thomas Barber's house but the darkness would much better suit his purposes. He left, thinking that Barber lived very well on Scots blood money.

The sight of good food did little for Christin's appetite. Instead of eating lunch, she removed her dress and wrapped herself in a flowing robe as white as the snow outside. She removed the pins from her hair and shook it to stream down her back. Then she brooded before a narrow window on the second floor.

Rome was as unpromising as Patrick these days, for she had only sent Scotland another papal bull to end its rebellion. Edward Plantagenet had been counseled to review his position with his earls. Bloodshed between the two countries must be stopped, but truce seemed farther away than ever.

Not for much longer would Christin be able to conceal the presence of Patrick's child. She could hardly hook her dresses about her waist. Richard had faithfully relayed her circumstances to Patrick, and the Scot's child continued to grow inside her. Christin pressed her flushed cheek against the cold window. Why had Patrick not sent word? He said he would talk to her father. *Where was he?*

"Tildy, if you make that sound and shake your head at me one more time, I vow I'll scream!"

Tildy, ever since she had become aware of Christin's condition, had taken to clucking to herself with a sorrowful wagging of her head. As she busied herself with tasks that Christin would much rather have done for herself, the old woman mumbled doleful predictions about children being born with curses on them. The sins of the fathers upon the children. Mark her words, the child would pay. At her wits' end, Christin had finally threatened Tildy with the kitchens if she didn't cease.

"Beg pardon, m'lady," Tildy bridled. "I was just grievin' how bad the Scots heathen is treatin' you. Not a word all these weeks. Very pitiful it is."

"What do you expect him to do, of a mercy? Come down here so Edward can hang him?"

"I can think of worse things."

The woman snatched at the edges of her mutch with offended hands as a subtle rebuke. Christin straightened to her tallest height.

"Tildy, your tongue is much more nimble than your wit."

Tildy didn't reply, but she made more noise shutting the door than was necessary.

Restless, Christin peered once more upon the white-blanketed Ure Valley. Far across the dale, in a simple formation, approached a party of horsemen. They looked like tiny wooden soldiers with painted uniforms; a dozen men caparisoned in gold and white, the royal insignia blazoned on the cloaks and banners. They made a very neat picture.

In seconds, Christin knew they were from the king, and that their presence unquestionably concerned her relationship with Payne Comyn. What other possible reason could there be?

She thought her nausea had subsided, but it treacherously thrust upward, and Christin feared she would be sick. Tearing herself from the window, she opened the door to her room a crack like a burglar. Unseen, she slipped out to the stairs where she could eavesdrop upon the hall below. In her nervousness, she dropped her hairpins and felt like weeping when she stooped to pick them up.

Laurence's voice carried distinctly.

". . . most extraordinary," he said. She heard him offer the men-at-arms ale and fresh bread, but she couldn't distinguish their reply.

In a moment her twin's steps receded but returned with her father. It seemed like an hour, but the soldiers stayed at Greystone only the better part of fifteen minutes. William, standing in her direct line of vision, swept his eyes over a folded document, covered his mouth for a moment, and lifted his face in the direction of the upper floor. Christin moved from sight; she already knew what the message said.

Almost before the men had shut the outer gates, she dashed down the stairs, decorum forgotten.

"What was that about?"

"That man you told us about?" began Laurence, his expression denouncing her. "That Comyn fellow of the Highlands? He's done exactly as he said he would do. You, my dear sister, have been summoned to court."

"Oh!" She swayed. "Oh!" Perhaps no one would shout if she fainted.

But her father was sinking before her eyes, groping behind himself for the safety of a chair. Laurence helped his father steady himself. Christin stooped to prop her father's feet on a stool and stood before him, not meeting his eyes, picking distractedly at her robe.

"He'll be all right," Laurence diagnosed after listening to the heaving chest.

Christin doubted it as she held a chalice of wine to William's lips. She doubted he would ever forgive her.

"Now," William swallowed, his words cracked but audible. "I'm still the head of this house. I should have done this sooner. Christin, I will speak with my friend, Edwin Penmark. I've known him for forty years and—"

"What?" Flinging her hair back from her face, Christin knelt at her father's feet in a cloud of skirts. "What are you saying, Papa?"

William cleared his throat, wishing he could find another way. "I don't have all that many years left, daughter. You will bear a grandchild before I die, God willing, and I don't want to leave this earth without knowing you will be honorably wed and cared for as I cared for your mother."

"But, Papa—"

"Edwin will do this for me. He's a kind man and has loved you like his own daughter ever since you were born. I don't speak of him as a . . . real husband. Please give me credit for that. But he would marry you and give your child a name."

Christin placed her palms together and closed her eyes as if she were praying. But she wasn't praying; she was trying to believe that this could be happening.

"But he's . . . so old, Papa," she whispered.

"Father," hesitated Laurence, tugging his lower lip out of shape, "I will admit that it's a possible solution. But for Christin's sake, could we give this a little time? Maybe we can make another arrangement—someone who lives away. A younger man? You'll have to agree it's a drastic step, even for Christin."

Standing abruptly, Christin glared at him. "Laurence, please."

The room seemed completely unable to protect them from forces outside that were changing their lives. Laurence coughed his distress and paced the rug. William covered his eyes as if he couldn't bear to view her sin any longer.

"I want only what's best," the elder Winchelsea mumbled behind his hand. "It may be that if we press Edward to reconsider the Scot's petition . . . No, I doubt that. As for the excommunication being lifted, I think that's hopeless, too. I'll wait for a few more days, Christin, but in the meantime I am sending for the abbot and Edwin. You, daughter, will talk to them."

Both pairs of masculine eyes studied Christin. They watched her fingers thread the ribbon on her robe and begin rolling it into a tiny cylinder.

Laurence moved too quickly and bumped a table. As if some omen, a vase of his mother's toppled to the floor, rolling, slowly coming to rest as if it were dying. He held his twin in his arms, awkwardly at first, until Christin's head lowered to his shoulder.

"Oh, Chrissy, I'm sorry. I admit I hate the man—I

can't help it. But I don't want to see you miserable all your life. I'm so sorry."

Tears stung his eyes, and he stared over her shoulder into nowhere. "I wish Mama were here," he said softly. "She would know what to do."

Christin almost felt safe in Laurence's arms. The hard muscles of his waist reminded her of the protection of Patrick's body when he held her. She and Patrick had been wrong, even though their act had begun as a means to correct a wrong. They should not have been so simple in their love.

She had trembled and lowered herself upon him, crushing her own breasts in her hands because she had wanted him so. He had filled his hands with her buttocks and arched himself upward to meet her, thrusting deep, saying her name softly, over and over as his eyes grew drugged with desire for her. They had perverted the act between a man and a woman, using it for pleasure instead of the begetting of children, as it was meant to be. Now they would both pay.

"Whatever you want, Papa," she agreed tonelessly, disengaging herself from Laurence's embrace. "I will talk to them, but pray God it never comes to marrying Sir Edwin. I've known him all my life, and it's true, I have honest affection for him. But I don't know if I can do what you ask."

Christin hesitated outside the door to her father's chambers, her face blanched, her knuckles poised to knock. Nearly two oppressive hours had crawled by since Abbot Donney and Edwin Penmark had shut themselves behind it. Downstairs, silent and understanding, Margaret, Richard and Laurence waited for her. Now, she was unable to interrupt, and she slumped at her own weakness and went back downstairs.

"I feel as if I've been tried for treason and am waiting for a verdict of death," she admitted as she entered the room where they were.

For the dozenth time she straightened her long blue sleeves and her stiff collar. Then she poured a glass of wine which she simply stared at.

"Papa's doing what anyone of us would do if we were in his place," Laurence justified.

"That's awfully easy for you to say, Laurence, since you're not being asked to wed someone more than twice your age."

"Nobody asked you to get with child by some outlaw whose name is never spoken without an oath!"

"Both of you, stop it!" Margaret cried.

She glared at her offended brother and swept across the chilly room to force Christin down in a chair. Margaret placed the wine to her sister's lips. While Richard stoked the fire, Christin sipped, and clenched her hands in futility.

"You look terrible," blurted Margaret.

At her words Abbot Donney stepped into the room, and all their eyes riveted on him, as if he had the power of life or death. His flowing robes were black serge. Quite fitting, thought Christin. Last rites were administered in black.

"Christin"—he flourished a gold signet ring—"your father wishes to see you now."

"The fallen lamb led to the slaughter, Father?"

"Try not to be adverse, my dear." His disapproving brows cut a ridge between his eyes.

"Forgive me."

Her father's receiving room upstairs looked like anything but a sentencing room. Comfortable leather chairs beckoned near an inviting fire, and the masculine smell of good living was both comforting and irritating.

Edwin Penmark had been a guest and a friend in her father's house ever since she could remember. He wasn't a tall man, nor was he at all handsome. His face, with its ruddy cheeks, still managed to appear rather frail. Yet Christin could hardly recall a time when he didn't smile. As she stood in the doorway now, afraid that her

entire body painted her a wicked woman, Edwin
stretched out his hand.

"Christin." He took her fingers with reassuring firm-
ness. "William has told me everything. I want to help
if I can."

With her back so stiff it hurt, yet refusing to lean
against anything, Christin waited until Abbot Donney
closed the door.

"I'm sorry, Lord Penmark. I don't know whether I'm
more sorry for me or for you." She forced a perfectly
dismal smile.

Edwin was nervous, for he smoothed the edges of the
buttons on his vest repetitiously. Christin felt better,
just knowing he was nervous, too. Intimately, then, as
if it were just the two of them seeking a solution, Edwin
drew a chair beside her rigid knees.

"Do you remember when you were a very little girl
and you came to spend a day with Elaine and me? And
you stuffed your tiny stomach so full of green apples
that you became ill?"

Christin's hands gripped the chair arm, harder and
harder, as a drowning man clutches a lifeline. She was
powerless to let it go; she couldn't tear her eyes away.
Quickly, Edwin covered her hands with his—hard, almost painfully. And then he pulled them free and sat
smoothing them until she calmed.

"Life isn't always fair, is it, my dear?"

Behind them, William cleared his throat noisily.

"Your father loves you a great deal to ask me this
favor," Edwin continued. "And I love him, too, and
Caroline, bless her heart. Had I known you were in
trouble, I would have come to you both. What is the life
of an old man for but to bring comfort to those he loves?
I have built a good name and a sizable fortune. If that
will help you now, I give it to you freely. I'll not live
too many more years, I think, and I know of no better
thing to do with my worldly goods than to leave them
in the hands of a fine young lady."

If Christin could have stopped herself from weeping, she would have. How could a man be so kind, asking nothing for himself? She wanted to hide her eyes, for she feared they revealed her love for Patrick. And that love seemed out of place in this room.

"I don't know what to do anymore," she whispered.

"Do what you must do, my dear. What we all must do from time to time—put someone else's needs before our own. That is what I do, and what you will do. And if the truth were known, it is probably what the father of this child has been forced to do. I know that if you love this man, there must be much good in him."

With difficulty then, they talked about the future of her child, they skirted the overpowering desire that had created such a delicate situation. She swallowed down a wild, blinding anger that made her want to strike out at everything in her path. Christin wanted to scream that no one could possibly understand the pain she suffered.

But she smoothed William's graying hair back from his eyes. "I'm sorry, Papa. There are some things I can't say I'm sorry for, though."

She spun about at Abbot Donney's murmur of reproach. "Well, I was honest in this, Father! It was the only thing I could do."

"I understand," he said, but she knew he didn't.

"I know what I have to do," Christin yielded. "Set the wedding anytime you want to. Tomorrow. It doesn't matter. I'll be ready, and I will smile. I'll be as good a wife as I know how to be."

Holding her skirts wide, she bowed. After an awkward pause she spoke with clipped precision. "If you gentlemen will excuse me, I have certain things I must do."

Before any could stop her, Christin opened the door and shut it behind her. Then she slumped back against the wall and pressed her fingers against her lips until her teeth cut through the soft flesh.

The sense of failure that washed over her was degrading. Patrick *had* to know by now how badly she needed him. Well, it was time to pay for her mistakes; they could not be hidden any longer. But this baby was half his. How could he care so little?

At the head of the stairway her father's favorite hound bounded up to meet her, his friendly tail wagging. He nuzzled a moist nose against her fingers.

Christin strode past without a word, and when the sympathetic animal licked her trailing hand, she slapped him sharply across his nose. The poor thing yelped in surprised pain, hastily moving himself away to lick his wound in puzzled dignity.

Once in her room, Christin placed a candle on a table by her bed. Candle wax dribbled onto the grained wood like a small conspirator in the destruction of her life.

"I will write Patrick," she said aloud, searching through a drawer, tossing things carelessly until she found a piece of paper. "Midnight. How fitting. He seduced me at midnight. I will denounce him at midnight."

Somewhere she had a quill and some ink. At last she found the frayed pen beneath some yarn in her knitting basket. The moment she touched quill to paper, she made a large blot and swore how much she hated Patrick Mowbray.

To Patrick Mowbray, Knight of Fealty to Robert Bruce, Scotland.

On this day, December twenty-nine, in the Year of Our Lord, 1318, I write this Letter. Far better that I had Died when you took me to Scotland in the summer. Now I carry the Child which you Swore you wanted. My greatest Sin was believing you when you said you loved me. This is the last Time I will write you, for I am to Wed a man who is twice my age. At least he will not hurt me. I do this so my father will not die and so my Family will not hate me. I swear to the Holy Mother Virgin that I will never Forgive you.

> This is written in my own hand,
> Christin Anne Winchelsea,
> Yorkshire, England.

Creagen must take the letter to Richard, and Richard must seal it, for she had no suitable wax. As Christin folded the short epistle a soft but insistent knock interrupted her action. For a second she chewed on her thumbnail, then slipped the letter into her pocket.

"Who's there? It's late."

"It's Laurence, Chrissy. I have to talk to you."

They measured each other levelly across the threshold, both near tears. He knew about Edwin Penmark. For so many years the twins had been closer than any parent and child could possibly be. Whatever had happened between them, Christin knew her brother loved her deeply.

"Come in. I'm preparing for my wedding day."

She laughed bitterly, gesturing at the clutter from her search. A few discomfited moments ticked past before Laurence disregarded their recent quarrels and took her in his arms.

"Oh, Chris," he whispered into her hair. "I know you don't want any of this, but I do think you're a brave girl to do it."

She leaned back in his arms and blinked hard. "True, true. I'm very brave."

Laurence awkwardly released her and moved about the room. "Papa only wants you to be happy."

"I know that. But the only way I'll be happy is for Patrick Mowbray to pay for this."

Making a short whistling sound, Laurence's gray eyes widened. "That's the spirit! God's blood, I thought you loved the man!"

"Laurence, I think I'll go to bed now. I'm terribly

tired. I know it's late, but if Tildy's still up, would you send her upstairs?"

The handsome twin started to say something, then changed his mind with a shift of weight. "This will all work out for the best, you'll see. You're very strong."

Yes, she was strong, she thought, as she watched Tildy trudging her way through the bright moonlit snow to the stables where Creagen's quarters were. Patrick had told Christin in the most emphatic way possible—his silence—that he rejected her. The only thing which remained of their love was the child inside her.

As if by some motherly miracle she could touch something of Patrick, Christin pressed both hands against her belly. Would this baby look like him? Would it be a curly, blond-headed rebel like him?

In spite of her panicky attempts to hate Patrick, Christin pulled the covers beneath her chin. Her anger had dwindled to a raw, aching hurt. She imagined Patrick's face when he received her letter. She pictured his frown puckering his forehead, then his shrug. At least Payne Comyn had wanted her!

Tears stung her eyelids. She didn't want to remember Patrick's kisses, the way his lips touched softly first, then eagerly opened to taste her. But she did.

Chapter Nine

The streets of any seaport city were dangerous at night, even for a man as accustomed to misty alleyways and characters of the night as Patrick was. Almost every week witnessed a murder somewhere. So Patrick protected his back, a deeply imbedded instinct by now.

Tonight he would leave Scarborough. Entering Thomas Barber's house was only a matter of dexterity. From the beginning, Patrick realized he had changed, and taking Barber didn't exhilarate him as it once would have. Danger was no longer a challenge. It was something which could separate him from Christin forever. Shifting his weight to keep warm, waiting for Barber's household to retire, Patrick wasn't certain he liked what he was doing anymore.

Thick twisted ivy allowed Patrick to climb up the townhouse walls with ease. Once he reached the second floor, he edged sideways along a narrow ledge until he stood shivering outside a window. The fog made him nearly invisible.

Below him slithered an alley. Only an occasional voice from the streets interrupted the drowsy city. After twisting the latch off a shutter, Patrick stepped into the welcome warmth of a luxurious boudoir.

A lavishly figured screen across which were draped

petticoats and finely stitched woman's undergarments, divided the chamber. Barber's wife's bedroom, obviously. As he paused beside the door to the hall voices outside sent him back behind the screen where he held his breath, his knife in his hand.

". . . until he's feeling better."

As the steps faded away, Patrick closed his eyes. His plans didn't include a useless confrontation with a woman. When he inched toward the door and reached for the knob, the brass object slipped from his fingers. Patrick stood face to face with a woman who had to be Barber's terrified young wife. Before she had time to do more than open her mouth to scream, Patrick's fingers closed over it.

"Be still, madam, and I'll not hurt you. Play false and I'll break your neck."

She froze in his arms like a statuette, and Patrick was forced to drag her back into her bedroom. With his free hand he shook her, balancing her upright, then he flipped her chin up with a thumb.

"I beg your forgiveness," he said wanly, as he searched about the room for something to gag her with.

The muffled attempts to talk behind his hand grew frantic, then tearful. With some distaste Patrick gagged her with one of her stockings. Then he pushed her onto a chair and towered above her. She was a small woman with a mouth which hinted of practicality.

"I didn't come to rob you, madam. I came to see your husband. Thomas Barber is your husband?"

At first she didn't answer, but when Patrick took a step toward her, she nodded vigorously. Her face was white, her coiffure a shambles, her gown twisted. As she timorously reached one hand to push away tendrils of hair from her eyes, Patrick's thought darted to Christin.

Immediately, he realized his mind was playing him false. Was this what love did to a man, softened him to the point that he couldn't deal with the wife of a murdering spy? He hooked his hip on the edge of her dresser and folded his arms.

"If I thought you'd behave yourself and not scream, I would let you loose."

Her eyes went blank, and he snapped his fingers. She flinched.

Patrick tugged at his lower lip. "Actually, your memory might be more disposed than your husband's. Have you ever met a man named deHughes, Mistress Barber? A Yorkshireman?"

Patrick let his Border burr slip unmistakably into his voice. She couldn't help but realize he was a Scot. As she did, she grew terrified. When she nodded yes, he smiled.

"Ah, very good. Now, do you know that your husband witnessed at deHughes's trial and as a result deHughes was executed?"

When she didn't immediately agree, Patrick paced, pondering. Still, she did eventually nod yes, and Patrick touched her gag. "If I loose you, will you give me your word you'll be quiet?"

She agreed with her eyes.

"Ohh, you're a beast," she choked when he removed the stocking. Grabbing for a jar of cream from off her dresser, she gingerly dabbed at the corners of her mouth. Then she glared at him. "DeHughes deserved to die."

"Whether he did or not is not why I'm here. What I want to know is where your husband got his information about deHughes."

"DeHughes was a traitor!" she raised her voice.

"Shh!" Patrick strode to the door and bent his ear to listen. "That doesn't matter to me. Do you know how your husband learned of deHughes?"

"A man told him," she snapped, then looked at Patrick's darkening frown and grew more prudent.

"What—man—told—him, madam?"

"I don't know his name. Are you going to attack Thomas? Thomas has a terrible head cold. His temper is vile, and he'll surely do something terrible."

Rotating full circle, thinking that he might do something terrible if she didn't stop wasting his time, Patrick braced his fists on his hips. The vivid thought rankled him—that this entire episode was a colossal waste of time.

"Mistress Barber—"

"Lady Barber," she corrected.

"All right, *Lady* Barber. Can you describe this man who told your husband about deHughes?"

She thought a moment, started once to speak and formed her words slowly. "He wasn't a tall man, as I remember. And he had rusty colored hair. I saw him only once. You can't expect me to remember everything." She blinked at Patrick's tight mouth. "He had a square jaw," she said quickly, tracing the shape of her own.

"How did he talk, Lady Barber? Like a Scot or a Saxon?"

"That's difficult. All I really remember about him was that he had good table manners. He liked oranges."

Patrick's eyes narrowed for a moment. "Oranges? *Oranges?*" His big shoulders slumped, and he presently leaned an elbow against the wall.

"Are you going to speak with Thomas?"

"Don't worry about Thomas. Now, I don't want you to think I'm ungallant, Lady Barber, but I do feel obliged to tie you up until I can get out of this house. I won't hurt you, and someone will find you very soon. I'm sure you understand."

"No, I don't understand!" Lady Barber almost came off her chair. "I told you what I knew, you filthy liar! You said—"

Before she could utter the first shrill beginnings of a scream, Patrick clipped her chin neatly with his fist. She slipped back down into her chair as easily as if she had meant to do it. Gently lifting her, he laid her on the bed, drew a cover neatly beneath her chin and bent to squint at her chin. She would hardly have a bruise.

His search downstairs proved absolutely futile, and

207

the risks warned him that half an hour in this house
was too long.

"Oranges," he swore under his breath. "All this, to
learn the bloody traitor liked oranges." Then he consoled himself by relieving Thomas Barber of a dozen
gold pieces he found in a drawer in the sitting room.

"For deHughes's wife, you swine," he said and slipped
through the hall to Thomas Barber's room.

The figure who jerked upright in the canopied bed
was bleary-eyed from a cold. As if he looked at a ghost,
Barber's puffy eyes blinked, and his jaw dropped. He
sneezed twice.

"Get yourself a few handkerchiefs, mate," advised
Patrick coldly, slipping his knife from his boot. "Robert
Bruce has a few questions he wants to ask you."

Hovering over a tiny fire in the outlying thickets
skirting Scarborough, Weryn blew on his cupped hands
and waited for Patrick. He had expected him the day
before. When the Scots-English spy finally did locate
him, late in the evening of December thirtieth, the large
man hugged Patrick like a relieved brother. Weryn
clapped him hard about the shoulders and frowned at
the sullen stranger cursing them with ice-blue eyes.

"That is—"

"Barber."

Patrick rubbed his hands over the meager flame and
ignored his prisoner.

"In Scotland traitors don't live long," Weryn smiled,
his one eye gleaming wickedly.

The well-bundled Barber lifted his chin fearfully.
"What will you do with me?"

"You will receive the same justice as deHughes," answered Patrick without looking at him.

"I have money," Barber whispered. "I will pay you
well to let me go."

The two Scots turned to stare at the frustrated tears
sparkling in the man's eyes.

"Tell me who sent you into Edward Plantagenet's

court with evidence of treason," advised Patrick, "and I will let you go."

Weryn busied himself with transferring equipment to the horse Patrick and Barber had doubled. Thomas Barber moved jerkily, clutching Patrick's sleeve, then jumping back as if it were an accident.

"He'll kill me if I tell," he whispered.

Tossing his head back in a throaty laugh, Weryn pointed a finger at Patrick. "What do you think he'll do?"

"Enough!" clipped Patrick. "What do you hear from Ireland?"

Weryn knew Patrick was asking about Payne Comyn, not Edward Bruce. "It's not good, m'lord. The Bruce is greatly vexed over it and wonders, so 'tis said, that his brother's Irish kingdom will prove to cost too much. Some of the troops have returned to Scottish soil."

Patrick's head snapped up. "By Saint Andrew, I want to go home," he said. "I want to see Christin."

They filled their stomachs with oatcakes and Patrick kicked snow over the fire. Somewhere in the west Christin lay sleeping, and he ached to see her. Lately his thoughts had grown so tormented that he had practically given up sleeping altogether.

"We could ride that way if you wish it, m'lord. 'Twould only be a few days."

Scratching at the beard he'd grown, Patrick shook his head. "First I must get this man off my hands. Then I must report to The Douglas and see what's happened in my absence. Surely the good friar has had word by now. Then, if the king doesn't send me off on another witch hunt, perhaps we can go to Yorkshire."

Weryn saddled Patrick's horse and fed it a small handful of oats. Then the men pulled their chins far down into knitted scarves. Thomas Barber sneezed, and they bowed their heads against the blast of the frigid North Sea. Everything was gray—the snow they trampled beneath their feet, the open sea stretching miles beyond and, Patrick thought, his life until he saw Christin again.

By the time they reached Newcastle-upon-Tyne the year 1318 was dwindling. The fortress was one of the few English towns Patrick felt safe in, though its key position on the frontier made it heavily guarded. But it was a religious settlement, and the mention of John's name gained him access.

Patrick had known Friar John since he was a boy, the Friar was one of the few clergymen he truly liked. Inside the old monastery would be warmth, food and a comfortable place to sleep.

They were escorted into a private area of the monastery, a sparsely furnished room with a low ceiling. A fire roared and cast eerie reflections onto dark, polished paneling.

"Patrick," John's robes whispered on the floor, and he clasped both Patrick's hands in his. "Please sit and thaw out. Who's that?" He pointed to Barber.

"Just put him in a safe place, Father," mumbled Weryn, already shedding his jacket and wet boots. Without removing his garments, Patrick slumped on his spine and smiled the first contentment since he had departed for Scarborough weeks past.

"You remember Weryn, John? It's hard to forget something that big."

"Of course I do. I'm having food sent. You didn't have a beard when I saw you last, Patrick. Tell me now, what of Edward Bruce in Ireland?"

Patrick arose to catch at the monk's arm with cold fingers. "John," he said, "have you had any messages for me?"

Pausing with a gentle laugh, laying down his burden of jackets and boots, John inclined his head. He was a tall, distinguished man.

"As a matter of fact, Patrick, I have three. Where have you been?"

"On a wee errand for the king. The messages—where are they?"

John shrugged at Weryn. "I think the man is eager." In a few minutes he returned with a tray of hot food and three sealed packets with nothing written on their outsides except the initial 'M'. They were all unopened.

"Would you like to go in my chamber, Patrick, for a little privacy? By the look on your face, I would say yes."

Patrick winked his gratitude and followed the monk into a close room where a meager brazier of glowing coals radiated the only heat. Drawing the single candle beside the warmth from the coals, Patrick tore into the topmost letter. It was the blotted one Christin had written. Patrick's eyes scanned it quickly, feeling his smile disappear and hard lines of cruel disappointment drawing down the sides of his mouth.

God's precious blood! He read more, then tore open another. Christin was with child. Another—Christin was summoned before the English crown. Sir Edwin Penmark . . . I don't think I will ever forgive you . . . Christin, Christin!

Unaware that he had sunk to a low kneeling stool, Patrick held her letter in a clenched hand. How could life punish him for something he had no knowledge of? For several moments he sat motionless, his lips moving silently to form her name.

Everything, the entire universe from heaven on down, had been against them. How could she? He would kill Penmark!

Patrick ate only because he knew he must. As Weryn and John made decisions about the prisoner, Patrick twirled an empty cup in his fingers and remembered Christin. When had a day passed that he had not recalled the way she hugged him from behind, and pressed her breasts against his back? What traitorous little bitches they were—to promise faith forever, then give themselves to another for the sake of something called propriety.

"Patrick?" repeated John.

When Patrick stumbled out of the room, the monk arose to follow his long angry strides. Patrick turned as he jerked on his jacket. John shook his head. The flaxen-haired Borderer hardly recognized anything, except perhaps some inner demon, which tormented his peace.

"You can't go out, my lord."

"Let him go," Weryn advised, and Patrick shut the door.

Snow was falling again, and he stepped a few paces to brace both palms against the heavy stones of an archway. As he dropped his weight against them, considering the white fluff collecting on the tops of his boots, a low wail of anguish slipped past his lips.

Deliberately Patrick scraped his palms downward until he felt the comforting reality of stone biting into his flesh. For *what* had he lost this woman? A war? A tight-lipped prisoner? It was for nothing—the love of honor and . . . obedience to his king, and . . . duty. It was the bloody treachery of the English! Never had they had a loyal inch of flesh on their bodies. What had he expected?

Well, this was one treachery Christin would face him with! If he got caught and hanged for his troubles, he would have her stand before him and swear to his face that she didn't love him anymore.

Later, with only one hour's troubled dozing before the fire, Patrick and Weryn left their prisoner with instructions to have him taken to Stirling. Then they mounted fresh horses and headed toward southern Yorkshire in the foulest weather either had ever seen.

"We'll get fresh horses and sleep tomorrow," announced Patrick after his own wheezing mount nearly foundered.

"I've ridden the Border with you for years, laddie," Weryn shouted, his face blistered raw by the wind's bite. He pointed to the dim light of human habitation in a valley at their feet. "I'll be damned if I'll ride past that burgh tonight!"

"You'll do as I tell you or I'll haul you off that beast

and thrash some prudence into you!" Patrick vented his temper like a testy youth.

Jerking up his head, Weryn pulled hard on his reins, causing the animal to halt abruptly. The last miles had been a trial. Patrick was in such a vile humor that if he spoke at all, he was crude and offensive. Weryn wasn't of a mind to pay any more for Christin Winchelsea's grip on his lordship's affections, despite the younger man's suffering. Weryn flung his great body to the ground and stood in the snow as Patrick's horse pranced and sidled in a small circle.

"You big oaf! You think I can't tarnish some of that glittering on your angel wings?" Patrick mocked his friend's burly stance.

"A suckling puppy, bearing his milk teeth to a grizzly bear!" Weryn taunted. "Patrick, if you had as much sense as you have mouth, you wouldn't be in this mess t' begin with. I tried t' warn you about tossing that wench, but you refused to listen."

Patrick leaped off his horse so vigorously that he fell with his full weight on his hands.

"You mention her name again with that filthy tongue of yours, and you won't talk for a week, you half-blind cur. You've a mind for a fight? Come on, then, let's have a bit of it, if you can." Motioning with half-frozen fingers, Patrick challenged Weryn. "Come on, come on. I've listened to your complaining and mewling all the way from the Tweed. You can throw that blade away, too. You've got the honor of a bog-trotting Highlander, and I don't want an eight-inch slit in my gullet. Throw it aside, I say!"

Weryn tossed his head back and roared with laughter. In the eerie whiteness of the forest the sound seemed silver and dead.

"This is th' first good thing that's happened to me since I spent a week in the bed of a countess in Kelso. Matter of fact, she reminded me a bit of your lady, Patrick, with that round little rump."

"I warned you, Weryn."

Patrick threw himself at Weryn with all the force he was capable of. The snow was so impeding that it made them both practically immobile. The heavy weight of Patrick's blow landed against Weryn's stomach with a thick *whoof*. Fighting hand to hand with a man as large as Weryn resolved into nothing more than a grueling wrestling match. Both men strained until arms and legs became hopelessly tangled.

When Weryn's fist finally did connect with Patrick's jaw, it nearly blinded the younger man. For a few seconds he went limp. Weryn, thinking he had the lighter man bested, struggled to his feet only to topple as Patrick hurtled at the parted legs. Patrick threw both his arms about the stout calves and the giant crashed into a white drift.

Snow was packed inside their boots, inside their clothes, and still they twisted the arms and legs of the other until small grunts of pain dwindled into silent, agonizing determination.

"Say you're sorry!" choked Patrick, grinding snow into Weryn's face. Weryn's only reply was to close his teeth down on the heel of Patrick's thumb, wrenching a blistering oath from Patrick's frostbitten lips. Once he shook his hand free of those jaws, he caught Weryn in his good eye with an elbow, causing the great man to roll onto his stomach with a howl. Feeling the chill of the wind on the small of his back, Patrick extricated his legs from between the weakening ones of his companion and managed to crawl some feet away.

Weryn dragged himself into a half-sitting position and spat blood out on the snow. "A curse on your miserable hide."

"You'll burn in hell for this, if not for your other crimes," promised Patrick, grabbing a handful of snow and holding it against a small split on his cheekbone.

"I think you broke my wrist." Weryn pulled up his sleeve and squinted at it in the moonlight.

"I hope I did," Patrick muttered, tenderly inspecting the crotch of his thick trews. "I swear to the Virgin you've ruined me. Christin's is the last child I'll ever sire."

Both men dragged themselves backward and leaned against the trees, gasping for breath, glaring at each other until Weryn smiled and adjusted his patch which had miraculously managed to stay in place.

" 'Twas good for you, laddie. A woman wields the keenest blade ever whetted by man."

Patrick coughed, held his pained chest and sighed softly. "My backside is frozen." Looking sorrily at his feet, he swiped at his nose. "I could wring her neck, but I swear I love that little wench."

"Aye, I know it." Weryn reached over a meaty hand and placed it on Patrick's shoulder. "A good night's rest. You'll get over it."

"And then I have a few choice words I plan to say to Madam What-ever-her-name-is."

Chapter Ten

The first two days after Christin's wedding were spent not in the luxury of Penmark's castle, but in the familiarity of Greystone Manor. At first she thought Edwin had postponed returning to Erskill Castle because of the new snow that was banked in powdery drifts waist high. Later she reasoned the unhurried days were offered as a time to accustom herself as the Lady Penmark.

When Lord Penmark finally assembled his retainers and led them by horseback to Erskill, ten miles north of Greystone, Christin crossed herself, faithfully vowing she would be like her mother. Caroline Winchelsea had been irreproachable, faithful in small matters, generous with all who knew her, uncomplaining in hardship.

Erskill Castle had gone to considerable trouble to please its new mistress. As Christin entered the cobbled courtyard, not having been there in many years, she nervously requested to enter through the kitchens rather than the grill-worked gates at the front.

"If that is what you want, my lady."

Edwin, pleasantly surprised at her swift assumption of wifely responsibilities, balanced himself on a polished cane and allowed a servant to remove his long cloak.

Bowing, a woman stepped to Christin's side to brush off the snow from her cape.

The new mistress ignored Tildy's sniff at her airs. Lifting her chin, Christin moved past them with the brisk efficiency of a woman who knew her place.

Female domestics and embarrassed knaves stared to see their new lady inspecting the buttery and pantry. Sweeping through the reek of pitch torches instead of the candle-lit main hall, she approved of the well-scrubbed look. As she left the work quarters, Christin heard them whispering. Whispering, she resigned herself, was something she must tolerate for awhile.

"The staff went to too much trouble, my lord," she smiled. They were past passageways which smelled of cooking food and sweating stones. Apples and nuts were perched on the great hearth in anticipation of their wants. Even the plates and goblets were placed on the table, ready to be filled.

"It's been far too long since they've had a mistress to fuss over. I fear they have grown slovenly with only a doddering old man."

Edwin's eyes glowed with pride. He gave his trim girth a satisfied pat.

"John, fetch your ladyship something warm to drink, and quiet those hounds. They will waken the dead, by heaven."

When Edwin arose after their meal to accompany Christin to her chamber, a sensation of foreboding chilled her. Until this moment the meaning of her situation floated somewhere above her, impersonally. Once she saw her bed and her own familiar clothes in a strange setting, the future was swiftly cast in iron. Could she truly see this through?

Christin's living quarters consisted of two rooms, the second of which she assumed to be Tildy's, until Edwin told her it would be refurnished for the baby. Completely private, beautifully appointed with handworked pieces, it was set apart in a corner turret. Already its fireplace blazed, inviting her in. Pale green tapestries covered the walls to discourage drafts. A single window was taller than she was, and Christin wrote her new name in the condensation. Edwin laughed.

"The only thing which might come as a surprise to you, my dear, is this."

Moving to a table beside her bed, he opened the lid to an old cask rimmed with tarnished brass studs. Christin's eyes widened. The chest spilled over with jewels— family pieces, some incredibly valuable and very old.

"These jewels have been in my family for four generations. Elaine and I had no children, so of course they will be yours to give to your children."

"I couldn't, Sir Edwin." Christin shook her head. "I just couldn't."

He considered a moment. "Perhaps not now. Whatever you decide. Whenever."

Properly, though a bit winded from his climb, Edwin lifted her hand to his lips. "I chose these rooms for you with much thought. They are what I would have selected if I were you. You will need time. You'll bring much comfort to my last days. But," he chuckled, "I'm afraid this is the last time my old legs will brave that stairway. From now on, if you want to visit, you'll have to do it in the accommodation of the lower level."

Christin's smile was brilliant, and she blinked hard. "I don't see how you do it, my lord. I hope I never do anything to disappoint you."

"Then call me Edwin. Now," he braced a slender hand on the door frame, "I'm sure you have things to occupy your time. Myself, I have a stack of accounts that I've neglected for far too long. Good night, Christin."

One at a time, he took the stairs carefully. In an unconscious, protective gesture, Christin folded her arms across her thickening waist.

"Good night, Edwin."

"Erskill is such a lovely place, Christin."

For the past few days Margaret and the children had

stayed with Christin, helping her to unpack and to slip into a life much more demanding than the routine pace at Greystone. Edwin's household was a large one. Lord Penmark, though his age prevented active participation in the Parliament, was still taken into counsel. Nobility often requested his time.

"I'm scared to death I'll make a mistake," Christin gestured about the dark cellar where sacks of food were stored along with extra weapons for the servants if they were ever needed. "I must know everything. So much protocol. I never dreamed. Yet Edwin is easy to please."

Christin had been married over a week. As large as the castle was, she was making an inventory of it. Whether due to the care of Edwin's first wife, she didn't know, but her new home lacked for nothing. Silver plate was in abundance. Candelabras, platters, knives and linens were also plentiful. Twelve bedrooms were furnished comfortably and the kitchens and bakery could run as well without her supervision as with it.

"How easy to please is easy?" smirked Margaret.

Glancing at the children as they scrambled in a barrel for a perfect apple, Christin drew Margaret near a wine cupboard.

"If you're asking me if Edwin places any wifely demands on me, he doesn't. We have pleasant meals together every evening. He sits before the fireplace in his chamber and reads while I knit. Sometimes we play chess. Then I excuse myself and go up to my room."

"No servants' remarks about a young fortune huntress marrying an old man for his money?"

"How would I know? But even so, that would be kinder than the truth."

Absently, Christin withdrew a corked cask of wine, dusted it off, looked at it without seeing, and replaced it. "How could I have been so *wrong* about Patrick, Maggie?"

"Faugh! You weren't wrong about Patrick. The time wasn't right for you two, that's all. Don't you ever see yourself being . . . a real wife to Edwin? I mean, Christin, that after a woman lives with a man for a time, she grows accustomed to certain things. It wouldn't be out of the ordinary for you to go to your husband's bed. And it wouldn't be very often, obviously."

"Margaret! How can you suggest that to me? It would be a . . . a profanation of everything Patrick and I meant to each other. I know that's gone now, but my honor, my life—"

"Life is a very long time, sweet," Margaret said, pressing her cool fingers against Christin's blood-rouged cheeks. "The man will be kind to your baby, Christin. You will soon learn how that grows on a woman."

"I don't want to talk about this."

Christin lifted her skirts and called for the children to come. To even consider sharing Edwin Penmark's bed would be adultery.

As Patrick and Weryn stood mounted upon a hill, the younger man pulled his knitted cap low. There wasn't much of a moon, yet he could view the distant castle jutting against a cloudy southern horizon. He sniffed the night breeze.

"At least it won't snow tonight," he predicted. "It took us long enough to find this place. Snow would undo me completely."

Erskill's wall was high, and even if Patrick scaled it, there still remained the formidable task of finding Christin without bringing the place down upon his head. He grinned to himself; unauthorized entries were his strong point.

"There'll be hell to pay for this, my lord," grumbled Weryn.

"You were the one who suggested it, dolt. Give me the rope. And don't expect me back before dawn."

Weryn didn't like the thoughts of Patrick using a grapnel; the clattering of metal upon stone sounded like a garrison attack in the dead silence of night.

But Patrick had done it all many times before. The only difficulty lay in scrambling over the point where the rope joined the stone's edge. When he slithered over it, twisting his jacket and scraping his bare stomach in a six-inch burn, even leaving some of his knuckles behind, he swore fervently. Hobbling to the safety of the shadowed parapet, he energetically sucked on a barked knuckle. Then, with only a whisper, he dropped down into the courtyard and adroitly avoided the sleepy guard.

In less than a half hour, after a search of the second floor, he spied a small pair of boots neatly cleaned and sitting outside a doorway at the top of a twisting stair.

The boots could only be Christin's. Now the problem was, would he find her alone if he entered? It was not yet eleven o'clock, and voices murmured below him from two different directions.

Holding his breath that the door would not be locked, Patrick leaned his shoulder against it. It moved, and he slipped into a spacious room bathed in deep shadows. The only light was a dwindling fire. From a large bed, Christin's breath came steadily.

Where, he wondered, was his thorn-in-the-flesh, Tildy? After assuring himself that the woman was not in the adjoining room, Patrick relaxed with a long sigh, locked the door, and pulled off his jacket.

What did he feel as he stood over Christin, spying on her slumber as her mouth parted slightly? She was even more lovely than he had dreamed her. Long, frilly lashes rested upon her cheeks, framed by brows that arched, not at their centers, but more over the edge of her eyes.

He stooped beside the bed to smooth a tendril of her chestnut hair between his fingers. She stirred, and Patrick hooked a finger to slip the cover down beneath her chin. He memorized the way her neck curved into her shoulder. Looking upon her, he decided, was too much of a torture. Already a crucifying ache spread through the lower part of his body. Yet powerless to help himself, Patrick inched the cover even lower and tightened his jaw at the sight of her hair spilling over her breasts.

"Damn you, Christin," he trembled.

Stealthily, slowly, Patrick's fingers closed over her mouth. It took only a few seconds for Christin to struggle awake, thrashing at his hand, her eyes flaring and terrified.

"Shh! Don't fight, Christin. It's Patrick. Shh, wake up now, and I'll take my hand away."

With a feeble whimper, Christin slumped back against the pillow, unable to believe the nightmarish form bending over her, its knee braced on the bed beside her hip. He was completely in black, and the blond hair and beard against the firelight made him look like a fallen angel.

"Are you awake?"

She nodded her head against his hand, and Patrick withdrew the offensive fingers, straighting to loom above her.

"Are you mad?" She clutched at her gaping gown and shrank back against the headboard. "They will *kill* you if they find you here!"

"I'm sure they will. Where's Tildy?"

"She's down another hall. What in sweet faith's name do you think you're doing?"

Patrick, taking the precaution of double-checking the door, moved to stir the fire and light a candle. Christin was so stunned that she could hardly believe any of it. She drew her gown close up to her chin and padded in bare feet to warm herself before the fire.

Neither of them spoke as the fire grew noisy. But the guilt had not changed—her tresspass for not crying out in moral outrage at his crime of breaking into a man's house at night to see his lover. Instinctively, Christin's hands moved to her belly. They found each other depressingly difficult to read.

"Motherhood becomes you," he spoke at last, flatly, as though he approved yet hated her for being so beautiful.

Something in his voice made Christin stiffen. She began inching away from him, her eyes never leaving the intensity of his face. Patrick was different. She had never seen him so absolutely dispassionate.

"How did you get in?"

"Your husband's guards could do with some instruction."

"Oh."

With an awkward flutter of awareness, Christin's eyes lowered to the neck of her gown. Its looseness did little to enhance her modesty. Ever so discreetly, she slid her fingers upward, not wishing to call attention to it, pretending a gesture of touching her throat.

"Don't touch that gown," he ordered.

Patrick's unthinking display of strength was like the unexpected whirring of flexible steel. Both were certain now, if not before, that this encounter would end in disaster.

Knowing he read her mounting anger, Christin spun from his dark examination, her hair shimmering gold and rust. She heard him take one step, then stop where he stood.

"Why didn't you come to me, Patrick? I did everything I knew to reach you before I married. You can scarcely deny that."

Before he could answer she put words in his mouth, facing him, flying at him with pent-up rejection.

"You didn't care enough! Curse your Scot blindness! And now, you come here to what? To cast blame upon *me?*"

Defiantly, in the only gesture she knew, Christin snatched her clothing tightly shut, crushing the full curves.

"I said to not touch that gown."

Christin feared him now. The low harshness of his words was a warning of a new pain unlike any she had known before. He was as hurt as she, and he was far too strong for her to escape, if it came to that. And it certainly would, for his hand darted to trap her wrist in a painless, but hopelessly unbreakable grip.

"You can't make me do this," she said. "You don't have the right. Not anymore."

Christin resisted his embrace as Patrick ignored her protest. He caught her tightly to his waist with his free arm, and as she pushed against his chest, he captured that hand, too. Then, with a swift movement, he imprisoned it behind her back with the other.

"Couldn't you wait a few weeks for me?" Patrick didn't smile as he spoke. "You speak of betrayal? *I believed you!* And yet you took my words to be a lie. Does not a fool deserve vengeance for that? For believing the lying lips of a woman?"

"I didn't lie. Everything has changed now. Please don't do this. Even before, in Scotland, you never did anything like this. Patrick, let—me—go!"

He smiled then, not a real smile but showing his teeth in glittering self-mockery.

"One thing hasn't changed between us, sweetheart. Even after your woman's treachery, our need for each other hasn't changed. I had hoped for your sympathies and your love." He laughed mirthlessly. "And—forgive me—your loyalty."

He crushed her then, in a sinewy strength, snapping her head upward, and he bent it back to almost touch her mouth with his.

"So, lambie, I will console myself with your body. And you won't deny me. Be still, sweetheart, and feel your heart beating."

Christin despised the hammering pulse that coursed through her.

"This isn't right." Her mouth drew down at the corners.

"Right?" he mocked. *"This* is right."

Patrick's mouth dipped, brushing across her lips in a breath of a kiss. His beard was soft, the smell of him intoxicating. Patrick always smelled the same: soap, leather, and wood smoke, the faint sweat of horses. Collapsing against his chest, unable to keep the masculine erectness from pressing against the bones of her body, she smiled faintly.

"Kiss me, then. You know I can't stop you—a mighty, triumphant conqueror who needs to prove he's stronger than a pregnant woman."

For a few seconds, Patrick's face paled with gaunt anger. Her taunting was dangerous. He stepped back, his jaw bunched hard. His eyes moved over the promise of her bosom only half-visible to him, for she was ripe with months of carrying his child. When he brushed her gown aside, touching one peaked nipple, it was no longer soft in his fingers, but sensitive and suddenly firm. Its springing life gave the lie to Christin's eyes, even as she struggled to steady her breath and to pretend that his touch didn't arouse her desire.

"Justice is important to me," she protested. But her words were already husky.

"And to me, Christin, love," he murmured lazily, teasing the tiny orb of flesh almost beyond her ability to bear it. "I belong to you. You belong to me. Justice."

The abruptness of his embrace, his sudden passion, was a shock. She knew it would be in her eyes—her weakness to the spell of his lips, lowering slowly, hot, and parting with the certainty of his ability to undo her.

Long minutes later, when he released her, she forced her eyes to focus.

"I can't," she breathed.

Sweeping her up in his arms, Patrick walked soundlessly to the bed. He stared long at her. "What you cannot do, lassie, is stop me. I've starved for you all these months, dreamed of you, and remembered the night when you awoke and searched for my mouth even as I slept."

Christin buried her face in his chest.

"If it weren't for a capricious king, you would have my name now. Instead of Penmark's. And you tell me I *can't*? I will spare his life. Then, by heaven, he can't begrudge me for taking what is mine."

She was lost. She knew it, and still her pride prevailed. Christin fought against her gown as he pulled it tightly above her bare hips. And when she attempted to escape from beneath the entrapment of his big body, Patrick twisted great tresses of her hair in one hand and pinned her still. He touched her everywhere, eventually invading the satiny woman's flesh between her legs until she stilled. Sensations blurred, and Christin moistened her lips. She whispered his name, and he didn't have to entangle her hair anymore.

"Oh, Patrick," she yielded. She felt her body when it surrendered—melting with his, blending with a physical symmetry so different from hers.

"I came," he said, wrenching his tunic over his head, "to hear you say you love me. Only that. I would never force you against your will, lassie. No matter how I wanted to."

Tears collected in her eyes as Patrick stretched himself upon her, still clad in his trews, bracing part of his weight on the palms of his hands.

"You could have made it easier for me to be noble."

"I don't want a noble lover. Chris, say it. I have needs that are apt to slay me if you don't."

"I have always loved you." She gave him the words. "I've never been dishonest about that, Patrick. I wanted to have your baby. But . . . I couldn't defy my family and the church. I had to marry Edwin. Please believe that. I had to!"

"I don't want to talk about Edwin. I want time. I want you to kiss me and make me feel like the most important man in the world. I want to love you and make you feel things you've never felt before."

Even as Patrick spoke, he shifted his weight to pull off the rest of his clothes. Christin shrank from the ardent, probing part of him that she still didn't quite know. He whispered husky senseless things into her ear and drew his weight upward upon her, parting her legs with a knee and slowly filling her with the thick warmth of his own body.

"Don't move for just a minute," he whispered.

226

He was at her mercy then. His need was too great, bringing him to the level of a man, not a warring conqueror. This need filled Christin's hands with a power which she could have used, in those moments, to her own advantage. She could have damaged Patrick. She could have bruised the inner man who intuitively returned to the source of physical comfort and freedom of his soul.

But she only stilled when he stilled and moved when he moved, returning kiss for kiss and breath for breath. It was a moment of building up and ebbing away, ending in inevitable self-doubts of whether enough was given to the other.

With their immediate hunger appeased they both understood what they had done was like looking at a jewel in daylight—valuable and beautiful, but not as satisfying without the glitter of candlelight. How large was their guilt in satisfying their hunger in Edwin Penmark's own house? Where was the line, given their circumstances, which separated right from wrong?

Cradled in his arms, the warmth of his naked length soothing and peaceful, Christin trailed her fingers up the line of Patrick's jaw, across his forehead.

"Patrick?"

"What?"

"Where did you get that scar?"

She touched the faint mark, and when he opened his eyes she smiled and leaned to kiss him. Patrick hugged her and rested his chin in the curve of her neck.

"You smell good," he said. "The scar? Shall I make up some story of heroism? Would you think me valiant if I said I received it dueling with the earl of Surrey?"

Christin giggled. "Tell me the truth, varlet."

"It was a silly accident, when Malcolm and I were small boys. It was my fault, really. Malcolm and I were throwing small pieces of iron over the roof of a building. Somehow I didn't get out of the way soon enough. But that wasn't the terrible part of it."

"What was terrible, my sweet bonny lover?"

227

Christin toyed with his ribs until he growled his misfortune and rolled his weight onto her. For heated seconds they wrestled, and she squeaked at him, "You're crushing me. Please, finish your story, and do get off me."

"Scots have ways of handling rowdy young lassies who don't know they go too far," he threatened, moving aside and grabbing a handful of flesh inside her thigh.

"I said I'll be good. The story, please."

"Oh, yes. Well, my father was so upset that he threatened Malcolm with a thrashing, and Malcolm hit me. In the stomach." Patrick's tone sobered. "I think his blow hurt me more than the cut on my head. There I was, my head bleeding all over the place with Mother quarreling with my father. It always grieved me when they fought. At first I blamed my father and later, when I was old enough to realize that Malcolm and I had different mothers, I somehow blamed myself."

"You always say 'my father' or 'our father,' Patrick. Didn't you ever call him 'Father' or 'Papa'? I don't think you liked him very much."

Patrick rolled onto his back and was quiet. Sensing he was troubled, Christin slid her knee across his waist and laid her head on his chest. With automatic familiarity, Patrick settled his palm on the curve of her hip.

"Malcolm was always my father's favorite son. I never understood it. It's just the way it was. When I was eight years old, my mother returned for a time to Scotland. I know now that my father didn't force her to do it, but then I thought he did. Anyway, I grew closer to my grandfather than I ever was to either of my parents. My father left the bulk of his money and estates to Malcolm, as you probably know. I threw my part of it in Malcolm's face and told him to do whatever he wanted to with it. I never did go back, and I haven't seen Malcolm since."

Christin propped herself on her elbows, unaware of how the sight of her bare flesh stirred his desire for her. "You're young to have seen so much death, Patrick."

228

He drew her face to his with both hands and kissed her eyes and nose and the tiny crevice of her upper lip. With a sensuality which amazed her, he sucked the tips of her fingers.

"And I don't intend for my son to grow up like that. Christin. I want you to return to Scotland with me. To-night. If you want to talk with your . . . husband first, I don't mind. Personally, I don't care if they think I stole you again."

Christin's whole body stiffened from his unexpected demand. Their moralities were so different. Because he had defied a king of the right to control his conscience, he expected that she was capable of the same.

"Patrick! What are you saying? How can you—my family—how can you put me in such a position?"

"Put *you* in a position? What about me? Sweetheart, when you told me you would find a way to work things out, I never dreamt you meant . . . this." Patrick flicked his hand over his head, haphazardly.

"Well, I wasn't considering living in mortal sin."

"Damnation, Christin! I won't ask you forever. I've never crawled to a woman before, and I won't do it now."

She could no longer be in the same bed with him. Groping her way about the darkening room, she found the discarded gown. But before she could slip it over her head, Patrick towered over her. He flung it to the floor with a harsh sound.

Their nakedness stripped the pretenses from between them. Once again the impression of catastrophe settled heavily upon her. Christin found it impossible not to wrap her arms across her bosom.

"What you're telling me is," he wiped his mouth, "that you love your father and Laurence more than me. Or our child. You choose their hypocritical ideas of conduct before you will dare to live with a man you love."

"That's not hypocritical, Patrick. That's unfair. I want my child—our child—to grow up in a normal home, free from slander. If you weren't so selfish, you could see I'm right. You knew when we conceived this baby that I couldn't live in common law with you. We agreed we would wait for the truce—"

She bit her lip and blinked at the dying fire. Inside her, too, things were dying.

"Yes, we did agree to wait, didn't we? And then you married Edwin Penmark."

Christin wished she could say she despised Patrick, and she moved in the direction of her gown.

"No!" He jerked her about. "Look at your belly, Christin! Already it grows round with my flesh and blood. No woman has a right to keep that from a man."

His distress stilled the turbulent seconds, and Patrick slowly spread his hand over the expanding curve below Christin's waist. Cruelly, at this ill-fated moment, nature thrust another wound into the vulnerable Scot. A faint flutter of life stirred beneath the hard, callused palm, and he froze in awe.

The tiny ripple of life flowing from her body into his was as profound as every risk Patrick had taken in his life. Christin could only gaze up at the golden-bearded man in wonder. She shrank from his fingers which bit into the softness of her arm, hurting her.

"Be still!"

Even the sound of their breaths shocked them, and presently Patrick smiled.

"I've never felt a bairn's wee kick before. I'm over thirty years old, and I never felt it before. Do you know what it's like, Christin, for a man to feel the life of his very first child?"

"Much the same as it is for its mother, I suspect." Her voice broke, and she wriggled to escape him. Tears sparkled in her eyes, then spilled.

Patrick drew her tightly against him and brushed the diamond drops with a bent knuckle. "Please, sweetheart. Don't deny me. Come with me."

When she dropped her face onto his shoulder, the very hiding of her face voiced her refusal. Patrick's breathing grew labored. He retrieved the gown, jerking it over her head with ungentle hands.

"You, madam, will have no small amount of accounting on Judgment Day."

Unable to stop the trembling of his hands, Patrick began pulling on his clothes. Not once did Christin lift her head, listening as she stood, to the movements of his dressing. When he was finished, he tipped her head up roughly. His eyes were pitiless and very dark.

"It's a mistake to ever want anything. I was happier when nothing was sacred to me."

In a moment so long that it had neither beginning nor end, reaching back to the first time he had stood over her head in the glen and she had covered herself with his garment, they stood helplessly. Neither could bridge the chasm gaping between them.

"Remember . . . the last time we were together . . . I hated you." His voice was like muted thunder, promising a storm.

The finality of the door closing was irrevocable, like standing before a bier. Quite abruptly the room drained of light and grew uncommonly cold.

Payne Comyn jerked the bit in the tender mouth of his horse. He was etched on a hill overlooking the Ardle River, and if Christin had seen him now she wouldn't have recognized him. He was displayed in full war panoply, garbed in tartan plaid and a horned helmet. Rawhide thongs bound calfskins about his legs, and a piece of Celtic jewelry gleamed on his chest. Swarming about him, covering the hill, were four hundred men, all in war regalia.

Moonlight glinted off the ribbon of water beneath them as it slithered through the valley, and to the northeast, Braedeen gasped its dying breath. To Payne's knowledge not a single sheep or lamb had escaped the executioner's sword, or the herds, or the dogs. The belligerent population had threatened no problem, fighters though they were.

This destruction was a time-honored tradition. If he didn't do it himself, his son would do it. No honorable Highlander would tolerate being lied to before his king, of being tricked, made a laughingstock. How could Mowbray have left his town undefended? Didn't he know that Christin Winchelsea's refusal to go to Edward's court had sealed the fate of this manor?

"What of the wind?" Payne inquired of the Highlander beside him, a burly man with the soft eyes of a woman and the hands of a killer. He, like all of Payne's men, did their killing efficiently and quietly.

"It will freshen soon, my lord," assured the man-at-arms.

"Your first task will be to fire the stables, the town next and the manor last. Two hours is the most I will allow. Do ye have flint and tinder ready?"   ·

"Aye."

The man's horse sidled fitfully. To the west warriors were regrouping, but the ones to their east had already formed their position. A mist rolled in from off the river, and within the hour a distinct breeze wafted from the west. Payne smiled and lifted his arm in a signal.

As his hand plunged downward, Highlanders poured off the hills, circumventing Warrick Manor and spilling into the hardened street of the burgh. Payne had decided upon mercy; no more slaughter than actually necessary. A full-scale war with The Bruce was one thing he didn't relish.

Bruce wouldn't rally his army for a mere burning; it was too common a practice. And the king couldn't risk aligning the Comyns and the MacDougalls this time of year. No army, no matter how strong, could venture into the Highlands during the winter. A stranger caught in a snowstorm north of the River Forth was almost certainly a dead man.

"This, Christin Winchelsea, is your reward for damaging a man's pride," Payne murmured to himself.

If Mowbray had stayed out of the affair with Christin, none of this destruction would have been necessary.

Where had the whoreson Saxon traitor gone while his mistress was pledging her troth to some aging old fool?

Isolated shouts of battle echoed through the river valley, and Payne sniffed the tangy smoke before he saw its thin blue film. Unfortunately for them, no crops stood in the fields, but Payne had strategically chosen his attack. Warrick's snow had melted days ago. The countryside would burn before the night was over.

"Clifford's havin' trouble with the trees to th' north."

Payne noted the still-blue haze. The flames would be murky brown if they were affording destruction.

"Get more men over there. Cut brush and pile it high. Drag timber, but get those trees burning."

"Aye, m'lord, but it'll take time."

From the vicinity of the town a red glow pulsated. Payne grew weary with watching, and he hurled himself from the hillside, ploughing his way into the thick thunderheads of smoke. They burned his lungs and stung his eyes.

As the burgh began retching forth its peasants, who were outnumbered twenty to one, its meager number of fighting men futilely spilled their blood in an effort to save the manor house. Old men and women fled from wheeling horses, faces grim and their eyes red.

Hiding in the forests they watched thatches pulled off their roofs to burn in the street. Stored hay and grain fed greedy flames while beasts and poultry were slaughtered. Systematically the destroyers worked their way to the outlying crofts sprinkled throughout the fields.

Only small pockets of youngsters gave any resistance out in the fields. Glynnis crouched behind the dark side of an untorched croft. In the distance, less than a quarter of a mile away, Dame Haggitt's tiny dwelling etched a rectangular pattern of red. More than likely the old woman was dead.

Glynnis had no idea where Gideon's mother was, for they had become separated when the melee started. But the MacKenzie house was burning. Gideon had come for only a moment; he and David were on horseback.

"Don't try to save anything, Mother!" he had shouted, his hair singed, his sword drawn. "Glynnis, go with Mother to th' forest. Things are too wet t'burn. Take some blankets and keep movin' toward Perth. I'll find you."

"But Tag!" she had screamed. "'Tag can't find 'is way. He'll die, Gideon!"

Now, she didn't even know if Gideon were alive or dead. Peg MacKenzie was a strong woman and could take care of herself, and Glynnis had refused to go with her. Someone had to help Tag out of the inferno.

"I'll get him and meet you at th' bog."

Glynnis had flung her hand in the direction of a mire where all the children were forbidden to play.

From shadow to shadow she dodged now, moving ever closer to the manor. Tag's old wattle house wasn't too far from where Christin had lived behind the kirk, and Glynnis dragged herself toward it, half-strangling, her lungs near to bursting.

"Oh blessed Virgin," she wept. "They've fired Warrick."

Slumping to the ground to catch her breath, she gaped at the timbered east wing of Warrick outlined in the haze. Where, oh God, was Warrick's laird?

"Tag?" she shouted, stumbling again, holding the heaviness of her swollen belly. "Tag?"

Glynnis pressed hard against her unborn child. It hurt her but she couldn't stop. Horsemen with swinging torches were making progress in the forests now. And the burgh itself would burn until everything was devoured or the rains quenched it.

The walls of flames seemed between her and everything. She screamed Tag's name again. Miraculously, from somewhere in the heavy pall, Glynnis heard the old man answer.

"Tag! *Where are you?*"

"Glynnis? Is that you, lass?"

"Yes. It's me! it's me, Tag! Keep calling. I'll find you. Don't stop calling!"

Tag's voice drifted through the smoke like that of an apparition haunting the pits of hell. Why had he wandered so near Warrick? Couldn't he hear the marauders in the forest beyond it? The whole sky was alight now.

Sometimes stepping over a body she couldn't recognize, Glynnis picked her way, pausing every few steps to listen.

Horses! Swiftly the thunder of hooves burst about her. She began running madly, but flames turned her back again and again. She could hear the wild yells as the destroyers bore down upon her. As they plunged through the brown curtain they never saw her in their path. The lead horse knocked her aside as easily as a toy doll. Over and over she rolled.

"Gideon!"

The Highlander jerked on his reins and pranced in a circle, listening. He heard nothing except the steadily increasing roar from the forests, and he charged onward. Near the kirk, Tag inched his way from tombstone to tombstone, his second sight guiding him, telling him where not to venture.

"Glynnis? Answer me, lass. They're gone now. Call out, call out. Glynnis?"

When Tag found Glynnis, he fell over her senseless body. Crawling, feeling with his fingers, he bent over the girl. Her clothes were rent from the upper part of her body, and soft wet patches of flesh marked her shoulders and arms. Hoof marks.

"Saint Andrew will help ye, lass," he breathed over her, making the sign of a cross. "Keep fightin'. You're a strong lass."

Gnarled old fingers found her legs. No broken bones, but the warm trickle of blood already bathed her knees. Tag staggered to his feet, gripping her hands, and he began dragging her where he guessed the stone kirk had to be. Fortunately, Glynnis remained unconscious, for he knew he hurt her terribly.

The Highlanders didn't torch the church, probably fearing it would call down the wrath of Saint Fillian.

After Tag heaved Glynnis inside, he began moving about to gather the linens Christin had washed. As well as he could, he padded makeshift compresses where Glynnis' unborn child was slowly dying.

Then Tag held her hand in his and slowly rocked back and forth, humming an ancient chant of supplication. Perhaps the dawn would bring help. He knew raids. The Highlanders would leave with dawn.

The chances of Gideon and David reaching the stables before the raiders was so fragile it hardly existed.

"Saul! Ride south!" Gideon shouted. "Get word to Patrick and Douglas."

"I don't know where the laird is," Saul shouted, tethering a spare hill pony.

"He'll be somewhere between here and Scarborough. Don't come back 'till you bring him. Leave word at Perth and tell Douglas to come."

"Aye. Can you hold them off?"

Twenty fighting men were swiftly leading the terrified beasts into the safety of the trees. If the horses couldn't be kept together in the outlying bogs, they would be turned loose and the survivors gathered later.

"We've no chance at fightin'. There're too many. Save the animals and the people. And yourselves. Rankin, take three men and go to Braedeen. God help us, I fear 'twill be too late."

In less than two minutes the dispatches were obediently on their way. Gideon wrestled with Triste and her terrified colt. Before he could lead them outside, the muted thunder reached his ears.

"Holmes! Scatter them out! Anywhere. David and I will hold 'em off as long as we can."

It was suicide. But if they were quick, the men could save Warrick's horses. Gideon snatched a rope from the wall and he and David sprinted for the pathway coming off the hills. Highland torches were blinking down the hillside like fireflies. They would pass between two wooded thickets some fifty yards from the river.

"We'll run a rope. That's worth a couple minutes of confusion!" Gideon decided.

Hastily they strung the rope, knowing the most it would do was cause the lead horses to stumble. But that might be enough. By the time the hemp stretched fetlock high, the Highlanders were a hundred yards away. The two men dived for the underbrush and scrambled for cover.

It was almost asking more than a man could do—to lie in the direct path of onslaught. The first horses heaved into the rope, throwing their riders over their heads. The rope didn't hold, as Gideon had known it wouldn't, but the next riders stumbled, trying to avoid stepping on their own men.

Brandishing their swords, the two Warrick men dashed to the point of greatest confusion.

The next seconds were bedlam. Highlanders crashed to avoid each other and their slashing attackers. David took a sword in his chest before he was knocked from his feet. A hot spurting in Gideon's shoulder spun him about, making him drop his weapon, and he felt steel deep in his hip.

Loudly cursing the pain, Gideon lunged for a riderless horse and threw his good leg half over the saddle. With a quick motion he wrapped his wrist in the reins and held on.

"Let the devil take him!" Gideon heard the shout behind him. "He's a dead man!"

He didn't doubt it. Behind him there was nothing but roiling holocaust. "Glynnis, pray God you're safe," he breathed and hoped that he would live long enough to reach the river.

Chapter Eleven

Only fifteen miles stretched between Patrick and Warrick. A frosty haze shrouded the winter moon like the veil of a mourning woman. With the fresh horses they would reach home before midnight.

Christin had made her decision, Patrick reminded himself dully. He shoved the knitted cap to the back of his head, which lent him an impudent air. When a man needed more of a woman than the comfort of her body, he deserved what he got! It wasn't only that Christin's legs tangled with his when he awoke. It was her drowsy smile and her lazy eyes which said, "I'm glad that you begin my day."

Aye, when he had taken her from Miron he had known he would regret it.

"Weryn?" Patrick pointed north, squinting at the pink glow rimming a jagged line of hills. "What do you think that—"

Both men reined suddenly and stared at each other for unbelieving seconds.

"Fire!" breathed Patrick. "Sweet Jesu! Why do I feel the devil's own hand on my shoulder?"

"It's too far t'be certain, Patrick. Come on!"

The glow arched a good twenty miles in width, and after a half hour of breakneck riding Patrick accepted the sinking in his stomach as the truth. Warrick was burning! The whole sky was red, and the country smelled of blackened timberland.

"Ho!" shouted Patrick to a figure pounding breakneck toward them on the narrow road. The two men swerved aside, and the frantic rider drew up seconds before crashing headlong into them. His small pony reared, thrashing its forelegs.

"Saul!"

"My lord?"

"God's mercy, man, what's the matter? It's Warrick, isn't it?"

"Oh my lord!" choked Saul, slumping over to catch his breath. Dappled with flecks of sweat, the Border mount flared its nostrils.

"I was tryin' to reach Stirling, to get help! It's that devil-worshippin' Highlander! He's slaughtered the whole of Braedeen. One of the tillers told me." The tough bearded man began weeping shamelessly. "The herds—Johnnie, Hayes—dead. The murderin' bastards burned most of Warricktown. Some of th' women are dead. Rankin tried to fight, and he's dead."

Patrick's breathing was harsh. A rage was boiling so deeply inside him that he had to steel himself to hear the entirety of Saul's account.

"Did you actually see Comyn? Are you sure it was him?"

Saul swiped at his eyes and nodded, still gasping.

"Gideon?" demanded Patrick, shuddering with black visions of Gideon writhing in flames.

"I dunno, m'lord. He and David were tryin' to save th' horses. That's the last I saw of him."

With a loss of control Weryn had never known of him, Patrick wrenched off his cap and buried his face in it.

"Go to Stirling, Saul," commanded the one-eyed man. "Jamie was there or nearby."

Weryn didn't doubt Comyn would pay with his life for this. He stiffened at the sight of Patrick straightening, his face cold and perfectly devoid of pity.

239

"A physician from Perth, if you can!" Patrick yelled back at Saul.

As they neared Warrick's inferno, seeking an entrance through its walls of shooting flames, Weryn leaned from his saddle.

"Did he really do this because of th' lass?"

"He may have burned because of her," Patrick said tonelessly. "But he will die because of me."

At Patrick's return, his people crept from the hidden places of the land. They were beaten and hungry, some of them wounded. Weryn led them through the burning debris to the manor.

When Patrick surveyed his smoldering lands, staring glassily at hundreds of slaughtered sheep, dead shepherds with their faithful dogs beside them, he turned back, sickened.

Warrick's east-wing roof had caved in, and some of the wall had collapsed. The keep still blazed, and though Patrick was certain it couldn't be saved, he commanded teams of villeins to fight it under control.

Perth sent three of their monks who were versed in the ways of healing. Patrick dispatched two of them to scour through the town and the crofts to bring all sick and wounded to the intact wing of the manor house. Patrick's upper chambers remained untouched, and he transformed the second floor into a makeshift hospital.

He discovered Tag hunched cross-legged in the kirk beside Glynnis where he had sat all night, holding her limp hand in both his own. With his wits dulled from grief and fatigue, Patrick collapsed onto the floor beside him.

"Poor lassie," Patrick shook his head at the hideous marks upon Glynnis' shoulders.

She stirred as she drifted in and out of consciousness.

"Are you awake, wee one? It's Patrick. Wake up. I've come to help you, lass. Do you know who I am?"

Patrick shook Tag's arm. "'Tell me what you know. How did you get here?"

"The bairn is dead, m'lord," Tag said without moving anything but his lips. "I needed to fetch her some things, but I was afraid t'leave her. She's bled mightily."

"The monks will tend her now. She'll be taken to the manor. You've done well, Tag."

The old man had lost his stick. Brushing aside Patrick's attempts to help him, he twisted upward and squared his frail shoulders. Patrick swore the man read everything in his soul with those sightless eyes.

" 'Twas th' same with MacCauley, m'lord, when the devil from the Highland got 'im. I warned you. You should never ha' brought the English lass here."

"Hush your superstitious babbling! MacCauley was drunk and fell into the sea and drowned."

"Eyes that see not. Ears that hear not," chanted Tag.

"My lord?" Glynnis awakened again, and Patrick knelt to touch her bruised cheek. "Tag said you can't find Gideon."

"Men are looking. We'll find him."

"Our bairn is gone. It was only so big. I couldn't do nothin' to help it at all. Nothin'."

Her bosom heaved with soundless sobs. For a moment Patrick considered the altar beyond them, an angry muscle flexing in his jaw. Warrick's holy place should lend comfort to the grieved, not witness the death of a babe before its time.

Weryn found Gideon by the river, hidden under a crevice of rock, more dead than alive. He carried the younger man tenderly in his arms across the docks, up the hill to Warrick, toward Patrick who issued terse orders for breaking out Warrick's few remaining stores.

The kirk housed the dead who awaited burial. Dame Haggitt was one of fifteen people killed. Peg MacKenzie was another. David's body lay covered on a shield. Monks passed among battered mourners offering comfort and prayers.

Ten minutes after a young boy walked into the main hall with Triste and her colt. The Douglas arrived with a troop of forty amored men. His usually lithe countenance was vexed.

"'Patrick," he clasped the hand of his old friend. They sat over tasteless ale, and Douglas drew off his helmet. Burghers leaned against the castle walls or lay on soiled blankets.

"This has happened to me," The Douglas said, trying to sympathize. "More than once. And to The Bruce many times. The first is hard. Listen, I've little time. I bring a message and will leave ten men with you. That's all I can spare."

"I don't need your men, Jamie. I can do whatever must be done."

Patrick rubbed sandy eyes with the edges of his hands and watched his prize mare prance. He had thought never to see her again.

"Find a sack of grain below, Locksey," he called. "I'm in your debt."

"Patrick, d'ye mind? I *must* talk to you!"

"I know what you've come to say, Jamie." They left the hall with strides that hinted of calamity yet to come. "I don't care what anyone says," vowed Patrick, "I'll confront the whoreson, damn his miserable soul, then I'll open up his throat."

"Nay, you'll not, Patrick," The Douglas said once they were outside. "The king forbids it. It will start a war, and Comyn knows it. That's why he did it. I know how you feel. This is a subtle political move, not really aimed at you. Or the Englishwoman. Damnation, Patrick, Bruce means it!"

"These people don't need food in their stomachs as much as they need an accounting for the deaths of their kin, Jamie. Until Comyn pays, do you know what they'll do? They'll refuse to plant crops. They won't go to battle. They'll sit here, whipped, and they'll eventually die. They look to me to avenge them. *I have to.*"

"No one sympathizes more than I do." The Douglas sighed. "You're so much like Wallace. Once we had to literally drag him off the battlefield. He would have died because of the injustice of the moment."

Douglas took the blond man's wrist in a tight circle of

thumb and forefinger. "Listen to me. There are other ways. Other ways beside a sword."

Patrick moved to hook his thumbs in his belt and stare far to the north, past the Grampian Mountains.

"I thought of looting their abbey," he confessed. "But gold is too heavy to handle. Even if I buried it, Bruce would still know I did it."

James grinned. "Don't touch an abbot's gold. The Comyns are wealthy, and they're invincibly protected up there in those fastnesses. Calla came to me after a late audience with th' king. I've ridden all night to tell you."

They leaned their weight against gravestones and considered the charred carcass of Warrick, their breaths coming frosty white.

"Don't give me riddles," said Patrick.

"All right, then. Comyn's uncle possesses a fortune in jewels. Calla saw them once. She claims he keeps them in a hidden vault in the chapel. The chapel is an added wing beside the lord's chamber, and it will be almost as difficult t'reach as the castle itself. Calla doesn't know how to actually get to the jewels. Only this: somewhere to the right of the high altar they lie behind the cornerstone."

"Are you sure? How could Calla know a thing like that?"

Douglas grinned. "Patrick, you don't think you were the only man in lovely Calla's bed? For years after she married deMohr, she frequented Comyn castle for weeks at a time."

Patrick pondered, his mind far ahead of Douglas.

"A man could carry jewels," he said at last. "And if it were Comyn's *uncle,* the nephew would be like a cuckold stuck with a bastard child. Unable to talk without looking like a fool."

Patrick's laugh was whipped in the wind, and James chuckled, too.

"Calla is sure they're behind the stone?"

"She's sure. And these are her exact words. 'Tell him

I do this for the Saxon girl. Patrick's a philandering cur!' "

Patrick leaned his head back and smiled. Calla had had no illusions about what he and Christin had done in Stirling Castle.

"*If* I could remove that stone," he mused.

"And *if* you didn't get killed trying to get away."

"Look at them," Patrick flung his arm wide. "Look at my people. And the wretch went to Edward. He has forced Christin into the most ridiculous mess of a marriage. For that alone I should kill him. Did Bruce tell you to have me do this, Jamie?"

"That," chuckled The Douglas, "is something you'll have to ask the king."

Patrick didn't press his friend farther. He knew the king could not openly condone an affront to Comyn, any more than he could give Patrick leave to ravage the Highlands. Traditionally, a feud had laws unto itself; a chieftan such as Comyn was a small king in his own right.

They spoke of Barber's imprisonment. As Patrick suspected, the man refused to speak. But at least his capture had threatened his agents; the killings had stopped.

Three days after Comyn's ravaging assault, bitter wind poured down from the Grampian Mountains. The rites pronounced over the shriven were hearty and blessedly brief.

In Warrick's hall great fires roared, and huge suspended pots simmered with barley gruel. Patrick, drawn with grief, demanded the silence of his people. Because of his intimacy with the king, though he possessed little wealth, he was a powerful man in Scotland. They might blame him for Comyn's vengeance, but they listened with respect.

"We have been dealt a blow," he raised his voice. "This burgh is, from this moment, under martial law. Food will be rationed. Everyone is promised one meal a day, and clothes will be upon every back. The sick are to be kept separate, and any person suffering from so much as a toothache will report to the monks at once."

Patrick braced his fists upon his hips. "We will be living in close quarters for the remainder of this winter. I want no epidemics of flux or fevers sweeping through this camp. Places for bathing will be set up in the laundry room for the women and young children. The men will use the river. See to it."

His posture defied their sullen faces. He would force them to survive.

"We will live off the river. If you have problems, come to me. By my word, the first man who attacks his neighbor or steals so much as a crust of bread will hang."

There wasn't a person in the hall who doubted Patrick's words.

"Gideon." He motioned with a crooked finger and strode to his chamber.

Gideon hobbled up the stairs to Patrick's room where men already pressed for an audience.

"How's the hip?" inquired Warrick's laird.

Patrick closed the door and stripped off his clothes and changed into the remaining garments he hadn't given away. The pale youth tried to smile. Patrick waved him down onto the bed.

"I fear you'll be no good to me. Tell me the truth."

Gideon coughed gently. "Glynnis is in a bad way, sir. Not from the scars she'll have. It's her mind. She stares at her knees for hours without moving. She will hardly let me touch her. She blames . . . Lady Christin."

Patrick doused cold water over his face. "She should blame me, not Christin. Give her another bairn, and you'll see the loss slacken soon enough."

Gideon shifted the bandage on his shoulder as if he weren't so sure. "Mayhap."

"Now, Gideon. When do you think you can ride?"

"Oh, I can ride now, sir. I don't know how good, but I can stay mounted. Why, m'lord?"

"I'm riding to the Highlands tonight."

"What?"

"I'm going to enter into Comyn's castle and make him pay ten times over for what he's done to Christin and this town."

"You're a dead man, m'lord." Gideon whistled and shook his head.

"Don't be so quick to bury me in the Highlands." Patrick lathered his face and frowned at the dull edge of the knife he was using. "I don't need a man who can ride. I will be the bait. All you would have to do is pull in the net."

Patrick turned to gaze down at the tousle-headed young man. Mowbray's eyes were clear, and he spoke his heart, which was rare for him.

"We're a sorry pair, Gideon. Both our women have been hurt by this man. I warrant we have this coming to us."

Gideon found himself unable to swallow down a foreign knot in his throat. He didn't fully understand the implications of the moment, only that Patrick was reaching out to him as an equal—man to man. He stood and cleared his throat.

"Aye, sir," he agreed. "We will do it. Or there will be two dead men in the Highlands."

The younger man's need for revenge was as soul-consuming as Patrick's. It would be personal, sweet and ruthless.

The two men who plowed through the heart of the Grampians were lean and weather-beaten. The air was dull and cold, wet with occasional sleet. But not enough snow fell to make them lose their way. Over a period of years, disappointment had refined their abilities to survive the wild land, and they wound through Lord Atholl's domains without being discovered.

Patrick was mounted on Triste, a calculated part of his strategy, though a risky one. Triste was bred for the fast run, not for clambering about in rough Highland terrain. She balked at filing between towering jaws of two-thousand-foot rock and around foaming cataracts. Patrick's diligence to hold her under control intensified.

One night and day later Gideon threw back his head and gaped at John Comyn's invincible fortress.

"The devil's own folly!" he breathed. "I've never seen anything like it. My lord, you'll never get up there, much less get down alive."

"Only a mad person would try to scale it in this weather." Patrick hunched in his saddle. "That's why the guard will be small and careless."

The castle was a clump of living rock high above their heads. Its tower spread so high it was dizzying. Sheerly cut, in the face of the cliff, a long zigzag of steps mounted the steep incline. Without so much as a rope for guidance, the climb was not for a squeamish man.

Scaling the cliff at night would be impossible, in daylight only barely possible without a rope dropped from above. And, minus the cover of darkness, even if a man mastered his way to the crest, he would face certain death at the hands of guards.

"How can you think of it, m'lord?" mourned Gideon, completely overwhelmed with the hopelessness of it.

"With a few misgivings, Gideon. We'll find a place to rest for the remainder of the day—and make plans."

Not daring a fire, Patrick placed Gideon under a tight jutting of rock and fed the horses. Then he and Gideon huddled together to keep warm and slept for two hours. When they awakened, the skies threatened an early dusk.

As they chewed on dried fish and considered the treachery of the cliff, Patrick pointed.

"What if a man climbed the face of it in daylight and waited on the top steps, out of sight until dark? Then he could go over without being seen."

"You mean, just *stand* there, hugging that rock two hundred feet up?"

Patrick nodded. "Aye."

"No man could do that," Gideon gravely shook his head.

"Perhaps not. But for Christin I'm angry enough to try it. Now, Gideon, I want you to take your horse and hide it well. Go to the base of that last hill. Wait in the ravine until my work is done. When I come back down I will place the jewels . . . here."

Patrick unfolded himself from under the rock and bent over a tree whose heart had been splintered many years past.

"You see?" Patrick reached his hand into the hole and sifted through rich tree-rot. "If they follow me, I'll lure them away. Then you return. Take out the jewels and head for Warrick. Don't get yourself caught. Understand?"

Impatient now to begin, Patrick grinned. "I'll take Triste to a safe place and tie her. Once I'm on horseback, it's up to you, Gideon, whether I make it or not."

Allowing himself an hour before nightfall, Patrick removed his gloves, unwrapped the extra rawhide wound about his boots and shed his bulky leather jacket. Then he filled a bag with fine gravel from the streambed nearby and slung it about his neck.

"If th' fall doesn't kill ye, m'lord, you'll die of frostbite." Gideon rubbed his palms briskly and slapped his arms.

"Keep a keen ear, and don't get addled. I'll be all right."

Patrick held out his hand to the younger man, and Gideon wiped his mouth. "I'll pray," he said.

The face of the cliff seemed to stretch to infinity as Patrick hugged it. He was diligent to not avert his eyes. The crags beneath him yawned like hungry jaws. For thirty minutes he inched upward noiselessly, praying with every breath that he wouldn't find ice on the rocks.

Twice he did, and he tipped the bag about his neck, sifting chance silt everywhere and working his feet into it with care. When he clung two feet from the top, astounded that no strange head bent over the side to thrust him over, he steadied his breath.

For the next half hour, as darkness suspended him

between heaven and earth, Patrick kept perfectly still and felt sweat running down the sides of his body, though the wind was freezing.

When he finally heaved himself over the top, Patrick simply lay there, flat on his stomach, and rested. He thought of Christin, of how she might have been forced to live here if she had married Payne Comyn. Enough of that, he told himself. There was work to do.

After a thorough examination, Patrick decided, that the risk of walking in the rear quarters was unavoidable. The windows were inaccessible, the doors hopeless, and he spotted three guards from where he stood. The woman who shook her mop at the kitchen door was so weary that she hardly lifted her head when he stumbled in.

"Don't ye know better than t'leave a door open, old woman?" he scolded a rude garble of Gaelic and Highland burr, stamping his feet. "Any cur dog could track up th' place."

The kitchen maid grimaced at his back.

"Your muddy feet don't help none," she snorted and slapped down her mop.

Once he was inside Patrick increased his pace. He wouldn't be hanged if he were caught; he would be killed in a slow manner known only by Highlanders.

Shuffling noises from the passages beyond indicated people were up and about. He darted from one wall to another, pausing long moments to listen. Having no idea where the chapel was, he wasted more than an hour looking for it.

The sanctuary was immense. But then, the Comyns had so many sins to confess, Patrick grimaced to himself. A hazy pattern of moonlight splattered on the floor, and he knelt almost reverently before the enormity of the cornerstone. From the wall it jutted out to form the lower dais of the altar. Chipping it free would take the better part of a night.

"Christin," he whispered, wiping sweat from his forehead, "no matter what I said before, I forgive you. Lord, I don't want to die in this place."

The one tool Patrick had allowed himself was a broad-bladed chisel. When he struck the first hammering blow of his knife handle, it echoed like a crack of lightning before thunder. It took him four hours to free the two-foot stone from its cavern. Removing it was an entirely different matter.

Prying his knife between stone and wall served only to snap the steel blade.

"Damn!"

Gouging the jagged edge of the blade into the stone, Patrick braced his back against the altar and heaved with all his strength, until his veins corded and muscles knotted with effort. Over and over he strained until he finally collapsed on his stomach.

"It would ha' been easier t'kill ye, Comyn."

Gradually, after he dislodged it enough to hook his fingers over the edges, the stone moved. It finally scraped across the floor with a grievous complaint, leaving ragged craters in the timber.

Kneeling before the black hole, Patrick was surprised to find no corresponding wall on the other side. Obviously he faced a passageway running behind the altar itself, down into the interior of the underground chambers. After removing a candle from the altar he slithered along on his belly. Shortly before dawn he discovered, not only the other entrance from the sacristy interior but six containers of varying shapes as well.

Several casks contained gold, and for a few seconds he was tempted to devise a way of stealing it.

"Dolt!" he scolded himself and pried open the remaining container.

The old cask containing the jewels was endlessly more than Calla's word had led Patrick to expect. Awed, he rummaged through its contents. Most of the jewels were set in pendants, with rings and jewels for the ears. A few were stones removed from their settings; a large handful were uncut rubies, some smaller diamonds and a half dozen large emeralds.

Here was more wealth than the whole crown of

Scotland possessed. "This, Chrissy," he said, holding the most splended emerald by its chain, "is for you."

The sleeping hounds which blocked the kitchen doors constituted Patrick's newest hazard. They would crash the entire castle down on his head if he tried to slip past. His decision to go through a high window wasn't made a moment too soon. One of the dogs bayed a warning, and sleepy feet stumbled past as Patrick held his breath and flattened against a wall.

With one sharp blow, he struck the glass with his knife. The tinkle sounded enormous. Again he struck. And again.

Ignoring the shards of glass which stabbed through his trews, Patrick heaved himself through and dropped the nine feet to the ground. For one moment he feared he had broken his ankles as he struck hard on his feet and rolled over.

Making sure he still had the jewels in his shirt, Patrick picked himself up and sprinted for the cliff. Harsh voices came from nowhere. He ran headlong into a burly man as tall as he was. The guard was so surprised that Patrick's blow to his stomach doubled him.

Once Patrick was at the mercy of the cliff, he forced thoughts of jewels, of Gideon, Christin, and everything else from his mind. Men yelled at him, and he glimpsed a Highlander climbing hand over hand down a rope.

By the time he was two-thirds down, the descending guard began sweeping toward him in huge, swinging arcs, attempting to kick him. Patrick's fingers fumbled for the bag of gravel around his neck. Not daring to move, he loosened it with his teeth, filled one hand, and dropped the bag fifty feet below him. He would only have one chance.

When the Highlander made his next sweep, cursing him in violent Gaelic, Patrick settled his feet, counted three seconds, and threw blindly. As the bits of stone caught the man in his face, he cried out in disbelief.

He struck the bottom of the cliff like a soft thump on a fat pillow, hardly audible at all.

Six feet from the bottom, shaking so badly he could hardly hold on, Patrick jumped. For a full ten seconds he stared at the gray-blue dawn.

I'm alive, he thought with wonder.

Crawling on all fours, he buried the pouches of jewels in the rotted tree soil, knowing Gideon was watching from somewhere. He counted six men halfway down the cliff. Still hurting from his fall, Patrick sprinted for Triste. They spotted him. He knew horses would be hobbled in this cove.

Triste's descent was steep, tearing great long strides down the hillside. Against the skyline were shouting men. Patrick swept his broadsword from its sheath on his saddle as four men approached from his right. The momentum of his horse plunged them forward, with Triste sliding, almost sitting on her haunches at times.

Patrick stood high in his stirrups. Left and right he swung, unhorsing two men with his first blow. Once they reached enough flat terrain for Triste to take her head, they would have a chance at least. But the animal was terrified by the clamor and biting steel. It took nearly all Patrick's strength to hold her.

A third man bore down on him, and Patrick took a blow to his shoulder that numbed his whole arm. Standing as high as he could, seeking the warrior's chest, Patrick heaved his weapon like a spear. It found its mark.

Patrick slumped to cradle his arm to his chest. When he groped inside his sleeve with his right hand, it withdrew soaked with blood.

With no hand on her reins, Triste took her head. She dodged clumps of rock and most of the branches. A few caught Patrick's head, but Triste strained her great heart and skidded to the bottom of the last hill. A good five miles of winding moorland lay beyond them. Patrick heaved a sigh of relief as he felt her stride lengthen.

Patrick had not misjudged his stakes when he gambled. Triste gobbled up the miles with a magnificence that no Border mount could match. Birch trees soon folded the pair into their arms, and from there it was only a matter of clever wits and patience.

At nightfall, Patrick stopped to pad his shoulder and button on the leather jacket from behind his saddle. Weak, half-freezing, he ate enough to keep him in the saddle all night. He was a Borderer, toughened to this brand of misery. But at this moment, gazing at stars in a cold sky and feeling blood trickle down his side, Patrick wished terribly that he could lay his cheek on Christin's breast and go to sleep.

As Lent ended, so did the Yorkshire winter. Early wheat grassed numerous fields, some for sheep grazing, some for harvesting. The Hartleys and the Winchelseas both planned to celebrate Easter in Edwin's chapel at Erskill.

Christin moved heavily with Patrick's child these days. Once Easter was past, Edwin insisted, she must begin her confinement. And to make sure she did, the guest chambers were prepared for her. Christin had wearied so of the stairs that she moved in at once.

At the end of Holy Week, Christin's eye found the sight surrounding her to be perfect. Except that Patrick was separated from her by the everlasting Border. On the floor, Johnnie and Sissy argued over chess. Margaret stitched baby blankets and embroidered an elaborate "P" on a corner of each. Edwin and Richard invariably compared points of history and debated upon the possibilities of the truce.

"Robert Bruce," Edwin said, pausing to cough into a handkerchief, "has one of the most practical political heads I've seen since the early days of Edward the First. Scotland could easily have found itself at civil war over the Comyn disturbance. I despair of what would have resulted had that been Edward the Second and one of his English earls."

"Personally," Richard nodded, leaning to advise his son of a chess move that drew squeals of protest from

253

Sissy, "I think Parliament should force Edward to acknowledge the inevitable. England should withdraw its claims to suzerainty. Scotland has earned it, and this war is costing us a fortune."

Thinking she couldn't possibly bear talk about Scotland, Christin said, "Did Edwin tell you he's teaching me to read Latin?"

She arose to move about the room, bending to speak to the children, seeing that chairs were comfortable and refreshments were near at hand. Richard trailed behind her and watched her pause to span her hands against her spine.

"Will you *please* sit, Christin? I can do that."

He practically forced her down into a chair and scooped up her feet. With a foot, he pushed a stool beneath them.

Edwin had afforded his wife a magnificent wardrobe, and Christin had been careful in her choice of colors, as her hair seemed to better compliment greens and blues and black. But she hadn't gained as much weight as they all thought necessary. She had lost weight, and she wore her hair up, which only made her appear more frail with her slender neck and shoulders.

Even though Christin looked lovely and she spoke cheerfully, her hands were never still. Margaret confided to Richard under her breath that if Christin were ever caught without something to keep her fingers busy, she would shatter into a dozen pieces.

"Christin, the way you attack with that needle, it's a wonder you don't wound yourself," she chided. "Must you spend every waking moment doing something?"

An intensity flamed Christin's cheeks scarlet. She dropped her eyes, taking small swift stitches. "If I don't keep busy, I think about things." She didn't say she thought about Patrick, nor did she miss Margaret's change in breathing. "And if I let myself think about things," she mumbled softly, hoping no one would overhear, "I will go mad."

The winter months hadn't been good for Edwin. He

tired very easily. These days, he coughed almost incessantly at times. When it rained, Christin hardly saw him without a fresh handkerchief in his hand.

Turning so she couldn't see Christin intimately bending over the back of Edwin's chair, Margaret stretched her sewing thread taut and studied her needle. The familiar sight of Christin's slender hand reaching for his arm, and the solemn manner in which Edwin's eyes sought hers, were too poignant. Margaret sighed grimly and returned to her stitching.

"You'll excuse us, won't you?" Christin smiled. "I'll be back in a few minutes. Johnnie, one of Edwin's friends brought him some lovely sketches of foxes. They're on his desk."

"Thank you," the lad grinned and fidgeted in his clothes. He was outgrowing his jacket.

"Do you see how careful she is with Edwin?" Margaret asked her husband the moment the door shut. "It breaks my heart."

"Don't stand so close to the fire. And yes, I think she's being wonderful about the whole thing. William says she's cheerful and doesn't complain. She's even refused to go to Cornwall, saying she doesn't care if everyone in Miron believes this is Edwin's baby."

"Richard!"

Margaret's eyes warned him to guard his talk in front of the children, but Johnnie glanced at his mother with a knowing rebuke.

"Little enough do you men know," Margaret scolded. "Can't you see the nose on your face? Christin is making herself sick, smile or no smile. If you ask me, she's pining for Patrick. There, I said it, and I could wring his neck."

Edwin allowed Christin to take his arm, and he chuckled as she walked him to his room.

"We make a pair, don't we Christin, girl?"

"Faugh! My aches and pains will be over in a few weeks, Edwin. It's that cough I don't like the sound of.

What you could do with is a bit of hot summer sun. Do you think we should have gone to Cornwall after all?"

"I'm fine, dear. One learns to accept the inconveniences and label everything 'old age.' "

But Edwin didn't resist when Christin helped him into his chair and summoned John to prepare him for bed. Moments later, when she returned with a cup of warm herb tea, Edwin was propped up with four pillows.

"This room is drafty," Christin complained, frowning at the stone walls. "We should hang it with tapestries." Edwin coughed and motioned her to his side.

"You miss your young Scot, don't you?" he asked bluntly.

He caught her off guard, and she bumped against his bed. "Oh, I'm sorry," she said and nervously smoothed her hair back off her forehead.

"I'm trying to grow up a little, sir." Christin lifted her head honestly, still not looking at her husband's eyes. "I think life is a matter of learning not to fight things. It takes so much energy to fight." She twisted her mouth out of shape and shrugged. "Well, I say that with my mind, but I don't think my heart knows it yet. In that respect I still do fight. Many things, I suppose."

"You have it all wrong, Christin. Life *is* fighting. Not scolding or fretting, but fighting. Even now, I still fight."

"You?" She shook her head. "What do you have to fight about?"

"Ahh," Edwin leaned his head back and closed his eyes as he spoke. "I fight the anger of getting old. I fight to see my country freed of this war. And narrow minds that can't let people do things a different way. Aye, time is against me on that, I warrant. People are very slow to learn."

His sigh was heavy and pessimistic. For a few seconds Christin thought he was falling asleep. Carefully, she lifted his arms and placed them over his chest. As she drew the cover to his shoulders, she stopped, quite suddenly, and stared down at the handkerchief folded in

Edwin's palm. Unmistakable flecks of blood darkened its stark whiteness.

Her brain rebelled. No, she reasoned, there were many reasons for a bit of blood upon a handkerchief. Edwin would tell her if something—or would he? Edwin was such a private, honorable man.

Before Edwin suspected what she had seen, Christin nestled the comforter beneath his chin, and he opened his eyes. Their wise depth of experience disguised their fading age. She smiled and kissed his forehead.

"You go to sleep, now. I'll play the gracious lady without you. I may even be brave enough to read a bit of Latin. See, I'm not so grown-up that I don't enjoy showing off!"

"You're a comfort to me, girl. I thank God for you," he said and closed his eyes again.

As Christin returned to her guests, she grew acutely aware of the injustices in her life. She was sorry that she could not fall in love with her husband.

Over the years, Christin had learned that whenever Richard had something on his mind, he laced his hands behind his back and pondered the ceiling. He did it now, and when he finally stooped, hesitantly kneeling beside her chair, she lowered her knitting. She first looked at Margaret, then back to Richard.

"What's the matter?"

"Nothing's the matter, Chris," protested Richard. "I have something for you that Friar John gave me. I was just waiting for the right time, that's all."

Once again, Christin studied her sister. "Do you know anything about this, Margaret? *Has something happened to Patrick?*"

"No! Of a mercy, Christin, I don't even know what he's talking about. Why didn't you tell me this, Richard?"

"Because it's a letter. Christin has a right to see it first. It's not sealed, Christin, and I must admit I know what it contains, but I didn't read the letter. You know I wouldn't do that."

257

"Give it to me."

Fishing about in his pocket, Richard withdrew a well-handled fold of paper, a thick one. He placed it in her lap, upon her pile of knitting. Christin haltingly began to peel back its edges, as if she dreaded what she would find. Within the letter itself was enclosed a smaller fold of paper. The letter was from Patrick, for Christin glanced at once to the signature scrawled at the bottom of the paper.

Swiftly she flipped it face down, moistened her dry lips, and opened the remaining packet.

"Oh!"

She lifted out a chain of gold with a single emerald the size of her thumb, in the shape of a tiny egg.

"Oh, Mama," breathed nine-year-old Sissy, tiptoeing to peer at it. "Isn't it beautiful? Who sent it to you, Auntie Chris?"

"A friend, sweetheart. A friend I met in Scotland. Yes, it is lovely."

The chain threaded itself intimately through her fingers as if it were a mysterious part of him reaching to touch her. Closing her hand upon it so tightly her knuckles whitened, she bit her bottom lip hard. Her smile hurt her face.

"Do you mind if I read the letter in my own room?" she whispered huskily. "I won't be but a minute."

Margaret reached over to smooth back an unruly wisp of hair.

"Of course. Take all the time you need."

Even shutting the chamber door didn't separate Christin from them enough. She sagged back against the wall of the corridor. Her loyalties were so torn between Erskill and Warrick that she felt ripped apart sometimes. When Robert Bruce took a force of men into the Highlands, her own helplessness sickened her. At times she wished that Richard didn't have such reliable sources of information.

How could Patrick have written her after telling her

258

he hated her? How could he ask her to examine all the love and pain again?

She was so upset to find Tildy preparing her room for the night, Christin stammered a ridiculous errand for the woman to attend to downstairs. Then, drawing a footstool beside the fire, Christin sat, rigidly unable to relax. When she could breathe again, she turned the paper to the light.

His handwriting was bold, like everything else about him—the way he walked up behind her and cupped his hands about her breasts, the way he laughed and grabbed her when she bent over. Wiping her sweating hands on her skirt, she began to read.

Christin, I have never given you anything. I wouldn't have this, except I stole it. But then, you already know I am a thief. I once stole you. And then you stole part of me, which is where all my troubles began. I hope you are happy. I am doing better, now. There are some nights I can sleep through without waking up to think about you. Gideon and Glynnis lost their baby, but I think they started a new one. I would like to have a word when our bairn is born. I hear that Edward has increased the price on my head since I went into the Highlands. That makes me an extremely valuable father.

Patrick

For some minutes Christin tried to stop the tears, but they dropped on the swell of their baby. Patrick was hurting for her.

"Oh, Patrick," she whispered and cradled the clear green stone in the nest of her palm. "Did you send this to make me sorrier than I already am?"

The rules choked her sometimes—rules of how to live, how to dress, whom to marry, which king to obey. How could rules be good which gave people the right to make judgments on a man's soul? Or to baptize or not to baptize his children?

"What did he say?" Margaret demanded upon her return.

Drawing the chain from beneath her collar, Christin smiled. "He said he stole it."

Richard laughed heartily. "From Comyn. How fitting."

"Richard!" his wife scowled.

"Stealing is not always stealing." Then Richard told them of Payne Comyn's attack upon Warrick and Patrick's looting.

"Payne will only hate him more," sighed Christin. "In the end, Patrick will be such a burden to the king that even The Bruce will wish him gone."

"Little chance of that," laughed her brother-in-law, smoothing his jaw. "A good portion of that theft went to the crown and Bruce deserved to receive it. The Bruce's jaunt north warned Comyn he'd better take his losses and keep still."

"Richard will you stop with all this war talk? We've all heard it before." Margaret pushed her sister into a chair.

Christin's shoulders drooped and she toyed nervously with the jewel at her throat.

"Here, darling, sip a little wine and try not to think of it now. Patrick's all right. He lived through it, and Father John told Richard that as soon as the winter breaks, the town will begin rebuilding."

Christin shook tears off her face.

"I don't see how Patrick keeps getting away with things like this. One day someone will kill him. What will I do, Margaret, when somebody kills him?"

Chapter Twelve

The last four weeks of Christin's pregnancy were a concern to the entire household. At nights when the unborn baby kicked so hard she couldn't sleep, she arose and paced the floor with an aching back. In the wee hours, Tildy, who slept in her room now, brought hot herb tea to make her rest. But she couldn't.

Only with Tildy did Christin lose her composure enough to reveal the contents of her heart.

"Why is it Patrick I despise, Tildy? He's the father of this child. For Edwin I feel patience, and I would bear anything. I try not to complain or let him see me look grumpy. But if Patrick were here, I think I could strangle him."

"Someone should've strangled him long ago."

"You used to take up for him!"

"That was before he—Someone should've gelded him before he got you in this condition. Go back t'bed, dearie."

During the last plodding days Christin's guilt about marrying Edwin began to tell. She confessed it over and over, expressing her sorrow of using another human being to share in her own mistakes. Father Donney was powerless to comfort her at all.

Often she slipped into Edwin's room at night. He

261

slept little more than she did. Though he dressed every day, carrying on his appointments in a routine fashion with those who sought his counsel, his nights were a different matter.

"Please forgive me, sir," Christin often said as she sat on the edge of his bed and held the unsteady pulse of his wrist to her lips. "I don't mean to be so difficult. I really don't."

"A little longer, Christin. Once the babe comes, everything will be different."

"Mama had difficult births. Do you think I'll die, Edwin?"

He shook his head. "I know little of those matters, my dear. All I can remember is your father's grief. It was such a bleak despair. I could hardly bear to watch him."

Tildy found Christin, one rainy afternoon, heaving herself up and down the turret stairs.

"Lord have mercy—what are you doin', child? D'you want to kill yourself?"

"I want this baby to come!" Christin blurted. "It should be coming, and it's not. Look at Triste. I was with her when she foaled. She walked, Tildy. To the very last, she walked."

"But you're not a horse, my lady."

"Well, I feel like one," Christin wept, her grief not that she was quitting the stairs, but the bittersweetness of one of her fondest memories.

"It's those horrible raids. Sir Richard should never have told you anything about them." Tildy pushed Christin into a chair and placed a cup of ineffectual tea into her hand.

Richard brought news of the first spring raids himself. They decided to picnic by the river, a short excursion on a beautiful day. It might be her last chance before the baby came, Christin said.

Never, in the history of the warfare between the two nations, had Scotland struck the northern counties so savagely, Richard reported. They walked slowly along the grassy river bank as he described huge raiding parties that swept over one hundred miles deep into England.

Patrick's name was closely linked with The Douglas and Thomas Randolph. Randolph, England cried out in offense, had sworn fealty to England. But he was Robert Bruce's own nephew, the lord of Nithsdale. Once the young man had been captured from Edward's ranks and converted to the Scots cause, his daring escapades were as notorious as Patrick's.

"For five years we've not seen the likes of this!"

Richard and Laurence strolled back toward Erskill with Margaret and Christin, while William and Edwin took advantage of the spring morning to examine the orchards. As May sunshine popped the blooms wide, the older men remembered, to the number, the years in which a freakish frost killed all the fruit.

"The prior of Irthing reports one thousand raiders, superbly mounted," Laurence announced. "He said Thomas Randolph and Patrick rode into Lanercost and took a fortune in gold, silver and jewels from the abbey."

"Oh, Jesu!" Christin bent to hold her belly, as if she could prevent the unborn child from hearing such things of its father. "It's because of me. He takes his anger out on the valley of Irthing because I married Edwin. If I had gone to Scotland and lived in sin with him, none of this would be happening!"

"Don't be silly, Christin," scolded Margaret. "Laurence, did you have to tell her all that just now? Can't you see what it does to her to hear about Patrick?"

"I think she's right," Laurence defended his position with an angry flush. "In less than two hours, everything at Lanercost was destroyed. They broke down the masonry, trampled the gardens and orchards and slaughtered every living beast."

"Not the abbey!" For once, Christin made no attempt to hide her tears. "Patrick wouldn't burn an abbey!"

She leaned on the drawbridge and grasped its rusty

chain. She grew more impatient with her twin by the minute.

"You forgot to say what Edward's high-and-mighty Clifton did, Laurence. Be fair, at least. He destroyed three of Bruce's towns. And he didn't spare the women, or the children."

Richard swept her up in his arms, striding rapidly through the main hall.

"Richard, Patrick didn't . . . they . . . not the women?"

Richard bent his head. "He spared the abbey, Chris. As far as I know, none of the townspeople was killed. A few men, only, who fought them. Damn Laurence's stupid thick head!"

After he set Christin on her feet, Margaret drew her down on a bench. Christin's throat thickened. Because she loved Patrick, the hatred he bore crushed her, too. If he cared about her, he wouldn't subject her to this!

"Tell me everything, Richard," she choked. "I want to know it all."

"I myself spoke with the abbot, yesterday. I actually rode up there hoping to find Patrick, but the camp had moved on. The abbot was calling down every curse heaven had to offer, but he had to admit that the Scots were ordered by their own captains, under penalty of death, to not touch a single innocent."

"What kind of a child do I carry?" Christin touched her distended belly with pitying fingers. "Tell me, Margaret; if it's a boy, will he follow in the ways of his father?"

"You've been listening to Tildy again—that old witch! I'll have her neck if she doesn't stop filling your head with such nonsense!"

"Well"—Richard made a sound between his teeth—"one really can't blame the Scots all that much. After all, much of Lanercost's wealth was taken from Scotland to begin with. If Rome would simply admit that Bruce is king, the raiders would go home and everyone could live in peace."

"Fools! You think that The Black Douglas will honor

a peace treaty?" cried Laurence. "One week and he'd be back over the Border. Royal freebooters!"

"Rome! Scotland! Bruce, Edward! I can't stand anymore. I'm going to bed." Christin heaved herself up and leaned heavily against the table.

Once she was in her room, she refused to sit, lacing her hands at the small of her back and pacing the length of the long chamber. With the instinct of a wild creature, she knew her time was near. Back and forth she dragged herself.

"I'm sending for some valerian," Margaret declared. "I've heard Mama took it to help me along. And pennyroyal, too."

"You must go to bed, my lady," Tildy frowned.

"Leave me alone," Christin replied wearily.

Margaret and Tildy exchanged helpless glances, and Tildy knowingly gathered the supplies she had placed away weeks ago. The men exchanged resigned shrugs in the hall, mumbling things about "a woman's time." Margaret told everyone they might as well prepare themselves for a long wait.

Christin dutifully sipped her tea and visualized Patrick with his leather helmet in place, seated on his horse and issuing orders for ropes to tear down monuments and for huge blades to slash art masterpieces.

Tildy wasn't surprised when Christin's labor began slowly. Long after water had streamed down her legs, bringing tears of helpless frustration, her contractions began—spasmodically, accomplishing little.

"I expected this," clucked the faithful maid, shaking her head the next morning at Christin's exhaustion. "It's th' strain the poor thing's been under. 'Twouldn't be half so bad if th' scoundrel was here by her side where he belongs."

The two women were aproned. They had had things in readiness for hours. Occasionally Christin moaned softly from her bed, her skin dry, her lips beginning to peel.

Margaret, eyeing Tildy sharply, pinched her lower

lip between her fingers as she considered. Her decision was abrupt. Without speaking, she swept from the room.

"Richard, I want to talk to you." She pulled him from the table where the men sat with their legs crossed and frowns on their faces, their eyes intently studying the swirl of ale in large flagons.

"What's wrong?" he asked, allowing himself to be drawn from the hearing of the others.

"First of all, put Edwin to bed. He looks terrible. Christin's suffering far more than she should, Richard. I know it's a first baby and all that. But I was thinking —really, it was Tildy thinking—perhaps if Patrick were here, things would go easier for her. I know I do much better when you're sitting by my bed."

Margaret watched her husband straighten and smooth his belt as he turned the possibilities over in his mind. "She swears that she never wants to see Patrick again as long as she lives," he protested.

"That's only bitter war talk."

"Damnation, Maggie! What about Edwin? I can't say, 'I want to bring Christin's lover into this place.' That's immoral!"

"Immoral or not, I say Edwin cares about Christin's well-being more than gossip. Miron hasn't exactly held its collective tongue about this situation, you know."

Rubbing at his jaw, Richard squinted at her logic.

"Patrick wouldn't have to do anything except sit by her. And speak to her." Margaret pleaded her case. "Christin's certain the man hates her. I think inside her head somewhere she's fighting even having this baby. I could slap Patrick's face for ever telling her such a lie."

"I don't know. These raiders don't stay in one place long enough. Granted, this is an awfully large party. They're probably camped somewhere. But that doesn't mean I can get there before they move."

"Send Creagen to look. What can it do except cost the man a few hours of riding?"

*   *   *

Edwin answered Richard's knock himself, leaning on his cane, his handkerchief crumpled in his hand. He coughed and covered his mouth.

"William," he said, for Richard insisted that William accompany him to Edwin's rooms, not at all certain that Margaret's request was wise.

If Edwin was appalled at Margaret's request, he never allowed it to show. With a wave of his finger, he motioned them to be seated.

"Times are changing, aren't they?" Edwin smiled. His eyes were calm but almost drained of vitality.

"My daughter knew what she was doing," said William. "I don't excuse it, but I do understand it. However, I understand your position too, Edwin. And, then there's Laurence. His own guilt devours him. If he were to come face-to-face with the man, I don't know . . ."

"It all may be a moot point, gentlemen." Edwin blotted his mouth. "Your man may not be able to even find the Scot. But if we do intend to try, there's no time to waste. Do what you will about Mowbray. I wish only to see the baby born and Christin at rest."

Richard bowed, wondering as he did so if anyone had ever truly appreciated this old man. "Your understanding amazes me, Lord Penmark," he said. "Thank you."

Creagen, because of his size, tethered a large relief horse and left within the quarter hour. Greystone Manor knew that Lady Penmark was in travail with her first-born child, and half the staff was at Erskill making preparations for a celebration the minute it was born. When he clattered across the bridge those who knew the truth of Christin's baby glanced at those who only guessed. They had never thought to see the day a Scot would be welcome within these walls!

Patrick Mowbray was not on the Scottish side of the Border, as Margaret had said he probably was. He was with Robert Bruce in Durham, destroying South Tyne with the same systematic thoroughness of William Wallace's early campaigns. Newcastle, Creagen learned after several inquiries, had seen the Scots from a distance. But Newcastle was so strongly fortified that the invaders had chosen not to attack.

Creagen galloped swiftly, enjoying the evening mist wetting his face and satisfied with the thudding of rhythmic hooves beneath him. He didn't often get the chance to ride. The camp shouldn't be much father. He swept his gaze across a blood-red horizon which had burned for a night and a day. The sight was frightening, even to Creagen.

Escaping victims filled the narrow roads, making the thoroughfares practically impassable at times. They were more than eager to describe where the accursed marauders had last been seen.

Finding the Scots camp was easy; getting near enough to speak to Patrick would be almost impossible, Creagen thought when he rode near the tents stretching in all directions. Corbridge was less than a mile away.

Slowly then, from all sides, a cluster of men approached him, looking like anything but an organized fighting force. Some had not unblackened their faces, and they stank of acrid burning. In a few short minutes, Creagen was surrounded.

The Scots could easily have killed him, and at one point he feared they would. At the mention of Patrick's name, however, the surly men grew more prudent. With shoulders which drooped at the oft-repeated ritual, they escorted Creagen into the camp.

"Dismount," he was told curtly. "And wait here."

Scot heads bent, discussing the Englishman's presence loud enough so he could hear it. From the corner of his eye, Creagen saw one man lift his head and flick his gaze up and down. The smith stared straight ahead and said nothing.

Patrick emerged, surrounded by laughing men who all spoke at one time. At the sight of a stranger in the camp, they stopped. The tall blond man was grimy and blood-stained. His hands were unwashed.

"Creagen?" Almost as an afterthought, Patrick dismissed his men. "Have you ever been in a camp of war before?" he asked as he shook Creagen's hand.

"No, m'lord," he admitted. Creagen took one suspicious glance, to make sure the Scots weren't following, and ducked low under the flap of the tent. Inside, one small table was cluttered with maps of England, weighed down with a short-handled ax. A spluttering lamp of melting fat and a wick was the only light. It stank.

"I'll say what I come to say, sir."

"You always do, Creagen," Patrick quirked a humorous eyebrow.

"It's Lady Christin, sir."

The grimness that drew Patrick's face amazed Creagen. Putting up a hand to silence his efforts to explain, Patrick stepped to the outside, called to a young man with an order that made no sense to Creagen, and returned. Patrick poured a pan of water and began washing his hands.

"What about Christin?"

"Her time is upon 'er, m'lord. Things aren't good. Sir Richard and Lord Penmark sent me t'find you."

"Me?"

Patrick's surprise wasn't in the least pretended. Creagen almost asked him if he wouldn't sit down.

"I haven't slept in nearly two days," Patrick offered the excuse, as if it were a reason for his paleness.

"It's a four-hour ride to Erskill. A hard four hours," Creagen informed him generously.

Patrick smiled. He knew exactly how many hours' ride it was.

"She must be very bad for Penmark to do this."

"Aye."

Patrick's fist slammed the table, and water sloshed on the maps. He shook his head as he wiped it off. "I can elude a king who amuses himself by trying to kill me. I can ride into England and . . . do this." He flung the towel in a great arc. "Yet I can't keep her from suffering."

"No, sir."

Working the shoulder which still hurt from his wound at Comyn's castle, Patrick pondered for a few vexed minutes.

"I'll be right back," he assured the smith. "Have something to eat while I'm gone."

Creagen did that gladly enough, though he wasn't sure what he was eating. Within fifteen minutes Patrick returned, having trimmed his beard and changed into a surprisingly fashionable suit becoming any traveling Englishman. Its color was deep blue, and Patrick grimaced at the hat with its feather before he irritably jerked it over his curls. Creagen knew better than to smile.

"Thank you for coming, m'lord."

"Don't thank me yet. This may cost me more than the war."

Even as Patrick rode the forty miles to Erskill Castle, the Scots broke camp and pulled back nearer to Berwick. Though The Bruce thought it unlikely, he couldn't chance Edward's massing a large enough force to strike his flank.

As he and Creagen clattered across Erskill's lowered bridge only a few minutes before midnight, Patrick guessed that this was one of the most difficult things he had ever been asked to do. His disadvantage at showing himself so openly was extremely dangerous.

Never had Patrick's life encountered an absolute defeat—one that he could not cope with or force to bend in some retribution. It had never occurred to him that Christin would bring him to that point. But this woman, whom he loved and who was now threatened with the same early death as her mother, was as impossible to control as the wind that whipped his face.

Everyone in the Erskill hall, who wasn't in bed, knew who Patrick was when he entered with Creagen. Patrick's strides were long and brusquely defiant as he strode through heavy gates and beneath the portcullis which could trap him, if Edwin played false.

Some distance away, near the wing where Christin

lay, Edwin Penmark moved to greet him. They had been waiting for him. Patrick's fingers curled about his swordhilt, for he instinctively knew who Edwin was, so meticulously dressed, carrying his years with such weary grace. Richard, too, approached, his hands outstretched in a manner which Patrick found relieving.

"I expected it would take you longer, my friend," said Richard.

Patrick looked past him, searching for some evidence of Christin's whereabouts.

"No, it's not been born yet," Richard answered the unspoken question.

Patrick hardly heard himself being presented to Edwin Penmark as his mind clicked off mental escape routes. As a vague afterthought, he bowed to Christin's husband, growing aware of Richard's scowl at his rudeness.

"Forgive me," he said lamely. "From habit I fancy my blood's remaining in my body. Where is Laurence Winchelsea?"

"Cleverly plied with spirits and put to bed," laughed his host.

At the man's subtle tone, Patrick's wits started. He measured Edwin with a spy's instinct. Could it be, Patrick wondered, that he sensed covert alliance here?

From a side doorway, then, appeared the one man Patrick dreaded facing more than the English king: William Winchelsea. The stooped man walked slowly. The nearer he drew, the more alert Patrick became to his thinly controlled outrage. The old gentleman was perilously proud. At the sight of him Patrick understood the Winchelsea children. Like some cornered young culprit, Patrick ground his jaw and inclined his head.

"The circumstances should be far better, sir," he muttered. The Scot's years of defying authority made him sound impossibly arrogant.

"If my daughter weren't fighting so hard to bear this child, sir," William drew himself up, touching his chest lightly, "I would deliver your head to Edward myself."

"Threats have never done much to frighten me, Lord Winchelsea."

"Then perhaps fatherhood will, by God!"

Patrick's lips thinned with embarrassed rage. Penmark shifted his weight, his face a turmoil. Tapping the same discretion he displayed with Payne Comyn, and accepting the public defeat he swore to himself he did not deserve, Patrick forced himself to stand corrected.

"You have every right to wish me dead. Unfortunately, sir, I am not. And I wish very much to see your daughter."

Edwin Penmark came gallantly to his rescue. "The young man's presence speaks for his sincerity, William. I'm sure it will be all right."

"In my day," William thrust at the Scot in a parting riposte, "only blood would pay for a crime so foul."

Patrick's temper exploded, but he spoke quietly, with deadly control.

"Must we wait then, Lord Winchelsea, for a generation of you to die before men learn their own petty problems are not the single point to which every compass turns?"

"Patrick!" Richard snapped, jerking him away before William lifted his hand in affront. Even Edwin's scholarly cordiality could not let such an insult pass without comment.

"You are a guest in my house, Sir Mowbray. For the sake of the innocent, I suggest we sheathe personal prides."

He didn't threaten Patrick with being refused his seeing Christin, but the tall Borderer knew that his insolence would cost him that privilege. Again, he yielded.

"I will repay courtesy with courtesy, my lord."

Edwin seemed reconciled to even that much of an acquiescence and drew William tactfully to the opposite side of the hall. No one followed Patrick and Richard to Edwin's ground chambers. Richard was furious.

"I expected better of you than *that*, Patrick!"

Lustily, and a little angry at his own behavior, Patrick

swore. "I have English blood on my hands, Richard. What would you have of me?"

"Compassion for the helpless. God help you, if you hurt this girl."

"I'll not hurt her. I've never meant to hurt her."

When Patrick entered Christin's room, he moved past an open-mouthed Tildy and a woman he guessed to be Richard's wife, Margaret. But if he expected to be given privacy with Christin, he miscalculated. Tildy withdrew gladly, for she still feared Patrick; but Margaret took up her sewing and, after a subdued nod, settled herself in a corner of the room.

At a glance, Patrick saw soaked bedclothes twisted in great knots. He was stunned, and the smoldering anger drained from his whole body as he stooped over Christin.

She looked terrible—her eyes deep and her skin gray, as if she were dead already. When he softly spoke her name, her eyes fluttered open. Finally, she focused upon his curly blond head above her and felt the weight of his body easing to the bed as he sat. She began to cry.

"Oh, Chrissy, sweet," he groaned, his face hovering so near that she reached to touch his beard. "My sweet, sweet lassie."

"Patrick?" Her voice was so cracked and dry she could hardly say his name. "Oh, Patrick, it hurts so bad."

Slipping his arm beneath her neck, Patrick cradled Christin in his arms and held her to his chest. He forgot Margaret and rocked Christin, whispering soft, shushing sounds into her hair, the wetness of his tears upon her cheeks.

"Don't cry," she whispered. "Don't cry. It will be—"

Christin's nails dug hard into the leather of his jacket, and she pulled against him with such strength that Patrick's eyes darted to Margaret's, pleading for something he couldn't possibly know. Margaret flew to the bedside and tried once to unclench Christin's hands from around Patrick. But it was hopeless. Christin buried her face against his waist and muffled her scream.

"If she could try to help, Patrick," said Margaret. "She's so tired that she just can't try anymore."

"Yes she can," Patrick's eyes flared with the first real terror he had ever felt in his life. "Please, Chrissy, for me. Have this baby for me, sweet girl."

"Stay with me!" Christin struggled to control herself. Promise . . . *don't leave me.*"

As if he would keep the life in her body, Patrick slipped behind her back and wrapped his arms so she could hold tightly to his hands. Margaret was busy doing something to help Christin, but he couldn't bear to watch. He wasn't even aware that he was whispering that he loved her—over and over—leaning his face against the side of her head.

"Tildy!" Margaret cried. "Come quickly!"

Christin shifted her position, twisting in her efforts to bear an unwilling baby, but when Patrick tried to draw away, fearing he was more in the way than helping, she clawed at him, begging him not to leave her.

"Help me," she wept.

And there was nothing he could do but accept the pain of her fingers crushing his—for hours, it seemed.

Margaret kept repeating things for Christin to do, with Patrick only half-aware. The birthing was among the three women. He held her, but he was not part of it.

"It's coming, Christin," said Margaret.

Patrick closed his eyes and wrapped Christin's arms around his bent knee and braced himself. Christin hugged his thigh as if it were a mast in the midst of some terrible storm. He never dreamed a woman could possess such strength. Memories of the afternoon he and Christin had helped Triste birth her foal came flooding back, and he felt ashamed that he could not be her strength as she had been his strength.

When the infant cried the first squeaking sound, Patrick blinked. Christin lay limply in his lap. For a moment he feared she was dead. He didn't cast the first glance at the baby.

"Chris," he mourned, smoothing strands of wet hair

back from her forehead. "Oh, Christin, I'm sorry. I'm sorry, lassie."

Without opening her eyes, Christin smiled palely and lifted one floppy hand toward him. Caring nothing of how much he exposed his human frailty before these women, Patrick caught the slender hand to his lips.

"I love you," he whispered into her palm and held it to his cheek.

Christin opened her eyes—gray eyes which miraculously came back to life, truly *seeing* him, searching for the tiny squirming piece of humanity which sounded like a kitten—half-mewling, half-crying.

"Maggie is—"

"Don't talk. It's a boy, Chris." Margaret laughed. "Sir Mowbray, may the Lord have mercy upon us, there're two of you."

Stone still, exhausted, half-lying on the bed beside Christin, Patrick looked as if he couldn't comprehend it all. Once he started to speak, but no sound would come. He cleared his throat.

"Could you," he finally croaked, "do you think I could—"

"See it?" finished Tildy, wrapping the small thing in a square of blanket. "Aye, more than that. Hold him a mite while I see to his mother. Ah, m'lady, 'twas a time of it, eh? Just like your own mother. Faugh, you're a stronger girl than she was, rest her soul. Let me put you to rights. They're born wantin' to suck, th' little angels. Nature knows about her own. Aye."

With deft hands Tildy arranged Christin on the large bed—smoothing, fluffing, straightening, and Margaret changed Christin's gown. Quickly she braided Christin's hair in one heavy plait. As Tildy gave the new mother's face a cool washing and added an extra pillow, Patrick stood gaping down at his arms full of a strange bundle.

He felt humbled and weak in his knees. How did it come to be that he who had spent years battling to take the lives from men's bodies, now stared at an unwashed infant with wet ringlets of reddish-yellow hair? The baby

275

had a wrinkled face that he didn't find at all attractive. Yet, with a curious finger, he touched the round cheek. The newborn worked its tiny mouth, reaching to try and suck the tip of his finger.

Patrick drew his hand away, fearing the puzzling phenomenon. He wanted to say "thank you" to someone, or do something, but he wasn't certain to whom or how.

Slumping against the wall by the head of the bed, he watched Christin nuzzle her breast to his son's cheek. How did they know what to do—these women who immediately became mothers?

Christin smiled at him. "I don't look very good."

"You're beautiful."

The tiny mouth tugged hard at her nipple. "Ohh, that hurts," she laughed.

"It's supposed to hurt," approved Tildy, proud of her handiwork.

Margaret wasn't watching Christin and the baby, she was watching Patrick. Seeing a man observe his first-born child was not new to her, and she sensed the same grateful strength in Patrick that she had seen in her own Richard. He truly loved Christin.

"He'll be beautiful after he has a bath, Patrick," Christin murmured. "See his little eye lashes? Here, sit down on the bed. Isn't he long?"

The new father reached out a hand which was larger than his son's head. With a forefinger, he traced down the small arm to the tiny hand and slipped it beneath the soft palm. Silky fingers slowly curved over the steely one, and Patrick felt a foreign sensation slither through his body.

"We'll have to think of a name," he said thoughtfully.

"I already have." She lifted her face and cradled Patrick's bearded jaw.

"Really, now? All by yourself?"

He grinned, feeling the first complete happiness he thought he had ever known—except for his time with her.

"And what will our son be called, little mother?"

"Nigel," she said. "I name him Nigel."

Margaret ceased tidying the room, and Tildy turned to stare at them. Dawn filtered a bluish-gray haze into the room.

Patrick hadn't the faintest idea if the two women knew the significance of Christin's choice: that of Robert Bruce's brother, whom he loved more dearly than himself. But Patrick understood. He felt his eyes stinging, and he felt the future awakening with the dawn. His heart felt as if it would burst in his body.

"I never loved anything as much as I love you." His voice broke.

Margaret turned away, blotting at her eyes. She wanted to be with Richard. As an afterthought, she grabbed Tildy's arm and pushed her forward. Then Margaret softly closed the door behind them.

Chapter Thirteen

While Christin rested, Patrick slept in a guest chamber in a wide comfortable bed. When, four hours later, a manservant discreetly awakened him, the Scot was surprised. But the servant was surprised, too; Patrick's blade at his throat was neither hesitant nor insincere.

Mumbling his apologies, which didn't comfort the gangly lad overmuch, Patrick proceeded to indulge himself in the first hot bath he had had in two weeks. He decided upon the removal of his beard, though he shaved it off himself. He didn't trust the unsteady hand of the shaken servant.

Patrick gingerly rubbed his smooth jaws, feeling slightly exposed, and his attempts to subdue his curls with a hairbrush were halfhearted.

"Lord Penmark wishes to speak with you when you've finished, sir. Food is waiting."

The youth arranged Patrick's fresh clothes over a chair back and cast an envious glance at the muscles of his legs. They were the sinewy, lean legs of a man who spent many of his hours astride a horse.

"Are—"

Patrick glanced up from buckling his belt. "Go on."

"Are you really what they say? An . . . uh?"

The boy diligently concentrated on his feet, and Patrick smothered a smile. Old stirrings of a youth he had hardly known radiated a warmth through him. He was a father.

"Are you trying to say the word 'outlaw'? Yes, I think that's what they call men when they carry a price on their head."

"I thought an outlaw would be . . . different."

"Don't look at me like that. There's no glamor in doing all of your riding at night."

"Oh, I didn't mean there was. I . . . well."

Patrick laughed, then paused to debate whether or not to buckle on his sword. He decided against it.

"When I was your age, I thought William Wallace was God. Do you know why I'm here?"

The awestruck boy blushed to the soles of his feet. "Y-yes."

"Then you understand. Don't ever get a price on your head, laddie. Border romance dulls a wee bit when you look down at a son you can't keep."

"Aye. I warrant so."

Patrick almost envied the boy his innocence as he ambled along behind him, down the stairs, along the hall into a strange alcove. He couldn't remember when his only worry had been to avoid getting caught toying with the laundry maids. The lad's hand poised to knock on the aged oak door.

"What was your father, boy?"

The youngster blinked and smiled, not understanding. "A servant, sir."

"Oh." Patrick nodded his head. He wondered if he wanted his own son to follow in the footseps he had made. Far better to be a servant, as this boy was, than a wanted man. "That's all right," he said and clapped him briefly on the shoulder. "You may go now."

Even with his lack of sleep Patrick was alert and thoughtful. The prospects of entering a chamber where Edwin Penmark waited for him were hardly comforting. Patrick dropped his hand to the doorknob. Penmark was wealthy, he was English, and he was now the legal father of Patrick's son. Penmark might have a reputation for honesty and fair play; but by his birth and his politics, he was automatically an enemy.

The room, a small chamber, caught the earliest morning sun. Patrick's head almost bumped the rafters sloping toward the side of the door. He ducked and glanced about himself in surprise.

A table was set for three people. Patrick's gaze encompassed the whole room at once. Standing erectly officious beside Edwin's long shelf of books, manuscripts and maps, was a third man: the priest who rode with Laurence to bargain for Miron. Edwin, his impeccably clad legs crossed as he sat, smoothed a manuscript book and marked his place with a finger.

"I trust you slept well, sir." Edwin rose.

Immediately, Patrick's eyes darted to the tall window. About twenty feet wide, it hovered a good fifteen feet above the ground outside. One cautious brow arched at the old man, and Patrick locked his hands behind his back.

"Homer?" he indicated Edwin's book.

"You surprise me."

"Why? Because I shaved my face or because I can read?"

Edwin laughed and waved the clergyman forward. Patrick bowed, and the abbot commented that he was well informed upon the progress of The Bruce's raids. After listening, his face expressionless, Patrick offered the priest his back. He accepted a plate of sliced venison, bread, cheese and fruit from a servant. As he glanced up at the loose-jointed servant, he hid his smile when the man unconsciously retreated several paces.

"Have you seen my son, sir abbot?" he asked abruptly.

"Yes, I have."

"Will you baptize him?"

"Of course. Are you a straightforward man in everything, Sir Mowbray?"

Abbot Donney accepted his food like a woman who ponders over which garment to wear, and he tidily began his eating. But Edwin only sipped from a chalice of wine and leaned back in his chair to study the contrasts of his guests.

"I have been told I am," replied Patrick.

As Patrick drank off his ale and blotted his mouth with a napkin, he mentally ticked off possible reasons for being summoned. Then he placed both his big hands upon the table. Five hours ago, he had held Christin in his arms, fearing she would die. Now he would leave his son in this man's house. The grievance cut a deep groove between his brows.

"I don't suppose you remember much of Edward the First," began Edwin. "You had to be a very young man. Few of his subjects understood why he allowed his own bitterness to taint his judgment. I wondered myself. But this son of his is not so . . ."

He left the sentence unfinished as Patrick leaned forward, hardly believing his ears.

"His son is not so . . . proud?" he supplied with pretended casualness, and answered his own question. "What else could drive a man to Edward's length but pride? It . . . drives me sometimes."

The Englishman lifted his chalice ever so slightly, as if he approved of the admission. The hinges whispered behind Patrick's back as the servant left.

"Christin has been strictly reared according to your standards, Sir Mowbray," the abbot said and watched the effect of his words. "Her family's opinions influenced her to make decisions that she might not have made if she were of less integrity. You defy what you do not agree with. She cannot."

Leaving part of his food uneaten, Patrick stood to prowl about the room, pretending to examine a large oil portrait.

"Are these two subjects supposed to be connected, my lords?"

"Connected?" repeated Edwin. "Ah, yes. I certainly hope so. For everyone's sake."

"You tell me nothing new about Christin's upbringing. In my country we could raise this son as our own without disgrace. Customs differ. Christin needed a name. She found one."

"You resent that."

"I wish I could have prevented it."

"But you're grateful, are you not, that she had someone who was in a position to help her?"

Patrick smiled coldly. "I think I begin to see now. You wish for something in return for playing the gallant, Lord Penmark. What is your price for being a father to my son?"

Edwin's chin tightened. "When you live as long as I have, you will learn." He gave a pointed frown at Patrick's fingers thrumming upon the frame of his first wife's portrait. "One doesn't close a door until he knows what is behind it. Not if he's wise."

"You're now going to tell me what's behind the door."

Refusing to be baited, Edwin gestured for Patrick to be seated. "Don't be foolish. I didn't marry Christin to have a young wife in my bed. I wanted to help her. I *did* help her. And"—his generosity attempted to penetrate the wall of suspicion Patrick had erected between them—"I can help you."

"It can't be money you want." Patrick laughed quickly, then sobered.

"We want nothing, sir! We wish to give *you* something."

Quite suddenly, Edwin's voice was weary and disillusioned. His habitual correctness was replaced with something Patrick was not certain of. So, with a skill learned over years of trial and error, Patrick kept his face a mask.

"We, you say? And what do *both* of you wish to give me?"

"The ear of the English king."

Lazily, with a remaining crust of bread, Patrick mopped up a bit of gravy and chewed thoughtfully.

"You have a great deal to lose in this situation with

Christin, Sir Mowbray," the abbot broke into his thoughts. "A great deal. Not only your head, but now a son that you cannot claim. I assure you; the slightest thing you do or say will attract the ear of the king."

Though Patrick twirled an empty chalice, his thoughts were racing, wondering if he dared to explore what these men were hinting at. "Why?" he asked. "Why am I so different from other men?"

"Because, unlike Edward's earls who distrust him as much as the devil himself—and the reverse—you have nothing to gain by playing false with England. You *need* this truce, both as a man and as a Scot. An Englishman, intimate with the Scots king, needing the authority of an English law? Unheard of!"

Patrick's laugh was rich with mirth. "English *law?* But, sirs, I have no need of English law. I have no wife. She has a husband already."

Slowly, as if he wished the occasion to be a solemn one, Edwin walked to a cabinet and withdrew a box with a padlock looped through its latch. Then, from his pocket he took a key and worked it into the keyhole.

"Abbot Donney also has a key to this box. He and I are the only ones who know its contents. Christin does not know, nor does her father."

Slouching against the wall, Patrick casually drew a forefinger across the moist space between his nose and his mouth. He pulled himself up then, and accepted the sheaf of papers. He began flipping through the authorized, carefully worded documents, glanced upward, then slowed down and read. After ten minutes, he looked at Abbot Donney. To Edwin he said, "You knew this when you married Christin?"

"Yes."

"And no one else knows?"

"There are times I suspect that Christin guesses at it. She's an alert young woman who often sees more than she's told."

"How long have you known that you're dying, Lord Penmark?" Patrick asked bluntly.

"For many months before Christin was . . . left Miron. Before you say anything, let me say that I did what I felt was right. As you see by my will, when I die your son will be an extremely wealthy young man."

Either Patrick was too exhausted to absorb all the facts, or his inborn prejudices against the English clouded his judgment.

"Why do you tell me this? Why *did* you marry Christin?"

"For the obvious reason. At the beginning," explained Abbot Donney, "Edwin knew he had little time left to live. Secondly—"

"It was more than that, Sir Mowbray," interrupted Edwin. "I'm not that noble. I loved my first wife very much. And when she died, I was lonely. You see, when a man knows he is dying, he begins to reflect upon his life. He realizes that he's afraid, that most of his life counts for nothir . At the tir t was—and still is— a comfort to know that I have helped Christin. Look at yourself. It wasn't nobility that drove you to conceive this child, though it perhaps served a decent purpose at the time. It was a human need. No motive is clear-cut."

Unused to such honesty from an Englishman, Patrick sighed and tapped the papers on the back of one hand. Then he slumped, unable to organize his thoughts.

"I understand that," he gestured abstractly. "Believe me, it is the one thing I *can* understand. I think I understand what you offer me. Bluntly put, Christin. When you die. But I couln't marry her once, and I won't be able to marry her then."

With both hands outstretched, Abbot Donney stopped the conversation.

"Edwin and I have discussed at great length, for a number of years, our desire to see this war end. After he married Christin and became acquainted with your own personal circumstances, it occurred to us both that perhaps you would . . . help us."

"Help you?" Patrick made a harsh sound. "I can't even help myself!"

"Patience!" the abbot raised his voice. "If you, Patrick Mowbray, will use your circumstance to negotiate between Edward the Second and Robert Bruce, we think we can use this to free you of your excommunication. Edward will listen. We all win, sir."

Patrick's jaw was hard, his eyes accusing them of naivete. "Forgive me of being wary of the Greek who bears the gift, my lords," he said, "but suppose I decline to negotiate. Will you then refuse to die, Lord Penmark?"

Abbot Donney slammed his fist on a table.

"All right," Patrick inclined his head. "That was rude. But I must tell you now; I have no intentions of facing Edward."

The abbot was angry now. "No one is asking you to face Edward personally. We have a prelate in very high position who is willing to do that for you. But, Sir Mowbray, if you wait until Edwin dies, your bargaining power will be cut in half."

The period of silence was not a short one nor a comfortable one. Each of them knew the decision made in the next moments would affect many lives.

"There are no guarantees, Sir Mowbray," Edwin eventually broke the nerve-wracking quiet. "But for the sake of Christin and for your son, who for a short time will bear my name, you cannot refuse to take the risk."

Without a doubt, the opening wedge had been driven in, with bold, unerring blows.

"Edward will think I'm begging for mercy," Patrick observed.

"This is not a time for personal pride."

"Pride," snapped Patrick, "is all we have left!" Patrick folded his arms and considered for a moment. "Edward must agree to recall the blockade at Berwick. He must call off Hereford and Pembroke. We will agree to any reasonable terms for patrolling the Border. But The Bruce will be called by one title and one only.

King! And from the halls of Edward's Parliament. If your man is what you say, all of Edward's terms will be repeated without treachery or prejudice in the Scottish court. Bruce has always gone the second mile. But *King* Robert it will be. Nothing less, you understand?"

"Aye, sir. It will be done. We will contact you again, and you counsel with your own king."

The abbot smiled at his use of The Bruce's title, and Patrick relaxed his stance an iota. Edwin walked to the door.

"I feel you have been in England long enough, sir. Your safety is a matter of concern for us all, now."

As Patrick paused by the table to drink a last swallow of ale, his mind staggered at the implications this conversation held for Scotland. He hardly dared hope for its personal promises. At the soft rapping upon the chamber door, his head snapped up. Three pairs of eyes swiftly searched the other, and they all wondered the same thing. Had they been overheard?

Almost dragging her off her feet, for her hand was still poised upon the knob, Patrick wrenched open the door.

"Christin!"

She swayed, her face as colorless as water. Edwin made some sound of movement, and Patrick heard footsteps running down the hall. Then the call of Margaret's voice.

"Christin, are you possessed?" she shouted.

With her fingers pressed over her mouth, Margaret stood awed as Patrick swept Christin up in his arms. He chose to ignore the abbot's working brows and inclined his head to the two men.

"You are correct." He allowed his eyes to drop to Christin's disarray of hair spilling over his chest and shoulders. "Much could be lost here. I will take my leave quickly."

He didn't wait for the door to shut, nor did he glance back to see if Edwin and Abbot Donney watched him carry Christin to her rooms.

"Sweetheart, what do you think you're doing? Will you tell me that?"

Christin allowed her head to loll back in the crook of his arm. For a moment she thought nothing mattered, not even the soreness spearing through her body. He was holding her. Already she grieved for the moment he would lay her down and separate himself from her.

"I woke up," she said with the simplicity of a child, "and you were gone. I wanted only to see you one more time."

"Put her down quickly, Patrick. She's lost too much blood as it is," Margaret ordered briskly.

As Margaret held the door and as Tildy finished changing the linens on the bed, Patrick stepped inside. His responsibility, the enormity of it, hurtled down upon him with the impetus of a boulder from a great height.

In the corner, out of the draft, near the small blaze of a fire, slept his son. Thoughtfully, Patrick moved beside the cradle, still holding Christin. She craned her neck to look down at Nigel. He squeaked tiny birdlike sounds.

"Isn't he beautiful, Patrick? He's had his bath now. I was afraid you would go without seeing him again."

"If you hadn't just had a baby, madam, I would turn you over and paddle your bottom until it was very brilliantly red."

"She deserves it," her sister grimaced. "Put her on the bed. You've waked your son, and he will wish to be fed. Not that you're much help yet. Try hard, darling. Perhaps you can trick him into thinking he's had something. Then I want you to get some sleep."

"One more stunt like that one, m'lady," Tildy grumbled, "an' you won't need t'worry about sleep."

With an expert flick of her wrist, Tildy snatched down the sheet, and Patrick lowered Christin to the bed.

"Do you want me to go?" he asked awkwardly as

Tildy arranged the pillows and Margaret scooped up the tiny bundle of manhood.

"Yes," Tildy said.

"No!" Christin exclaimed at the same time. She frowned at Tildy. "Tildy, have a lunch packed for Patrick."

"She's recovering," Tildy shrugged at Margaret. Her march from the room informed Patrick in plain terms that she heartily disapproved of his presence in Christin's room, or even at Erskill. England, as well.

As Margaret placed the baby beside her, Christin thought she would never walk or run again without pain. Yet, when she turned on her side, motioning for Patrick to sit beside her, she whispered smiling love-words to her tiny son that meant nothing at all except how glad she was that she had him.

Curious, Christin opened Nigel's blanket and inspected him—the first real look she had had since his birth. His red face was screwed up in a wrinkled squint. He had perfect legs and plump wee arms. His fingernails needed trimming, and the miniature fingers reached and clawed at nothing.

"He's so soft, Patrick. Touch him. Isn't he just like silk?"

Almost as if he were afraid, Patrick smoothed a hard knuckle up the side of Nigel's small thigh. A tear splashed on Nigel's chest, and Patrick didn't blot it away, but glanced at Christin's brimming eyes.

"Oh no," he shook his head, shushing her.

"You'll leave me now," she smiled and cried at the same time, her face twisting out of shape. Patrick felt his heart tearing in a way he had never dreamed possible.

"But I'll always have part of you," she nodded vigorously. "Scotland can never take this from me. Nor Robert Bruce. Nor The Douglas."

"The Douglas?"

"Nothing. What were you talking about with Edwin and the abbot?"

Patrick watched absently as Christin uncovered her breast and nestled Nigel to her. The little mouth seemed contented once it found her, and before Patrick could concoct his answer, Christin's eyes widened.

"You shaved off your beard, Patrick."

"Do you disapprove?"

"I liked it."

"It will grow back."

As Margaret discreetly closed the door and left them alone, Patrick bent forward to find Christin's lips. He kissed her with a gentle, persuasive yearning he didn't often allow her to see. Her lips parted slowly. Her whole body melted as she let his tongue tantalize her.

"I love you," she smiled when he finally straightened.

"And I love both of you," he sighed.

"Did you see my father?"

He nodded. "Earlier. Before Nigel was born. He was . . . unnerved. As any father would be."

"You didn't quarrel, did you? Oh, Patrick, you promised me you would explain things to him. Gently. So he would understand."

"I'm afraid your father isn't much in the mood for explanations right now. Perhaps later, when—"

"When, what?"

"Nothing."

"Patrick, you mustn't resent Edwin. He's been so understanding. He's never once purposely made me feel guilty for what happened between us. I know he's had to bear talk. Yet he protects me from all that."

"I don't blame Edwin." Patrick drew away from her. Hiding things from Christin became more difficult. "In fact, I think he's a fine man. I'm grateful to him for . . . a number of things."

The silence grew heavy with his leaving. When Christin's fingers absently twirled Nigel's fuzzy thatch of hair, she spoke as if she were musing.

"You're not coming back, are you?"

Patrick knelt beside the bed, roughly turning her face to his. "How could you say a thing like that?"

"Because of the way you avoid everything I say. Oh, Patrick, it was wrong for us to make love in this house. I've felt guilty about it ever since it happened."

"Stop changing the subject. I will come back!"

Patrick considered the things he would like to tell her—that Edwin Penmark was dying, that Patrick was considering placing himself in a more dangerous relationship to Edward than ever before. That everything was for her now, instead of for pride and country. That he was going to grovel before Edward—for her and for Nigel.

"And as far as avoiding what you say," he teased, "a man is a fool if he tells his wife everything, lassie."

"Wife? You said 'wife.' " Christin stared at him in amazement.

"Did I? All this birthing of bairns has gone to my head, I think."

"Then would you put Nigel in his cradle?"

Without a word, he lifted the tiny bundle of boy, so small Patrick could balance him in the palm of one hand. To kiss his own son was a thing he had never considered. Now that he did, Patrick was embarrassed. But he wanted very much to do it, and even Christin's awareness could not bring him to deny this one need. The round cheek beneath his lips was softer, even, than Christin's, and he had thought nothing was that soft.

"It's very frightening isn't it?" Christin smiled as he set the cradle rocking with his toe. "He's worth all of it—the misery, the fear, the bitterness, the war—all of it."

Edwin's final warning rang louder in Patrick's ears, now. It was dangerous to remain with her much longer.

"I have to leave you now, Christin."

"No!" she cried. "Not yet! Please, just a few minutes more."

"Oh, sweetheart."

Slipping his hand beneath the back of her head, he

lifted her lips to his again. Christin grasped both his hands and covered them with kisses.

"You didn't really hate me, did you? When you left me that night?" she asked.

"An angry lad said that, Christin. No, I could never hate you. It's painful loving you, sometimes, but I don't think I can stop now." He grinned.

"When will I see you again?"

"I don't know. Oh God, I don't know."

Christin refused to watch his even, lonely steps to the door. Like a wilted rose, she dropped her empty arms down to her sides and sank against the pillows. Deep in her heart she knew she would always be reaching for him. He was a Borderer, and he would always be leaving. And every time he left, part of her would die, all over again.

Chapter Fourteen

During the weeks after Nigel's birth, Christin submerged herself in work. Besides the care of Nigel, which she insisted doing herself, Christin filled every waking hour with activity.

If she didn't, she grew so lonely for the sights and sounds of Patrick that she felt she could hardly go on living. Out of necessity, then, everything assumed an excessive importance to her.

Unconsciously, her smiles became not only beautiful; they bloomed with compassion. Her concern for Erskill and its people grew not only friendly, but solicitous. Though Christin was not completely happy, she learned to be cheerful with the portion of pleasure she had. With each passing day, Christin grew to be more a woman.

Nigel grew plump. He was contented with Christin's movement near him and alert to the sound of her voice. But once he began to creep from the confines of their room, she found herself almost scheming for a few minutes with him to herself. Everyone from the laundry maids to the lads who carried firewood invented excuses to steal him away.

"She's spoiling him, Margaret," Christin complained of Sissy, who dominated Nigel like a tyrant when she visited. "She'll have that child convinced she's his mother."

Margaret smiled as her laughing daughter charmed Nigel by blowing a feather and catching it as it floated down. Bearing Nigel had lent Christin an added depth, Margaret mused. Her sister's face didn't look like a girl's anymore. Her cheekbones were more finely drawn, and her back was proudly straight, accentuating the new fullness of her bosom. Even her walk was changed, and the way her hands moved.

Having spent the entire morning outdoors, the two women were weary. Fall nipped the air and put the last touch of ripeness to late pears and persimmons and wild grapes. As they trudged across the creaking drawbridge back into the bustle of the courtyard, Christin absently slipped Patrick's emerald back and forth on its chain. She didn't bother with dropping it beneath her dress anymore.

"I dread cold weather," Christin said as they folded their pallets and unpacked the picnic paraphernalia. "Edwin's cough grows worse in winter. He doesn't eat as well. Old age, he says."

"Edwin is remarkable for his age, Christin. Do you realize that? He's such a wise gentleman. Richard says that many of the young upstarts in London value his opinions quite highly."

"Enough to keep him from resting when he needs to."

Christin kicked off her slippers and rubbed her feet together, then stretched them out to study her toes.

"Almost every week someone calls, and they shut themselves in that room of his. Edwin isn't as strong as he was, and if those men were more courteous, they would realize that."

Margaret laughed at her wifely complaint and motioned Tildy forward from the opposite side of the hall. The woman was craning her neck to find Christin.

"Tell them to go home then, Christin."

"I did once, but Edwin treated me like a child. In that polite way of his, he warned me not to interfere."

"That's not your childhood, my sweet, that's your sex! Men think our brains are so delicate that we shrivel at obscenities or swoon at the complexities of politics. Politics are inseparable from men's bodies, anyway. And we know those well enough!"

"Margaret!"

"It's true. More decision affecting affairs of state are made in bed than in Parliament."

"You say that because there's a man in your bed," giggled Christin. "Do you know what I do in bed? I study. Can you imagine what Edwin announced when Nigel was a month old? 'You'll be left a widow someday, Christin,' he said. 'We both know that. So I will teach you to do everything.' I swear he is, too. Everything."

"That's exaggerating, Christin."

"Oh? I keep accounts for every soldier in his hire, I'll have you know. And rents and outstanding debts. It's endless. Do you realize Edwin supports a family whose great-grandfather once saved a Penmark child from drowning? Yes, Tildy, what is it?"

Tildy bowed in Margaret's direction. "You'll never believe who's just ridden up to th' castle."

For a moment Christin tugged on her shoes, and Tildy smoothed her hands on her apron officiously. Snapping her head up, Christin's hands flew to her cheeks, her eyes wide with apprenhension. Her foot caught in her skirt as she rose too quickly, and she stumbled.

"Patrick!"

"Oh no, Lady Christin. I'm sorry." Tildy caught her arm. "I didn't mean that. It's . . . that captain fellow of The Douglas's. Swythen."

"Becket Swythen?" Christin repeated "What for, of a mercy?"

"I don't know, m'lady."

Tildy began explaining, but Christin already swept across the busy expanse. Why would Becket Swythen be here? He wouldn't be unless something dreadful had happened to Patrick!

Nausea spurted through her vitals. One day the stony-faced messenger would arrive from Scotland with news of Patrick's death. She was no different from any other Border woman who existed in perpetual fear of watching her husband carried home on his shield.

Lifting her skirts in both hands, Christin sped out the doors. Becket stood in the sunlight, his rusty hair catching its rays. He talked with the castle guards who formed a half-circle about him, puzzling over a right of passage signed by Edwin Penmark.

"It's legal enough," Tom shrugged, placing the paper in her hands.

So often had she strolled about the castle with her ledger tucked in the crook of her arm that the servants assumed it to be a natural thing to turn to her for approval.

"Captain, is it Patrick?"

"He's fine," Becket nodded quickly. "He's busy with The Douglas. That is why I've come, madam. I've brought you a gift."

"A gift?"

As the man stepped from her line of vision, he gestured toward the stunning bay mare with her black markings. A strange man held her reins. She was nervous, prancing and jerking her head with majestic resentment. Beside her, almost as large, stood her colt; the same splendid lines, the same excellence.

"Triste!"

Christin didn't realize when she reached for the captain's arm for support. Completely overwhelmed by the enormity of Patrick's gift, Christin almost felt she should be able to look northward and see his love spinning out toward her—an unbreakable gold thread over the hundreds of miles which separated them.

"I can't begin . . . I really—"

Moving to the horse, realizing that the beast couldn't possibly remember the sound of her voice, Christin looped her arms about the high arched neck. She crooned and whispered nonsense into the twitching ears.

It was almost like holding Patrick again. Christin imagined him standing before Triste, taking his last look at her, knowing that she would place her own hands where his had been. Carefully, she placed her spread hand upon Triste's shoulder, envisioning Patrick's touching, too. Then she felt foolish and drew it quickly away.

Once begun, the memories refused to stop: warm, sun-filled moments when the colt had been born and Patrick was so tired; Patrick's arms about her knees, almost making her stumble; Patrick turning his face into her thigh.

"Ohh!" she said again.

She must have made the milling guards uncomfortable, for they pretended to occupy themselves at some senseless task, gradually wandering away until Becket shifted his weight beside the man who held the horses.

Christin cast a nervous glance at the stranger, then away. "Tell me . . . everything he said, captain."

Becket cleared his throat. "He said to tell you that this is the only thing he could give you that he hadn't stolen."

Christin laughed and quite unexpectedly began weeping. Her struggle to keep her face intact failed disastrously. She turned so all he could see was the slump of her back, and she choked down the sobs.

"He said," Becket continued awkwardly, "that he uh . . . wants his son to know who his real father is."

She dared not let their eyes meet, so she blotted her tears on her sleeve. But Becket didn't embarrass her by offering to help her; he only stood mutely patient until she was finished. Once she felt repaired enough to turn around, Christin forced a broad smile on her face.

"Now!" She sniffed. "How is he, Captain Swythen? Really, how is he? Is he happy?"

"Mayhap." Becket shrugged his eyebrows. "He's rebuilt all th' damage that Comyn did t'Warricktown.

Th' people have done fine with the summer crops. All th' sheep have been replaced. But then, I guess there's th' dead. You can't replace them. I don't know if I'd call th' laird happy."

The gray crags to the north seemed to mock her. They were the enemy. But she did not lose control again.

"Tell him I will do as he asks. And that I'm very sorry."

"I also have a word from Lord Douglas, madam. He said 'thank you.' He said you'd know what he meant."

Christin wasn't sure she did know what The Douglas meant. Was he thanking her for naming Patrick's son Nigel, or for staying out of Patrick's life? It didn't matter; The Douglas didn't frighten her anymore.

When the stablemen realized that Christin had finished speaking with the Scot, they gathered around the mare and colt, commenting that they had never seen such magnificent horseflesh.

"Her line goes back to Norway," Christin caught herself explaining. "Must you go back immediately, captain? I would like to keep you for hours and drain you of every piece of information you have. You do have time to see my son, don't you?"

Before he could refuse, Christin lifted her chin and corrected herself. "Patrick's and my son. You must see him. He's part Scot."

"Aye," he grinned. His blue eyes softened, and he allowed a glimmer of amusement to show. "I'll take that long."

Though Becket seemed uncomfortable inside an English castle the size of Erskill, he accepted Christin's hospitality. Tildy fetched Edwin and Laurence to join them. When Christin placed Nigel into Becket's arms, her twin glowered and stuffed his hands in his pockets.

Becket ruffled Nigel's cottony curls politely, and commented how solid he felt for six months. He was a right bonny laddie. Christin did manage to coax Edwin out—

side to admire Triste. If Edwin held any resentment about Patrick's gift, he didn't express it. But no one could misconstrue Laurence's disapproval.

Christin was disappointed when, after Becket and the other Scot had eaten, Laurence strolled with them through the orchards. She hoped to take advantage of Becket's blossoming friendliness to learn more of Patrick.

"You're a man of few words, captain," she said, hoping if she made small talk Laurence would leave.

Becket was hardly taller than she was. When he talked, their eyes were level. "All I know is war, m'lady. And there's little t' gossip about war."

"Have you always been a soldier?"

"Forever, I warrant. I would do anything to end it."

Laurence contemplated Becket with some perplexity. "Scots love to fight. It does something for their blood."

"It does little for their blood, m'lord, except to spill it."

Expecting temper, Christin was amazed that Becket's movements, like his words, gave the impression of lengthy premeditation. After he reached to snap a pear from a branch near his head, he sliced it with the same meticulous gravity with which she would have measured medicine for a sick child.

"You *must* believe Scotland will win," Laurence disagreed. "Otherwise you wouldn't continue fighting."

"Scotland has been at war for decades. Since after Alexander's death. And if she continues to fight this one"—Becket wiped a bit of juice from a corner of his mouth—"the Border won't be where you see it now. It will be along the rim of the Low Highlands, along the Forth. In another ten years, everything south of the Forth will look exactly like your Northumberland. Wild. Desolate."

"There's the truce, though," Christin reminded.

"Truces are made to be broken, Christin," Laurence

snapped. "I agree with this man. A postponement is no good for either country."

"Only a solid victory and a clear defeat will end it."

"Scotland's victory and England's defeat," Laurence predicted sarcastically.

"Perhaps."

As Christin drew back to see if she actually heard a Scot consider anything less than blazing triumph for Robert Bruce, Becket grinned and wiped off his knife.

"I think it's the pears. I vow they've loosened my tongue. Now, with your leave, m'lady, I must return. The Douglas expects me."

"Yes," Christin said, deep in thought. "Please explain to Patrick . . ."

He could explain nothing to Patrick, so Christin simply bowed and watched him mount. When she later gathered up a fretting Nigel and ambled toward her room, she was still thinking of the captain. "Becket Swythen is a very strange man," she said.

Richard would arrive tomorrow to take Margaret and Sissy back to Northallerton. Though she loved her sister dearly, and eagerly looked forward to her visits, Chrstin now craved time to sit in solitude and ponder Patrick's gift. She needed to imagine everything about him—the brashness with which he swung open a door, the studious way he picked up a harness, the wide stride of his legs as he paced and thought. She yearned to feel her loneliness melting in her mind like a sweet dissolving in the warmth of her mouth.

"What's so strange about him?" Margaret interrupted.

"You're your daddy's man, little one," Christin crooned as Nigel gurgled back at her. "Well, for one thing, Margaret, Laurence spoke to him with courtesy. You must admit, *that* is strange."

"Everything about this war is strange lately."

"What have you heard?"

"Nothing. Except that Richard refuses to talk about

it anymore. I always grow suspicious when Richard
doesn't talk."

"Edwin refuses all the time."

"Yes, but you and Edwin are—I'm sorry, sweetheart." Margaret wished she hadn't said anything.

As Christian unbuttoned her dress, Nigel quickly
found the object of his search. She smiled down at his
chubby hands holding her and drifted into liquid, swirling memories.

"By the mass!" Margaret exclaimed, causing Christin
to start. "I've heard Richard mention that man's name.
That's what it was. Ever since he came here, I've been
trying to fit him into some . . . puzzle. I remember now."

Pacing the room in a halting manner, the older sister
absently repinned her hair, continuing her talk with
a mouth full of pins. Christin found it impossible to
understand her garbled words.

"Richard was talking to Father—"

"Will you take those pins out of your mouth?"

"Richard was talking to Father, I said. Very important names. Douglas . . . some prelate from Canterbury. And I'm sure this Swythen man was mentioned.
Even Patrick, if I recall."

"And?"

"That's all."

"But if there were to be a meeting somewhere and
Patrick was—"

"Wait a moment, Christin. I never said there was a
meeting."

"Of course there is. What else could there be—Canterbury and The Douglas? And"—Christin tapped the
end of her nose thoughtfully—"it wouldn't be in Scotland. Not with Canterbury involved. So, it must be in
England. And not in London, either. Isn't that strange?"

Margaret glared at her sister's reasoning and lifted
Nigel from her arms. He was full and only toying. Christin hardly seemed to notice. "You're strange, Christin,"
she said.

"I only meant, if Becket Swythen's name were mentioned with a group of men that impressive, it's strange that he should hold such a different view of the war. From Scots in general, I mean."

"Different, what?"

"He doesn't believe in the truce. That's odd. He thinks it won't work. And he doesn't believe—or so it seemed to me—that Scotland has much chance of defeating Edward outright. I never saw a Scot who didn't think he could win *everything*."

Margaret, dusting her hands, wasn't as convinced as Christin. "Frankly, I think you're letting this get out of proportion, Christin. First of all, you don't know if there will even *be* a meeting. And the man is only one of The Douglas's officers."

"Perhaps." As if to free her head of fancies, Christin shook it. "But, I'm keeping my eyes and ears open anyway. If Patrick Mowbray comes into this country, he surely had better not leave without seeing his son."

Christin denied to herself that she ever spied on her husband's comings and goings. No fact of Edwin's daily routine hinted that something was afoot regarding the truce. He took pleasure in Nigel's babyish antics and proudly planned his future. When Edwin spoke of Patrick, it was without blame.

Christin loved Patrick and she loved Nigel. And her unselfish devotion whetted her instincts razor-sharp. She examined Edwin's words with the ear of a lawyer, not a wife. She consoled herself that she would know when something threatened. Even a dumb animal sensed when a storm brewed in the distance.

For weeks she moved through her life like a blind person—walking into a room and feeling with outstretched arms, expecting to find certain familiar objects slightly out of place. Edwin's health grew steadily worse; at times Christin feared he was dying. When she suggested, with great tact, that he take to his bed for a season, he grew agitated and intimated that he had important things to occupy his mind. He would be fine in a few days, he promised. She was not to worry.

When Edwin mentioned, in an overcasual manner, that he was leaving Erskill for an afternoon—perhaps until late at night—Christin prudently kept her eyes lowered. She continued feeding Nigel his gruel and worded her objection to sound detached.

"The weather is not overpromising, my lord."

Edwin fussed over his papers more than was necessary. "The weather, my dear, is never right for anything. But I don't think it will rain."

"Probably not."

For a worried moment, Christin wondered if she shouldn't just blurt out all her uneasiness to her husband. Edwin wished only to protect her from concern. It was some manly honor with him. She made a flimsy excuse and swiftly went searching for Tildy.

"I have a marvelous idea," she beamed, holding Nigel at arm's length to the older woman. Christin set him briskly into Tildy's arms.

"I shall spend the day with my father. This may be the last chance I have to see him for awhile. It's going to rain."

Tildy, grabbing at her mutch as Nigel yanked it off with a curious fist, blinked at her ladyship. "It's not going to rain, Lady Christin."

"Of course it will."

Without another word, Christin marched to her room and furiously searched through her wardrobe as Tildy stumbled along at a puzzled pace.

"Papa loves this color. What do you think, Tildy?"

Christin flung wide the skirt of an apricot gown and held it against herself, twirling about the room in what she hoped looked like excitement.

"We'll probably go to mass, too. I haven't been to mass with Papa in ages. Plan to have Nigel all to yourself today—everyone has been after me for weeks to take some time for myself."

302

Her heart throbbing, Christin strode to the tall turret window. Her need to see Patrick was nearly choking her. No matter how small her chances were of seeing him, she would take them.

"My, I really feel well today," she said.

"Faugh!" Tildy didn't bother to shut the door as she left.

The second Tildy disappeared, Christin shut the door, shivering with the danger of the unknown. She locked the door and darted to the window. Already Edwin and his escort of four guardsmen twined their way through the courtyard toward the front gates.

Hardly had she buttoned her dress when Tildy rapped urgently at the door. "Just a minute!"

"The door's locked, m'lady."

"Oh, is it? Just a minute. I'm coming!"

Swirling her cloak about her shoulders, the black velvet one she had worn on that long, all-night ride into Scotland over a year ago, Christin opened the door. She laughed breathlessly.

"I just wanted to tell you that his lordship's leavin'," Tildy announced. She studied the room suspiciously, only her eyes moving. Christin stood remarkably still and smiled sweetly.

"Thank you. He told me he was leaving."

Second by interminable second, the silence thudded heavily. "I told him it would rain," she added. Then, to her horror, she giggled.

Without a word, Tildy clumped down the stairway. Christin allowed her only one minute out of sight before she, too, skittered down, slipping out the chapel door. She strode into the stables with her cloak furling about her boots. At the sight of her, several men stumbled to their feet from where they sat mending Erskill's trappings.

"Be still," she said. "John! Where are you?"

A red-haired youth, hardly fifteen years of age, appeared in a doorway near the rear of the building, searching for her voice. Drawing nearer, he buttoned on a jacket and quizzed her with his eyebrows.

"Your ladyship?"

"I want you to saddle Triste, John. I'm riding today." Everyone knew she had never sat the horse before, but only John dared object to her demand.

"Perhaps another, Lady Christin," he suggested. "That mare 'as a strong 'ead. As strong as a 'orse!" He laughed briefly, saw that she did not, then sobered.

"Saddle her," she repeated. "And quickly, John. I'm late."

The other men busily ducked their heads and occasionally stole a glance over their shoulders. Christin paced through the strewn straw until John drew the dancing horse from her stall. Triste was magnificently spirited, so the stablehands kept a safe distance. Smiling, Christin pulled on her gloves and stepped beside the mare's head.

"Do be a very good girl today, Triste," she murmured.

Christin was an excellent horsewoman. Laurence had taught her, and there were few better than him in Yorkshire. Before John could help her into the saddle, she seized the high pommel and swung her leg over. Holding back a horse of Triste's spirit was not something many men would relish, and Christin had to exert all her strength as she guided the beast through the courtyard.

"John! Come with me!"

She saw dismay written all over his face, but she also knew he would follow her. He wouldn't dare allow her to ride alone.

Edwin and his escort had ridden south, toward Whitecorm Forest. "Hurry along," she called back to John who was on a dappled mare.

"Lower the bridge, please," Christin ordered the guard. "We'll return late. Make sure your man is at his post to let us back in."

The guard thrust out his chin at the sight of two people riding out alone. Castle gossip about Lady Christin Penmark's impulsiveness was not without foundation, even though they did respect her. He shrugged and set the heavy chain creaking. Once they clattered across the drawbridge John pointed a finger.

"Mistress, Greystone is in that direction."

"I know where Greystone is. Just do as I say, and we'll get along wonderfully."

"But—"

"If we don't catch sight of them soon, we may have wasted all this effort."

"Aye, your ladyship," he replied glumly.

John had no idea what she was about, but he had no doubts that he was in trouble already. He fervently hoped she wasn't about to do something really dreadful, like meet a secret lover. Edwin Penmark would hold any servant to a harsh accounting if she came to harm, even from herself.

Both Triste and her rider were delighted when she took her stride. As the wind caught Christin's hair and tossed it in all directions, whipping her cloak out behind her back like an exuberant banner, her laughter rippled back to John.

"I'll race you!" she cried.

John, no more powerful than any other mortal man to resist such a charming challenge, shouted his acceptance, and they rode until both horses wheezed. Winning easily, and laughing at her triumph, Christin reined Triste to a standstill.

"You are a bonny girl!" she gasped for breath and bent her cheek against the silky mane.

They rested upon the crest of a J-shaped string of hills. The valley floor sloped steeply below them, and the forest draped into it from both sides of where they stood. Through the trees, in a fairly straight manner, was hacked a road. Presently, John caught Christin's eye, pointing to the figures moving slowly, far beyond them.

Edwin's escort stopped, waiting apparently, until it was joined by another, much larger escort. From a richly canopied litter slung between a pair of Spanish horses, a strange figure alighted. Even from a distance, there was no mistaking that the scarlet-robed man was an ecclesiastic of some importance.

For a moment Christin was afraid, wondering if her mischief would double back upon her. What was Edwin involved in? Attempting to twist her hair into a semblance of order, she reasoned Patrick was somehow involved in all this. She was part of Patrick, so she was involved also. Her mouth felt dry. She wondered absently if Nigel were taking his nap.

After an hour of tedious following, fearing to lose them and hesitant to draw too near, Christin realized where Edwin and his important companion were going. They were practically on top of an old hunting lodge of Henry III. It had been abandoned long ago.

Once picturesque, the ruins had been nearly overrun by the forest. Part of a broken-down chancel still stood, and traces of garden terraces remained. Scattered blocks of pavement approached what had been the central hall. But, for the most part, moss swaddled the paths and benches, and creeping vines smothered the broken gates.

"What is this?" whispered John.

"It's important, whatever it is."

At least twenty men were present, some in litters like the one Edwin's companion arrived in, some on horseback. The men of rank clustered in a group separate from their retainers and guards. No fires were lit, and no women were present that Christin could see.

"The minute it gets dark enough, I'm going closer," she announced, dismounting and securing Triste in a huge clump of spruces. Christin strode to the edge of the slope and dropped down to clasp her hands about her knees as John knelt beside her.

"Lady Christin," he begged, "I really don't think—"

"You don't what?"

"Nothing," he sighed. "Am I supposed to stay 'ere?"

"Yes. Do you have a knife?"

"Well, then, you're armed. Why do you worry?"

John gazed at the afternoon sky as if he were praying. And Christin thought he shivered.

Chapter Fifteen

Becket Swythen urged his horse into the cold waters of the Ure River, far downstream of Miron. When he approached the burgh from the south, he did so with foreboding, leaving the road and picking his way to a group of pine trees behind the small church. The work of the night ahead could well change the course of the war. He didn't want it bungled.

Laurence Winchelsea might refuse to meet him. The youth was less than receptive to the request for a meeting, the courier had reported. Their brief exchange of words at Erskill, even if the young lord had not known it, had laid bare a sympathetic comradeship that Becket was not above using.

Becket's instincts of men and strategy spanned many years. He knew that if he could deceive a man as brilliant as James Douglas for over four years, and if he could consistently elude a spy as practical as Patrick Mowbray, he could manipulate Laurence Winchelsea. Winchelsea was emotional, and was caught in a family crisis.

After hitching his horse to a small tree and flinging himself flat on the ground, Becket inched forward, his wet pants squishing in the pine needles. He waited for an hour, listening to the river as it gurgled along its path, unconcerned. The sun sank low.

An hour's wait was not long for a man like Becket. He was patient. He had waited two weeks before he finally smuggled himself into Thomas Barber's cell at Stirling Castle. Patrick Mowbray hadn't taken the Englishman's death easily. Becket knew how the English-Scot agent worked; Douglas would have eventually learned who deHughes's informant really was.

Killing, thought Becket as he scanned the valley, was something he had little personal taste for. James Douglas didn't hesitate to kill. Enough people had died in the war.

Laurence Winchelsea etched a clear outline against the sunset as he topped the hill. Becket viewed the youth's tall grace in the saddle with envy, and watched him rein, sitting quietly as his horse pawed the ground. Swythen smiled, allowing Laurence to fidget for two full minutes.

"Dismount and step into the trees, Lord Winchelsea."

The twin's head wrenched to the side, and the vigilance of eyes raking along the leafy green shelter was an indication of the flashing point of his temper.

"I'm alone. I said I would be," Becket reassured him.

"Show yourself first." Laurence fondled the hilt of his sword. "Keep your hands out where I can see them."

With a soft thud Laurence dismounted and held his body ready for Becket to reveal himself. After several doubtful glances over his shoulder, the younger man spotted the source of his search. His stance refused to relent an inch, and he examined the sandy-haired Scot with unconcealed suspicion.

Becket had seen the look before. He didn't appear the sort for clandestine meetings and mysterious messages. That was why he was good at his job. He kept his voice soft, and his manner unobtrusive.

"I'm not a danger to you, Lord Winchelsea. I wouldn't ha' sent the message if I wanted you dead."

"Why *did* you send the message? 'You can prevent

rivers of blood, Lord Winchelsea.' You should have been a playwright."

"You had the same worry on your face when we talked before, Lord Winchelsea. I believe we've something to say. I warrant you've kept your eyes and ears open since we spoke at Erskill."

Laurence's failure to hide his brimming tension didn't perturb Becket. The boy was honest, but he had the finesse of a dazed wrestler.

"I've no wish to bandy about the point like a tiptoeing virgin," Laurence announced curtly. "I'm no fool. I know there's something underfoot. Faith, both my sisters' husbands are involved in it!"

"That's true."

"And now I know you're involved in it. This . . . *great* meeting. I know where it is and who will be there. I wasn't invited."

Becket grinned, and Laurence slapped his reins over a branch.

Motioning Laurence to enter the safety of the shadows, Becket withdrew a small flask from his leather breeks and sipped a long drink of rank river-brewed whiskey. When he offered it, Laurence stared down his nose in offense.

"I like a man who comes to the point," Becket nodded. "You're right about the noble heads puttin' themselves together tonight. You did well to learn of it, for it's not widely known. Neither is th' fact that, less than ten miles away, a garrison of forty English cavalry waits to escort the earl of Lancaster to London."

"How do you know that?"

"I saw them. I've been in Yorkshire a week."

Laurence glanced aside quickly, then back, as if he did not believe it. "Who are you?"

"A man with the same hopes as you—to see the war end. But my politics are far different from your own, Lord Winchelsea. Make no mistake about that. Scotland hasn't a bairn's breath of a chance of winnin' this war, though, and we both know it. This truce the noble heads are spittin' out is only one more in a line of many. Delays cost a lot of blood, sir."

"A fine speech." Laurence smiled almost contemptuously. "How does that affect me?"

Becket swallowed more whiskey and replaced his flask, making a small sound between his teeth.

"The forty cavalry, my lord. I want them led to Whitecorm Forest within th' next two hours."

Whirling from the man's bald frankness, his thoughts struggling to grapple with the horrifying implications, Laurence dropped his jaw.

"A massacre? Holy God!"

As Laurence turned to leave, Becket grabbed his shoulder. Laurence jerked it free, his mouth curling down at the corners in disgust.

"You misunderstand, sir," Becket said quickly. "I don't deal in massacres."

"Then what do you deal in?"

"Pinpricks, my lord. Pinpricks—so that Scotland can see where she stands. So that she can have the time she needs to accept the inevitable. As long as men like Douglas and Mowbray and Randolph run back and forth across the Border, Scotland will go on dreaming and go on bleeding."

At the mention of Patrick's name, Laurence unconsciously hesitated in his departure. He slowly examined the cinch of his saddle. His disgust, Becket guessed, waned a wee bit.

"I can't talk to you." Laurence shook his head.

"Then go."

As if the conversation were ended, Becket began walking toward his own horse. "All I want is for Mowbray to be put away somewhere safe, in a nice English prison. The Douglas, too, if they can catch him. But since I work for The Douglas . . . well—"

"You know what happens to Scot traitors."

Becket shrugged. "The first Edward killed them. His son's not quite so bloodthirsty. I warrant you have as good a motive as anyone for catching Patrick Mowbray.

I was with The Douglas the day Mowbray took your town. But we heard the talk. They said he made you look like—"

Becket stopped speaking, for Laurence's eyes were somewhere else. A year in the past, no doubt. Wiping a careful hand over his mouth, Becket rested a hand on his stirrup and gave Laurence's wound time to re-open.

"Revenge is sweet," he said softly. "And it's not for children."

Laurence did not reply.

"Justice doesn't always come like it's supposed to," Becket urged. "Sometimes it needs a kick along the way. You don't even need to dirty your hands, Lord Winchelsea. Just ride to fetch them and let them do the work. You can wait somewhere if you want the satisfaction of seeing him trapped. Sometimes that's worth it, sometimes not."

With a great sigh, Laurence slumped down to the base of the tree where he stood and dropped his head into his hands. He sat until the sky was nearly dark, until a wolf howled his lonely sympathy across the hills. When he finally spoke, he didn't lift his head but mumbled into his lap.

"I couldn't stand it if my family found out I did such a thing. It doesn't matter how much I would like to see the man hauled off to London. Tell the English yourself."

"I can't. The Douglas expects me with him, and it will arouse his suspicion if I'm gone much longer. He thinks I'm standing outpost guard now."

Laurence laced his fingers, his face twisted with the battle raging inside his conscience. When he slapped his thigh, it was abrupt and decided, making the horses snort.

"I will take them to the place. No more."

Becket squinted at the rising sliver of moon. "You'd best be quick about it, then." He swung into the saddle and it creaked its complaint. "Oh," he added, his reins outstretched, "the officiate is from the archbishop of Canterbury. He is not t' be harmed."

Despite her vantage point on the hillside, and no matter how hard Christin strained her eyes, she could not distinguish Patrick from any of the men among the ruins. Perhaps she had misinterpreted Margaret's fragment of information. Perhaps Christin had come for nothing.

"I can't see or hear anything, John. You stay here. I'm going closer."

John gasped and he clutched her arm in both hands. "You'll get caught for sure, and his lordship will thrash me!"

"*I* will thrash you, John, if you don't stop complaining."

The small fire someone had lit was both fortunate and unfortunate. It decreased her chances of being seen as she cautiously crept down the hillside. But it also clustered the members of the counsel about it, necessitating Christin's drawing even closer.

When she first heard Patrick's deep voice, she thought she would be sensible. She would view Patrick in the light of history: a man of peace daring to reason with some of the most powerful men of the realm.

Such a thing was not possible. She could view Patrick only as the man she loved, and whose life was forever interwoven with her own. She huddled, feeling small and forgotten She marveled at the dignity of his voice and remembered how earnestly it had hoarsened when he said, "I love you, Christin."

Old cloister benches seated a number of men, and lesser attendants leaned against broken pillars. As she inched nearer she finally saw him—dressed in riding leather and almost out of sight behind a black-robed Dominican friar who recorded everything on a large scroll of parchment.

"The trade agreement alone between Scotland and

England could replenish Edward the Second's war debts," Patrick proposed with authority.

He was certain of himself, but he looked out of place —a fighting hawk among peacocks. She recognized the earl of Hereford, the earl of Angus, and the son of Lord Berkeley. Behind Patrick she glimpsed Becket Swythen and Richard. From the Scottish court there was another man she did not know, but recognized. Edwin was seated almost out of her line of vision.

"And if we lift the blockade on Berwick and open up that seaport?" asked an English voice. "What is to keep the Scots from taking their coal to Europe?"

"We've a need for your iron, Lord Berkeley," answered Patrick. "The Bruce is prepared to relinquish sixty thousand pounds of confiscated English landholdings along the West Marches. That, in exchange for a capitulation between England and Spain for the lifting of the Scottish excommunication."

"The terms seem heavily weighted on the Scots side, Sir Mowbray." The representative from Canterbury sounded unconvinced. "The attacks on Carlisle and Newcastle must stop. Outstanding monies still exist from the reign of John Balliol. You must consider your own obligations."

"You call off Hereford and Pembroke, and we will consider our obligations, my lords." Patrick's voice was perfectly controlled, but Christin recognized the familiar anger.

"Would Robert Bruce consider an annual payment to Edward for this title of king he wishes so much?" the Earl of Angus drawled.

Patrick paused. "That depends entirely upon the effectiveness of your envoy to Rome, my lord. Robert Bruce has made it clear for many years that he is willing to negotiate whatever is necessary. Present a complete list of Edward's demands. They will be considered."

"I expect you will see to it, young man," chuckled Hereford. "Why not ask Edward yourself?"

"I'm not that big of a fool, my lord," smiled Patrick.

For nearly an hour the issues were debated. The ground was cold and damp. When the twelve men finished with their points of question and the clerics had dutifully recorded them, they left in the pomp accorded their rank. Of the higher-ranking lords, only Edwin remained, with the ecclesiastic, James Douglas, Patrick, Richard and the guardsmen and captains.

Several times, deep in earnest conversation with the Canterbury cleric, Patrick pivoted to pace the mossy floor. The fire had nearly died, and the moon rose a dull glow behind the drifting clouds. His curls caught what light there was. His head was bowed, as if he were deeply troubled. His gestures were emphatic and impulsive.

"No," Christin heard him say. "I cannot do it."

"You're a proud man to have such a price on your head!" The man raised his voice, and Patrick thrust out a finger.

"I'm not asking Edward to remove the price on my head! I would do much to see it gone, but even I will only go so far, Your Grace. Use your influence. Forget the bargaining. The words spoken here were all true, but only what they wanted to hear. Edward cannot afford to maintain his armies any longer. It is ruining the English economy, and you know it. You are suffering. We are suffering. *But we will fight!* Do not be mistaken about that. We will have honor, even if it costs us dear."

"He speaks the truth, Your Grace," Edwin Penmark urged. "I believe the man when he says that The Bruce can be taken at his word. We have everything to gain by petitioning the pope in their behalf. Edward can only gain favor with his earls. Pembroke will come around. Lancaster, too, in the end."

"And you, Sir Mowbray, what about your end?"

"My end will take care of itself once the excommunication is lifted. Until it is, I lose. But I give you my word; even The Bruce's enemies will support him in this truce. Those who have supported Edward in the past are not in as favorable a position as they were two years ago."

With an impressive flourish, the wealthy Englishman swept his robes about him and nodded, appearing to be in some eagerness to leave.

"I trust Edwin Penmark. I will do what I can, but I will not be held accountable. As we know, Edward is sometimes capricious."

From where she sat, Christin watched The Douglas pull Patrick aside. Patrick inclined his ear without facing his general.

"I don't think you should linger here, Patrick," The Douglas said. "It's hard t'tell a friend from an enemy in a situation like this."

"What? Do you know who murdered Barber?" The two men faced each other deliberately; then Patrick glanced behind himself.

Though the mysterious killings had ceased during the last weeks, The Douglas's caution and suspicions had not. His opposition to Patrick's negotiating with Canterbury had received his approval only upon the condition that he be present, too.

"No, I haven't learned anymore. But I'll tell you, laddie. If I had it t'do over again, I'd have advised the Bruce to send someone else after Barber."

"You worry too much, Jamie," smiled Patrick.

For a moment, during the curt amenities of departure, the delegates spoke so softly that Christin couldn't hear anything. She flattened herself on her stomach and forced herself to wait. That was when she glimpsed the movement of another person besides herself on the hillside.

Christin's fright was so intense that she didn't move or breathe. Her own life was probably threatened, but Patrick's vulnerability outweighed any thoughts she had for herself.

The figure drew closer, creating only a flitting shadow which blended with that of a tree, detached itself, and blended once again. The person was so near that Christin could discern the tiny crackles of spruce needles crunching under his feet.

As the intruder paused to observe the scene below, his face lifted. Christin saw it clearly: a handsome face, the exact image of her own.

"Laurence!"

"You!"

Like some current of lightning between its source and the object of destruction, the twins clashed. Laurence's distress erupted from the guilt for what he had planned and Christin's guilt was for being discovered eavesdropping.

Laurence lumbered up beside her and sank down next to her.

"What in God's name are you doing here?" he whispered.

"What are *you* doing here?"

"Nothing! How did you know of this?"

"The same as you, probably. I followed Edwin."

Laurence smoothed his rumpled hair and laughed breathlessly. "I could hardly keep from knowing. Father and Richard kept going off to secret conferences. Patrick Mowbray seems to be the key in all this. At least, the ambassador appears to think so."

"Yes." Idly relacing her boot, Christin watched the clerics gather their quills and ink.

"Richard knows you're here, does he?" she asked.

"Ah, no. I got bored at Greystone. I came much later." He moistened his lips. "You surely don't plan to speak to the . . . Patrick?"

"Why not?"

"No reason," Laurence said quickly. "But it wouldn't be wise, do you think? The nature of the affair and all."

"Shh."

Becket Swythen drew Lord Douglas aside from the small cluster of remaining attendants, and their heads bent. Becket made a wide gesture, and The Douglas motioned at Patrick.

Arising quickly, Laurence began moving from tree to tree.

"Will you sit down, please?" Christin whispered. "You're driving me mad!"

"Christin," Laurence returned to grip her arm, and she leaned back to stare at him. "I think you should leave now. Everything is finished here, and—"

"I came to see Patrick, Laurence. If I can. When the men leave, I'm going down."

"No!"

Swiftly, he looked away, then back again. He released her arm and lifted his hand in a gesture of disgust.

"What kind of a woman are you that you can flaunt Patrick in your husband's face? My lord, Christin!"

"What's the matter with you, Laurence? You have no more business here than I have!"

Henry III's old hunting lodge was cupped in an oval valley. Christin assumed the alertness of a nervous doe as she sensed imminent disaster. Rising, suffering from an anxiety she didn't understand, she threw the heavy folds of her cloak loosely behind her shoulders. The men appeared to disperse, and some wandered toward their horses.

"Something . . . something is wrong," she muttered, at a loss. "I feel . . . terrible. Something is wrong."

"No! Nothing is wrong. I think you should go now, Christin."

Christin and Laurence were little different from other twins. A constant association and a sharing over the span of a young lifetime had honed the sensitivity between them.

Laurence was deeply disturbed, she realized. He didn't wish her to be here because of something he dreaded. And what could that be? How could Laurence dread something of the future—*unless he knew what it was?*

As if her memories were minute iron shavings attracted by a magnet, all the humiliations Laurence had

318

suffered, all his angers and bitternesses, seemed to congeal into a ponderous lump of iron misery. Laurence had reason to hate.

She flew at him, twisting his shirt in her hands, nearly bowling him over. "You tell me what's going on here!"

"No! I—"

"You're lying! It's all over your face, Laurence. You've done something. You hate Patrick and . . . Holy Jesu!"

Christin wrenched away from him and began running down the steep incline of the hill. But she stumbled and fell. Before she picked herself up, her twin was practically on top of her.

"You can't go down there. God, Christin! They're waiting for him. They'll kill you if you go down there!"

It was an action of purest reflex. Christin screamed as loud as she could—a piercing outcry that she didn't dream she was capable of. It shattered the vale with alarm.

"Patrick! *Run, Patrick.*"

When Laurence's fingers clamped over her mouth, it was too late. Men appeared from nowhere in seconds and Christin could hardly grasp the ensuing confusion. She fought off her brother. He clutched at her cloak, pulling her back down, and she struck him hard with her fist against his temple.

"He can't escape! Stay here!" Laurence thundered.

As her twin rolled head over heels for twenty feet, she sank onto the grass, stunned. Laurence sprang to his feet and gave a great shout.

"No! It was a mistake!"

But the forest was spewing out English cavalry in pairs, some climbing trees with deadly longbows, some darting for places of ambush near the ruins. Laurence struggled with two men trying to enter the melee on horseback, striking wildly and accomplishing little good. One kicked him aside with a heavy boot.

Christin was beyond caring anything for her brother's

safety. Pandemonium was bursting like a river in spate. Horses whinnied, and well-dressed diplomats scurried into the shadows and disappeared.

"God help you, Patrick," she wept, stumbling toward the onslaught of men.

One English hand grabbed at her, dragging her back, but she fought him off and pummeled herself through the mass of bodies, trying to reach Patrick.

When he heard Christin's scream, Becket Swythen tried to withdraw inconspicuously. Before he retreated thirty yards, he glimpsed The Douglas slashing his way toward his horse somewhere to the right. Becket snarled his anger and felt hands grappling about his knees.

"Call them off!" Laurence screamed, battling to wrestle Becket to the ground.

Witnessing this amazing exchange between his captain and the Winchelsea youth, The Douglas was deterred from reaching his horse. Sword against sword, he strained against an Englishman. They were caught in the confinement of several trees with scarcely enough room to wield a blade at all. With his toes digging into the ground, his whole body rigid, the Scots general instinctively grasped what was occurring between the two men.

"*Beckeeet!*" he roared. He stumbled.

Fighting to keep from falling, The Douglas regained his balance in time to see his foe slump to the ground as Laurence stood over him, a stone the size of a man's head in his hands. In spite of the border separating them, the quick-witted Scot met the mind of the impetuous twin. It wasn't difficult; the younger man's face was twisted with the bitterness of his remorse.

"Douglas, save yourself!" Laurence cried.

As the twin instinctively stepped toward the Scot whom he wished to save, Becket dragged himself from the grass. Baring his teeth, the traitor hurled himself at the span of Laurence's back.

The Douglas's arm struck Laurence aside with only inches between life and death. For one moment, the

320

impact of what had happened escaped Laurence. When he turned, horrified at the impersonal silence of the dead Becket at his feet, he lifted agonized hands toward his own head. They were clawlike, white-knuckled —the image of his conscience.

Everything was hopeless. The Douglas glimpsed Patrick slashing back and forth powerfully. As nine men drew their circular net tight about the fair-haired Scot, The Douglas moved in to die with him. Perhaps they could hold them off for a minute, he thought.

"No!" Laurence screamed. He clutched at The Douglas's arm. From several directions at once now, men moved toward them. High in the trees, archers positioned themselves. "You must run!"

"For thirty pieces of silver?" The Douglas cursed him, even as he sprinted for his horse.

The chances of Douglas escaping were almost as desperate as Patrick's. As Laurence threw himself between Douglas and an Englishman, Douglas mounted and hacked his way toward the protection of the forest.

Patrick glimpsed his fate in the seconds between Christin's scream and the creeping trap of horsemen. He didn't begrudge ending his life with a fight; a Borderer accustomed himself to the immediacy of death. But a man's death should count for something.

Precious days had been squandered when Christin needed him. For what? Climbing into Barber's house to learn that Becket had eaten too many oranges? The people of Warrick had died and had been burned out of their homes. For a truce that couldn't be agreed upon? DeHughes was dead. Others, too. Barber had been murdered. For all *this*?

A man should make his death his own matter!

With a recklessness born as a result of an unyielding, capricious fate, Patrick hurled the sword from a man who crouched to engage him. Amid the cursing, the ringing of blades and perilous shouting from the trees, he systematically fought his way toward his death.

"Stop!" rang a gravelly voice. "Don't kill that man!"

"Scots ain't worth nothin' alive!"

"Kill me, then," shouted the bareheaded Borderer, mirthlessly working his blade toward the Englishman who had spoken. The swirl of Christin's cape flashed in his peripheral vision for a second.

Two Englishmen were down, one was crawling out of danger, several more tightened the lethal circle.

"Knaves! To him!" shouted a thick-chested captain waving directions with one arm, his sword in the other. He glanced at the aimed longbows in the trees and motioned archers into position on the ground. Cloth-shafted arrows fitted to the strings.

Surrounded by fifteen swordsmen, Patrick craved one more look at Christin. As he turned, his sword went spinning from his hand.

Christin couldn't see Patrick within the tight circle of men, but she saw the man drop down from the tree limb above, and she heard shouts of victory when he landed upon his target.

"No!" she wept, beating at their backs. But men swarmed over Patrick, grabbing his arms, his legs, the hair of his head.

"Patrick!"

"Get her out of here!" he shouted, but he was silenced by a fist to his mouth.

Shoving his way where Christin struggled hopelessly, Richard grabbed her into his arms. Her hysteria was a garble of pleas and blame for Laurence.

"I can't do anything, Christin. Get out of the way."

"Edwin!" she screamed. She knocked Richard's arms loose to dart toward the small stooped form sitting on a broken stone bench. "You can't let him die, Edwin!"

Edwin's look was so pitying that she wanted to take him into her arms, but he only shook his head and huddled down into the coughing spasm of his own slow death. When she saw Laurence trying to reach her, to pull her out from the tangle of men, she kicked at him.

"I will never forgive you for this. Not for the rest of my life. Let me through! Let me—"

"Stop!" roared a command. A tall, compelling figure strode forward across the ruins wearing a splendid red cloak thrown back over massive shoulders. As he removed his plumed helmet, the circle of men quieted, and loosened enough to allow him passage to yield a view of Patrick.

A good many unnecessary blows had managed to find the Scot's face. Blood streamed down one temple, and he had taken a knife wound in his side which bled copiously. Patrick squinted through trickles of blood to view Robert Clifton, a close confidant of the earl of Lancaster, and one of the best military minds in England.

"Don't you do your own killing, my lord?" Patrick spat out dirt and blood with his words.

"Ah, the Scot has a tongue as sharp as his sword," the Englishman retorted. "Edward doesn't want your corpse in this valley, my young rebel. He will hang you as high as Wallace. He told me so himself."

"Lord have mercy."

Christin slumped to her feet, her cloak billowing out, almost hiding her in its velvet cloud. Patrick's eyes met Richard's through the opening of men. At last they bridged the Border, for the older man drew nearer, willing to do anything.

"Take her out of here," Patrick coughed.

"What will you do with this man?" Richard demanded.

Lord Clifton stared at Richard. "Who are you?"

"I am Richard Hartley. What are you going to do with this man?"

"He will be taken before the king, of course, and given a fair trial. What do you think?" Richard watched him make a mental note of his name. "Who is that woman?"

"Lady Edwin Penmark."

At the mention of the English monarch, Christin jerked up her head. As if she were sleepwalking, she staggered to her feet. She finally reached the towering man whose cape kindled an irrational fury inside her.

323

"A fair trial? Is that what you said?" she mocked. "What do you know about fairness, you who have descended in your hordes until Scotland was nothing but black wilderness?"

Edwin's cough startled Christin. When she saw her husband's efforts to walk, she took his arm, helping him stand before the indignant nobleman.

"Sir?" she whispered to Edwin.

"I can stand," he said gratefully.

Adjusting his clothing, Edwin drew himself as tall as possible before Clifton. Patrick didn't make a sound, but he hardly could, for a man's arm around his throat was nearly strangling him.

"My lord." The old man bowed, not waiting for an acknowledgment. "We will fight you on this. I do not know who gave you the order to capture this man, but matters of great import took place here tonight. If this troop delivers this Scotsman into the hands of the king, you will do more to destroy our hopes for peace than anything you've ever done for it."

The commander looked at Edwin as if he were a raving madman needing to be put out of his misery. As Christin stood there, clutching her husband's arm, the guards dragged Patrick to his feet, mouthing mockeries and deliberately lurching against him, shoving him from hand to hand.

The bitterness on Patrick's face made him look as if he were possessed by a demon who didn't care if they killed him on the spot. When he managed to free one arm, two of his captors sprawled against their companions before they realized he had wrested it loose. Four Englishmen took their place, landing meaty blows about Patrick's waist until he sagged heavily against the several hands which held him. His head lolled to his chest. A man on his left yanked it upright by his hair.

As they dragged him past her, Christin tried to touch him, but her hand was callously brushed aside. To humiliate Patrick more, the cavalrymen hauled him up to weave before her. He strained to see through the swollen slits of his eyes.

"Madam?" he mumbled.

Christin summoned more strength than she had; he had always drawn out the actress in her. Her chin lifted with the poise of a queen, and she smiled. Her heart was breaking, and she gave him the only gift she could: that which her pride had kept from him all this time.

"Your son, Sir Patrick," she said with exact clarity. "I will give him the best that I have."

Something passed over his face; only she knew it to be the triumph that it truly was. Turning his head to the side as much as he could, Patrick addressed himself to Edwin.

"See to her, my lord."

Chapter Sixteen

Not since Edward I executed William Wallace, along with the brothers and officers of Robert Bruce, had London been so involved in a trial. The captured traitor cured the boredom of a lingering fall. Well-dressed lords gossiped in the streets beside richly canopied litters. Hardly a shop swung open its doors that didn't hear at least one heated discussion about the crimes which Patrick Mowbray had committed against the state.

Some Londoners still remembered the gruff old patriarch, Cecil Mowbray. He had inherited some of the best lands in England through a clever marriage to Yolande Hildemeir. Those who didn't recall, gathered in the street and regarded the lofty White Tower with grave clucking sounds and tales of other promising young men who had turned out to be a disappointment.

Leaving Nigel in Tildy's care at Erskill diminished Christin to the point of depressed monosyllables. The only hours she had spent away from him were those disastrous ones at Patrick's capture.

But Edwin insisted that they all go to London, though he suffered untold pain from the trip. Laurence and Richard haunted the offices of influential clerics and lawyers reputed to take hopeless cases. Margaret had her hands full simply coaxing people to eat and keeping Laurence from within speaking distance of Christin.

Inside the smoke-stained kitchen of Edwin's London townhouse, Christin paced before a fire. Completely oblivious to her appearance, her fingers fussed with the buttons of a blue gown. The king had refused to see her. She hardly knew where to turn.

"Christin," Margaret warned as she and a maid prepared ingredients for a mutton stew, "this isn't getting you anywhere."

Christin snatched open the shutters to a window opening onto a side street.

"Look at them out there—nobles and their smiling ladies. Women carry bread and children romp. They laugh, while my Patrick rots in that prison until Edward kills him. I don't think I can stand this!"

"I think you'd better stop worrying about Patrick long enough to get a doctor for Edwin. Christin, he's not doing well."

"I've already sent John for one."

Her gray eyes traveled more slowly along the street, to women accepting the hands of their gentlemen, worried only about clearing their skirts of the gutters. She slumped against the sill, her hair escaping from the severity of its knot. Her whole body felt weighted down with stones.

"Edwin's dying," she said bluntly.

"Don't say that."

"He is; he knows it. When they took Patrick that night, he began vomiting blood. He cries and keeps saying that Patrick came to Whitecorm because he trusted him. I will *never* forgive Laurence. I don't care how sorry he is."

Examining the vegetables on the table without really seeing them, Christin picked up a piece of dry bread and nibbled at the crust.

"Women are so helpless, Maggie. When it comes down to the line, we really can't do very much. Do you know what they do to men when they draw and quarter them? They cut them open and—"

With the wail of a tortured animal, Christin dropped the bread and stood helplessly alone, covering her ears and squeezing her eyes tightly shut.

"I can't stand it!" she screamed.

Margaret grabbed her tightly, crushing her to her breast as if she could force the agony to leave her.

"No, no! Please, sweet, you mustn't."

"My beautiful Patrick! God in heaven, Nigel Bruce and Christopher Seton killed and dozens and dozens more. If I had done as Patrick wanted me to and lived with him . . . there was the king, but we could have run away and lived together somewhere and had our son. Then he would never have come—"

As if she were a beaten child, broken and bleeding, the women guided Christin to a chair and hovered over her, saying words that told her she was loved but didn't comfort her. With her head upon her arms, Christin poured out all her horror of the most hideous death a human can suffer. Finally, from exhaustion, her groans subsided, and she breathed deeper. And ceased her weeping, at last.

When the doctor came, she was almost herself. She and Margaret waited outside Edwin's room, and when the physician came out he only looked at them grimly and advised keeping Edwin quiet. After Christin plied him with questions, he said it was hard to tell. Margaret asked him point-blank if Edwin could die. He said he wasn't God, but to not give up hope. He had bled his lordship, and that was all anyone could do.

Christin washed her face after he left, splashing water on her swollen eyes. Margaret found her standing before an open window in her bedroom, brushing her hair.

"Out of this huge city," she said tonelessly when Margaret closed the shutters, "no one cares that Edwin is dying. In the whole country, Patrick has no one but me . . ."

Poised, her hairbrush in the air, she repeated slowly,

"No one but me. And *Malcolm!* Maggie!" She whirled. "I forgot about Malcolm!"

Without further explanation, Christin snatched open the wardrobe and pulled out her cloak. She twisted her hair in a haphazard knot. With a movement more determined than anything she had done for days, Christin swirled her cloak about her shoulders and tugged on her gloves, leaving Margaret to follow her down the stairs.

"Where are you going?"

"Tell Edwin I've gone to find Malcolm. And as soon as it's dark, Maggie, I want you to make sure the rear door is open. Creagen got word to a patrol on the Border that we would be waiting to hear some word from Scotland."

"They will never come here. It's too dangerous."

"They will. Robert Bruce is already threatening to end all negotiations if Patrick isn't released. London must be crawling with spies this very minute. Besides, The Douglas will not leave me here without some word. He wouldn't do that."

Christin took Wattie, the first scullery boy she found to ride with her through London's streets to seek the address of Lord Malcolm Mowbray.

He was not difficult to locate. By dusk Christin and Wattie had learned Malcolm's address and had drifted, along with the mist rolling off the Thames, to the outskirts of the city. Promising rain, the wind grew more irritating. A pale moon lit their way as the cobblestones ended and their hoofbeats drummed softer.

The Mowbray estate was set back from the dirt street —many years old, almost covered with ivy except for the roof and four chimneys. The side wings were dark; only a faint glimmering came from the ground floor at the back. It was not yet ten o'clock.

"What do you think?" she asked of the thin freckle-faced lad as they sat studying the great house which seemed to dare them to intrude.

"Servants is up, per'aps, mum. D'you want me t'knock?"

"I will."

Dismounting, smoothing her gloves, brushing distractedly at her cape, Christin squared herself and marched briskly to the front door. She knocked five times before footsteps grew louder on the other side.

"Who's there?"

"I am Lady Christin Penmark. Please open this door."

"Just a minute."

Christin waited, not too patiently. Presently a gentler, more educated voice addressed her. The door opened a slight amount.

"I'm Christin Penmark. I'm looking for Lord Mowbray. I've been riding for over an hour just to get here."

She supposed her weariness was of no concern to him if he didn't know Malcolm Mowbray. To her relief, however, the door opened fully, and a tall slender man glanced over her head to the young man waiting by the front gate.

"May I ask your business, Lady Penmark?"

He was seven or eight years older than Patrick. He let his eyes wander over her face, down to her throat and back up. Christin wished she looked better.

"It's about . . . Patrick Mowbray."

At the mention of his name, Malcolm's whole person changed—his posture grew stiff, the lines on his face deepened.

"You may have your servant come in, too, if you like," he replied, opening the door wider.

"Thank you. You're Malcolm, aren't you?"

He looked down at her with the same brown eyes that Patrick had. Other than that, they hardly resembled each other at all. Malcolm smiled with even white teeth.

"Yes," he said. "Please forgive my caution. But as you can imagine, with Patrick being brought into the city, I've been beleaguered with all kinds of people."

Christin pushed a lock of hair from her face and preceded him, allowing him to direct her into a room whose furnishings were nearly all leather. A beautiful dog lazed near the fire, the draperies were drawn tightly, and candlelight reflected off silver appointments on a sideboard.

"Pray sit, Lady Penmark. I'll get something."

While he was gone Christin studied the aging furnishings, part of which could have been Patrick's. How could he have given his fortune away? However, many years had passed since then. Perhaps when she knew Malcolm better, she would think Patrick had good reason to scorn it.

As she removed her cloak and gloves, tossing them carelessly onto a chair, Malcolm returned carrying a large tray with two wineglasses, bread, apples, and an exquisite cut-glass decanter of red wine. Until then she hadn't realized how hungry she was.

"Bobby is feeding your man," he grinned, sitting opposite her while Christin selected an apple. She bit into it with a crunch.

"Do you have any idea why I'm here?" she asked bluntly.

"Only that it must have something to do with Patrick."

She sighed and rested her hand with its half-eaten apple in her lap. "It's a very long story, Malcolm. I don't even know where to begin."

"A man doesn't have to know everything. You want to help him, don't you?"

"Yes, don't you?"

Malcolm leaned forward to pour wine into the glasses. As if she were mesmerized, Christin watched his hands. They were the most beautiful hands she had ever known a man to have—long slender fingers, smooth knuckles and delicate tips, like a lute player who had once come to Yorkshire with some Benedictine monks.

"Of course." He smiled and held out her glass.

Christin turned it in her fingers then arose to walk about the room. "You mean you'll help me?"

"Yes," he chuckled. "Why shouldn't I? He's my

brother. I've already met with three men of the law. But I'm not sure what help they can be."

"That's one of the things I came to talk to you about." She gestured broadly as she spoke. "I tried to see Edward, but he won't grant me an audience. Do you think you could do something to get me an audience with the queen? You know they'll execute Patrick. He hasn't a—"

"Lady Christin, I'm sorry to interrupt, but I really don't think there's much hope from the courts. My brother has committed treason against the crown."

"But—"

"There are many counts against him now, any one of which carries the death penalty."

"How can you? His brother?" she cried, stumbling toward him and jarring the tray. "You just sit there and say it as if"—she waved her apple core before her eyes, as if they hurt—"as if he were a horse that had to be put out of its agony."

"I didn't say that!"

"You don't like Patrick, do you? Admit it, Malcolm! Do you think I don't know? Do you think Patrick hasn't opened his heart to me about you? His father treated him like dirt, and you just . . . give up!"

Malcolm lurched from his chair, and Christin caught a glimpse of the Mowbray temper she had so often caught raging in Patrick's eyes.

"I have not given up, your ladyship! I said there seemed no hope through the courts. Yes, I know what my brother thinks of me. It doesn't really matter. My father was a terrible man. I never wanted the estate he gave me. Oh, it's too much to tell."

"Try," Christin said gently. She didn't flinch when Malcolm probed the depths of her eyes, though she wished after a moment that she could duck her head. One couldn't hide much when Mowbray men inspected.

"What are you to him?" he demanded.

With a wan smile, her fingers making a steeple,

Christin spoke with as much courage as she could gather.

"Patrick Mowbray is the father of my son. You are an uncle, Malcolm. Nigel is nearly seven months old."

During the incredible silence Malcolm poured the other glass of wine and sipped several times. "Why didn't he marry you?"

"He couldn't." Christin shrugged. "At least, not by English law. At the time I didn't feel I could live in Scots common law. That all seems many years ago, when I was young."

"Come with me. I want to show you something."

She hardly knew what to say, so she meekly followed Malcolm upstairs and waited as he unlocked the door to a room facing the front of the house. He opened it, pushing it back for her to step into its dark cavern, and she grew afraid. But Malcolm quickly found a candelabra and struck flint to tinder. When he lifted the light above her head, Christin glanced about herself.

Canvases—large, small, completed, half-completed—filled the studio to overflowing.

"Oh!" she said and moved to look closer at some of them. Splendid portraits, many whose faces she recognized, gazed back at her. Beautiful women and children standing beside them. Edward II. And one portrait of his father and the queen.

"Malcolm," she breathed, daring to smooth her fingertips along the edge of one. "They're absolutely the finest work I have ever seen. Patrick never told me about these."

"There's much that Patrick doesn't know about me. And what he thinks he knows . . . well."

She spun about to study the tall man. He was slender to the point of gauntness. She wondered if the sadness she now saw around his eyes had been there before. They stared at each other until they grew uncomfortable.

"It's good to see you," she said softly, and his brows questioned. "It's almost like being . . ." She waited until she could speak without trembling. "It's almost as if I were with Patrick."

When she dropped her face into her hands, desperation consumed her whole body until she could hardly stand up. The moment Malcolm's arms went about her, she clung to him fiercely. So vivid was the memory of the guards leading Patrick away that she hardly realized when Malcolm guided her back down the stairs into the sitting room.

As Christin sipped her wine, Malcolm paced the width of the room. "I've thought of this several times. The only reason I haven't already done something is because it would take men. Those I do not have. Hiring men is a risky affair in a case like this. It's just an idea, of course."

"What idea?" Christin came alive, vibrant with raw nerves. "I can get men, Malcolm. What idea?"

"What men can you get?"

"Scots, of course. Do you think Patrick has no friends? They would die for him. They've probably been trying to get him out for days. When is Patrick's trial?"

"One question at a time. You can get Scots, you say. When?"

Christin shook her head. "I don't know. But I left word where to find me when I arrived in London. I'm sure someone will come. Maybe even The Douglas."

"The Douglas?" Malcolm's jaw hung loosely. He was incredulous. "The *Black* Douglas?"

"Yes, yes. What idea do you have?"

"Well," Malcolm swallowed, "Edward has a . . . friend, Hugh le Despenser. In fact, Christin, half the kingdom would help us in this if they knew."

"Go on, please!"

"Since the Scots are so good at kidnapping, why don't they take Despenser and demand Patrick as the mail for his release?"

Her dark eyebrows arched in disbelief. *"That* is your idea?"

"It's as good as any." Malcolm frowned at her. "Edward is mad about this man. He would do anything or pay anything if he thought Despenser's life were in danger."

Rising quickly, Christin gathered her cape and gloves. Malcolm glanced about himself, as if he were searching for the reason for her haste.

"Where are you going?"

In a businesslike fashion Christin shook his hand. "It's a good idea, Malcolm, but I don't think it will work. I must go home now and wait for someone to come to me. I'll tell them what you think. You will want to talk to someone, I suppose."

Though Malcolm didn't appear very sure he wished to meet with uncivilized Scots, he finally nodded. "If you think so, all right. The trial is one week from today."

Her whole body froze. "I didn't think it would be so soon," she whispered.

Not trusting herself to talk anymore, she hurried into the hall, forgetting to say any of the polite things she had been taught. During the ride back to Edwin's townhouse the wind whipped her cloak. Trash from the street slapped into the horses's legs and made them shy.

She refused to glance at the Tower of London. When her hair blew loose, like a banner, announcing that she had borne a son to a Scot, she wished a thousand times over that she had stayed in Scotland. Part of Patrick's nightmare was her own fault. She would have her pride to blame if he died.

But before she went inside the townhouse, Christin took one look at the Tower's grisly spires half-hidden by the gathering storm clouds.

The next night, at eleven o'clock, the kitchen maid tapped softly upon Christin's bedroom door and whispered hoarsely that someone downstairs wanted to see her. Bolting upright in bed, Christin rubbed the sleep from her eyes. As she pulled on her robe and inquired about Edwin, the maid explained that Sir Richard was sitting with him.

"Bless his heart. Richard is a godsend." She smoothed over her hair, praying that the man downstairs would be The Douglas.

It wasn't The Douglas, but a straggly looking young man of about twenty who badly needed a haircut and who had dirt under his fingernails. He slouched against the wall and crossed boots with half of one sole missing. The other was laced with a piece of blue twine. He frowned at the kitchen knave who at first had refused to let him in because he was a filthy scoundrel and Lord Penmark was a proper gentleman.

"Be you Lady Penmark, ma'am?" he asked in a thinly pitched voice, his accent one of the incomprehensible Cockney dialects typical of the more squalid sections of London.

"Yeess," Christin hesitated. "Wattie, you and Mary go on back to bed now. I will speak with this . . . man."

Mumbling under his breath, and giving her a wounded glance, the knave drew Mary out the door. By the time it closed Christin was stoking the fire in the cookstove. When it blazed higher, she placed water on to boil.

"You have business with me?" she asked finally and motioned the man into a chair at the table.

"I need to ask one thing," he said in deep, perfect English.

Christin's eyes devoured his face. "You're from The Douglas, aren't you?"

"Mistress, I'm to ask if you own a horse." He bowed —a half-comical snap from the waist.

Laughing, Christin said, "Yes, her name is Triste. Oh, I knew The Douglas would send someone. I will feed you! There's no time to lose. Patrick's trial is in less than a week. Who are you?"

She sliced meat as she chattered, and she remembered to fetch mustard and plenty of bread and ale. The man was Geoffrey, a Douglas spy, and once he shed his Cockney accent, Christin noticed he appeared older than she had first thought. He grinned at her as he chewed.

"This is good. I haven't eaten all day."

"There's plenty. I've met with Patrick's brother."

It took only five minutes for Christin to tell all she knew of Malcolm's plan. Geoffrey agreed that it might work, if one believed in miracles. Taking Patrick by force was out of the question.

James Douglas had not even come into the city. He was in hiding near a small English burgh twenty miles away, but Geoffrey didn't know exactly where. Queen Elizabeth had violently opposed his stealing into England at all.

"It is an awfully risky plan, though, mistress." Geoffrey cut some more venison and took a large bite. "First of all, we'll have to get in the palace itself. We've got two men in there already, but taking a man like Despenser will be suicide."

"You can do it, can't you?"

"I didn't say we couldn't do it. But it will take us a day to set it up with our men. We'll have to take Despenser at night. If something goes wrong, it could cost another day. Then there's the problem of getting someone to tell the king that his favorite has been snatched."

Leaning upon her propped fist, Christin pondered what he said. "I'll tell the king."

"Oh no, madam. But one of us surely can't."

"I see," Christin sighed. "Then Malcolm will just have to do it."

Geoffrey wiped his sleeve across his mouth. "What if Edward throws him in irons? After all, he's another Mowbray."

"There are always risks, Geoffrey! Malcolm will do it—I know he will. Shall we go see him now?"

He grinned at her. "You'd better get dressed mistress."

"Oh!" Christin looked down at her robe. "I won't be but five minutes."

As the two men discussed the plan for kidnapping Hugh le Despenser, Christin thought that it sounded more and more like a hopeless child's prank, stupidly unrealistic. The problems grew more complex by the minute, and the risks ran murderously high.

"It won't work," she said dismally. "You put me in mind of David and Goliath. Be honest. No one could save Nigel Bruce, and no one can save Patrick."

Malcolm took her hands in his as they sat around a large table with only two candles to light the spacious room.

"The Scots weren't so experienced then, Christin, and they didn't have as much money as they do now."

"But Malcolm, if Scotland has spies in London, what makes you think that London doesn't have spies in Scotland? They might know everything we do."

Geoffrey screwed up his face. "I'm sure they do. They expect us to try something. But through the king, probably. Anyway, they don't know who our men are or where they are. Tomorrow I will make contact myself."

Everything was for nothing. Christin learned it the very next day. Hugh le Despenser was not even in London!

Whatever gossip, that was not centered around Patrick, reported that the king's lover suffered an ailment of the stomach. Others said Edward was angry and was having him punished. Many hoped he would not come back, but Christin, ironically, prayed that Hugh le Despenser would remain in good health. And that his return to London would be mercifully soon.

Growing hysterical demanded too much of her. Christin spent many of her hours beside Edwin's bedside. It was a discipline she felt she deserved, and Edwin deserved her care.

Edwin spoke to her of his private affairs, telling her

where his papers were, whom to see, and where he was to be buried. At first she rebelled, saying she wouldn't listen. But death, in its way, was steadying, like the path of the sun.

"I'm not afraid of dying, my dear. I've lived a long, good life. I've had your cheery company these last months. I have someone who will grieve over me when I die. I am blessed."

Even though he was so weak he could hardly lift them, he held her hands in his; sometimes he held one against his frail cheek; sometimes he kissed it. He asked about Patrick, and she lied, telling him that Edward would consider hearing an appeal if one were made.

"That's good," he smiled and slumped back against his pillows. "Perhaps this will not end badly, after all."

"No," she forced herself to smile, her eyes haunted. "I'm sure everything will work out for the best, Edwin. You did the right thing."

"Thank God," he whispered, and his smile faded as he drifted into a fitful slumber.

At one-quarter hour before midnight, Christin stepped down from a litter owned by Malcolm Mowbray. Malcolm dismounted from a horse which pranced daintily beside it. He tossed the reins to a blank-faced retainer, and mumbled a quiet order that Christin was too distraught to hear.

"This will never work," she said.

She gnawed at the inside of her cheek and stared forlornly at Traitor's Gate, the watergate which separated them from the complex network of gray-stoned defenses comprising the Tower of London.

Malcolm took both her hands in his and pulled her into the murky shadows of a wall that skirted the southwest corner of the city. There was nothing of leisure about either of them. They both knew the chances of disaster. But he spoke firmly.

"These guards are well bribed, Christin. Our plan *must* work."

Malcolm had come for her himself with the news, not trusting it even to his most worthy servant. For two days, without her knowledge, he and Richard Hartley had worked to procure Christin admittance to the cell where Patrick was being kept prisoner. When Christin learned of it, she was speechless.

"I don't know if I can do it," she tried to explain, suffering visions of getting caught, of magnifying Patrick's crimes. "I used to think it was clever to outsmart people. But I don't anymore. I will do things badly and upset Patrick. You see, don't you?"

Malcolm hurt her hands he jerked on them so hard. "Patrick needs to see you, and you *will* control yourself. You *will* give him the courage to see this through. *Do you hear me?*"

Her gray eyes seemed to see into the depths of his soul. "You love him, too, don't you?"

He didn't answer.

As Christin looked at the network of guards at this single entrance, she nearly collapsed. Two thousand pounds or not, she didn't believe she would ever reach Patrick's cell.

"Prepare yourself now," Malcolm whispered in her ear.

He strode boldly forward to present a folded paper to one of the guards. Christin pulled the hood of her cape as far over her head as possible, and stood immediately behind Malcolm's right shoulder. Almost amused, she recalled how frightened she had been when the Scots had chased her across the glen. She wished the same thousand men were here, and that they could somehow rescue Patrick from this place.

Malcolm placed a coin in the warden's hand and, miraculously, they passed through the gate. Six times the procedure was repeated before Christin, who could hardly place one foot before another, heard the screech of the hinges on one of the central keeps. She had lost count of how many "Hail Marys" she had repeated under her breath and how many archways and connecting passageways she had gone through. Now, she just breathed "Thank you," and grew alarmed when she realized Malcolm was not permitted to come with her.

"It will be all right, Christin. Go to Patrick. You don't have very much time."

"Malcolm?" In a vague manner, lost in a strange world, she lifted her face to his. Malcolm took her in his arms and kissed her.

"Don't be afraid. It's all right."

At the gruff demand of the Tower guard, she flung open her cape for inspection. He hardly glanced at her —he was too well pleased with his extra coins.

The stairs of the Tower were narrow and clammy, and the warden, when he reached the landing, jammed his torchlight into an iron bracket on the wall. His keys jangled, then the heavy iron door scraped harshly against stone.

The cell was hardly ten feet square, and at first glance it appeared empty. When the guard retreated a few steps, he heaved himself down to wait. Christin turned to question him.

"Go on, go on," he waved her forward. " 'E's in there."

She inched into the small space, not sure what to expect. "Patrick?" she called softly.

At the same time she heard a faint rustle; her eyes strained to adjust to the near-darkness. A tall shadow which had been flattened against a wall detached itself. It moved and then paused.

"Christin?"

Everything was bright: sunshine glinting upon wild Scottish rivers, the emerald brightness of grass that sees rain nearly every day, the laugh of stablehands at a newborn colt jutting its hindquarters in an effort to stand.

She met the torment of Patrick's kiss with all her strength, wishing she could get closer to him, that she could change bodies with him, that she could be inside his flesh and take all his hurt upon herself.

Patrick's tears were not those of weakness, or even of fear. They were of disbelief that heaven had blessed him enough to taste her once again before he died. He covered her with starving, eager kisses, moaning a primitive sound of pain that only those who have lost everything could possibly understand.

She touched him everywhere—blindly, with exquisite intimacy, making promises with her hands that she had no way of keeping.

"How did you get in here?" he asked against her mouth. Christin pulled his face nearer and kissed his eyes and his nose and his cheeks and his ears.

"Malcolm," she whispered. "Oh, Patrick, we're working so hard to get you out of this place."

"Malcolm?"

"Yes, darling. He's done the most miraculous things." She leaned back against Patrick's arm and beamed at him with tears streaming down her face. "He's bribed men. He's working—"

Both her hands clamped over her mouth when she remembered the warden outside on the steps. "Everything will be all right, sweetheart," she nodded vigorously. "You mustn't worry."

Patrick held her in his arms with the reverence he would have shown his mother. "I love you," he said with a slow sigh. Then, not wishing to see the pain in her eyes anymore, he turned her head into his shoulder. His face twisted.

"I don't want you to come to the trial, Chrissy. Promise me you won't come."

She could hardly believe him. She wanted him to need her to be there, and she shook her head hard. When she shoved herself from his chest, hurt that he couldn't share his fear like he shared his triumph, Patrick grasped her shoulders and lifted her free of the floor.

"No, Chris. Obey me. I mean it! I don't think I could bear to see the grief on your face."

His courage was second nature, but even that had its

limits. The set of his jaw was a brittle strength; his shoulders were heavy, almost defeated. "Because I love you, I don't want you there," he said gruffly. "I don't want you to see me . . . to remember me like that."

He forced her wet eyes shut with his lips. "Don't think about the trial anymore," he murmured. "Let me hold you in my lap like a wee lassie. Keep your eyes closed and pretend we're not in this place at all."

She obeyed, for what she wanted didn't matter. Looping her arms about his neck, she clung hard as Patrick slowly lowered himself to the floor. She wouldn't think about the unfairness of his life; she would memorize the tightness of his arms wrapped about her waist. Snuggling herself deep into the hollow between his legs, she slowly let out her breath when his hand found the gentle comfort of her breast. Patrick cradled her like a baby, as if he could erase the pain in her heart with unhurried tenderness.

"Tell me about Nigel," he said, needing the pretended detachment of her words. "Tell me about everything."

The things Christin spoke of were trivial—only words coming quickly, one after another. She saw him studying her mouth intently while she spoke, and she paused, unable to bear the hungry futility about the edges of his eyes, the grief set in the curve of his lips.

"It's all right, Patrick." She took his mouth with a fierceness he could hardly match. Both of them tried to ignore the meanness, the threats of the stone walls hovering about them. "I can see you in my mind. I can see you naked and strong, and I can see us loving each other. I see myself giving all that I've been afraid to. I can see all that."

"Hold me tight. Forever. Don't let me go."

But she was already holding him as tightly as she could. Almost frantically she forced his hand loose from her back, drawing it beneath her skirt. The desperation she felt was not one of passion, only a need for the oneness that an intimacy would give them. She wasn't even certain he understood why she parted her legs and trapped his hand there. They had made love; they had borne a child. And this could be the last touch, the last kiss, the last time she would hear his breath grow harsh from the nearness of her.

"He'll come back," whispered Patrick, finding her ear with his teeth.

"I don't care."

"I love you."

"I know you do. I'm sorry for everything. Please, just touch me. Love me."

It was, in a way, like returning to a sweet, familiar memory of the past. Patrick held her against him as carefully as if she were a part of his own body and slipped his fingers into the soft, tight secrecy that was uniquely her.

Christin accepted that it was as close as they could be. The caress was small and good; it was right and she belonged there. Neither felt the surge of passion. When she touched his dormant manhood, knowing they were surpassing the needs of human flesh, she felt as if they touched somewhere deep inside their souls.

"Oh, Chris." His face buried in the curve of her neck was incredibly sad. "My bonny, bonny girl. I've made love to you a dozen times a day in my mind since I came to this hell. I know every inch of you. Every bit of you. Even this. Even the unphysical love that would let you die to spare me this. I know you."

Moments later, at the first movement of the guard, Patrick lifted his mouth from hers, struggling to blink his eyes into focus. Vowing she would not cry, Christin made her body rigid. But still her shoulders shook. Patrick placed her forcibly from him and stood them up, holding her face between his hands.

"Be strong, Christin." He exposed his face to her, unashamed that she saw him at his most needful. "If something should happen to me I—"

"No!" she whimpered. "I won't listen to that. If I had you again in Scotland—oh, I would love you, Patrick.

I would live with you. I wouldn't care about people and customs. Oh, I would love you!"

She pressed herself against him, knowing she had the right to possess him with her hands, the tips of her fingers. His back was too taut, his knees too forced in their strength. She smoothed the backs of his legs, the lean flatness of his buttocks as the muscles flexed. She traced the curve of his spine as it reached upward to frame the shape of his back. His back would protect her from the whole world if it could.

"What does a man do to deserve this? A man loves a woman and asks her to share all his misery."

"Love isn't just for the good things, my darling. Everything you are is part of me now." Her lips began trembling with the dread of parting.

"Listen." Patrick's intensity sounded more like anger. "You must be strong. You must do what you must do. For Nigel. Listen to me!"

He shook her hard, and Christin went limp in his hands, her hair tumbling about them. She would do anything he wanted her to, even be strong in her weakness. Half-drugged with sorrow, she gathered what remained of her courage. He loved her, and that doubled his pain. So she straightened and blinked bitterly and set her mouth.

"Ye 'ave t'leave now," came the voice from the landing of the stairs.

Patrick's hands shook when he adjusted her cloak about her shoulders. His whole body felt as if it would break.

"I'll be all right," he said in a dull monotone. "Thank Malcolm for sending you to me."

"Patrick?"

"No, Christin."

He didn't kiss her good-bye. He twined his fingers in her hair and tried to tell her with tear-filled eyes a thing so large the whole world could not contain it.

Christin remembered, though she stumbled trying to find the door, to remove the pieces of gold from the pockets of her cloak. She turned back to press two of them into Patrick's hand and close his fingers over them. The other she gave to the guard. She was glad the rough man pushed her forward. She didn't think there was any way she could force her feet to move away on her own.

Christin had never seen anyone die before. After midnight, in the early morning hours on the day of Patrick's trial, she sat beside Edwin's bed, praying for his death. It seemed abhorrent to wish for such a thing. In life Edwin had been a meticulous man. Now, his mouth open with its slow trickle of blood at its edges, she knew he would want it to end quickly. Since Christin loved him in an entirely different way from anyone else in her life, she prayed he would die.

Mary offered to relieve her vigil; Margaret demanded to. But she shook her head no.

"He stood by me through everything. I promised him I wouldn't leave, and I won't."

Whenever Edwin stirred from his half-comatose state, Christin lifted his frail fingers to her lips and spoke his name. She had no idea whether he heard her or not. Death, she discovered, had its own set of instincts, and though this was a new part of life's mosaic, she knew when it was happening.

The room was close with the heat of the fire and the odor of dying. No sound came from the street except a bell which tolled the hour. The house was silent except for Edwin's rattled breathing.

As his feet began to tremble violently, and then his hands, Christin snatched up her head, fully awake. For one moment his pale blue eyes opened wide, and he lifted his head from the bolster of pillows with uncanny strength. He didn't speak to her, but she sensed somewhere deep inside herself that he realized she was there.

For the full space of three seconds he stared straight into her eyes, as if he were saying, *I'm glad I'm not alone.* Then he slumped back, twisting his head oddly.

Crossing herself, a knot in her throat which threatened to choke her, Christin bent over him to straighten his neck. She smoothed the thinning wisps of hair from off the forehead which was peaceful at last.

Edwin had been shriven, but the priest must be called now. For several moments, Christin sat beside the man who had given her his name. He had known the intents of her heart. Never once had he condemned her by the tone of his voice. For that, she loved Edwin in a special way that few people enjoyed.

"Good-bye, Edwin," she said hoarsely. "I will always remember the man you were."

Her thoughts turned to the man who waited in the Tower to stand trial for treason. "Oh, Edwin," she whispered, wiping her tears off his hands where they dropped. "Sometimes there are worse things than dying."

She did not go to bed that night. She sat in the kitchen with a quill and ink and listed the things she must do as Edwin's wife. There was his funeral; his body must be taken back to Erskill. There was the litany he wanted, and papers to put in the hands of men she did not know. She would do them all, for she could not think of Edward's court.

So, because she knew Patrick would wish her to do it, Christin assumed an extraordinary strength. It was not natural with her, but she forced herself. In her own heart, in the mass of wounds she suffered, she prepared for her own death. For when Patrick Mowbray was executed, her spirit would cease to exist. And, if it weren't for Nigel, she would make certain her body died as well.

Chapter Seventeen

The day of Patrick's trial was a test of the keenest order. Time was measured in ponderous seconds, each one carrying its individual torture as physical as a blade under a thumbnail.

Several times Christin neared collapse, but Margaret, as ruthlessly as a general, demanded the utmost of her sister. Maggie prodded Christin to activity, driving her forward in her business of grief, refusing to allow her solace in her self-pity.

The day dragged on and on until Richard came with the news. Edward had found Patrick guilty of high treason against England. The execution was to be the following day, with all the pomp and splendor of a first-class hanging.

All faces riveted to Christin, at her terrible eyes which stared—transfixed. At this moment reaching her was not possible. She did not hear Geoffrey enter the townhouse from the rear; she did not hear Richard pull Margaret aside and whisper urgently; she did not see six men furtively arrive at the stables in fifteen-minute intervals.

Margaret left Christin in her suspended state of mind for two hours. Christin sat, properly stiff-backed, on a chair, her hands folded. When Margaret entered briskly with a tray of hot food, placed a napkin in Christin's lap, and pulled a chair beside her, she didn't move.

"Christin?" Margaret shook her shoulders. "I know you're suffering, but we need you now. Patrick needs you. Pull yourself together. Eat this."

Christin gazed at the napkin in her lap, at the hot soup on the tray. "I can't."

Margaret sopped a bit of bread in the liquid. "Open your mouth. I have things to tell you." Christin obeyed, like a child, and forced herself to swallow.

"Hugh le Despenser is returning to London. He will arrive sometime this evening by boat. I know the chance is frail, but we must take it. The Douglas has sent men."

So immersed in pain was Christin, that the words hardly registered. She remembered Patrick's courage in the meanness of his cell; her own courage reaching outward, as if they could entwine. He suffered for her, and she for him. They were both alone.

"Edwin is dead," she announced, as if it closed something of her life.

"Yes, darling. Edwin is dead."

"What do you want me to do?"

Margaret smiled. "We must make ourselves as unrecognizable as possible. Malcolm says the more people crowding the docks, the better. In fact, it's crucial. Are you ready to try?"

Their fingers, threading together, grasping hard until they hurt, were comforting. They could do something. That was a blessing.

The strip of docks flanking the Thames was always bustling with activity. When Christin and Margaret, dressed as servant women with shabby shawls and hovering white caps, mingled with the dockers, they didn't see any familiar faces.

The red sun sparkled off the murky waves of the Thames, and the evening air sharpened, crisp and chill. The two women lingered patiently, their backs against a rough timbered warehouse. They watched small anchored craft bouncing, and large docked ones unloading merchandise. Shouts in foreign languages occasionally caught their attention.

Despenser's galley was a large, elaborate one. It employed at least one hundred rowers, fifty on each side. The dripping chorus of oars caught the sunset, and the women watched the vessel slip through the dozens of ships like a haughty mistress.

"We're much too far away." Christin pointed. "She will drop anchor out there."

Hardly had she spoken when Richard quickly appeared, pausing as if he asked directions.

"Move slowly down the docks. He will come ashore with less than half a dozen men. The king's guard will take him off the docks immediately."

They walked as rapidly as they could without running. Despenser's standard fluttered brazenly from the ship, mocking England. "I take taxes from your hands," it declared. "I control your fates."

"I'm afraid," Christin whispered.

"So am I."

The small rowboat bearing Edward's favored minion slipped through the water. Christin could see Despenser's face. All around them, men-at-arms with spears buffeted commoners aside with curses and threats, clearing a path. They were on horseback, and Christin narrowly missed being stepped on.

Hugh le Despenser was helped ashore. He was dressed in black plate armor. His helmet was black-chased with scarlet ostrich plumes, and his swordbelt—even his spurs—were of gold. Christin hated him.

Helmeted guards kept perfect order as Despenser took the reins of his horse. Swinging into the saddle, he shouted to a guard being thrust forward by the press.

"Get this riffraff away from me!"

The royal residence was not a quarter mile from where they all waited. As the elder Despenser pompously led the processional, winding toward the Tower of

London, the crowd grew abusive. It hated both father and son.

"English whore!" someone shouted behind Christin.

"Jamie!" screamed a woman in a drab dress no one would remember. She darted feverishly, and a small boy clutched her hand. She waved and clawed at the guard who tried to bar her with a spear turned sideways.

"Keep yer distance!" he bellowed. "Back! Back!"

The woman struck at him again, and at the precise moment she did, the boy threw a squalling, scratching tomcat onto the shoulder of the guard.

"My cat!" His shrill scream shattered the pressing townspeople. "Mother, my cat!"

"Sodomite!"

"Pervert!"

"Corrupters of the people! Kill 'em!"

Screaming, shoving, their bitterness erupting like a flash of oil in flames, the onslaught overflowed. The cat, flung into the street by the burly guard, darted between the horses' feet. They shied and reared, bumping against the shoulders of those behind.

Hugh le Despenser was dragged from his mount, and no one noticed or cared that the hands who handled him were Scottish—not English. Christin couldn't see anything. She grabbed the arm of a guard and began screaming gibberish, then slapped his face. The poor man gawked at her, pushed her backward and battled hopelessly to reach the street.

The crowd was dangerous, and several times Christin feared for her life. Order was not restored until someone had the good sense to ride fullspeed for reinforcements. By the time they arrived, Hugh le Despenser was nowhere to be found.

Eventually the two women straggled to Edwin's townhouse. Large bruises and scrapes hurt them, and Margaret feared that several of her toes were broken.

Maids swiftly prepared steaming tubs of water. Except for the fact that Huge le Despenser had actually been smuggled off the docks, they knew nothing. They

351

bathed and dressed and ate. Then they waited until nearly midnight.

"Poor Patrick," Christin repeated, pacing and twisting her hands until they hurt almost as much as the rest of her body.

"Christin, please. You're driving me to distraction!"

"I'm going out to look for someone."

"You'll do no such thing. Sit down and be quiet!"

The kitchen door crashed back against the wall, and Richard, with Geoffrey and Malcolm, hobbled inside. Laurence shut the door and Christin called for servants. Food was rushed in along with water for washing.

"Did you do it?" cried Christin. The men were exhausted, and Richard waved her demand aside.

"Yes! The Douglas has him by now, in a cottage at Dover overlooking the sea. He's negotiating the exchange of Patrick for Despenser. Our job is to convince Edward that he will never see Despenser alive if he doesn't comply."

Christin felt herself gawking. "Will he see Despenser alive?"

"If he touches one hair of Patrick's head he—"

Richard refused to meet her eyes. Christin's breath caught. "Oh my God!"

"One of us must go quickly to Edward now," continued the exhausted man as Margaret picked debris from his hair. "The castle has a net of iron over this city. No one can get in or out. Everyone is suspect."

"I said I would go," Malcolm mumbled, his head bent on his arms over the table, his hands limp.

"No," objected Laurence. "This is my doing. I must go."

Christin spun about; a dish shattered on the floor. This was the first time she had really looked at her twin since the disaster in Whitecorm Forest. Her heart told her that Laurence's grief had been almost as keen as Patrick's. But she had to have something to blame.

"No," said Malcolm, lifting his head listlessly.

"Let him go!" cried Christin. "This is Laurence's fault. Let him go."

"Christin," Richard pleaded. "A little compassion. He's paid ten times over, for God's sake."

"I want to go." Laurence's words were full with regret. "I hope Edward takes me instead. I hope he kills me."

"Laurence!" Margaret darted to hold her brother. "She didn't mean it. It's the pain, sweetheart. The suffering. And Edwin. Everything. One person can't bear so much."

Throwing back her streaming hair, Christin stood perfectly still in the center of the room. "It doesn't matter what you did, what any of us did. I think I've always known that Laurence had just cause for hating Patrick. It's my fault that any of this happened."

Christin's memories of childish jealousy multiplied until the weight of guilt hurt her body. "Your crimes seem very small when compared to mine, Laurence. I'm sorry."

"It's settled then," Laurence agreed, nodding. He moved to place his palm against her cheek for long, silent seconds. They had never needed many words. She knew the wound between them would heal in time. And she wanted it to.

"None of you will go," she said. "One thing Edward respects is a show of strength. Perhaps it's because that's all he's ever had in the wake of a father like Edward the First. A man might threaten his weakness too much. But a woman wouldn't be a menace to his pride."

They watched as she drew herself tall. Her mature beauty was unconscious. "I will be courageous," she promised them, her eyes seeing something they could not. "I will stand before the king with my head up. He will listen. Besides," she smiled at Richard's dark scowl, "since Despenser is taken, he can't risk the scandal of misusing a woman to save his lover. A man? Perhaps he might. I will go."

Though they all argued for a heated five minutes

more, in the end they all knew Christin had a better chance of reaching Edward than any of them. At this very moment, the archbishop of Canterbury was placing a request before the king to receive any requests by the petitioners for an audience. If he failed, if the the king grew capricious, thinking he could recover the Despenser his own way, Christin could be in as much danger as Patrick.

Margaret wept as she dressed her sister in the black velvet of mourning. They used every woman's trick they knew to make her beautiful. After all, the court was composed of human beings, and they couldn't help being moved by the sight of a beautiful woman risking her life to plead for the father of her son.

When her grooming was complete, Christin carefully descended the stairs. The men inspected her critically. Somewhat awkwardly, Malcolm kissed her hand.

"You're exquisite in black, Christin. I only pray that Edward's pride is greater than his wisdom tonight. God willing, he won't relish being outdistanced in dignity by a lovely young woman. I've done all I can do for Patrick. If you'll excuse me, then—"

"But," Christin protested, "if Patrick . . . when Patrick is released, he will want to see you, Malcolm. Meet him, please."

Richard interrupted. "Margaret, Laurence and I will take Edwin's body back to Erskill. Douglas will come with Patrick and Christin up the coast by boat to Berwick. Come with us, Malcolm. We'll meet them at the Border together."

The artist smiled and shook his head.

"Not now, Richard. Perhaps another time. Wounds between brothers don't heal in the batting of an eye. I did what I did for Patrick because he never deserved our father's treatment of him. Someday, when the time is right . . . someday, yes."

His manner wasn't happy, but it was resigned. Christin embraced him with a love that even she didn't fully understand. "It shouldn't be this way," she said into his neck.

"We don't always choose, Christin." He straightened and kissed her forehead, touching her cheek with his fingertips. "Take care. What you do is very dangerous."

An excruciating hour passed before Christin was granted an audience with Edward II. Exactly as Richard and Geoffrey instructed her, she presented a sealed letter to one of the guards outside the royal residence. Once the chamber doors closed behind her, she felt that she was in the great jaws of a trap. Walking out alive would be more a matter of luck than justice.

The king's chamberlain, his heavily ringed hands not out of keeping with his blue satin tunic, ushered her into an anteroom. After nearly an hour's wait, Christin thought he had forgotten her. When he returned he gave her a look not entirely unsympathetic and drew open a curtain. Before her spread the court of England, and though its chamber was smaller, its attendants fewer, Edward's majesty was not diminished. The queen's chair beside him, on a raised dais, was noticeably empty.

When the curtain fell shut behind her, the half dozen groups of barons, knights, clergy and advisers ceased talking and glanced up at her. As if ordered, they formed a passageway to the throne.

Edward was an enormous man, the image of his father, yet without the strength of will marking his face. His fair hair, his broad forehead, the weakness about his mouth—none of it fit the anger which glittered in his eyes.

Lifting her fingers slowly, Christin pushed back the hood of her cape. Her hair spilled, her uplifted face catching the soft glow of candlelight, her beauty startling the sea of faces.

With a gesture which was calculated to portray respect, Christin pulled aside the heavy folds of her cape. The sculpture of her body was visible, her perfection capturing them all. She bent low to the floor—a black velvet bloom against the inlaid tile.

If Patrick had any fate left him at all, it now rested in her hands. She would crawl on her hands and knees before this man if she must.

"Your Majesty," she murmured. "I am your servant, though the message I bear is not worthy of you."

"Indeed, my lady?" snapped Edward. "Do you come here in folly? A small blade in a jeweled sheath kills just as dead as another. You think to dazzle the mercy of our court?"

"That would not be possible, sire," she said, feeling as if her entire body was in revolt. She needed to retch.

The tone of Edward's voice, in spite of the displeased murmur rippling through his attendants, seemed pleased with her submission. But as he did not command her to stand, Christin remained bowed. She was aware of his rising and the slow circle he walked around her. His shoes were of soft cordovan leather.

"You fear us, my lady?" he asked softly, though she knew the entire court heard him.

"Yes, sire."

"Then why did you come?"

"Only to tell you what you wish to know, Your Majesty."

He stepped aside, said something to his chamberlain and bade her rise.

"We have read the letter, madam. We have even spoken with this . . . diplomat from Canterbury. Tell me, how do you dare? Do you not know what we could do to you?"

Heavy tapestries and carved furniture seemed to blur with heavy stomachs and blunted eyebrows. She was not without enemies in this room, but neither was the king. She felt him testing her. Only the right degree of courage must show. Too much would ruin her, and ruin Patrick.

"A woman puts aside her own fears for a child or a man she loves, sire. Just as a king puts aside the workings of petty men for the good of his kingdom. I do what I must. I follow my heart."

"Her heart!" tittered a man standing near Edward. He crossed his arms and awaited her fall with obvious relish.

Edward's jaw tensed, but he only settled himself in his chair. "By all means, continue, Lady Penmark. You have our full attention."

She flushed at the sarcasm. "What was done is not treachery, Your Majesty. Not as before."

A gasp floated through the room at her nerve to remind Edward of Piers Gaveston's murder. The frown marking Edward's face darkened. She hurried on.

"Patrick Mowbray was betrayed while seeking a noble peace, sire. We wanted only an audience." She swallowed. "I know I could die here, Your Majesty. But you are not your father. You are Edward. King. Now."

Christin spoke only the truth, and when she met his eyes it was with honesty. She had touched him somewhere.

"Aye, we are king. The terms in the letter are not displeasing to us. But we still do not know the whereabouts of our friend."

"The Douglas has him at Dover, Your Majesty," she said without hesitation. "He has suffered no harm. He is in no discomfort, except for a small temper."

Shocked at her boldness, Christin thought she glimpsed a small smile toying with the edges of his mouth.

"And this exchange, it will be a complicated little affair. Yes?"

"Yes, sire."

The king bent again to counsel, and she stood as tall as she could, not daring to show a shred of weakness. One of the king's men presented him with a crisp roll, which he read quickly, signed and returned to the chamberlain. He rolled it back up, his rings flashing impressively, tied it, and presented it to Christin with a wary look. She didn't know what to do; she didn't know what had happened.

"We will spread the rumor, madam," Edward's voice rang over the room, "that Mowbray will be sent to France. But, by God, we will not lift the price off his head!"

She felt her knees buckling, and she pictured herself sprawled on the floor, unconscious.

"Neither will we remove the blockade from Berwick! However," Edward's voice lowered, and she nearly crushed the paper in her hands, "we wrote His Holiness in Rome. A copy will be sent to the man who calls himself Robert Bruce. That will satisfy the demands of the fools who have sent you."

People ceased talking and gesturing signals to each other. Eyes stared as if they could not believe. Christin could hardly believe her ears. Patrick had won! Perhaps not as he expected to, but *he had won!*

If the king worried about repercussions with Parliament the following day, he didn't show it. None of the officials in the court chamber dared question his decision.

"T-Thank you, sire."

A ponderous silence filled the room. Christin realized that she was supposed to leave. Slowly, she began backing from his presence, her head bowed deeply, aware that every eye in the room was dissecting her, some even hating her.

"Lady Penmark!"

Christin froze and lifted her eyes. "Sire?" she whispered.

"Your family is in disfavor with our court. Except for your father's, all lands will be held in forfeiture until a period of truce or my discretion. One indiscretion and you will find *yourself* banished to France in fact instead of rumor. Permanently."

"Yes, Your Majesty." She let out her breath slowly, aware now that she had been holding it.

She wished to know if excommunication were really

possible. But Edward wouldn't tell her more, even if he knew. Her decision to go with Patrick would be in spite of it, not because it would be easy. As she left, the chamberlain lifted the curtain for her departure.

"Your ladyship," he spoke softly, "the escort to Dover for the return of Despenser will be a large one. I suggest that you finalize your affairs quickly and wait outside the city gates. Alone."

London's heavy gates could only be opened at night upon the king's order. Once outside them, Christin shivered. The night was cold, the sky littered with millions of stars. Things could still go wrong, and she was afraid.

Once they reached Dover and the exchange of prisoners was made, they would be together. When Patrick and The Douglas were together again, she would feel safe. And when Margaret brought Nigel to Berwick, the three of their lives would touch. Patrick didn't know his son. His first act of fatherhood would be to take their child across the Border, changing their worlds, changing their lives.

Twice a heavy bell pealed, its sound rippling out to shimmer upon the crisp night. Her horse snuffled and looked about unsuccessfully for something to eat.

When metal sounded on the other side of the gates, with voices and the clatter of many horses, Christin darted to the side of her horse. She wanted to run. Though she had risked everything fighting for it, she could hardly believe they would actually let Patrick go free. As the great oak swung outward, for a second her eyes closed, fearing disappointment.

The fifty-guard escort was led by two men, one a standard bearer. Behind these two rode Patrick, surrounded by an armed guard. Completely at a loss, Christin waited until the troop rode past the gates and they swung shut. She didn't expect Patrick to dismount, but as the formation halted, he swung out of the saddle.

Immediately, the guard was before him, swords

drawn. Her breath caught. Patrick, tall and golden in the starlight, was still very far away. He towered over the man and showed no signs of retreating from the point of the blade in his chest.

The night had been long and taxing; Christin felt her frailty of womanhood overpowering and exhausting her.

"Hold!" shouted the guard at the figure which symbolized everything destructive in Scotland.

"Let him go to her," countered a captain, reining his mount beside them.

Except for the fact that Patrick was so thin, and was running to her with great long strides, Christin realized nothing. Everything was too incredible. He was alive! He was free! Their anguish had not been for nothing; Edward was addressing himself to the excommunication.

Patrick swept her up in his arms and laughed down at her, as if it were only the two of them. "I'm filthy!"

"I don't care."

Christin pulled his face down with both her hands and kissed him for long, unbelievable seconds. In the grief of dealing with his death, she had almost forgotten the wonder of his mouth. She didn't care if the whole world watched her.

"Has there even been enough time?" she whispered, reluctantly releasing his lips, touching his face, wondering at his dignity.

His answer was to bury his face in her hair. The men began to fidget at their whispered caresses.

"Not until now," he chuckled with his cheek against the crown of her head. "Now is forever, I think."

"We ain't got all night, Scot," reminded the captain. Patrick grinned without turning his head. "It's a good ride to Dover."

"Despenser won't go nowhere, more's the pity," someone grumbled.

"We aren't out of it yet, lassie," whispered Patrick, his inspection of her never wavering. "We have many problems."

Christin smiled as he drew her to her horse. She reached for the pommel and paused, distracted in her nearness to him. "Problems are like the poor," she said softly. "We have them always."

"Your haste, my lady," advised the guard, motioning with his sword.

Christin let Patrick swing her up into the saddle, tingling at the lingering caress of her backside. She knew they would not prevent her from riding beside him. She wondered if she and Patrick weren't somewhat extraordinary in the eyes of the English guard—they who had dared to kidnap the king's own lover—Patrick, a wanted Scotsman risking his life for peace.

Bending from her saddle, Christin touched the curls on his forehead with her fingertips. Between the two lovers spun out a future together, problems and all. But they would face the problems. They would raise their son together, conceive and bear more children. All the people they knew, and the ones yet to come, like this escort who would take them to Dover, would see them together.

Watching the man who would be the rest of her life, Christin realized what people thought didn't matter. The lifting of excommunication would come in its time. The wars men fought and the injustice of kings could all be borne. She and Patrick could meet anything the world had to offer . . . as long as they were together.

Dear Reader:

Would you take a few moments to fill out this questionnaire and mail it to:

Richard Gallen Books/Questionnaire
8-10 West 36th St., New York, N.Y. 10018

1. What rating would you give *The Satin Vixen?*
   □ excellent □ very good □ fair □ poor

2. What prompted you to buy this book? □ title
   □ front cover □ back cover □ friend's recommendation □ other (please specify) _____

3. Check off the elements you liked best:
   □ hero □ heroine □ other characters □ story
   □ setting □ ending □ love scenes

4. Were the love scenes □ too explicit
   □ not explicit enough □ just right

5. Any additional comments about the book?

   _____

6. Would you recommend this book to friends?
   □ yes □ no

7. Have you read other Richard Gallen
   romances? □ yes □ no

8. Do you plan to buy other Richard Gallen
   romances? □ yes □ no

9. What kind of romances do you enjoy reading?
   □ historical romance □ contemporary romance
   □ Regency romance □ light modern romance
   □ Gothic romance

10. Please check your general age group:
    □ under 25 □ 25-35 □ 35-45 □ 45-55 □ over 55

11. If you would like to receive a romance
    newsletter please fill in your name and
    address:

    _____

    _____

    _____